Johannes Ockeghem and Jacob Obrecht

Garland Composer Research Manuals
Volume 13

GARLAND COMPOSER RESOURCE MANUALS

General Editor: Guy A. Marco

Johannes Ockeghem and Jacob Obrecht
A Guide to Research

Martin Picker

GARLAND PUBLISHING, INC.
NEW YORK & LONDON
1988

LIBRARY OF CONGRESS CATALOGING-IN-PUBLICATION DATA

Picker, Martin.
  Johannes Ockegem and Jacob Obrecht : a guide to research / Martin
Picker.
    p.   cm. — (Garland composer resource manuals ; v. 13)
  Includes index.
  ISBN 0–8240–8381–4 (alk. paper)
    1. Ockeghem, Johannes. d. 1496?—Bibliography.   2. Obrecht, Jacob,
  d. 1505—Bibliography.   I. Title.   II. Series.
  ML134.O3P5   1988   88-4175
  016.78'092'2—dc19   CIP
                                                                        MN

Printed on acid-free, 250 year-life paper
Manufactured in the United States of America

GARLAND
COMPOSER RESOURCE MANUALS

In response to the growing need for bibliographic guidance to the vast literature on significant composers, Garland is publishing an extensive series of research guides. The series, which will most likely appear over a five-year period, encompasses almost 50 composers; they represent Western musical tradition from the Renaissance to the present century.

Each research guide offers a selective, annotated list of writings, in all European languages, about one or more composers. There are also lists of works by the composers, unless these are available elsewhere. Biographical sketches and guides to library resources, organizations, and specialists are presented. As appropriate to the individual composers, there are maps, photographs or other illustrative matter, and glossaries and indexes.

CONTENTS

PREFACE

Johannes Ockeghem (ca. 1420-1497) and Jacob Obrecht (ca. 1450-1505) are among the most important composers of the late fifteenth century. Their names are often associated by historians, partly because of the accident of their alphabetical proximity in music dictionaries and encyclopedias, but also because of their prominence and near-contemporariety. Both were Netherlanders, born and educated in the provinces of the Low Countries ruled by the Duke of Burgundy, and both represent the highly-developed polyphonic tradition of their native land. As their countryman Johannes Tinctoris noted around 1473, they cultivated a "new art," the origins of which he traced to English composers led by Dunstable, and which was developed in France and Burgundy by Dufay and Binchois. These masters were succeeded by Ockeghem, Busnois and others, praised by Tinctoris as "the most excellent of all the composers I have ever heard."

Tinctoris mentions Obrecht only once in all his writings, but this is simpy because Obrecht was a full generation younger than Ockeghem and Tinctoris, who were contemporaries. Obrecht, however, even more than Ockeghem, was a direct heir to the traditions of Dunstable and Dufay, and was deeply indebted to Ockeghem and Busnois as well. Despite their similarities and the continuity their styles represent, there are profound differences between Ockeghem and Obrecht. Ockeghem served primarily at the French royal court under Charles VII, Louis XI, and Charles VIII, and his outlook was predominantly aristocratic and medieval. His highly individual style is characterized by emotional restraint and a deep spirituality, difficult to analyze but self-evident to any listener, and is widely viewed as the culmination of late-medieval polyphonic technique and its self-effacing esthetic philosophy. Obrecht, on the other hand, spent most of his life in the service

ix

of religious establishments in the commercial
cities of the Low Countries, while seeking and
finally obtaining a prestigious appointment at an
Italian court (Ferrara). Obrecht brought his
prodigious technique, rooted in the same sources as
Ockeghem's, to the expression of typically
Renaissance self-awareness and humanism by
emphasizing virtuosity, clarity of structure, and
aural sensuousness in his work.

The two composers are not contemporary
opposites, like Verdi and Wagner, nor are they
master and pupil, like Schönberg and Webern.
Rather, they represent successive phases in a
tradition that was continuous from the early years
of the fifteenth century until the end of the
sixteenth, and which underwent a transformation in
style from late-medieval polyphonic intricacy and
other-worldliness, well-represented by Ockeghem, to
a heightened consciousness of human feeling and
solidly balanced sonorities and forms, typified by
Obrecht, within a period of forty to fifty years in
the mid-fifteenth century. Study of the two
composers can illuminate that crucial juncture in
the history of Western musical culture.

This book separately surveys the lives and
works of the two composers, but gives the sources,
bibliography, and discography in a single listing,
since many of these items are concerned with both
composers. Printed sources and bibliographical
items are identified by sigla, explained in their
respective lists. All other abbreviations are
conventional and their meanings self-evident. The
information presented here is as complete as
possible through 1987. Since the **Collected Works**
of the composers with which this book is concerned
are still in the process of publication, it is
expected that the bibliographical data will
continue to grow, perhaps at an accelerated pace.

I am indebted to many individuals and
institutions for information, advice, and support
for the work presented here. I wish in particular
to thank Dr. Jeffrey Dean, Prof. Barton Hudson, Mr.
Leon Kessels, Prof. Chris Maas, Dr. Daniel Van
Overstraeten, Dr. Adalbert Roth, Prof. Richard
Sherr, Prof. Tom Ward, and Prof. Richard Wexler for
their prompt and courteous responses to my
inquiries and their willingness to share
information, often unpublished, with me. I also

wish to thank the staffs of the Laurie Music
Library at Rutgers University and the Music Library
at Princeton University for their assistance, and
the Research Council of Rutgers University for
their support of this project.

Martin Picker
Somerset, New Jersey
January, 1988

JOHANNES OCKEGHEM AND JACOB OBRECHT

I. JOHANNES OCKEGHEM (ca. 1420-1497)

A. BIOGRAPHY

The basic and still most complete survey of Johannes Ockeghem's biography is BrenetJ (1893), slightly revised in BrenetM (1911). Additional data, including the recently-discovered date of Ockeghem's death (February 6, 1497), is given in the 1970 exhibition catalogue **Johannes Ockeghem en zijn tijd** (JO). Further new information is contained in LesureO (1969) and WrightD (1975). No monograph on his works has been published, but particular aspects of his compositions have been the subject of a number of studies. A small book on him by the composer Ernst Krenek (KrenekJ) is superficial. Good general surveys of his life and works are to be found in standard historical studies, such as ReeseMR, and major encyclopedias, notably MGG (by Plamenac) and **The New Grove** (by Perkins).

1. Documents and Hypotheses

a. Name and Origins
"Okeghem" (or "Ockeghem") is the name of a village on the Dendre River near Alost in East Flanders, and is presumably where the composer's family originated. A family of that name is found in Ninove, near Okeghem, from 1165 (JO 99), and at Dendermonde, a little further away, from 1381. A "Johannes van Ockeghem" traced at Dendermonde from 1385 until 1416 may be a relative of the composer. Documents relating to the Ockeghems of Dendermonde are summarized in M. Bovyn, "(van) Ockeghem's te Dendermonde," JO 49-59.
There is, however, no evidence that the composer himself came from Dendermonde, despite frequent claims to this effect. Jean Lemaire from Hainaut calls him "neighbour and countryman" (see the reference in sec. 2 below), and Busnois's motet

"In hydraulis" locates his homeland as Burgundy
(which included the Low Countries during most of
the fifteenth century; see the entry for ca. 1465-
67).
    ClercxI examines the claims for Ockeghem's
Flemish nationality and finds them lacking in
documentary basis. Indeed, recent archival
research indicates that he may have been born in
Mons, in the French-speaking province of Hainaut
and near Lemaire's native town of Bavay. (An
announcement of this discovery by the archivist
Daniel Van Overstraeten of the Archives
générale du Royaume, Brussels, is projected for
publication in the **Revue belge de musicologie**,
1988.)
    A supposed autograph signature "J. Ockeghem,"
published in facsimile in 1885, has not been
authenticated (CauchieV). Various spellings of the
name (Ockeghem, Ockegem, Okeghem) appear in the
Rome Chigi MS, the most important source of his
works. Dozens of other spellings are known.
French archival documents most often give it as
"Jehan de Okeghem," but "Jean" and "Johannes" are
also found, with and without the "de" (see the
documents cited in JO 58-67, BrenetJ, and
PerkinsM).

b. Birthdate
    Ockeghem's birthdate is unknown. Recent
estimates range from ca. 1410 (PerkinsO-NG) to ca.
1425 (PlamenacO-MGG). The best guess is probably
ca. 1420, as suggested in PlamenacO-R.

c. Early Career (1443-50)
    The earliest documents of Ockeghem's career
indicate that he was a singer at the Church of Our
Lady in Antwerp from June 24, 1443 to June 23,
1444, a full year (JO 58). From 1446 to 1448 he
was a singer in the chapel of Charles I, Duke of
Bourbon, at Moulins (BrenetM 29). Thus his move to
France, where he was to serve for the remainder of
his life, occurred between 1444 and 1446. Charles
of Bourbon was the brother-in-law of Philip the
Good, Duke of Burgundy, and Ockeghem may have had
an early connection with the Burgundian court
through his patron.

d. The French Royal Chapel of Charles VII (1450-61)

In 1450 or 1451 Ockeghem became a member of the French royal chapel under Charles VII (PerkinsM 522). His service in that institution continued until his death in 1497. In the registers of 1453 he is listed first among singer-chaplains who are not priests (BrenetM 30, PerkinsM 522). In 1454 he is cited as First Chaplain and paid for a song-book given to the king:

A Johannes Hoquegan, premier chappelain dud. sgr., lequel a donne au roy notred. sgr., led. premier jour de l'an (1454), ung livre de chant . . . (7 jan. 1454) (BrenetM 30, PerkinsM 522-23).

The songs were probably his own compositions, and this notice may constitute the earliest document of his activities as a composer. (A similar gift to the king was made in 1459; see below.) Again in 1454 he was rewarded by the king beyond his normal salary (BrenetM 31, PerkinsM 523), a practice repeated regularly until at least 1475 (PerkinsM 523).

Among the works that may date from this early period in his career are his setting of "O rosa bella" and his well-known "Ma maistresse," both copied into manuscripts at Trent before 1456. (SaundersD 74-75)

Ockeghem retained the title of First Chaplain until his death. In the accounts for November 5, 1458, he and the other chaplains were paid for singing the Te Deum on the occasion of the election of Pope Pius II:

M. Jehan Okeghan, premier chapelain de chant de la chapelle du roy, pour lui et ses compagnons, le 5 novembre, en faveur que par ordre du roy ils sont chante solennellement le Te Deum pour les premieres nouvelles pour la creation du pape Pie, en l'eglise du chastel de Vendosme . . . (BrenetM 31)

On New Year's Day 1459 Ockeghem gave the king "a song (book?) very richly illuminated" (une chanson bien richement enluminee). (BrenetM 32, PerkinsM 523)

Later in 1459 Charles VII, who was hereditary abbot of St. Martin, Tours, named Ockeghem to the important post of Treasurer of St. Martin, a title he would continue to carry until his death. The

nomination is indicated in a document of July 28,
and on November 17 Ockeghem presented himself to
the chapter (JO 61). His appointment was resisted
but was finally confirmed by the Parlement of Paris
about 1462 (PerkinsM 524). Ockeghem's career as
Treasurer of St. Martin is summarized in an article
by J. M. Vaccaro, "Jean de Ockeghem, trésorier de
l'Eglise St Martin de Tours," JO 72-6. See also
PerkinsM 523-27, which gives details about the
income Ockeghem received from this benefice.

Ockeghem's composition of a lament ("Mort, tu
as navré") for Gilles Binchois, musician at the
court of Burgundy, who died in 1460, is further
evidence of a possible relationship to the court.
(See the entries for 1446-48 and 1461-67.)

On April 18, 1461, Charles VII released
Ockeghem from the obligation of residence in Tours,
since he was "occupied in service of the court":

> M. Jean de Okenghem, chapelain de la chapelle
> roialle, afin qu'il puisse jouir des fruits et
> revenus de la tresorerie de Saint-Martin
> quoiqu'absent, etant occupe au service de la
> cour. (BrenetM 35)

On July 22 of that year Charles VII died. Ockeghem
was among the officers of the court who ordered
black robes for the king's funeral (BrenetM 32).
Ockeghem may have composed his Requiem Mass for
this occasion (see WexlerW).

e. The Chapel of Louis XI (1461-83)

On January 28, 1464, Ockeghem is cited as
Master of the Chapel and furnished with a scarlet
furred robe suitable to his position:

> A maistre Jehan Okeghan, tresorier de l'eglise
> monseigneur Sainct Martin de Tours et maistre
> de la chapelle de chant du roy nostre
> sire . . . pour avoir une longue robe
> d'escarlate fourree de gris, pour estre mieulx
> en point et plus honnestement en sa compaignie
> et service . . . (BrenetM 37-38, PerkinsM 532)

Further designation as a Counsellor appears in a
document of 1477:

> Maistre Jehan de Okeghem, conseiller et
> premier chappellain et maistre de la chappelle
> du roy nostre sire et tresorier de l'eglise
> monseigneur Sainct Martin de Tours. (JO 65)

A similarly-worded document of 1481 informs us that
the house of the distinguished miniature painter

Jean Fouquet was situated on Ockeghem's property.
(JO 66)
     In ca. 1465-67, Antoine Busnois, singer of the
Count of Charolais, son of the Duke of Burgundy,
honored Ockeghem in the second part of his motet
"In hydraulis" with the following text:
     You, Ockeghem, who sing before all in the hall
     of the King of the French, strengthen the
     practice of your progeny as you perceive it on
     occasion in the halls of the Duke of Burgundy
     in your homeland. Through me, Busnoys,
     unworthy musician of the illustrious Count of
     Charolais, may you be greeted according to
     your merits as the supreme head of melody.
     Hail, true image of Orpheus! (Text and
     commentary in PerkinsL 364-65; fac. in MGG 9,
     Taf. 116.)
Since the Count of Charolais (Charles the Bold)
succeeded his father, Philip the Good, as Duke of
Burgundy in 1467, the motet must antedate that
event. As early as 1460 Busnois had been
associated with the cathedral of Tours, and in
April 1465 he was elevated from the position of
chorister at St. Martin of Tours to the order of
subdeacon of St-Venant, a nearby church administer-
ed by the chapter of St. Martin (HigginsI 69-76).
In view of Busnois's homage to Ockeghem, it is very
likely that Busnois was a pupil or disciple of
Ockeghem at Tours during the years between 1460 and
1465, and that he composed his encomium between
1465 and 1467.
     On June 2, 1462, and again between February 20
and March 5, 1464, the First Chaplain of the King
of France (i.e. Ockeghem) visited Cambrai. On his
second visit he was entertained at the house of the
canon Guillaume Dufay, his famous contemporary, as
the accounts make clear:
     . . . to the First Chaplain of the King of
     France in the house of master Guillaume Dufay,
     three lots of Burgundy wine. . .(WrightD 208).
Some time before 1472, possibly in 1464, Ockeghem
was ordained a priest at Cambrai (RothA). He may
have returned to Cambrai in 1468 with Louis XI, who
was joined there by Charles the Bold. If Ockeghem
and Busnois accompanied their patrons, there may
have been a singular meeting of both with Dufay,
thus bringing together the three most distinguished
musicians of the time (WrightD 209).

An unnamed "great mass" by Ockeghem was copied
at Cambrai in 1472, and lamentations (lost or
unidentified) by both Busnois and Ockeghem were
copied in 1475; these may have been liturgical
settings of Jeremiah, or possibly occasional pieces
in memory of Dufay, who had died the previous year
(JO 140, WrightD 209). In his motet "Omnium
bonorum plena" Loyset Compère offers a prayer for
a number of musicians headed by Dufay and including
figures at both Cambrai and the Burgundian court,
as well as Ockeghem. (See ReeseMR 227.) Thus the
motet, which must have been composed while Dufay
was still alive, suggests that Ockeghem had links
with both Cambrai and Burgundy. Ockeghem was a
principal benefactor of the College of Cambrai in
Paris (PirroH 103).

On August 8, 1463, Ockeghem received a canonry
at the Cathedral of Notre-Dame, Paris, and on
August 26 he appeared personally to be installed
(LesureO 147-8). His relationship with the chapter
was strained by his absence, however, and on August
22, 1470, the canonry at Notre-Dame was exchanged
for one at St-Benoît, Paris (LesureO 149).

In January 1470 Ockeghem was paid for the
expenses of a voyage from Tours to Spain. It was
presumably in Spain that he made a four-part
version of Juan Cornago's canción "Qu'es mi
vida." (A review of Ockeghem's relationship to
Spain is given in RussellM 6-9). In 1471 two
choirbooks were prepared for the chapel of Louis
XI, one of which opened with a "Noel de Okeghen"
(PerkinsM 535). No work of this title is known
under Ockeghem's name, but a monophonic "Noe, noe"
without attribution appears at the beginning of the
Burgundian/Flemish MS Brussels 5557, which also
includes a "Noel" by Busnois.

A letter of November 3, 1472, from Duke
Galeazzo Maria Sforza of Milan to "Domino Johanni
Oken" (probably Ockeghem) asks for help in
recruiting French singers for his chapel (MottaM
305-6). The Duke may have become acquainted with
Ockeghem during a visit to France in 1466 (BrenetM
28).

Louis XI died at Tours on August 30, 1483. On
September 8-9 vespers and mass were sung at St.
Martin in his memory (BrenetM 49). Ockeghem's
Requiem appears to have been composed at an earlier
time, however, perhaps on the death of Charles VII

in 1461 (see the entry for that year), but it may
have been sung again on this later solemn
occasion.

f. Late Years (1483-97)
Ockeghem continued to serve as First Chaplain
and Treasurer of St. Martin under Charles VIII, who
visited Tours in January 1484 (BrenetM 50). In
August 1484 Ockeghem and his fellow chapel singers
visited Flanders; on August 8 they were in Damme,
and on August 15 in Bruges (BrenetM 46). This may
have represented a homecoming for the elderly, and
by this time very distinguished composer.
On March 17, 1487, Ockeghem bequeathed his
property and income to the chapter of St. Martin.
On April 30 he was awarded benefices by Charles
VIII, and on April 3, 1488, he participated in the
Maundy Thursday ceremony at court (JO 67).
Little is known about the last decade of
Ockeghem's life, but he appears to have retired to
Tours. He died on February 6, 1497, as we know
from a document recording the appointment of the
chapel singer Evrard to succeed him as Treasurer.
The document, dated 1499, refers to:
. . . le trespas de feu M. Jehan de Obkeghan,
en son vivant tresorier d'icelle eglise qui
fut le VIe jour de fevrier mil IIIIc IIIIxx
XVI (1496 = 1497 n.st.; JO 279).
A donation was made to St. Martin's to celebrate a
mass in Ockeghem's memory (JO 68).

2. Reputation

a. Views of Contemporaries
In 1476 Johannes Tinctoris wrote his treatise
De natura et proprietate tonorum, dedicated jointly
to Ockeghem and Busnois, the leading composers at
the courts of France and Burgundy respectively. In
his **Proportionale musices** (ca. 1473) and **Liber de
arte contrapuncti** (1477), Tinctoris names Ockeghem
first among "the most excellent of all the
composers I have ever heard" (CoussemakerS 4: 16,
77, 154; TinctorisO 1: 65, 2: 12, 2a: 10).
Finally, in his **De inventione et usu musicae**
(Naples, ca. 1481) Tinctoris describes Ockeghem not
only as a distinguished composer but as the finest
bass singer known to him:

> . . . inter bassos contratenoristas: Joannes
> Okeghem; cujus (ut etiam compositoris eximii)
> supra meminimus.

(WeinmannJ 33)
In his **Naufrage de la pucelle** (1477), the poet-
musician Jean Molinet describes "the artful masses
and harmonious motets" of Ockeghem, Dufay,
Binchois, and Busnois, linking the names of the two
most distinguished composers of his time with the
leading figures of the preceding generation (JO
140).

Around 1477 the Italian humanist Francesco
Florio visited Tours and described the royal chapel
and its singers in performance of the daily
liturgy:

> The singers of the king sing mass and vespers
> daily. All the singers, chosen from across
> the kingdom, are judged excellent, among whom
> Joannes Okegam, Treasurer of the church of St.
> Martin and Master of the Royal Chapel,
> surpasses all in voice and art, just as
> Calliope, favored by Apollo, easily outshines
> the Pierides. I say that you cannot but love
> the man, since he is as distinguished by the
> beauty of his appearance as he shines by the
> dignity of his manner and speech, and also by
> his graciousness. He alone among singers is
> devoid of all vice and abounds in all virtue,
> and he alone, like the Arabian phoenix,
> deserves to be honored and respected. (The
> original Latin is in BrenetM 49-50; an English
> translation is given in MillerE 342, and a
> French translation in JO 75.)

Guillaume Crétin wrote a long Déploration
on Ockeghem's death (CrétinD, CrétinO 60). He
praised Ockeghem extravagantly as man and musician
and invited his colleagues Agricola, Verbonnet,
Prioris, Josquin Desprez, Gaspar, Brumel, and
Compère, as well as the poets Molinet and St-
Gelays, to join in lamenting his death "before he
attained one hundred years." Crétin describes
many of Ockeghem's works, including a thirty-six-
voice motet composed "without violating a single
rule." (The proposed identity of this work is
discussed under "Deo gratia" in the List of Works
below.) Crétin goes on to describe Ockeghem's
reception in paradise by famous deceased singers,
among them Dufay, Busnois, Fede, Binchois,
Barbingant, Dunstable, Pasquin, Lannoy, Baziron,

Copin, Regis, Joye, and Constant, who perform his
Masses Mi-mi, Au travail suis, Cujusvis toni, and
Requiem, after which Hayne (van Ghizeghem) performs
"with his lute the motet 'Ut heremita solus', which
everyone considers an excellent piece." He then
summarizes Ockeghem's career, stating that:
      For more than forty years he tirelessly served
      three kings . . . Without any vice, he had a
      fervent and simple heart, and was rightly
      called First Chaplain.
Crétin calls on Ockeghem's successor as Treasurer
of St. Martin, M. Evrard, to "build organs of great
sweetness" and play a motet for the deceased master
every day.
      Jean Molinet, perhaps in response to Crétin's
call, wrote a Déploration of his own ("Nymphes
des bois"), which was set to music by Josquin. The
musical setting contains a line added to Molinet's
text that vividly describes Ockeghem's appearance
("learned, handsome in appearance, and not stout"),
possibly written by Josquin himself (LowinskyMC,
no. 46). Molinet also wrote a Latin Epitaphium,
"Qui dulces modulando" (JO 141).
      The distinguished Dutch humanist Erasmus of
Rotterdam also wrote an Epitaphium for Ockeghem,
"Ergone conticuit," praising his "golden voice"
(aurea vox). (See J. Coppens, "Erasmus' treuerzang
over Johannes Ockeghem," JO 77-81, and MillerE 341-
43.) This was set to music by Johannes Lupi,
probably some years after Ockeghem's death, and
printed in 1547. (To be published in OckCW III;
see fac. in JO 212.)

b.   Posthumous Reputation
      References to Ockeghem's skill as a composer
continue throughout most of the sixteenth century.
The poet Jean Lemaire de Belges, in his La Concorde
des deux langages (1511), praises him for his
"armonie tres fine" (LemaireC 18), and in a letter
published with his Illustrations de Gaule (1513) he
compares Ockeghem to the distinguished poet
Guillaume Crétin, who had himself praised
Ockeghem (see above). Lemaire also refers to
Ockeghem as a "neighbour and countryman,"
suggesting that Ockeghem, like Lemaire, was a
native of Hainaut residing in France (but see above
concerning other theories of Ockeghem's origin).
Lemaire writes:

> . . . comment la langue gallicane est enrichie
> et exaltee par les oeuvres de monsieur le
> tresorier du bois de Vincennes, maistre
> Guillaume Cretin, tout ainsi comme la musique
> fut ennoblye par monsieur le tresorier de
> Sainct-Martin de Tours, Ockeghem, mon voisin
> et de mesme nation. (JO 138-39)

Nicole Le Vestu wrote a Chant royal in praise of
Ockeghem based on an argument possibly written by
Molinet concerning an "exquisite masterpiece of
nature," a thirty-six-voice motet by Ockeghem,
thereby winning for Le Vestu the first prize at the
Puy de Rouen in 1523. (See PlamenacA 37-39, JO 69-
71. This same motet is mentioned in Crétin's
Déploration, cited above. Concerning the
possible identity of this motet, see the entry
under "Deo gratia" in the List of Works below.)

   A manuscript copy of Le Vestu's poem is
illustrated with a miniature depicting Ockeghem
with the singers of the royal chapel, constituting
the only known portrait of the composer. Since it
dates from some thirty years after Ockeghem's death
(there is even some doubt as to which of the
figures in the miniature represents Ockeghem) it is
of questionable reliability as a likeness. (A good
color reproduction is found in MGG 9, Taf. 117.)

   Ockeghem's reputation was as great in Italy as
in France. The Italian humanist Cosimo Bartoli, in
his **Ragionamenti accademici** (1567), describes
Ockeghem as "almost the first in these times to
rediscover music, which was almost entirely dead,
just as Donatello rediscovered sculpture," and goes
on to compare Josquin, "disciple of Ockeghem," to
Michelangelo. (The original Italian text is quoted
in EinsteinI 1: 21.) This remarkable statement
identifies Ockeghem as one of the initiators of the
style we call "Renaissance."

   On a technical level, Ockeghem is cited and
praised for his contrapuntal achievements by
musical theorists from his contemporary Tinctoris
to Lodovico Zacconi (1592). For example, Glareanus
(**Dodecachordon**, 1547) describes him as one who
"excelled in skill" and "was admirable in invention
and in keenness of ability" (Glareanus 1547, p.
454). These views were still echoed as late as
Antimo Liberati (1685). (See HawkinsG 2: 658.)

   Nevertheless, with the reaction against
contrapuntal composition in the seventeenth

century, and again more strongly in the eighteenth,
Ockeghem came increasingly to be seen as a
representative of an outmoded, pedantic style.
Charles Burney, in his **General History of Music**
(1782), while recognizing Ockeghem's historical
importance and contrapuntal skill, feels that his
works demonstrate "a determined spirit of patient
perseverance" rather than a pleasurable aural
experience, which he considers the primary goal of
music (BurneyG 1: 727-31). Johann Nicolaus Forkel,
an admirer of Bach and no decrier of counterpoint,
echoes Burney's verdict in his **Allgemeine
Geschichte der Musik** (1801) (ForkelA 2: 533).

Revaluation of Ockeghem's artistic achievement
was a product of the Romantic movement in the
nineteenth century, exemplified by A.W. Ambros, who
in his **Geschichte der Musik** (1868) restored
Ockeghem's reputation to the position it occupied
in the eyes of his contemporaries and immediate
successors as that of the leading composer of his
generation:

> What places Okeghem above his predecessors is
> not the in fact astonishing sharpness of his
> canonic and other compositional skills. By
> virtue of his inherent musicality Okeghem
> instils in his music a singing soul; he
> creates a firmly articulated harmonic
> structure and clothes it in an artful web of
> ingenious thematic treatments, strict and free
> imitations, etc. One finds in Okeghem's works
> whole periods of wonderful melodic construc-
> tion, often in the middle voices, and of
> extraordinary delicacy and sensitivity of
> expression. (AmbrosG 3: 175)

B. COMPOSITIONS

1. Historical and Analytical Studies

a. General
The best general survey of Ockeghem's music is provided in ReeseMR 118-36. The masses, which constitute the most important part of his work, are studied in BorrenE 165-99, CrockerH 154-81, and HenzeS, and are available in a critical edition (OckCW). The motets and chansons are not yet available in a comprehensive edition and have been less intensively studied. StephanB examines the motets and FallowsJ the chansons in relatively brief studies. The latter, however, contains important new information. PlamenacJ is a pioneering work on the motets and chansons, but is over sixty years old and difficult to obtain. It is, nevertheless, the basis for its author's subsequent work on Ockeghem and for much of our knowledge of the composer's works. Note should be taken of the important article by Plamenac on the composer in MGG, and the excellent articles in **The New Grove**: "Ockeghem" (Perkins), "Mass" (Lockwood), "Motet" (Perkins), and "Chanson" (Brown).

b. Style and Technique
Analytical and stylistic study of Ockeghem's music is a difficult field of research and results have proven elusive. Among the more useful studies is KrenekD, dealing with Ockeghem's contrapuntal technique in relation to the teachings of Tinctoris, although Krenek does not differentiate Ockeghem from his contemporaries. Cantus firmus technique in the masses and motets is the concern of SparksC, a work of exemplary thoroughness. Stylistic aspects, primarily of the masses, are considered in ZimmermannS. The best study of a single work is BukofzerC on the Missa Caput. Ockeghem's rhythm, the most distinctive feature of

15

his music and the most difficult to analyze, is
discussed in HoughtonR (based on HoughtonRS),
BrennO, PlanchartR, and RahnO. Harmonic aspects
are studied in ApfelK, SalopE, and StrunkR.
Possible examples of word-painting in Ockeghem's
masses are cited in BorrenM 82. General questions
of style are taken up in MendelT 304-5, which
focuses on authenticity and chronology, and
LenaertsB, speculating on the possible influence on
Ockeghem of English music. Other general studies
include BesselerM 230-40, BorrenG 132-50, BridgmanA
239-60, BrownM 66-83, PirroH 100-14, and WolffM.
The difficulty Ockeghem poses to the analyst and
historian is pithily stated in TreitlerS 76-77.

c. **Performance Practice**
    Performance practice, especially the roles of
voices and instruments in the music of Ockeghem's
time, is examined in FallowsP, FallowsS, WrightV,
LitterickP, and BrownIV. The most important of
these are the two articles of Fallows, which treat
the problem of the size and make-up of ensembles
for polyphony in the fifteenth century, with ample
documentation. A broad range of stylistic and
editorial problems relating to the masses, as well
as their performance, are discussed in PlanchartF.

2. **Work List**

a. **Principal Editions**
    The first attempt at a critical edition was
undertaken by Dragan Plamenac: Johannes Ockeghem,
Sämtliche Werke, Bd. I, **Messen I-VIII**, in
Publikationen älterer Musik, Jg. I² (Leipzig:
Breitkopf & Härtel, 1927; reprint Hildesheim:
Georg Olms, 1968) (OckSW). A new edition of
Ockeghem's **Collected Works** (OckCW) was begun by
Plamenac in 1947 with Vol. II, **Masses and Mass
Sections IX-XVI** (American Musicological Society;
second corrected edition 1966), completing his
edition of the masses. (With original clefs and
unreduced note values, this edition is apt to be
difficult for the novice score-reader.) Vol. I,
Masses I-VIII, was published in a second corrected
edition in 1959 as part of the **Collected Works**.
Vol. III containing the motets and chansons edited
by Plamenac and Richard Wexler, is in preparation.
No single edition to date contains more than a

handful of Ockeghem's motets or chansons. The
largest collection of chansons (8) is found in
DrozR. For full references to editions, see
below.

b. **Alphabetical List of Works**
   (M = motet; S = secular work; doubtful works
are in parentheses.)
   Alma Redemptoris Mater (M)
   Aultre Venus estés (S)
   (Au travail suis) (S)
   Ave Maria (M)
   Baisiés moy dont fort (S)
   (Caeleste beneficium) (M)
   Credo sine nomine
   (Deo gratia) (M)
   (Departés vous, Malebouche) (S)
   D'un autre amer (S)
   Fors seulement l'actente (S)
   Fors seullement contre (S)
   (Gaude Maria) (M)
   Il ne m'en chault (S)
   Intemerata Dei Mater (M)
   J'en ay dueil (S)
   La despourveue (S)
   L'autre d'antan (S)
   Les desléaulx ont la saison (S)
   Ma bouche rit (S)
   (Malheur me bat) (S)
   Ma maistresse (S)
   Missa Au travail suis
   Missa Caput
   Missa Cuiusvis toni
   Missa De plus en plus
   Missa Ecce ancilla Domini
   Missa Fors seulement
   (Missa Le serviteur)
   Missa L'homme armé
   Missa Ma maistresse
   Missa Mi-mi
   (Missa Pour quelque paine)
   Missa Prolationum
   Missa Quinti toni
   Missa sine nomine I (3 voices)
   Missa sine nomine II (5 voices)
   Mort, tu as navré/Miserere (S)
   O rosa bella (S)
   Prenez sur moi (S)

          Presque transi (S)
          Quant de vous seul (S)
          Qu'es mi vida perguntays (S)
          Requiem
          Salve Regina I (M)
          (Salve Regina II) (M)
          S'elle m'amera/Petite camusette (S)
          Se vostre cuer eslongne (S)
          Tant fuz gentement (S)
          Ung aultre l'a (S)
          Ut heremita solus (M)
          (Vivit Dominus) (M)

c. **Categorical Lists of Works, with Sources and
    Literature**
    (1) Masses and Mass Movements - Authentic
Ockeghem's fourteen undisputed mass-cycles
represent the largest part of his surviving work
and are among the most impressive compositions of
the fifteenth century. Most are for four voices,
with some for three and five voices. In general
they illustrate the new homogeneous and vocal
character of mid-fifteenth century polyphony, as
well as its wider overall pitch range and
exploration of lower registers relative to earlier
music. Peculiar to Ockeghem is his tendency to
avoid sectional articulation by such techniques as
imitation of concise motives, cadences, or
homorhythm, and to maintain a "floating" quality
that tends to defy analysis and in which some
scholars see a musical analog to late-medieval
mysticism. (The classic statement of this view is
BukofzerC 291-92.)
     Ockeghem played an important role in the
development of the cyclic mass, a large-scale,
unified form made up of the five individual
sections of the Ordinary of the Mass (Kyrie,
Gloria, Credo, Sanctus, and Agnus Dei), created
mainly by English composers early in the fifteenth
century. Following the lead of his older
contemporary Guillaume Dufay, Ockeghem drew on
secular sources, especially polyphonic works, for
his cantus firmi as well as liturgical chants.
Four of his masses are based on polyphonic
chansons, at least two of them by Ockeghem himself.
One mass, the Missa L'homme armé, is based on a
popular song. Four others draw on plainsong, and
three masses are unified only by freely-invented

head-motives. Two other masses are based on
technical procedures that have contributed
inordinately to Ockeghem's reputation as a pedant:
the Missa Cuiusvis toni ("in any mode") and Missa
Prolationum, a cycle of double canons at every
interval in the octave and simultaneously deploying
four different "prolations," or divisions of the
tactus (measure). He also composed the earliest
extant Requiem Mass (see WexlerW).
References to sources and bibliography are by
sigla. Consult Secs. III-V below for full titles
and descriptions.

1. MISSA AU TRAVAIL SUIS. 4 v. OckCW I, no. 3,
   pp. 30-41. Cantus firmus from T. of chanson
   by Ockeghem or Barbingant.
   I. 1. Kyrie; 2. Christe; 3. Kyrie (38 mm.).
   II. 1. Et in terra; 2. Qui tollis; 3. Qui
   sedes (128 mm.).
   III. 1. Patrem; 2. Et resurrexit (215 mm.).
   IV. 1. Sanctus; 2. Benedictus (117 mm.).
   V. 1. Agnus Dei; 2. Agnus Dei (65 mm.)
   Sources: Barcelona 454 (anon.), Rome Chigi
   (fac. of Kyrie in OckCW I, BesselerS 111),
   Sist. 41, Sist. 63.
   Literature: BorrenE 169-72, ReeseMR 129-30,
   SaarL 141-43, SparksC 145-49, WolffM 39-40.
   Recordings: Mace 9030 Rehmann (Kyrie),
   Nonesuch 71336 Blachly.
2. MISSA CAPUT. 4 v. OckCW II, no. 11, pp. 37-
   58. Cantus firmus in B. is the concluding
   melisma of the Sarum antiphon "Venit ad
   Petrum" (see BukofzerS pl. 6-7, PaliscaN 1:
   164, PlanchartM viii). Head-motive in
   movements II-V.
   I. 1. Kyrie; 2. Christe; 3. Kyrie (72 mm.).
   II. 1. Et in terra; 2. Qui tollis (215 mm.).
   III. 1. Patrem; 2. Et incarnatus (255 mm.).
   IV. 1. Sanctus; 2. Pleni; 3. Osanna; 4.
   Benedictus (223 mm.).
   V. 1. Agnus Dei; 2. Agnus Dei; 3. Agnus Dei
   (153 mm.).
   Sources: Rome Chigi, Trent 88 (fac. in DTO 38:
   49-57).
   Editions: DTO 38: 59-79, PlanchartM 53-97,
   LenaertsA 22-23 (Kyrie), PaliscaN 1: 171-76
   (Agnus).

Literature: BorrenE 196-99, BukofzerC 278-92
(most important), GombosiJ 81-82, HarrisA,
HenzeS 122-40, MeierC 273-76, NowotnyM,
PlanchartG 1-13, SeayC 54-58, StrohmQ,
WagnerG 105-6.
Recording: Lyrichord 7213 Planchart.

3. MISSA CUIUSVIS TONI. 4 v. OckCW I, no. 4, pp.
44-56. A "catholicon" (Glareanus 1547) which
can be read in any one of four modes. A head-
motive is freely treated in the S. Copied in
1476/7 at St. Donatian, Bruges (JO 117-18).
I. 1. Kyrie; 2. Christe; 3. Kyrie (32 mm.).
II. 1. Et in terra; 2. Qui tollis (87 mm.).
III. 1. Patrem; 2. Et incarnatus; 3. Et iterum
(187 mm.).
IV. 1. Sanctus; 2. Pleni; 3. Osanna; 4. Bene-
dictus (2 v.); 5. Qui venit (3 v.) (116
mm.).
V. 1. Agnus Dei; 2. Agnus Dei (49 mm.).
Sources: Kraków 40634 (incompl.), Rome Chigi
(fac. of Kyrie in MGG 9 Taf. 118, OckCW I),
Sist. 35, 1539[1]. Theorists: Glareanus 1547
(Kyrie I, Benedictus), Wilphlingseder 1563
(Kyrie I).
Editions: AmbrosG V no. 1 (Sanctus, Benedic-
tus), GlareanusD 533 (Kyrie, Benedictus).
Literature: BorrenE 190-96, DahlhausM 3-5,
LevitanO 454-62 (most important), PerkinsM
540, ReeseMR 133, WagnerG 102-4, WolffM 41-
42.
Recordings: Arion 068 Meier (KGSA), Jubilate
15211 Heinrich (four versions), Mus. Her.
1035 Panterne (KSA).

4. MISSA DE PLUS EN PLUS. 4 v. OckCW I, no. 5,
pp. 57-77. Cantus firmus from T. of chanson
by Binchois.
I. 1. Kyrie; 2. Christe; 3. Kyrie (48 mm.).
II. 1. Et in terra; 2. Qui tollis; 3. Cum
Sancto Spiritu (192 mm.).
III. 1. Patrem; 2. Et incarnatus; 3. Et unam
sanctam (254 mm.).
IV. 1. Sanctus; 2. Pleni (3 v.); 3. Osanna; 4.
Benedictus (2 v.); 5. Qui venit (2 v.) (216
mm.).
V. 1. Agnus Dei; 2. Agnus Dei (119 mm.).
Sources: Rome Chigi (fac. of Patrem in OckCW
I), Sist. 14 (fac. of Kyrie in OckCW I).

Literature: BorrenE 172-75, HenzeS 161-79,
141-50, ReeseMR 128-29.

5. MISSA ECCE ANCILLA. 4 v. OckCW I, no. 6, pp.
79-98. Cantus firmus from latter half of
antiphon "Missus est Angelus Gabriel" (see
OckCW I, xxxv). Head-motive in S. A.
I. 1. Kyrie; 2. Christe; 3. Kyrie (110 mm.).
II. 1. Et in terra; 2. Qui tollis (185 mm.).
III. 1. Patrem; 2. Et resurrexit (247 mm.).
IV. 1. Sanctus; 2. Pleni (3 v.); 3. Osanna; 4.
Benedictus (2   v.) (145 mm.).
V. 1. Agnus Dei; 2. Agnus Dei (2 v.); 3. Agnus
Dei (99 mm.).
Sources: Modena a.M.1.2, Rome Chigi (anon.;
fac. of Kyrie I in OckCW I, MGG 2 Taf. 38).
Literature: BorrenE 176-78, BukofzerS 308-9,
CrockerH 160-64, HenzeS 180-90, 235-41,
PlanchartM 250-51, WolffM 146-48, WrightD
221.
Recordings: Harmonia Mundi 99600 Turner,
Lyrichord 7237 Planchart.

6. MISSA FORS SEULEMENT. 5 v. OckCW II, no. 13,
pp. 65-76. Cantus firmi and head-motive from
T. and S. of chanson by Ockeghem.
I. 1. Kyrie; 2. Christe; 3. Kyrie (76 mm.).
II. 1. Et in terra; 2. Qui tollis (138 mm.).
III. 1. Patrem; 2. Et resurrexit (200 mm.).
Source: Rome Chigi (fac. of Kyrie in OckCW
II).
Edition: HMS 3: 47-49 (Kyrie I, Christe).
Literature: CaraciF 199-201, CrockerH 165-67,
KreitnerV 473-74, PirroH 111-12, ReeseMR
126-28, SantarelliQ 337-40, SparksC 155-65
(most important).
Recordings: Counterpoint 5601 Levitt (Kyrie),
Lyrichord 7108 Zes, RCA 6016 Howard (Kyrie).

7. MISSA L'HOMME ARMÉ. 4 v. OckCW I, no. 7,
pp. 99-116. Cantus firmus from popular song
and T. of chanson by Morton(?). Copied in
1467/68 at St. Donatian, Bruges (JO 118).
I. 1. Kyrie; 2. Christe; 3. Kyrie (41 mm.).
II. 1. Et in terra; 2. Qui tollis (141 mm.).
III. 1. Patrem; 2. Et resurrexit; 3. Et unam
sanctam (178 mm.).
IV. 1. Sanctus; 2. Pleni (3 v.); 3. Osanna;
4. Benedictus (3 v.) (147 mm.).
V. 1. Agnus Dei; 2. Agnus Dei (3 v.); 3. Agnus
Dei (131 mm.).

Sources: Rome Chigi (fac. of Kyrie in JO 204,
of Et resurrexit and Agnus III in OckCW I),
Sist. 35 (anon.).
Editions: MPLSER I no. 6, HAM I no. 73 (Kyrie,
Agnus III), IMM 2 no. 15 (Kyrie), SmijersV
no. 1 (Kyrie).
Literature: BorrenE 178-82, CaraciF 178-86,
CrockerH 157-59, HaassS, HenzeS 24-28, 140-
60, 227-35, LockwoodA 107-16, PerkinsL (most
important), PlamenacZ, PlanchartF 9-13,
ReeseMR 125-26, StrohmM 129-31, TaruskinA
275 et passim, WagnerG 105.
Recordings: Mus. Her. 4472 Planchart, Mus.
Her. 830437 Stevens (Kyrie, Agnus III),
Musique flamande (Kyrie), Pleiades 251 Brown
(Kyrie, Agnus III).
8. MISSA MA MAISTRESSE. 4 v. OckCW I, no. 8, pp.
117-23. Cantus firmi and head-motive in S.
from T. and S. of chanson by Ockeghem.
I. 1. Kyrie; 2. Christe; 3. Kyrie (44 mm.).
II. 1. Et in terra; 2. Domine Fili unigenite
(2 v.); 3. Qui tollis (131 mm.).
Source: Rome Chigi.
Literature: SparksC 150-51.
Recordings: Nonesuch 71336 Blachly, Valois 909
Ravier.
9. MISSA MI-MI (QUARTI TONI). 4 v. OckCW II, no.
9, pp. 1-20. Head-motive in B. Copied in
1475-76 at St. Donatian, Bruges. The claim in
MiyazakiN that the mass is a parody of
Ockeghem's "Presque transi", which begins with
a similar motive, is exaggerated; the similar-
ities indicate the hand of the same composer
but need not have been deliberate. The
commonly-held interpretation of the title
("Mi-mi") as referring to the head-motive is
disputed in DahlhausM. It should be noted
that the B. of the Kyrie was borrowed by
Obrecht for the Agnus of his Missa Sicut spina
rosam, as pointed out in SparksC 276.
I. 1. Kyrie; 2. Christe; 3. Kyrie (52 mm.).
II. 1. Et in terra; 2. Qui tollis (162 mm.).
III. 1. Patrem; 2. Et incarnatus est (3 v.);
3. Crucifixus (2 v.); 4. Et resurrexit (262
mm.).
IV. 1. Sanctus; 2. Pleni; 3. Osanna; 4. Benedictus (2 v.); 5. Qui venit (3 v.) (108
mm.).

V. 1. Agnus Dei; 2. Agnus Dei (3 v.); 3. Agnus
Dei (123 mm.). Sources: Rome Chigi (fac. of
Kyrie in OckCW II), Sist. 41 (M. Quarti
toni), Sist. 63 (without title).
Edition: J. Ockeghem, Missa Mi-mi, ed. H.
Besseler, Das Chorwerk 4 (Wolfenbüttel:
Möseler, 1930).
Literature: BrownM 74-79, DahlhausM 1-2,
MayazakiN, PirroH 109-10, ReeseMR 131-33,
ZimmermannS 269-70.
Recordings: ARC 198 406 Knothe, Baroque 9004
Brown, EMI 38188 Hillier, Lyrichord 7108
Zes, Record Soc. 48 Blanchard, Valois 909
Ravier.
10. MISSA PROLATIONUM. 4 v. OckCW II, no. 10, pp.
21-36. Cycle of double mensuration canons at
every interval.
I. 1. Kyrie; 2. Christe; 3. Christe; 4. Kyrie
(125 mm.).
II. 1. Et in terra; 2. Qui tollis (144 mm.).
III. 1. Patrem; 2. Et resurrexit (173 mm.).
IV. 1. Sanctus; 2. Pleni (2 v.); 3. Osanna; 4.
Benedictus (122 mm.).
V. 1. Agnus Dei; 2. Agnus Dei (2 v.); 3. Agnus
Dei (85 mm.).
Sources: Rome Chigi (fac. of complete mass in
OckCW II, Kyrie in MGG 9 Taf. 94), Vienna
11883 (M. sine nomine, anon.). Theorists:
Heyden 1540 (Kyrie I, Et in terra, Osanna),
Zanger 1554 (Kyrie I), Wilphlingseder 1563
(Kyrie I).
Editions: HeydenA 74, 107-8, 123-26 (Kyrie I,
Osanna, Et in terra), ParrishM 53 (Sanctus),
Schmidt-GörgH 54-56 (Sanctus).
Literature: BellermannM 79-80, 88-89, GroutH
182-83, LowinskyC 186-88, PlanchartR 44-45,
ReeseMR 133-35, WallnerS 97.
Recordings: Accord 149167 Clemencic, Haydn
Soc. 9038 Møller (Sanctus), Mus. Her.
4026 Taruskin, Valois 964 Venhoda.
11. MISSA QUINTI TONI. 3 v. OckCW I, no. 1, pp.
1-14. Head-motive in all voices.
I. 1. Kyrie; 2. Christe; 3. Kyrie (49 mm.).
II. 1. Et in terra; 2. Qui tollis (160 mm.).
III. 1. Patrem; 2. Et incarnatus est; 3. Et
iterum (242 mm.). IV. 1. Sanctus; 2. Pleni;
3. Osanna; 4. Benedictus (167 mm.).
V. 1. Agnus Dei; 2. Agnus Dei (107 mm.).

Sources: Brussels 5557 (**M. sine nomine**, anon.;
fac. of Et iterum in OckCW I), Rome Chigi.
Literature: ApfelK, BorrenE 183-86, BrownM 79,
PirroH 106-7, PlanchartR 43, WegmanA.
Recording: Seraphim 6052 Otten (Kyrie).

12. MISSA SINE NOMINE I.   3 v.   OckCW I, no. 2, pp.
15-29. Head-motives in S., T.
I. 1. Kyrie; 2. Christe; 3. Kyrie (78 mm.).
II. 1. Et in terra; 2. Qui tollis; 3. Cum
Sancto Spiritu (162 mm.).
III. 1. Patrem; 2. Et resurrexit; 3. Et
exspecto (232 mm.).
IV. 1. Sanctus; 2. Pleni (2 v.); 3. Osanna;
4. Benedictus (2 v.) (183 mm.).
V. 1. Agnus Dei; 2.Agnus Dei (2 v.) (78 mm.).
Sources: Brussels Cons. 33.346 (Kyrie, anon.;
fragmentary), Verona 759 (fac. of Kyrie from
both sources in OckCW I).
Literature: ApfelK, BorrenE 186-89, PirroH
106-7, PlanchartR 43.

13. MISSA SINE NOMINE II.   5 v.   OckCW II, no. 14,
pp. 77-82. Paraphrases chants of the Ordinary
(Kyrie XVI, Gloria XV, Credo I).
I. Kyrie (12 mm.).
II. Et in terra (71 mm.)
III. 1. Patrem (chant); 2. Factorem; 3. Et
iterum (128 mm.).
Source: Rome Chigi.
Editions: J.v.Ockeghem, **Missa sine nomine**, ed.
J.A.Bank (Amsterdam: A. Bank, s.d.); Green-
bergA 23-8 (Gloria).
Literature: Brown 96-98, KreitnerV 474-5,
PerkinsV 540, ReeseMR 130, SparksC 139-40.
Recording: Epic 3045 de Nobel (Kyrie, Gloria).

14. REQUIEM.   3/4 v.   OckCW II, no. 15, pp. 83-97.
Paraphrases chants (LU 1807-8, GR 125-26, LU
753-54 and 1813-14). Possibly composed on
death of Charles VII (1461) (see WexlerW).
I. Introitus (3 v.): 1. Requiem (chant); 2.
Aeternam; 3. Te decet hymnus (chant); 4. Et
tibi (120 mm.).
II. 1. Kyrie (3 v.); 2. Kyrie (2 v.); 3.
Christe (2 v.); 4. Christe (3 v.); 5. Kyrie
(3 v.); 6. Kyrie (2 v.); 7. Kyrie (4 v.)
(155 mm.).
III. Graduale: 1. Si ambulem (chant); 2. In
medio (3 v.); 3. Virga tua (4 v.) (219 mm.).

IV. Tractus: 1. Sicut cervus (2 v.); 2.
    Sitivit (2 v.); 3. Fuerunt (3 v.); 4. Ubi
    est Deus (4 v.) (167 mm.).
V. Offertorium: 1. Domine Jesu Christe
    (chant); 2. Rex gloriae (4 v.); 3. Sed
    signifer (3 v.); 4. Quam olim Abrahae (4
    v.); 5. Hostias (chant); 6. Tu suscipe (3
    v.); 7. Hostias (2 v., optional) (142 mm.).
Sources: Rome Chigi (fac. of Kyrie, Rex
    gloriae, Quam olim Abrahae in OckCW II),
    Tarazona 5 (Sicut cervus only; anon.).
    (Louvain 163, destroyed in 1914, contained
    the Rex gloriae.)
Editions: J. Ockeghem, **Missa Pro defunctis**,
    ed. B. Turner (London: Mappa Mundi, 1978);
    J. Ockeghem, **Requiem**, ed. G. Darvas (Zurich:
    Eulenberg, 1977).
Literature: EckertO, EckartS, PirroH 112-13,
    ReeseMR 130-31, RobertsonR 29-36, RussellM,
    SparksC 140-41, WexlerW, WitteM.
Recordings: ARC 2533 145 Turner, EMI 38188
    Hillier, Harmonia Mundi 55999 Clemencic,
    Mus. Her. 4026 Taruskin (Hostias), U. of
    Illinois 8 Hunter, Valois 764 Venhoda.
15. CREDO SINE NOMINE. 4 v. OckCW II, no. 12, pp.
    59-64. Paraphrase of chant (Credo I). May be
    the "Patrem de Village" copied at Bruges in
    1475-76 (JO 117).
    1. Patrem; 2. Et incarnatus; 3. Et resurrexit
    (218 mm.).
    Source: Rome Sist. 26 (fac. of Et incarnatus
    in OckCW II).
    Literature: PirroH 110, PlamenacP 34, SparksC
    142-43.
    Recording: Baroque 9003 Brown.

(2) **Masses and Mass Movements - Doubtful**
Two masses bear conflicting attributions.
Neither of these is likely to be by Ockeghem.
1. MISSA LE SERVITEUR. 4 v. Probably by Faugues,
    to whom Tinctoris attributes it. Cantus
    firmus from T. of chanson by Dufay, all three
    voices of which are quoted or paraphrased in
    the Mass.
    I. 1. Kyrie; 2. Christe; 3. Kyrie (173 mm.).
    II. 1. Et in terra; 2. Qui tollis (287 mm.).
    III. 1. Patrem; 2. Et incarnatus (276 mm.).

   IV. 1. Sanctus; 2. Pleni (3 v.); 3. Osanna;
       4. Benedictus (3 v.) (252 mm.).
   V. 1. Agnus Dei; 2. Agnus Dei (3 v.); 3. Agnus
       Dei (175 mm.). Source: Trent 88 (attr. to
       Ockeghem; fac. in DTO 38: 83-94, also in
       FauguesO 9-20). Theorist: TinctorisL (Qui
       sedes, T. and B., attr. to Faugues;
       CoussemakerS 4: 146, TinctorisO 2: 143).
       Editions: DTO 38: 95-128, FauguesCW 5-46.
       Literature: ReeseMR 112, SchuetzeI 17-23, 32-
       37, 54-68, SparksC 177-81, 220-21,
       TinctorisA 130; WagnerG 107-10.
2. MISSA POUR QUELQUE PAINE. 4 v. OckCW II, no.
    16, pp. 98-115. Probably by Cornelius Heyns,
    to whom most authorities, including Plamenac,
    attribute it (in OckCW II: xxxvii). Cantus
    firmus from T. of an anonymous chanson. Head-
    motive in S.A.
    I. 1. Kyrie; 2. Christe; 3. Kyrie (115 mm.).
    II. 1. Et in terra; 2. Qui tollis (218 mm.).
    III. 1. Patrem; 2. Et resurrexit (224 mm.).
    IV. 1. Sanctus; 2. Pleni (3 v.); 3. Osanna;
        4. Benedictus (2 v.); 5. Osanna (220 mm.).
    V. 1. Agnus Dei; 2. Agnus Dei (3 v.); 3. Agnus
        Dei (122 mm.).
    Sources: Brussels 5557 (attr. to Ockeghem;
    fac. of Kyrie in OckCW II), Lucca 238
    (anon., incomplete), Rome Sist. 51 (attr. to
    Cornelius Heyns; fac. of Kyrie in OckCW II).
    Literature: BorrenE 199-202, PlamenacP 34-40,
    ReeseMR 136, RiemannH II[1]: 230-34, SparksC
    171, Strohm 131.

    (3) Masses and Mass Movements - Lost
    The following masses are known only from
    citations by theorists.
1. MESSA DELLE MADONNA (M. de Beate Virgine).
    Theorists: Zacconi 1592 (quotes T. of Credo),
        Cerone 1613 (quotes T. of Credo).
    Literature: OckCW II: xlii.
2. MESSA DOMINE NON SECUNDUM PECCATA NOSTRA.
    Theorist: Zacconi 1592 (quotes T. of Gloria).
    Literature: OckCW II: xlii.
3. MESSA JOCUNDARE.
    Theorist: Zacconi 1592 (quotes T. of Osanna).
    Literature: OckCW II: xlii.
4. MISSA LA BELLE SE SIET.
    Theorist: TinctorisL (quotes T. and Ct. of

Patrem; CoussemakerS 4: 145-46, TinctorisO
2: 142).
Literature: OckCW II: xlii; TinctorisA 129.

(4) Motets - Authentic
Although few in number, Ockeghem's extant
motets exhibit the same range of technical and
stylistic features as his masses. The motets will
be published in OckCW III.
1. ALMA REDEMPTORIS MATER. 2. Virgo prius. (119
   mm.). 4 v. Text and c.f. (paraphrased in
   A.): Antiphon B.M.V. (LU 273-74).
   Sources: Florence Ricc. 2794, Rome Sist. 46.
   Editions: BesselerA 5-9, GreenbergA 76-85,
   HüschenM 38-40.
   Literature: BesselerM 21, ReeseMR 121-22,
   SparksC 204-5, StephanB 74-5.
   Recordings: Lyrichord 7213 Planchart, Mus.
   Her. 1306 Venhoda, Mus. Her. 4179 Taruskin,
   Nonesuch 71336 Blachly, Teldec 6.41155
   Jürgens.
2. AVE MARIA. (44 mm.). 4 v. Text: Luc. 1: 28.
   Source: Rome Chigi.
   Literature: ReeseMR 122, StephanB 61-63.
   Recordings: Lyrichord 7213 Planchart, Mus.
   Her. 1306 Venhoda, Mus. Her. 4179 Taruskin,
   Nonesuch 71336 Blachly.
3. INTEMERATA DEI MATER. 2. Nec sine te. 3.
   Aspiciat facito. (136 mm.). 5 v.
   Sources: Rome Chigi, Sist. 35 (anon.).
   Edition: SmijersV 1: 3-11.
   Literature: KreitnerV 476-76, ReeseMR 123,
   StephanB 36-38.
   Recordings: Harmonia Mundi 99600 Turner, Mus.
   Her. 1306 Venhoda, Mus. Her. 7179 Taruskin,
   Music Guild 134 Blanchard, Seraphim 6104
   Munrow.
4. SALVE REGINA (I). 2. Eia ergo. 3. O dulcis.
   (239 mm.). 4 v. Text and c.f. (paraphrased
   in B.): Antiphon B.M.V. (LU 276).
   Source: Rome Sist. 42.
   Edition: J. Ockeghem, **Salve Regina**, ed. G.
   Hunter (New York: Assoc. Music Publ., 1973).
   Literature: BesselerM 238, RahnO, ReeseMR 122,
   SparksC 203-4, StephanB 75-76.
   Recordings: Mus. Her. 1306 Venhoda, Mus. Her.
   4179 Taruskin, U. of Illinois 8 Hunter.

5. UT HEREMITA SOLUS. 2. Ut heremita. (195 mm.).
    4 v. Cantus firmus in T. is notated as a
    puzzle-canon, which is realized in 1504[1].
    Although this work is anonymous in the
    sources, a motet of this title is cited by
    Crétin among works by Ockeghem (see
    CrétinD 34), and most authorities accept
    this as Ockeghem's. It reveals a striking
    thematic resemblance to the opening of
    the second part of Busnois's motet "In
    hydraulis," which pays homage to Ockeghem.
    One of these works may have been the model for
    the other, although it is not clear which came
    first. (See HigginsI 76-78, PerkinsL 369.)
    Sources: 1504[1] (anon.; fac. of T. in MGG 9:
      1831-4). Theorist: Finck 1556 (first part
      only, anon.).
    Edition: ScheringG 44-48.
    Literature: PerkinsL 369, ReeseMR 124,
      ScheringR, StephanB 43-44, WolffM 106-7.
    Recordings: Music Guild 134 Blanchard, Mus.
      Her. 1306 Venhoda (both perform this as an
      instrumental work).

    (5) Motets - Doubtful
    The following works, although without
conflicting attributions, are doubtful mainly on
stylistic grounds. They will be published, along
with the authentic motets, in OckCW III.
1. CAELESTE BENEFICIUM. 2. Caeleste beneficium.
    (257 mm.). 5 v. A c.f. appears to be present
    in the T. The text, of German-Lutheran
    character, cannot belong to Ockeghem's time or
    area of activity, and may be a contrafactum.
    The lateness of the source (ca. 1538), the
    unusual spelling of the composer's name, and
    the imitative style of the work, which is not
    typical for Ockeghem, render his authorship
    suspect. PerkinsO-NG 493 defends the
    authenticity of the work. See also "Gaude
    Maria" below.
    Source: Regensburg B.211-15 ([O]kegus).
    Literature: MohrH 18, StephanB 39-40.
    Recording: Mus. Her. 4179 Taruskin.
2. DEO GRATIA. (37 mm.). 36 v. (= four 9-voice
    canons). The attribution is based on various
    references to a 36-voice motet by Ockeghem
    (CretinD 29, OrnithoparcusC 197, GlareanusD 2:

532, et al.). A letter of Sebastian Virdung
(1504) describes Ockeghem's motet as
consisting of six 6-voice canons (WallnerS
97), while the present work is made up of four
9-voice canons. PlamenacA doubts that this is
Ockeghem's work, while LowinskyO accepts it.
TeramotoP suggests that the work may be by the
editor of 1542[6], Georg Forster.
Sources: Heilbronn IV-V/2 (anon.; T. only,
   copied from 1568[7]), 1542[6] (anon.; fac. in
   LowinskyO 176-77), 1568[7] (anon.; fac. in MGG
   9: 1835).
Editions: RiemannH 2[1]: 239-49, StamJ 21-28 (in
   both as "Deo gratias").
Literature: BorrenE 220-23, FeiningerF 45-47,
   LowinskyO 176-77, PlamenacA (the last two
   named are most important), ReeseMR 124,
   TeramotoP 347-48.
3. GAUDE MARIA. 2. Gabrielem archangelum. 3.
    Uterum tuum. 4. Erubescat Judaeus. (249
    mm.). 5 v. Text and c.f. (paraphrased in
    T.): Responsory (AM 1195). Authenticity of
    this work is doubted and defended for the same
    reasons as that of "Caeleste beneficium".
    Source: Regensburg B.211-15 (Johannes
       Okegus).
    Literature: ReeseMR 123-24, StephanB 39-42.
    Recordings: Mus. Her. 4179 Taruskin, Mus.
    Her. 1306 Venhoda.
4. VIVIT DOMINUS. (32 mm.). 2 v. Text: 2 Reg.
    22: 47 and Ps. 17: 47. Probably a contra-
    factum of a fragment from a larger work
    (mass?). The late date of the source and the
    style of this duo, which is imitative and
    displays the regular cadences and conjunct
    melodic motion typical for the early 16th
    century but not for Ockeghem, make its
    authenticity doubtful.
    Source: 1549[16].

    (6) Motets - Spurious
1. SALVE REGINA (II). 2. Eia ergo. (124 mm.). 4
    v. Text and c.f. (paraphrased in S.):
    Antiphon B.M.V. (LU 276). Attribution to
    Ockeghem is based on an erroneous reading of
    the mutilated name of the composer given in
    Rome Sist. 46, which HaberlB 156 and others
    read as "Jo. Okeghem." Jeffrey Dean has shown

that the name can be read as "P. Basiron", a
reading confirmed by 1520[1] (DeanO). The
relatively simple polyphonic texture and
clear-cut phrase-structure of the work are not
characteristic of Ockeghem, and there is no
reason to attribute this work to him.
Sources: Rome Sist. 46 (P. Basiron?), 1520[1]
   (Basiron).
Edition: PickerMB 160-68.
Literature: DeanO, PickerS, ReeseMR 122,
   StephanB 73-74.
Recordings: Lyrichord 7213 Planchart, Mus.
   Her. 1306 Venhoda, Mus. Her. 4179 Taruskin.

(7) Motets - Lost
1. NOEL. A choirbook copied for the chapel of
   Louis XI in 1471 began with a "Noel de
   Okeghen" (PerkinsM 535). No work of this
   title is known under Ockeghem's name, but an
   anonymous monophonic "Noe, noe" opens Brussels
   MS 5557, which also contains a "Noel" by
   Busnois (mod. ed. in IMM 2: 26-27).

(8) Secular Works - Authentic
Ockeghem's secular works, mostly rondeaux and
bergerettes, are generally for three voices, of
which the S. and T. play a more important
structural role than the Ct. Thus they exhibit a
more conservative aspect than his four- and five-
voice motets and masses in which all voices are
equally important. His personal style remains
evident, however, in their rhythmic intricacy and
contrapuntal freedom. A statistical summary of
Ockeghem's style based on a computer-aided analysis
of 11 chansons is given in TrowbridgeS. The
secular works will be published in OckCW III.
1. AULTRE VENUS ESTÉS. 3 v. (35 mm.).
   Rondeau.
   Source: Florence Ricc. 2794 (fac. in FallowsJ
      224).
   Edition: JonesF 2: 241-42.
   Recordings: Discophiles 330.222-4 Blanchard,
      Oiseau D254D3 Davies.
2. BAISIÉS MOY DONT FORT. 3 v. (58 mm.).
   Rondeau.
   Sources: Copenhagen 1848 (anon.), Florence
      Cons. 2439.
   Edition: NewtonF no. 48.

Literature: FallowsJ 222.
Recording: Oiseau D254D3 Davies.

3. D'UN AUTRE AMER.   3 v.   (45 mm.).   Rondeau.
    Text: Jardin no. 243, LöpelmannL no. 293.
    The attribution to Busnois in Paris 15123 must
    be incorrect, since Ockeghem is named in the
    early, central MSS Dijon 517 and Paris
    Nivelle, as well as other French and Italian
    sources, and the style of the work confirms
    his authorship.
    Sources: Bologna Q17, Copenhagen 291 (anon.),
    Copenhagen 1848 (anon.), Dijon 517, Florence
    178 (anon.), Florence Ricc. 2356 (anon.),
    Ricc. 2794, Paris 2245, Paris 15123 (attr.
    Busnois), Paris Nivelle, Rome Cas. 2856,
    Giul. XIII.27 (anon.), Seville/Paris (with
    alternative Ct.; anon.; fac. in TaruskinD
    7), Washington Laborde (anon.), Wolfenbüt-
    tel 287 (anon.; fac. in JeppesenK xvii).
    Tabl.: 1507⁶ (anon.).

    Editions: DrozT 72-73, JeppesenK 52-53,
    JosquinWM 2: 140, SmijersV 1: 12 (= PaliscaN
    217-18), TaruskinD 4-6 (2 versions).
    Literature: GroutH 191.
    Recordings: Bach Guild 634 (= W.W. Norton P8
    15483) Cape (instr. perf.), Oiseau D254D3
    Davies.

4. FORS SEULEMENT L'ACTENTE.   3 v.   (70 mm.).
    Rondeau. Text: Jardin no. 496, LöpelmannL
    no. 77.
    Sources: Dijon 517, Paris 1597 (anon.), Paris
    Nivelle (fragmentary; anon.), Rome Giul.
    XIII.27 (Frayres y dexedes me; anon.), St.
    Gall 461, Washington Laborde (anon.; fac.
    in PickerF), Wolfenbüttel 287 (anon.; fac.
    in PickerF).
    Editions: DrozT 48-49, GiesbertA 1: 2-3,
    GombosiJ Anhang 12-13, PickerF 1-5 (two
    versions).
    Literature: GombosiJ 16-18, HewittF,
    SantarelliQ 333-36, TrowbridgeS.
    Recordings: Accord 149167 Clemencic, Archive
    3052 Cape, Counterpoint 5601 Levitt,
    Lyrichord 7108 Zes, Oiseau D254D3 Davies.

5. FORS SEULLEMENT CONTRE.   3 v.   (63 mm.).
    Rondeau. Ct.= S. of Ockeghem's "Fors
    seulement l'actente". The authenticity of
    this work is doubted in GombosiJ but

reasserted in FallowsJ.
Sources: Copenhagen 1848 (anon.), Florence
    Cons. 2439, Paris 1596 (anon.), Paris 2245,
    St. Gall 461, 1538[9] (anon.).
Editions: GiesbertA 1: 4-5, GombosiJ Anhang
    14-15, PickerF 5-7.
Literature: FallowsJ 222, GombosiJ 18-19,
    HewittF.
Recording: Oiseau D254D3 Davies.
6. IL NE M'EN CHAULT. 3 v. (37 mm.). Rondeau.
    Source: Washington Laborde (fac. in EM 12:
    253).
    Recording: Oiseau D254D3 Davies.
7. J'EN AY DUEIL. 4 (originally 3?) v. (53 mm.).
    Rondeau. Since Bologna Q17 has a different
    Ct. than the other sources, it may represent
    an addition to a work originally composed for
    three voices. LitterickR suggests that
    Ockeghem may have made the revision of version
    B himself.
    Sources, version A: Bologna Q17 (anon.);
        version B: Brussels 228 (anon.), Brussels/
        Tournai (anon.; fac. of Tournai in
        LenaertsN 152), Florence Cons. 2439, London
        20.A.XVI (anon.), Washington Laborde
        (anon.), 1504[3].
    Editions: AmbrosG 5: 10-11 (version B),
        LitterickR 43-48 (two versions), PickerC
        226-28, 474-76 (two versions).
    Literature: LitterickR, PickerC 61-62.
    Recording: Oiseau D254D3 Davies (two
        versions).
8. LA DESPOURVEUE. 3 v. (32 mm.). Rondeau.
    Text: LöpelmannL no. 580.
    Sources: Florence 176 (anon.), Paris 15123,
        Washington Laborde (anon.; fac. in EM 12:
        241).
    Edition: PeaseE no. 133.
    Literature: FallowsJ 223.
    Recording: Oiseau D254D3 Davies.
9. L'AUTRE D'ANTAN. 3 v. (37 mm.). Rondeau.
    The Ct. is transmitted in two substantially
    different versions.
    Sources, version A: Dijon 517 (anon.), New
        Haven Mellon, Paris 15123 (anon.), Paris
        Cordiforme (anon.); version B: Bologna Q16
        (La trentana; anon.), Rome Cas. 2856.
    Theorist: TinctorisP (opening; CoussemakerS

4: 156, TinctorisO 2a: 14), Gafurius 1496
(opening, attr. "Olreghem"; GaffuriusP 159-
60, GafuriusP 173).
Editions, version A: DrozT 32-33, PerkinsMC
no. 20; version B: AmbrosG 5: 12-13.
Literature: BrownR 32-35, GareyC 16-20,
PerkinsL, PlamenacZ 381-13.
Recordings: Accord 149167 Clemencic, Archive
3052 (= Musique flamande) Cape, Mus. Her.
4472 Planchart, Oiseau D186D4 Rooley,
Oiseau D254D3 Davies.
10. LES DESLÉAULX ONT LA SAISON. 3 v. (31 mm.).
Rondeau. Text: Jardin no. 489, LöpelmannL
no. 121.
Sources: Dijon 517, Washington Laborde (anon.;
fac. in EM 12: 289).
Editions: DrozT 16-17, HaarC 141-42.
Literature: BrownG 8-10.
Recordings: London 9116 Rollin, Mus. Her. 4472
Planchart, Oiseau D254D3 Davies.
11. MA BOUCHE RIT. 2. Ha cuer pervers. 3 v. (72
mm.). Text: Jardin nos. 10 and 103, LöpelmannL no. 142.
Sources: Copenhagen 1848 (anon.; first part
only, textless), Dijon 517 (anon.), Florence
176, Ricc. 2356 (anon.), Kraków Glogauer
(anon.; textless), Munich Schedel
(textless), New Haven Mellon, Paris 15123
(anon.), Cordiforme (anon.), Nivelle, Rome
Cas. 2856, Giulia XIII.27 (anon.), Seville/
Paris (anon.), Washington Laborde (anon.),
Wolfenbüttel 287 (anon.; fac. of second
part in MGG 2: 515-16), 1501, 1538[9] (anon.;
textless). Tabl.: 1507[5].
Editions: DrozT 9-11, EDMR 4: 61, GombosiJ
Anhang no. 5, HAM 1: no. 75, HewittO 335-36,
MartiniM 29-31, PerkinsMC no. 30, WolfS 39-
40.
Literature: FallowsJ 223.
Recordings: Accord 149167 Clemencic, Archive
3052 Cape, Lyrichord 7213 Planchart, Mus.
Her. 4472 Planchart, Mus. Her. 830437
Stevens, Oiseau D186D4 Rooley, Oiseau D254D3
Davies, Pleiades 251 Brown, Seraphim 6104
Munrow.
12. MA MAISTRESSE. 2. Helas de vous. 3 v. (68
mm.). Bergerette. Text: Jardin no. 99 (Ha!
ma maistresse), LöpelmannL no. 214.

Composed before 1456 (SaundersD).
Sources: Cambridge R.2.71 (S., T. only,
    incomplete; fac. in FallowsJ 228), Escorial
    IV.A.24 (anon.; first part only, textless),
    Seville/Paris (anon.), Trent 93 (anon.;
    textless), Washington Laborde (anon.; fac.
    in FallowsJ 218-19), Wolfenbüttel 287
    (anon.).
Editions: HAM 1: no. 74, HanenC 3: 425-28
    (first part only), OckSW 124.
Literature: FallowsJ, SaundersD 74, WolffM
    194.
Recordings: Anth. Son. 4 Meili, Archive 3052
    Cape, Lyrichord   7213 Planchart, Mus. Her.
    830437 Stevens, Nonesuch 71336 Blachly,
    Oiseau 50104 Eeckhout, Oiseau D254D3 Davies,
    Pleiades 251 Brown.
13. MORT, TU AS NAVRÉ/MISERERE.   4 v.   (40 mm.).
    Ballade (motet-chanson). Lament on the death
    of Gilles Binchois (d.1460). Cantus firmus in
    T. and B. from final verse of Sequence, "Dies
    irae," from Mass for the Dead (LU 1813).
    Sources: Dijon 517 (anon.), Montecassino 871.
    Editions: IMM 3: 22-26, MarixM no. 54, PopeM
        no. 107.
    Literature: ReeseMR 121.
    Recordings: Arion 068 Meier, Mus. Her. 4472
        Planchart, Oiseau D254D3 Davies, University
        of Illinois 8 Hunter.
14. O ROSA BELLA.   2. Ai lasso mi.   2 v.   (46 mm.).
    Ballata. Text: Leonardo Giustiniani. Cantus
    firmus in S. from S. of ballata by Bedyngham
    or Dunstable.
    Source: Trent 90.
    Editions: DTO 14-15: 233-34, IMM 4: 8-15.
    Recording: Oiseau D254D3 Davies.
15. PRENEZ SUR MOI VOSTRE EXEMPLE.   3 v.   (35 mm.).
    Rondeau. Text: LöpelmannL no. 578. Canon
    à 3.
    Sources: Copenhagen 291 (anon.; fac. in
        BesselerS 127, MGG 9: 1829-30), Mantua (fac.
        in ScherliessM pl. 66), 1504^3, 1590^{30} (Fuga
        trium vocum). (Dijon 517 once contained
        this work, but the leaf on which it was
        written is now missing.) Theorists: Heyden
        1540 (Fuga trium vocum), Glareanus 1547
        (Fuga trium vocum), Faber 1553 (Fuga trium
        partium), Wilphlingseder 1563 (Fuga trium
        vocum).

Editions: AmbrosG 5: 18-19, DrozT 1-2,
GlareanD 532-33, IMM 2: 12-14, JeppesenK 62-
63, ReeseM 84-85.   BockholdtF 161-65
compares early editions (all incorrect) by
Hawkins, Burney, and Forkel.
Literature: DahlhausO, LevitanO, ReeseM 81-86,
ScherliessM 79-82, WexlerO.
Recordings: Accord 149167 Clemencic, Music
Guild 134 (= Record Soc. 48) Blanchard
(instr. perf.), Oiseau D254D3 Davies,
Seraphim 6104 Munrow.
16. PRESQUE TRANSI. 2. Helas, je suis. 3 v.   (53
mm.). Bergerette. Text: LöpelmannL no.
439.
Sources: Dijon 517, Washington Laborde
(anon.).
Edition: DrozT 98-100.
Literature: MiyazakiN.
Recording: Accord 149167 Clemencic, Oiseau
D254D3 Davies.
17. QUANT DE VOUS SEUL. 3 v.   (36 mm.). Rondeau.
Text: Jardin no. 316.
Source: Dijon 517.
Edition: DrozT 62-63.
Recording: Oiseau D154D3 Davies.
18. QU'ES MI VIDA PREGUNTAYS. 4 v.   (45 mm.).
Canción. S., T. from 3-voice canción by
Juan Cornago. Composed in Spain ca. 1470?
Sources: Seville 7-I-28 (anon.), Montecassino
871 (Cornago-Oquegan; fac. in PopeM pl. II).
Editions: CornagoC 69-71, GalvadáC 13-15,
HaberkampW 145-47, PopeM 131-35, PopeS 703-
5, StevensonS 218-23.
Literature: FallowsJ 222, PopeME 49-50,
RussellM 6 and 23 (n. 51), StevensonS 218-
23.
Recording: Oiseau D254D3 Davies.
19. S'ELLE M'AMERA/PETITE CAMUSETTE. 4 v.   (47
mm.). Rondeau in S.; popular song paraphrased
in T.
Sources: Brussels 11239 (anon.; S. and T.
only), Dijon 517 (anon.), Florence Cons.
2439, Montecassino 871 (anon.), Munich 1516
(anon.), New Haven Mellon, Paris Nivelle,
Seville 7-I-28 (anon.), Wolfenbüttel 287
(anon.), 1504[3].
Editions: GavaldáC 90-91, GombosiJ Anhang 8-
9, HaberkampW 256-58, PerkinsMC no. 4,

PickerC 437-39, PopeM 438-41.
Literature: ManiatesC 238-43, PickerC 81,
PlamenacP 36-37, RussellM 6 and 23 (no. 52).
Recordings: Archive 3052 Cape, Harmonia Mundi
990 Clemencic, Lyrichord 7213 Planchart,
Mus. Her. 4472 Planchart, Oiseau D254D3
Davies.
20. SE VOSTRE CUER ESLONGNE. 3 v. (44 mm.).
Rondeau.
Sources: Paris 15123 (fac. in PlamenacR 323),
Rome Cas. 2856.
Edition: AmbrosG 5: 16-17.
Literature: PlamenacR.
Recording: Oiseau D254D3 Davies (instr.
perf.).
21. TANT FUZ GENTEMENT RESJOUY. 2. Si haultement.
3 v. (65 mm.). Bergerette.
Source: Paris Nivelle.
Recording: Oiseau D254D3 Davies.
22. UNG AULTRE L'A. 3 v. (45 mm.). Rondeau.
Sources: Florence Ricc. 2794 (fac.in PlamenacR
321), Rome Giul. XIII.27 (D'ung aultre l'a).
Edition: AtlasC 2: 3-4.
Literature: PlamenacR.
Recording: Oiseau D254D3 Davies.

(9) Secular Works - Doubtful
The following works are attributed in one or
more sources to Ockeghem and, in equally or more
reliable sources, to another composer.
1. AU TRAVAIL SUIS. 3 v. (23 mm.). OckCW I, no.
3a, p. 42. Rondeau. Text: FrançonP 135.
Attributed to Ockeghem and Barbingant in
central sources, this work may be by either
composer. Ockeghem based his Missa Au travail
suis on it.
Sources: Dijon 517 (Barbinguant), Paris
Nivelle (Okeghem), Wolfenbüttel 287
(anon.; fac. in BesselerS 112, KonradM 39).
Edition: BarbireauO 2: 12-13.
Literature: FallowsJ 222, FoxB 98, PlamenacP
33-34, SaarL 137-40.
Recordings: Nonesuch 71336 Blachly, Oiseau
D254D3 Davies.
2. CE N'EST PAS JEU. 3 v. (55 mm.). Rondeau.
Attributed to Hayne van Ghizeghem in three
central sources, and probably by him.
Sources: Florence Ricc. 2794 (Hayne), London

20. A.XVI (anon.), Paris 2245 (Haine), Rome
    Giul. XIII.27 (Se mieulx ne vient; anon.),
    Rome Cas. 2856 (Okeghem), Segovia (Scoen
    Heyne), Washington Laborde (anon.).
    Editions: AmbrosG 5: 14-15, HayneO 10-11,
    MarixM 103-4.
    Recording: Oiseau D254D3 Davies.
3. DEPARTÉS VOUS, MALEBOUCHE. 3 v. (53 mm.).
    Rondeau. The attributions to both Dufay and
    Ockeghem are doubtful.
    Sources: Bologna Q16 (anon.), Montecassino 871
    (Dufay), Paris 15123 (Ockghen).
    Editions: DufayO 6: no. 93, PeaseE no. 115,
    PopeM no. 21.
    Literature: FallowsJ 222.
    Recordings: Oiseau D237D6 Davies, Oiseau
    D254D3 Davies.
4. MALHEUR ME BAT. 3 v. (59 mm.). Rondeau(?)
    Probably by Johannes Martini, to whom it is
    attributed in two early Florentine sources.
    Attributions to Ockeghem and the unknown
    Malcort are less reliable.
    Sources: Bologna Q16 (Dieu d'amors; anon.),
    Bologna Q18 (anon.), Florence B.R.229
    (Jannes Martini; textless), Rome Giul.
    XIII.27 (Jo. Martini), Cas. 2856 (Malcort),
    St. Gall 461 (Ockenghem), 1501 (Okenghen),
    [c. 1535]14 (anon.), 15389 (anon.). Tabl.:
    15076 (anon.).
    Editions: BrownF 2: no. 11, GiesbertA 2: 60-
    61, HewittO 353-54, JosquinWM 2: 66-67,
    MartiniS 53-55, ObrO 1: 226-27, ObrW 1: 189-
    92.
    Literature: AtlasC 1: 149-55, AtlasCA,
    FallowsJ 221-22, GombosiJ 85-86, HudsonT
    279-83, KarpS 457.
    Recordings: Accord 149167 Clemencic, Oiseau
    D254D3 Davies (instr. perf.), Oxford 128
    Venhoda.
5. QUAND CE VIENDRA. 3 (4) v. (33 mm.).
    Rondeau. Text: LöpelmannL no. 458.
    Attributed to Antoine Busnois in two central
    sources, probably correctly. PerkinsM 250
    suggests that the added Ct. may be by
    Ockeghem.
    Sources: Dijon 517 (Busnoys), Escorial IV.a.24
    (Hockenghem), Florence 176 (anon.), New
    Haven Mellon (anon.; with added Ct. si

placet), Paris Nivelle (anon.; erased),
Trent 88 (Gaude mater; anon.), Trent 91
(Gaude mater; anon.; with added Ct.),
Washington Laborde (Busnoys), Wolfenbüttel
287 (anon.).
Editions: DrozT 5-6, HanenC 3: 417-20,
PerkinsMC no. 16.
Literature: ReeseMR 102-4, FallowsJ 221.
Recording: Oiseau D254D3 Davies.

(10) Miscellaneous
Various works that are anonymous in the
sources have been attributed to Ockeghem on
stylistic or circumstantial grounds, without
confirming documentation. Some of these are
summarily listed below. (See also WegmanA.)
1. MILES MIRAE PROBITATIS. 4 v. Unpublished.
    Motet in praise of St. Martin of Tours.
    Ockeghem's authorship is suggested in AmbrosG
    3: 179 and PirroH 114, but rejected in
    PlamenacO-MGG 1835.
    Source: 1504[1] (anon.).
2. PERMANENTE VIERGE/PULCHRA ES/SANCTA DEI
    GENITRIX. 5 v. (30 mm.). Rondeau (motet-
    chanson). Cantus firmi: Antiphons ("Pulchra
    es" in LU 1606). Ockeghem's authorship is
    suggested in AmbrosG 2: 354 and accepted in
    StephanB 44. The work is listed as doubtful
    in PerkinsO-NG 495.
    Source: Dijon 517 (anon.).
    Edition: AmbrosG 2: 355-57.
3. RESJOIS TOY TERRE DE FRANCE/REX PACIFICUS. 4
    v. (42 mm.). Ballade (motet-chanson). C.f.:
    Antiphon (LU 364). Written for the coronation
    of Louis XI (1461)? Ockeghem's authorship is
    suggested in FallowsE 68, but the suggestion
    is withdrawn in FallowsJ 222.
    Sources: Montecassino 871 (anon.), Paris 15123
      (anon.).
    Edition: PopeM 391-94.
4. TOUS LES REGRETZ. 3 v. (67 mm.). Rondeau(?)
    The work survives with only an incipit, but a
    rondeau beginning with these words was written
    by the French court poet Octavien de St-Gelais
    for the departure of Margaret of Austria from
    France in 1493. Ockeghem's authorship of the
    music is suggested in PickerMR 85-86.
    Source: 1504[3] (anon.).
    Edition: PickerMR 97-101.

II. JACOB OBRECHT (ca. 1450-1505)

A. BIOGRAPHY

The only full-length survey of Obrecht's life and works is HoornJ (1968). Although rambling and overly speculative, it contains some useful information and facsimiles of documents not printed elsewhere. However, it should be used in conjunction with more reliable specialized studies. An earlier and still important monograph is GombosiJ (1925), which concentrates on Obrecht's style in relation to his contemporaries but not on his biography. Good but brief surveys of Obrecht's life are contained in the dictionary articles FinscherO-MGG and SparksO-NG, and in ReeseMR. The most thorough and up-to-date biography is contained in the unpublished dissertation BakerU (1978). Specialized studies of aspects of Obrecht's career include MurrayN, MurrayJ, and PirroO, and information may also be found in recent regional studies, LockwoodM on Ferrara and StrohmM on Bruges.

1. Documents and Hypotheses

a. **Name and Origins**
The name "Obrecht" (Hobrecht, Obreht, Obreth) is the Flemish genitive of "Hubertus," patron saint of Liège in eastern Flanders, and many families in that diocese bear the name (MurrayN 500, n. 2). Although it is most commonly spelled "Obrecht," many spellings are found in the fifteenth and sixteenth centuries. The greatest authority probably rests in "Hobrecht," since that spelling is found in the composer's autobiographical motets "Inter praeclarissimas virtutes" and "Mille quingentis" in the Segovia MS, a central source of his works (SmijersT 132). His actual birthplace is unknown. Efforts to locate it in Bergen-op-Zoom (PiscaerJ) are speculative.

39

b. Birthdate

The only document relating to his birth is the
text of his motet "Mille quingentis," written on
the death of his father Willem in 1488 (SmijersT
133-4):

Mille quingentis verum bis sex minus annis
Virgine progeniti lapsis ab origine Christi
Sicilides flerunt Musae, dum fata tulerunt
Hobrecht Guillermum, magna probitate decorum.
Ceciliae ad festum, qui Siciliam peragravit,
Coram idem Orphei cum Musis Jacobum generavit.
Ergo dulce melos succentorum chorus alme
Concine, ut ad caelos sit vecta anima et data
        palme. Amen.

(Translation:
Truly when fifteen hundred less twelve
[1488] years had passed since the birth of
Christ, son of the Virgin, the Sicilian muses
wept when the fates carried off Willem
Hobrecht, who was endowed with great probity.
Journeying through Sicily, he had a son,
Jacob, on the feast of St. Cecilia [November
22], in the presence of Orpheus and the Muses.
Therefore sing a sweet song, blessed choir of
singers, so that his soul may rise to heaven
and be rewarded. Amen.)
Archival documents in Ghent identify Willem Obrecht
as a city trumpeter from 1452 until his death there
in 1488, when "Jacobus Hobrecht, priestre" is named
as his heir (MurrayN 501 and ClercxL 155). Taken
together, these documents inform us that Jacob
Obrecht was born on November 22 while his father
was in Sicily, probably before 1452.

Another document in Ghent, of 1451, mentions
"een trompetter van Cicilien," possibly a reference
to Willem (MurrayN 501). PiscaerJ cites a
pilgrimage to the Holy Land undertaken by the
Marquis Henryk of Bergen-op-Zoom in 1450 as a
possible reason for Willem's presence in Sicily
(cited in MurrayN 501), but this speculation is
based on the undocumented assumption that Willem
lived in Bergen and served Henryk. It is not clear
if Willem was accompanied by his wife to Sicily,
but if such was the case, Jacob would have been
born there. Wherever he was born, the best
estimate of the year of his birth remains ca. 1450.

It is probable that his formative years were
spent in Ghent, from at least 1452 to perhaps as

late as the 1470s. Hypotheses concerning his
education are offered in MurrayN 502.

**c. Early Career: Utrecht(?), Bergen-op-Zoom(?),
and Cambrai (ca. 1476-85)**
     Many biographers state that Obrecht served as
"Zangmeester" at Utrecht in 1476 (for example,
FinscherO-MGG 1815), but no documentation for this
claim has been produced. He is also reported to
have been a teacher of Erasmus of Rotterdam (born
ca. 1466) during the late 1470s. The authority for
this belief is the Swiss humanist and music
theorist Heinrich Glareanus, pupil and friend of
Erasmus. In his **Dodecachordon** (1547), Glareanus
states:
          Jacob Obrecht is second to none in regard
     to prolificacy and to majesty of song in the
     opinion of our teacher, D. Erasmus of Rotter-
     dam, and also in our opinion. And he was the
     teacher in music of the boy Erasmus, as we
     ourselves heard many years ago from Erasmus's
     own lips. (GlareanusD 252)
Beatus Rhenanus, another friend of Erasmus and one
of his earliest biographers, wrote in 1540 that
Erasmus had been a choirboy at the Utrecht
cathedral (MillerE 343). This statement and that
of Glareanus have been linked together to draw the
conclusion that Obrecht taught Erasmus as master of
the choirboys at Utrecht. However, since no
documentation that Obrecht served in Utrecht has
been found, the place and date of Erasmus's
tutelage by Obrecht remain obscure (MurrayJ 125).
     A "Jacob Willemsone" living in Bergen-op-Zoom
in the late 1470s is thought to be the composer
Obrecht, as is the "Jacob" appointed Sangmeester at
the church of St. Gudule at Bergen in 1479 (BakerU
1: 112). On 23 April 1480 "Jacop de Sangmeester"
was paid for celebrating his first mass at the
church in Gastel, a dependency of Bergen (BakerU 1:
112-13, HoornJ 39), implying that he had recently
been ordained a priest. Other Bergen documents
list payments to "Meester Jacobe den Sangmeester"
between 1481 and 1484, while "Hobrecht" is recorded
as visiting Bergen in 1488, and "Meester Jacobe
Obrechts" is cited in Bergen documents for 1496-98
(BakerU 1: 113, 118-19). These documents are often
cited to show a special relationship between
Obrecht and Bergen-op-Zoom, lending support to the

suggestion that he was born there. Most authorities agree in identifying the composer with "Jacob
de Sangmeester," although Murray expresses doubt
that they are the same person (MurrayJ 128).

On 28 July 1484 the canons of the cathedral of
Cambrai, one of the most important religious
centers in northern Europe, named "Jacobus Obreth
de Bergis" master of the choirboys ("magistro
puerorum choralium"). (See fac. of the document in
PirroO 78.) Reference to him as "de Bergis" (of
Bergen) lends further credence to the belief that
he came from Bergen-op-Zoom.

On 6 September 1484 Obrecht assumed his new
position at Cambrai, and on 9 September received a
copy of his assigned duties to supervise the care
and education of the choirboys. According to his
contract, he is to teach them liturgy, plainchant,
good behavior, and Latin; to oversee their feeding,
clothing, and leisure; and to render an account of
his expenditures. He is also charged to instruct
certain adult vicars in music (PirroO 78-79). On
25 June 1485 he was assigned to teach a vicar from
Bergen to sing "super librum" (literally "on the
book," meaning improvised discant on a plainsong;
quoted in WrightP 313).

On 27 July 1485 Obrecht was reproved by the
canons for negligence in carrying out his tasks,
the first sign of serious difficulties with his
superiors. On 21 October they demanded to inspect
his accounts, and on 24 October the "master of the
lesser vicars" was sent to speak to the "master of
the choirboys" (i.e. Obrecht) and to recover such
monies of the church that he could (PirroO 79).

Throughout the period of difficulty at
Cambrai, Obrecht was negotiating for a position at
the church of St. Donatian in Bruges. The records
of the chapter for 7 February 1485 state that
"Master Jacob Obrecht, presently master of the
choirboys at the cathedral of Cambrai, greatly
desires to serve this church as succentor" (BakerU
1: 116-7). On 12 September he was invited to
Bruges, and on 13 October was installed as
succentor (assistant choirmaster) in absentia,
being paid for "traveling back and forth two or
three times" (BakerU 1: 117). On 1 November
Obrecht was relieved of his position at Cambrai
(PirroO 79).

d. Bruges and Ferrara (1485-91)
   In November of 1485 Obrecht actively assumed
the office of succentor at St. Donatian, the most
important church of Bruges (StrohmM 10 et passim).
His duties were similar to those at Cambrai:
supervision of the singers and training of the
choirboys (StrohmM 13). He continued in this post
through 1487 (MurrayJ 130).
   Obrecht's reputation as a composer had by this
time spread beyond the borders of Flanders to
Italy. He was cited as a composer of outstanding
merit as early as the 1470s by the theorist
Johannes Tinctoris, a Fleming who served at the
court of Naples (**Complexus effectuum musices**, ca.
1474; TinctorisO 2: 176). Obrecht is the only
composer of his generation mentioned in any of the
writings of the noted theorist; he would have been
about 24 years old. Further evidence of his
reputation while still a very young man is the fact
that his Missa Beata viscera was copied into Siena
MS K.I.2 around 1481 (D'AcconeL).
   In 1484 the music-loving Duke Ercole I d'Este
of Ferrara requested and received from Cornelius de
Laurentius of Antwerp, one of his chapel singers
who was then in Florence, a "messa de Jacob
Obrecht," which pleased him (MurrayN 509-10; fac.
opp. p. 515, also in HoornJ opp. p. 71). In
September 1487 Ercole sent Cornelius to Bruges for
the purpose of inviting Obrecht to visit Ferrara
(LockwoodM 163). Ercole's chapel was one of the
most distinguished in Europe and he undoubtedly
hoped to recruit Obrecht for it.
   On 2 October the accounts of the chapter at
St. Donatian show that "Cornelius de Lilloo"
presented letters from Ercole requesting permission
for "Magister Jacobus, succentor" to visit him.
The chapter granted Obrecht a leave of absence for
six months. This document is of great importance,
shedding light on Obrecht's career and reputation
and on Ercole's patronage of musicians (original
and translation in LockwoodM 163-64; a slightly
revised version of Lockwood's translation
follows):
      Letters from Ercole, Duke of Ferrara were shown
      to the chapter by a certain Cornelius de
      Lilloo, a singer of his chapel, which request
      the chapter to permit Magister Jacob the
      succentor to come to him for some months in the

near future. The chapter members have heard
from this Cornelius and also Don Johannes
Cordier, who affirmed that this Duke is
strongly devoted to the art of music, and
strongly favors the musical composition of
Magister Jacob over other compositions and has
for a long time wished to see him. Presently,
Magister Jacob having come before the chapter
and agreeing to the Duke's petition, the
chapter members allowed him to absent himself
for six months beginning on the next festival
of St. Donatian [14 October], provided that his
office and the singing would be provided for in
the interim period and not remain vacant. And
since Don Johannes Rykelin, chaplain, was hired
for this position, the chapter members were
content and ordered favourable letters to be
written to his lordship the Duke, and the
aforesaid Cornelius was presented with two
casks of wine and bread . . .

Obrecht journeyed to Ferrara in company with
Cornelius. On November 19 the Ferrarese ambassador
in Milan, responding to an inquiry from Ercole,
wrote that "if Cornelio and that other singer
[Obrecht], whom he is bringing from France, arrive
here, I will send him . . . to Mantua," where the
Duke was about to go (LockwoodM 163). On the first
of December Ercole wrote to his wife that "Dom.
Jacobo Obreth, excellent singer, whom we had
fetched from France," had arrived and would
accompany the Duke to Ferrara (original and
translation in MurrayN 510; fac. opp. p. 514, also
in HoornJ opp. p. 76).

Ercole made strenuous efforts through
emissaries in Rome to obtain benefices for Obrecht
from Pope Innocent VIII, undoubtedly in order to
persuade him to remain in Italy, but to no avail.
A letter of 17 January 1488 from Ercole to his
representative in Rome describes the situation
(MurrayN 513-15; see the extensive correspondence
on pp. 510 et passim, and the additional letters in
LockwoodMF 127-29):

. . . we have to thank His Holiness a hundred
thousand times for the reply given to you as to
our request concerning one of those two
benefices on behalf of Messer Jacomo Hobreth,
and for the good disposition and benevolence

that he shows towards us, for which we are
greatly thankful.
    However, since what we had asked of His
Holiness in this matter was such an exceptional
favor and one that could have the effect that
we ardently desire, we urge you to visit His
Holiness again and implore him on our behalf
that what was his pleasure not to grant for him
[Obrecht], he may be willing to reserve for us
the first of the two benefices that will become
vacant and to confer it on Messer Jacomo as
soon as the vacancy be known . . . And we beg
of you not to forget, if we may say so, to
remind every day every person concerned so that
this may never go out of their minds, because
we certainly desire above all that this Messer
Jacomo be favored. Our writing to you has
certainly made you understand that it is our
desire that he [Obrecht] may return to his
country fully pleased and that he may
appreciate how dear to us are his excellent
qualities, which certainly are highly
praiseworthy.
    Replying now to what His Holiness told
you, namely that he suspected we had seized
upon his "game," we say to you that we have not
engaged Messer Jacomo's services for ourselves,
but that we have invited him to visit us and
only with difficulty have persuaded him to stay
here for four or five months, after which he
will return to his own country. But we wish to
assure His Holiness that if we had been able to
persuade him to stay with us forever, and if
the recreation and enjoyment that we constantly
receive from him were any greater than they
are, they could never be such as to prevent us
from satisfying His Holiness's slightest wish,
and that more than willingly we would pass
Messer Jacomo on to him--finding more pleasure
and happiness in His Holiness's acceptance of
him than we would have in enjoying him
ourselves; always eager as we are to comply in
anything concerning His Holiness's will and to
obey any wishes of his accordance with our
devotion to him.
    A remarkable document of these negotiations is
Obrecht's motet "Inter praeclarissimas virtutes,"
uniquely preserved in the Segovia MS. Its text,

addressed to the Pope himself, names its author/
composer as "Jacobus Hobrecht." An abridged
translation, after NagleS 154-55, follows (for the
original Latin, see SmijersT 131-32):

> Among your excellent virtues and marvelous
> gifts of the mind, your piety . . . is
> outstanding. You always show a ready and
> benevolent heart, so that now . . . music is
> supported by your hand . . . Be strong in your
> fight!
>   Because of your fatherly behavior . . . I
> always sound forth with jubilation in my
> songs . . . And I humbly offer this present
> page, put together in a simple style of
> harmony, for the praise of God and your
> comfort. For what else I can give you as a
> service I do not know . . . Be strong in your
> fight!
>   Therefore kindly accept the present
> musical composition and me, Jacob Hobrecht,
> your very humble servant, with good will.
> Command and rule happily and long!

Ercole could not keep Obrecht in Italy, but he
continued to take an interest in him. In 1496 he
asked his ambassador in Milan to send him a mass by
the composer (MurrayN 506, 515-16), and in 1504 he
finally appointed him a singer and "compositore de
canto" in his chapel (MurrayN 507, 516; see below).

In the spring of 1488 Obrecht returned north,
having overstayed his leave by some months. He did
not go first to Bruges, possibly because of the
uprising there against the regent, the Hapsburg
archduke Maximilian, who was trying to assert his
authority over the city. Instead, he went to
Bergen-op-Zoom, a city that repeatedly attracted
him. On 12 June 1488 the authorities at St.
Donatian in Bruges urged him to return to his post
by the 24th of the month or "it will be necessary
for the canons to provide for another succentor"
(BakerU 1: 118-19). A second warning followed on
18 June, apparently to no avail. On 6 August the
canons received a letter from Ercole apologizing
for Obrecht's delay in returning, which he
attributed to the strife in Bruges, and promised
that he would be back by 15 August (BakerU 1: 119
and MurrayJ 130).

Obrecht returned to his duties in Bruges where
he remained until January 1491 (MurrayJ 132). In

1489-90 he and his singers were paid by the city to
perform in the "lof," or Salve concerts given daily
after compline at St. Donatian's (StraetenM 3: 183,
MurrayJ 132; concerning the Salve concerts, see
StrohmM 39). These public concerts, important as
they were to the cultural life of Bruges, must have
imposed an unwelcome burden on the succentor. In
1490 the canons decided to dismiss him, as had the
chapter at Cambrai some six years before. On 26
May they tried to persuade him to resign "in order
to preserve his own honor" (StrohmM 39). He seems
to have rejected their suggestion and held on to
his position, evidently with some local support.
On 15 October 1490 he was invited to perform, with
four other singers of his choice, by Count Philip
of Cleves at Sluis (StrohmM 39-40, MurrayJ 130).
However, in January 1491 he either was dismissed or
resigned, and a replacement, the former succentor
Pierre Basin, was named on 17 January (StrohmM 40,
182).
     Basin was a colleague of Obrecht in the choir
who in 1486 had endowed an anniversary mass in
polyphony dedicated to St. Martin to be sung in the
saint's chapel of St. Donatian's by the choirboys
and succentor "with two of the best singers."
Strohm believes that Obrecht composed his Missa de
Sancto Martino in response to Basin's request
(StrohmM 40). The Missa de Sancto Donatiano was
also written for Bruges, but not necessarily for
St. Donatian's church, since the saint was patron
of the city as a whole (StrohmM 146).

e. **Antwerp and Bruges (1491-1502)**
     Obrecht's delay in resigning his post at
Bruges was probably due to his desire to first
secure another position. Nevertheless, the earliest
documents specifically naming him as chapel-master
at the Church of Our Lady in Antwerp date from 24
June 1494 (MurrayJ 131-32). Probably that
appointment began in 1491, the year in which the
previous chapel-master, Jacques Barbireau, died.
Indeed, from 1491 until 1504 a "meester Jacop de
Sangmeester" received a salary from the Chapel of
the Holy Virgin; this cannot have been Barbireau
but may have been Obrecht (MurrayJ 128-33).
Obrecht maintained an amicable relationship with
Bruges after his departure, sending them a mass
from Antwerp in 1491, possibly the one that was

copied into a choirbook at St. Donatian's in 1491-
92 (StrohmM 40, 146).

Obrecht served as chapel-master in Antwerp
until 1498, visiting Bergen-op-Zoom in July 1497 to
direct the combined choirs of St. Gertrude's and
the Burgundian court chapel during the visit of the
archduke Philip the Fair (HoornJ 58). Other
evidence points to his presence in Bergen in 1497-
98 (MurrayJ 132). On 31 December 1498 Obrecht
returned to Bruges and resumed his duties as
succentor at St. Donatian's. Again, his musical
talents evidently outweighed his administrative
failings. Documents show that he was paid for
drawing the staves for a choirbook containing
masses "de Salve sancta parens et alii" in 1499-
1500 for St. Donatian's (StrohmM 148). A mass of
this title by Obrecht is not known, but the entry
may be an erroneous reference to his Missa Salve
diva parens.

On 3 September 1500 Obrecht asked to be
relieved of his post at Bruges because of ill
health. On 29 October the canons awarded a
benefice to "magister Jacobus Hobrecht, qui bene
famosus musicus esse noscitur" (master Jacob
Hobrecht, who is known to be a quite famous
musician), confirmation of the high regard in which
his musical achievement was held (StraetenM 3: 185-
86). Obrecht then returned to Antwerp, again
serving at the Church of Our Lady at least through
1502 (MurrayJ 130-33).

f.   Innsbruck, Rome(?), and Ferrara (1503-05)
On 6 October 1503 Obrecht is found at the
court of the Hapsburg emperor Maximilian I at
Innsbruck; the accounts show that he received
damask cloth in payment for an "Amt" (Missa?)
Regina coeli written for the court (StaehelinO 14):

> Maister Martin [Triemer], gib Jacoben Oppreht
> 14 ellen gueten Tamaschk; so wir ime
> schennckhen, von wegen aines Ambts **Regina coeli**
> so er unns gemacht hab.

Although no such mass by Obrecht is known, his
Missa Maria zart, based on a devotional song
popular in Germany at the time, may have been
composed during his stay in Innsbruck.

From Innsbruck Obrecht journeyed to Italy.
Documents found by Richard Sherr show that between
November 1503 and September 1504 Obrecht may have

been under consideration for, and perhaps even
received an appointment to the papal chapel of
Julius II. (Sherr, "Jacob Obrecht and Lupus
Hellinck: New Documents and Speculations,"
forthcoming in MQ. See also LockwoodM 208, n. 34.)
According to these documents, dated 1 August 1505,
benefices were vacated by Obrecht by his death
"outside of Rome," and one document describes
Obrecht as "perhaps a member of our chapel" (i.e.
the papal chapel of Julius II). Since the author
of the document was a member of the chapel himself,
this statement must be viewed as more than
speculation. However, this appointment, if it
occurred, was short-lived. Beginning on 2 October
1504 Obrecht received payment for service at the
court of Ercole in Ferrara, succeeding his eminent
contemporary, Josquin des Prez (documents cited in
MurrayN 516), who had received similar payments in
February and March.

Ercole was by that time seriously ill. He
died on 17 January 1505, and his son Alfonso, who
succeeded him as Duke of Ferrara, did not keep
Obrecht in his service. Obrecht received his last
payment on 31 December 1504 (MurrayN 507, 516),
although it is likely that he participated in the
memorial services for Ercole held on 5 February
1505. On 12 February the court paid a debt owed by
him, probably representing a final settling of
accounts (LockwoodM 208). A memento of the two
great composers who served Ercole during his final
years is the Ferrarese MS alpha M.1.2, a choirbook,
now at the Biblioteca Estense in Modena, compiled
around 1505 and devoted to works by Josquin and
Obrecht.

The last dated document of Obrecht's life is a
letter of 2 May 1505 from Ferrante d'Este to the
Marquis Francesca Gonzaga of Mantua recommending
Obrecht, who is coming to Mantua to present
compositions to Francesco (LockwoodM 209). There
is no evidence that Obrecht received an appointment
at Mantua, however.

Obrecht died in the summer, probably July,
1505 at Ferrara of the plague. The date of death
is suggested by the documents discovered by Sherr,
which are dated 1 August. Drafts of two epitaphs
by Gaspar Sardi, a Ferrarese poet and historio-
grapher, bear the date 13 August 1505 (HoornJ 106

with a fac. of the original MS). The second and
more polished version reads as follows:
    Musicus hic Hobreht doctissimus: Arte secundus
    Nulli alio tegitur, voce vel ingenio.
    (Here lies the most wise musician Obrecht:
    He is surpassed by none in art, voice, or
    genius.)
That Obrecht died in a Ferrarese hospital of plague
is indicated in a document of 1510 concerning the
execution of his will by the hospital administra-
tors: "msr. Jacomo Obreth, già cantore del Ill.mo
Sig. Duca . . . qui e morte de pesti" (StraetenM 3:
189, HoornJ 104 with fac.).
    Compositions that have been cited as possible
memorials to Obrecht include Josquin's "Absolve,
quaesumus/Requiem" and Verdelot's "Recordare,
Domine/Parce Domine" (see EldersJ).

g. Reputation
    Efforts to identify portraits of Obrecht are
based on a misunderstanding of a passage in
Vasari's **Life of Sebastiano del Piombo**, which
states that Sebastiano "painted in Venice some very
faithful portraits, among them that of the
Frenchman Verdelotto . . . and in the same picture
the portrait of his colleague, the singer Ubretto"
(EinsteinI 1: 155). Einstein identifies "Ubretto"
as Obrecht, but the name probably refers to Hubert
Naich, a madrigalist and younger contemporary of
Verdelot (see SindonaE). Gafurius (**Practica
musica**, 1496) includes him among many "very
pleasing composers" of the time (the others being
Josquin, Weerbecke, Agricola, Compère, Brumel,
and Isaac, all cited for their use of the well-
known procedure of moving the outer voices in
parallel tenths around a tenor; GaffuriusP 144). A
more penetrating evaluation, one of the earliest
humanistic attempts at music criticism, appears in
Paolo Cortese's **De cardinalatu libri tres** of 1510,
a treatise on the behavior befitting a cardinal of
the church. In a section dealing with the "the use
of music after meals," Cortese both praises and
criticizes the leading composer of masses (Josquin)
and outstanding composers of motets (Obrecht,
Isaac, et al.). Concerning Obrecht, whom he names
first among composers for excellence in motet
composition, Cortese states:

In this genre Jacobus Obrechius is considered
great for varied subtlety, but more crude in
the whole style of composition, and also the
one by whom more of the sharpest agreeableness
has been sowed among the musicians than would
have been enough for the pleasure of the ear --
like, in the field of taste, people who seem to
like those things that taste of unripe juice
better than sugar. (PirrottaM 104)
As Pirrotta points out, Cortese views music as an
entertainment rather than an autonomous art, and
his criticism reflects a diffidence toward any
music that requires intellectual effort on the part
of the listener.
     Obrecht's works were widely known throughout
Europe by 1500. In Venice in 1495 a mass by
Obrecht for four voices was performed with two
added bass parts played on trombones (StraetenM 8:
536-37). Petrucci published some of Obrecht's
works in his earliest songbook, the **Odhecaton**
(1501), and five of Obrecht's masses constitute the
entire contents of his **Misse Obreht** (1503). He
includes a variety of Obrecht's works in other of
his song and motet collections. A second book of
masses devoted entirely to Obrecht was published
posthumously in Basel around 1510, and major works
continued to appear in such collections as 1520[1],
1539[1], and 1539[2]. Glareanus cited and included
complete works by him in his **Dodecachordon** of 1547,
commenting on his "prolificacy" (see p. 41 above)
and the speed with which he worked. In the chapter
"Concerning the Skill of **symphonetae**," he turns to
Obrecht after discussing Josquin and Ockeghem:
     The third man in this class undoubtedly is
     Jacob Obrecht, and he is also a Belgian, who in
     fact was the teacher of D. Erasmus of Rotter-
     dam, whose opinion of Obrecht we have reported
     in [the chapter on] the Aeolian [mode]. More-
     over, it is said that he worked with such
     quickness of device and fertility of invention
     that in a single night he composed an excellent
     Mass, and one which was also admired by learned
     men. All the monuments of this man have a
     certain wonderful majesty and an innate quality
     of moderation. He certainly was not such a
     lover of the unusual as was Josquin. Indeed,
     he did display his skill, but without
     ostentation, as if he may have preferred to

await the judgment of the listener rather than
to exalt himself. There are many compositions
of his in this very book . . . (GlareanD 277-
78)

Obrecht's works continued to be cited by
theorists well into the seventeenth century. Many
examples, including some from works no longer
extant, are given in Zacconi 1592 and are again
cited in Cerone 1613. But his name and reputation
suffered eclipse in the two centuries that
followed, surviving only through Glareanus's
remarks until the 1860s, when the pioneer music
historian A. W. Ambros examined his works afresh
and found him "greater, more profound, more serious
and virile" than Ockeghem, who was still thought to
be his contemporary (AmbrosG 3: 182). Serious
attention has been paid to him ever since Ambros,
although when it was soon recognized that Obrecht
was not a contemporary of Ockeghem but belonged to
the next generation, he was somewhat overshadowed
by his true contemporaries. He remains outranked
in that generation by Josquin des Prez and Heinrich
Isaac, but he is often rated as their equal or
nearly so. More conservative than they, more
purely northern in his emphasis on polyphonic
structure rather than textual expression, but
sensitive to the new tendencies toward rich
textures and coherent harmonies, he is an outstanding representative of his age, straddling and
uniting the late Gothic and Renaissance styles as
perhaps no other composer of the late fifteenth
century. The normally objective Gustave Reese sums
this up in an unusual personal statement:

In addition to the technical proficiency shown
in his music, its sheer loveliness makes him
one of the greatest figures in a great
generation. (ReeseMR 204-5)

B. COMPOSITIONS

1. Historical and Analytical Studies

a. **General**
   Good overviews of Obrecht's works are
contained in the encyclopedia articles FinscherO-
MGG and SparksO-NG, and in ReeseMR 186-205. HoornJ
should be used with caution.

b. **Style and Technique**
   The most comprehensive and intensive study of
Obrecht's sacred music, albeit limited to works
based on cantus firmi, is SparksC 245-311, which
treats both structural and stylistic aspects.
Obrecht's style in relation to his contemporaries
is examined in GombosiJ, based on a selected group
of sacred and secular compositions. A brief but
wide-ranging study of his stylistic development and
the chronology of his masses is given in HudsonOT.
Representative masses are studied in MeierZ,
SalopM, and WagnerG 114-40. SalopM is the broadest
in its coverage and concentrates on Obrecht's
harmonic language. The cantus firmus motets are
examined in NagleS, which emphasizes external
rather than internal features, especially the
sources of texts and borrowed melodies. Most of
the general surveys neglect the sacred works that
are not based on identifiable cantus firmi or are
incompletely preserved. (RossM, a stylistic study
of the motets, has not been seen, and may be an
exception.)
   Source and attribution problems are considered
in NoblittF, NoblittT, StaehelinM, and StaehelinO.
Special aspects of Obrecht's technique and style
are studied in MeierH, NoblittC, SalopJ, and ToddR.
Individual or small groups of works are examined in
AntonowytschR, BukofzerC, HewittS, HudsonF,
LockwoodN, NoblittO, VellekoopZ and VellekoopP.
These studies are almost entirely concerned with
Obrecht's sacred music. Only GombosiJ discusses a
cross-section of his secular works.

53

A special problem in Obrecht research is his
use of number symbolism, often of a hidden nature.
There is convincing evidence of his concern with
this aspect in some of his works, such as those
discussed in LockwoodN and VellekoopZ. An extreme
view that sees such symbolism as omnipresent is
that of van Crevel, expressed in the elaborate
introductions to his editions of masses in ObrO.
Van Crevel's position is attacked in DahlhausZ and
elsewhere as overly speculative and unconvincing.
The matter remains controversial.

c. Performance Practice
     The most important issues in the performance
of Obrecht's music are the question of singing
multiple texts simultaneously in certain masses and
motets, the size and relative proportions of the
choirs that sang the music, the employment of
instruments, and the application of unwritten
accidentals (musica ficta). Broad aspects of
performance are dealt with in LenaertsM, NoblittC,
and WrightP. Application of musica ficta and
hexachord mutation (solmization, or the use of sol-
fa syllables to determine the appropriate intervals
to be sung) and their relationship to harmonic
structure are considered in BentD and CrevelV.

2. Work List

a. Principal Editions
     The first critical edition of Obrecht's music
was the **Werken** edited by Johannes Wolf between 1908
and 1921 in eight volumes and reprinted in seven by
the Gregg Press in 1968 (ObrW). This edition
consists of five volumes of masses, one of motets,
and one each of secular and miscellaneous works
(the reprint combines these last two items in one
volume). Out-of-date and deficient in many
respects, it remains the most comprehensive edition
of Obrecht's music to date.
     An attempt to bring the edition up-to-date was
made with the **Opera Omnia, Editio alterum** (Amsterdam, 1953-64) begun by Albert Smijers, who
completed only two volumes, one of masses and one
of motets, before his death in 1957 (ObrO). This
edition was continued with two further volumes of
individual masses edited by Marcus van Crevel
(1959, 1964) in an interesting but controversial

attempt to render the original notation in a
visually proportional score without barlines. (See
the critical reviews and commentaries in BankS,
DahlhausZ, and FinscherS.) The impracticality of
van Crevel's approach led to the discontinuance of
the edition.
A new start has been made with the Collected
Works (also called the New Obrecht Edition) under
the general editorship of Chris Maas (Utrecht,
1983-)(ObrCW). Five volumes of masses have been
published to date; a total of seventeen such
volumes are projected, as well as two volumes of
motets and one each of secular and textless works.
This promises to be a excellent and comprehensive
edition, but it is still many years away from
completion.
In his anthology of music by Netherlands
composers of the fifteenth and sixteenth centuries,
Van Ockeghem tot Sweelinck (Amsterdam, 1939;
reprinted 1952), and prior to his initiating the
Opera Omnia, Smijers published a selection of works
by Obrecht that had been omitted from Wolf's
edition (SmijersV). The Obrecht works are
contained in volumes 2 and 3 of this anthology.
Many works of Obrecht are still unpublished,
although eventually all will be included in the
Collected Works. An overview of its projected
contents is given in MaasT.

b. Alphabetical List of Works
M = motet; S = secular work; doubtful works
are placed in parentheses. Spurious and lost works
are not listed here.
Alma Redemptoris Mater (M)
Als al de weerelt (S)
Ave maris stella (M)
Ave Regina coelorum (M)
Beata es, Maria (M)
Benedicamus in laude Jhesu (M)
Cuius sacrata viscera (I) (M)
Cuius sacrata viscera (II) (M)
Den haghel ende die calde snee (S)
(Discubuit Jesus) (M)
(Ein fröhlich Wesen) (S)
Factor orbis/Veni, Domine (M)
Fors seulement (S)
(Haec Deum caeli) (M)
Helas mon bien (S)

Ic draghe de mutse clutse (S)
Ic en hebbe gheen ghelt (S)
Ic hoerde de clocskins luden (S)
Ic ret my uit spacieren (S)
Ic weinsche alle scoene vrouwen (S)
Inter praeclarissimas virtutes/Estote fortes
    in bello (M)
J'ay pris amours (M)
(Judea et Jerusalem) (M)
Lacen adieu (S)
Laet u genoughen (S)
(La stangetta) (S)
La tortorella (S)
Laudemus nunc Dominum/Non est hic aliud (M)
Laudes Christo Redemptori (M)
(Magnificat)
Ma menche vel ma buche (S)
Marion la doulce (S)
Mater Patris nati nata/Sancta Dei genitrix (M)
Meskin es hu (S)
Mille quingentis/Requiem (M)
Missa Adieu mes amours
Missa Ave Regina celorum
Missa Beata viscera
Missa Caput
Missa Cela sans plus
Missa De Sancto Donatiano
Missa De Sancto Martino
Missa De tous biens playne
Missa Fors seulement
Missa Fortuna desperata
(Missa Gracuuly et biaulx)
Missa Grecorum
Missa Je ne demande
(Missa Je ne seray)
Missa L'homme armé
Missa Libenter gloriabor
Missa Malheur me bat
Missa Maria zart
(Missa N'aray-je jamais)
Missa O lumen ecclesie
Missa Petrus apostolus
Missa Pfauenschwanz
Missa Plurimorum carminum (I)
Missa Plurimorum carminum (II)
Missa Rose playsante
Missa Salve diva parens
Missa Scaramella

Missa Sicut spina rosam
Missa Si dedero
Missa Sub tuum presidium
(Missa Veci la danse barbari)
Moet my laten u vriendelic schijn (S)
(Nec mihi nec tibi) (M)
O beate Basili/O beate pater (M)
Omnis spiritus laudet (M)
O preciosissime sanguis/Guberna tuos famulos
     (M)
Parce Domine (M)
Quis numerare queat (M)
Regina celi (M)
Rompeltier (S)
Salve crux/O crux lignum (M)
Salve Regina (I) (M)
Salve Regina (II) (M)
Salve Regina (III) (M)
Salve sancta facies/Homo quidam fecit (M)
Se bien fait (S)
Si bona suscepimus (M)
Sullen wij langhe in drucke (S)
T'Andernacken (S)
Tant que nostre argent dura (S)
(T'meiskin was jonck) (S)
Tsat een (cleen) meskin (S)
Waer sij di han (S)
Wat willen wij metten (S)
Weet ghij wat minder (S)

c. Categorical List of Works, with Sources and
    Literature
    (1) Masses - Authentic
    Twenty-seven masses by Obrecht are generally
regarded as authentic. Most are for four voices;
only two are for three voices, while one, the Missa
Sub tuum presidium, begins in three voices and by
adding a voice in each successive movement ends in
seven. Virtually all of Obrecht's masses are based
on cantus firmi, sacred or secular. Some cantus
firmi are divided into segments treated separately
in the various movements, then united at the end of
the mass (e.g. Missa Maria zart). In many masses
the cantus firmi are drawn from polyphonic models,
and voices of the model composition, in addition to
the cantus firmus, are quoted, notably in the Missa
Fortuna desperata, anticipating parody procedures
that will become common in the sixteenth century.

Other masses combine many cantus firmi and melodic
borrowings in a quodlibet-like texture (e.g. the
two Missae Plurimorum carminum, based on secular
tunes, and Missa Sub tuum presidium, on Gregorian
chants). Only one mass appears to be freely
composed, or at least is without an identifiable
model: the Missa Salve diva parens. Many of the
masses make use of a head-motive at the beginnings
of some or all of the movements to give an
additional measure of unity to the entire work.
The most striking example of such a head-motive is
the six-measure duo that opens each movement in the
Missa de Sancto Donatiano.

Unlike Ockeghem, Obrecht tends to write
clearly-defined phrases and employ sharply
delineated rhythmic and melodic motives, often in
imitative or sequential patterns. He also leans
toward harmonic structures of strong chordal
movement defined by the bass and in a unified
tonality. These features are characteristic of
many composers of the late fifteenth century, but
they are especially evident in Obrecht. On the
other hand his emphasis on schematic proportional
structures and structural cantus firmi and his
relative indifference to textual expression are
conservative features that separate him from more
progressive contemporaries such as Josquin des
Prez, Heinrich Isaac, and Jean Mouton.

References below to sources, editions, and
literature are by sigla. Consult secs. III-V below
for full titles.

1. MISSA ADIEU MES AMOURS. 4 v. ObrCW I, pp. 1-
   29. Cantus firmus from popular song and
   setting by Josquin.
   I. 1. Kyrie; 2. Christe (3 v.); 3. Kyrie (94
      mm.).
   II. 1. Et in terra; 2. Qui tollis (172 mm.).
   III. 1. Patrem; 2. Et incarnatus (186 mm.).
   IV. 1. Sanctus; 2. Pleni (3 v.); 3. Osanna (=
      Kyrie I); 4. Benedictus (3 v.) (142 mm.).
   V. 1. Agnus Dei; 2. Agnus Dei (3 v.) (71 mm.).
   Sources: Jena 32 (anon.; fac. of Kyrie in
      ObrCW I), Kraków 40634 (incompl.), Segovia
      (incompl.).
   Edition: SmijersV no. 12 (Kyrie).
   Literature: MeierZ 291-95 and 299-300, SparksC
      255-59.

2. MISSA AVE REGINA CELORUM. 4 v. ObrCW I, pp.
    31-69; ObrW III, no. 12, pp. 141-88. Cantus
    firmus from T. of motet by Frye. Also
    incorporates material from the S. of Obrecht's
    own motet of this title.
    I. 1. Kyrie; 2. Christe; 3. Kyrie (75 mm.).
    II. 1. Et in terra; 2. Domini Fili unigenite
    (3 v.); 3. Qui tollis (231 mm.).
    III. 1. Patrem; 2. Et incarnatus; 3. Et
    resurrexit (3 v.); 4. Et iterum; 5. Et unam
    sanctam (276 mm.).
    IV. 1. Sanctus; 2. Pleni (3 v.); 3. Osanna; 4.
    Benedictus (192 mm.).
    V. 1. Agnus Dei; 2. Agnus Dei; 3. Agnus Dei
    (137 mm.).
    Sources: Rome Sist. 160 (anon.; without title,
    incompl.; fac. of Kyrie II in ObrCW I),
    1539[2]. Theorists: Zanger 1554 (Osanna),
    Zacconi 1592 (many exx.).
    Literature: ReeseMR 200-1, SalopM 21-26 and
    131-33, SparksC 254-56, StrohmM 147.

3. MISSA BEATA VISCERA. 4 v. ObrCW II, pp. 1-31;
    ObrW V, no. 21, pp. 97-132 (incomplete).
    Cantus firmus is communion antiphon (LU 1268).
    Extensive head-motive in S. and A. (mvts. I-
    III, V).
    I. 1. Kyrie; 2. Christe (3 v.); 3. Kyrie (61
    mm.).
    II. 1. Et in terra; 2. Qui tollis (3 v.); 3.
    Qui sedes; 4. Cum sancto Spiritu (185 mm.).
    III. 1. Patrem; 2. Et incarnatus (3 v.); 3.
    Crucifixus (3 v.); 4. Et resurrexit; 5. Et
    unam sanctam (263 mm.).
    IV. 1. Sanctus; 2. Pleni (2 v.); 3. Osanna; 4.
    Benedictus (2 v.); 5. Qui venit (3 v.); 6.
    Osanna (145 mm.).
    V. 1. Agnus Dei; 2. Agnus Dei (2 v.); 3. Agnus
    Dei (93 mm.).
    Sources: Munich 3154 (incompl.; fac. of Kyrie
    in ObrCW II), Siena K.I.2 (anon., without
    title, incompl.).
    Edition: LenaertsA 26-29 (Agnus).
    Literature: NoblittCC, SalopM 27-28 and 135-
    37, SparksC 272-74.
    Recording: Opus Musicum 101/3 Hömberg
    (Agnus).

4. MISSA CAPUT. 4 v. ObrCW II, pp. 33-85; ObrW
    IV, no. 18, pp. 189-264. Cantus firmus is

concluding melisma of Sarum antiphon "Venit ad
Petrum," as used in the Missa Caput by an
anonymous English composer and formerly attr.
to Dufay. The opening of the Gloria quotes
the head-motive of that mass. (See BukofzerS
pl. 6-7, PaliscaN 1: 164, PlanchartM viii.)
I. 1. Kyrie; 2. Christe; 3. Kyrie (99 mm.;
c.f. in T.).
II. 1. Et in terra; 2. Qui tollis (227 mm.;
c.f. in S.).
III. 1. Patrem; 2. Et incarnatus (224 mm.;
c.f. in T.).
IV. 1. Sanctus; 2. Pleni; 3. Osanna; 4.
Benedictus (213 mm.; c.f. in A.).
V. 1. Agnus Dei; 2. Agnus Dei; 3. Agnus Dei
(183 mm.; c.f. in B.).
[Agnus Dei alterum. 1. Agnus Dei; 2. Agnus
Dei; 3. Agnus Dei] (243 mm.; c.f. in T., S.;
this movement is probably not by Obrecht).
Source: Modena a.M.1.2 (fac. of Kyrie in ObrCW
II).
Editions: PlanchartM 98-153 (lacks Agnus Dei
alterum), PaliscaN 1: 177-184 (Agnus).
Literature: BukofzerC 269-71 and 292-306 (most
important), GombosiJ 82-85, MeierZ 307-9,
NoblittCC, NowotnyM, PlanchartF 13-17,
PlanchartG 1-13, PlanchartR 44, ReeseMR 196-
97, SalopM 6-11, StrohmM 147.
Recording: Lyrichord 7273 Planchart.
5.   MISSA CELA SANS PLUS. 4 v. (ObrCW XIII).
Cantus firmi from chanson by Colinet de
Lannoy. Unpublished except for Osanna I.
I. 1. Kyrie; 2. Christe; 3. Kyrie.
II. 1. Et in terra; 2. Qui tollis.
III. 1. Patrem; 2. Et incarnatus; 3. Crucifi-
xus.
IV. 1. Sanctus; 2. Pleni; 3. Osanna; 4.
Benedictus; 5. Osanna.
V. 1. Agnus Dei; 2. Agnus Dei; 3. Agnus Dei.
Sources: Wrocɫaw I F 428 (anon., without
title), 1502² (Obrecht in Missa, Cela sans
plus = Osanna I), [c. 1535]¹⁴ (anon., Cela
sans plus = Osanna I, S. only).
Edition: ObrW VII, no. 5, pp. 12-3 (Cela sans
plus = Osanna I).
Literature: HudsonT 299-300, ReeseMR 189,
StaehelinG 24-25, StaehelinM 82-83,
StaehelinO 7-8.

6. MISSA DE SANCTO DONATIANO. 4 v. ObrCW III,
    pp. 1-32; ObrW IV, no. 15, pp. 41-84 (Missa
    sine nomine). Multiple cantus firmi, mostly
    unidentified. Cantus firmus in Kyrie I ("O
    beate pater Donatiane") is also used by
    Obrecht in his motet "O beate Basili"
    (compare hymn "Iste confessor," LU 1177).
    C.f. in Et resurrexit ("O clavis David") is
    antiphon (LU 341). An extensive S. A. duo
    appears as a head-motive in all movements.
    StrohmM proposes that the mass was written in
    1487 at Bruges.
    I. 1. Kyrie/O beate pater Donatiane; 2.
       Christe/O beate; 3. Kyrie/Gefft den armen/O
       beate (111 mm.).
    II. 1. Et in terra/Confessor Domini
       Donatianus; 2. Qui tollis/Cumque sacre (173
       mm.).
    III. 1. Patrem/O sanctissime presul; 2. Et
       incarnatus (2 v.); 3. Et resurrexit/O clavis
       David/Defende nos; 4. Et unam sanctam/
       Exaudi preces (201 mm.).
    IV. 1. Sanctus/O beate; 2. Pleni (3 v.); 3.
       Osanna/O beate; 4. Benedictus (2 v.); 5.
       Qui venit (2 v.) (145 mm.).
    V. 1. Agnus Dei/O beate; 2. Agnus Dei (2 v.);
       3. Agnus Dei/O beate (117 mm.).
    Sources: Jena 32 (anon.; without title; fac.
       of Kyrie II in ObrCW III), Rome Sist. 35
       (without title).
    Edition: HAM I, no. 77 (Missa sine nomine:
       Kyrie I, Agnus II).
    Literature: MeierZ 297-98 and 304-5, SalopM
       76-80, SparksC 472-73 (n. 46), StrohmM 145-
       47.
    Recording: Pleiades 251 Morgan (Kyrie I,
       Agnus II).
7. MISSA DE SANCTO MARTINO. 4 v. ObrCW III, pp.
    35-72; ObrW II, no. 8, pp. 117-50. Multiple
    cantus firmi from antiphons for the feast of
    St. Martin, Bishop and Confessor (LU 1746-50).
    StrohmM proposes that this mass was written at
    Bruges in 1486 at the request of Obrecht's
    colleague Pierre Basin.
    I. 1. Kyrie/Martinus adhuc catechuminus; 2.
       Christe/Martinus adhuc (3 v.); 3. Kyrie/
       Martinus adhuc (69 mm.).

II. 1. Et in terra/Dixerunt discipuli; 2.
Domini Fili unigenite/Dixerunt (3 v.); 3.
Qui tollis/Dixerunt (247 mm.).
III. 1. Patrem/O virum; 2. Et incarnatus/
Martinus episcopus; 3. Et resurrexit/Oculis
ac manibus (3 v.); 4. Et in Spiritum/O
beatum virum (273 mm.).
IV. 1. Sanctus/Ad oremus; 2. Pleni/Ego signo
crucis (3 v.); 3. Osanna/Martinus adhuc; 4.
Benedictus (3 v.) (254 mm.).
V. 1. Agnus Dei/O beatum Pontificem; 2. Agnus
Dei/Et non formidabat (3 v.); 3. Agnus Dei/O
sanctissima (109 mm.).
Sources: St. Gall 461 (Benedictus only;
anon.), Stuttgart I 47 (anon.; without
title; incomplete; fac. of Et incarnatus
in ObrCW III), Uppsala 76e (anon., without
title; S. only), ca. 1510 Concentus.
Edition: GiesbertA 1: 36-37 (Benedictus).
Literature: MeierZ 302-4, SalopM 80-86,
SparksC 278-82 and 297.

8. MISSA DE TOUS BIENS PLAYNE. 3 v. ObrCW IV,
pp. 1-24; ObrW V, no. 23, pp. 157-84 (Missa
sine nomine). Cantus firmus from T. of
chanson by Hayne van Ghizeghem.
I. 1. Kyrie; 2. Christe; 3. Kyrie (59 mm.).
II. 1. Et in terra; 2. Qui tollis (172 mm.).
III. 1. Patrem; 2. Et incarnatus; 3. Et unam
sanctam (159 mm.).
IV. 1. Sanctus; 2. Pleni (2 v.); 3. Osanna; 4.
Benedictus (2 v.); 5. Osanna (232 mm.).
V. 1. Agnus Dei; 2. Agnus Dei (2 v.); 3. Agnus
Dei (162 mm.).
Source: Vienna 11883 (without title; fac. of
Kyrie in ObrCW IV).
Literature: GombosiJ 45-47, ReeseMR 198-99,
SalopM 51-58, SparksC 249-54 and 288-94
(most important), ToddR 58-61.

9. MISSA FORS SEULEMENT. 3 v. ObrCW IV, pp. 25-
47; ObrW V, no. 22, pp. 133-56 (incomplete).
Cantus firmus from S. of chanson by Ockeghem.
I. 1. Kyrie; 2. Christe; 3. Kyrie (71 mm.).
II. 1. Et in terra; 2. Qui tollis (140 mm.).
III. 1. Patrem; 2. Et incarnatus (196 mm.).
IV. 1. Sanctus; 2. Pleni (2 v.); 3. Osanna; 4.
Benedictus (2 v.) (265 mm.).
V. 1. Agnus Dei; 2. Agnus Dei; 3. Agnus Dei
(69 mm.).

Sources: Munich UB 239 (copied from composer's
autograph MS; fac. of Kyrie in ObrCW IV),
Vienna 18832 (Benedictus; anon.). Theorist:
Glareanus 1547 (Sanctus, Qui tollis).
Edition: GlareanusD 303-6 (Sanctus, Qui
tollis).
Literature: GombosiJ 32-34, HudsonO, SalopM
38-41, SantarelliQ 333-49, SparksC 247 and
285-88.
10. MISSA FORTUNA DESPERATA. 4 v. ObrCW IV, pp.
49-91; ObrO I, no. 3, pp. 113-69; ObrW I, no.
3, pp. 85-135. Cantus firmi from T. and S. of
chanson attr. to Busnois. HudsonT proposes
that the mass was written in 1487-88 at
Ferrara.
I. 1. Kyrie; 2. Christe (3 v.); 3. Kyrie (155
mm.).
II. 1. Et in terra; 2. Qui tollis (218 mm.).
III. 1. Patrem; 2. Et incarnatus (218 mm.).
IV. 1. Sanctus; 2. Pleni (3 v.); 3. Osanna; 4.
Benedictus (3 v.) (259 mm.).
V. 1. Agnus Dei; 2. Agnus Dei (3 v.); 3. Agnus
Dei (267 mm.).
Sources: Berlin 40021 (anon.; lacks Agnus),
Florence 107bis (Christe, Pleni, Benedictus,
Agnus II; anon.), Florence Cons. 2439 (Kyrie
II, Sanctus, Osanna), Modena a.M.1.2 (with-
out title), Segovia (lacks Agnus), 1503
Misse Obreht, ca. 1510 Concentus (fac. of T.
in ObrCW IV), 1538[9] (Pleni, without text;
anon.). Tablature: St. Gall 530 (Benedic-
tus; anon.).
Editions: R. Eitner (Amsterdam, 1880),
GreenbergA 29-45 (Credo).
Literature: AntonowytschR, BrownM 157-58,
GombosiJ 112-16, HudsonT 289-300 (most
important), ReeseMR 201, SalopJ 300-9,
SalopM 58-63, SparksC 248-49, ToddR 61-62,
WagnerG 123.
Recordings: Harmonia Mundi 998 Clemencic, MCA
2508 Greenberg.
11. MISSA GRECORUM. 4 v. ObrCW V, pp. 1-33; ObrO
I, no. 2, pp. 69-111; ObrW I, no. 2, pp. 49-
84. Cantus firmus unidentified. Sequence
"Victimae paschali laudes" (LU 780) quoted in
Osanna, S.
I. 1. Kyrie; 2. Christe (3 v.); 3. Kyrie (73
mm.).

II. 1. Et in terra; 2. Qui tollis (237 mm.).
III. 1. Patrem; 2. Et incarnatus; 3. Et
resurrexit (202 mm.).
IV. 1. Sanctus; 2. Pleni (3 v.); 3. Osanna; 4.
Benedictus (3 v.) (204 mm.).
V. 1. Agnus Dei; 2. Agnus Dei (3 v.); 3. Agnus
Dei (118 mm.).
Source: 1503 Misse Obreht (fac. of Kyrie in
ObrCW V).
Literature: MeierZ 296-97, NoblittCC, PirroH
194, SalopM 44-51, SparksC 249-50,
StaehelinO 23-25, ToddR 65-69.
12. MISSA JE NE DEMANDE.   4 v.   ObrCW V, pp. 35-84;
ObrO I, no. 1, pp. 1-64; ObrW I, no. 1, pp. 1-
48 and Anhang iv-vii. Cantus firmus from T.
of chanson by Busnois, segmented. Head-motive
from chanson.
I. 1. Kyrie; 2. Christe (3 v.); 3. Kyrie (91
mm.).
II. 1. Et in terra; 2. Qui tollis; 3. Cum
Sancto Spiritu (234 mm.).
III. 1. Patrem; 2. Et incarnatus; 3. Et in
Spiritum (386 mm.).
IV. 1. Sanctus; 2. Pleni (3 v.); 3. Osanna; 4.
Benedictus (3 v.) (262 mm.).
V. 1. Agnus Dei; 2. Agnus Dei (two versions);
3. Agnus Dei (239 mm.).
Sources: Leipzig 51 (T. B. only; Agnus II-III
lacking); Munich 3154 (anon.; Kyrie, Agnus
incomplete; fac. of Et in terra in ObrCW V),
1503 Misse Obreht (Agnus II differs; fac. of
S. and T., Kyrie and Et in terra, in NG 13:
480-1). Theorists: Heyden 1537 (fragments
of T., Kyrie, Gloria, and Credo), Heyden
1540 (fragments of Gloria), Faber 1553 (Qui
tollis), Wilphlingseder 1563 (fragments of
Gloria).
Literature: BurkholderJ 510-11, GombosiJ 96-
99, MeierZ 290-91, NoblittCC, NoblittP,
ReeseMR 203-4, SalopM 66-72 and 97-125,
SparksC 262, WagnerG 116-18 and 124-25,
WolffM 49-51.
Recording: Baroque 9003 Brown (Gloria, Credo).
13. MISSA L'HOMME ARMÉ.   4 v.   ObrW V, no. 20,
pp. 53-93; (ObrCW VI). Cantus firmus from
popular song and T. of Mass by Busnois.
I. 1. Kyrie; 2. Christe (3 v.); 3. Kyrie (65
mm.).

II. 1. Et in terra; 2. Qui tollis; 3. Tu solus (145 mm.).

III. 1. Patrem; 2. Et incarnatus; 3. Confiteor (185 mm.).

IV. 1. Sanctus; 2. Pleni (3 v.): 3. Osanna; 4. Benedictus (3 v.) (163 mm.).

V. 1. Agnus Dei; 2. Agnus Dei (3 v.); 3. Agnus Dei (131 mm.).

Sources: Modena a.M.1.2, Uppsala 76e (anon.; S. only; Agnus III lacking), Vienna 11883.

Literature: GombosiJ 59-61, HaassS, ReeseMR 197-98, SalopM 42-44, SparksC 248, StrohmM 147, StrunkO, TaruskinA 274-75, ToddR 56-58.

14. MISSA LIBENTER GLORIABOR. 4 v. (ObrCW VI). Cantus firmus is antiphon (LU 1348). Head-motive in Kyrie, Sanctus.

I. 1. Kyrie; 2. Christe (3 v.); 3. Kyrie (96mm.).

II. 1. Et in terra; 2. Qui tollis (205 mm.).

III. 1. Patrem; 2. Crucifixus (212 mm.).

IV. 1. Sanctus; 2. Pleni (3 v.); 3. Osanna; 4. Benedictus (3 v.) (212 mm.).

V. Agnus Dei = Kyrie.

Sources: Kraków 40634 (anon.; incomplete), Segovia.

Editions: BakerU 631-724, SmijersV no. 11 (Kyrie).

Literature: BentD 34-41, CrevelV 119-21, LowinskyS 119 (n. 63a), MeierZ 296, SparksC 276-78.

15. MISSA MALHEUR ME BAT. 4 v. ObrO I, no. 4, pp. 173-225; ObrW I, no. 4, pp. 141-88; (ObrCW VII). Cantus firmus from S. of chanson by Martini (Ockeghem?), segmented. HudsonT proposes that the mass was written in 1487-88 at Ferrara.

I. 1. Kyrie; 2. Christe (3 v.); 3. Kyrie (86 mm.).

II. 1. Et in terra; 2. Qui tollis (225 mm.).

III. 1. Patrem; 2. Crucifixus (3 v.); 3. Et in Spiritum (287 mm.).

IV. 1. Sanctus; 2. Pleni (3 v.); 3. Osanna; 4. Benedictus (3 v.)(= Crucifixus) (264 mm.).

V. 1. Agnus Dei; 2. Agnus Dei (3 v.); 3. Agnus Dei (195 mm.).

Sources: Berlin 40021 (anon.), Kraków 40634 (incomplete), Leipzig 51 (attr. Agricola; T. and B. only), 1503 Misse Obreht, 1538[9]

(Christe, Crucifixus, Pleni, Agnus II;
anon., without text).
Literature: CrockerH 171-72, GombosiJ 91-93,
HudsonT 277-89, LenaertsM 621-22, ReeseMR
199-200, SparksC 260-65 (most important),
WagnerG 127-28, WolffM 45-47.
16. MISSA MARIA ZART. 4 v. ObrO Missae VII; ObrW
II, no. 7, pp. 41-109; (ObrCW VII). Cantus
firmus from German devotional song, segmented.
Composed at Innsbruck ca. 1503?
I. 1. Kyrie; 2. Christe (3 v.); 3. Kyrie (128
mm.).
II. 1. Et in terra; 2. Domine Deus (2 v.); 3.
Qui tollis (2 v.); 4. Qui tollis (377 mm.).
III. 1. Patrem; 2. Qui propter (3 v.); 3. Et
incarnatus (3 v.); 4. Et resurrexit (392
mm.).
IV. 1. Sanctus; 2. Pleni (3 v.); 3. Osanna; 4.
Benedictus (3 v.) (187 mm.).
V. 1. Agnus Dei; 2. Agnus Dei (3 v.); 3.
Agnus Dei (249 mm.).
Source: ca. 1510 Concentus (fac. of T. in
MeierZ, ObrO, MGG 9: 1815-18).
Literature: BankS, DahlhausZ, EldersS 136,
LenaertsM 622, ReeseMR 193-95, MeierZ 291,
SalopM 73-74, SparksC 262, WolffM 47-49.
Recordings: Anth. Son. 4 de Van (Qui propter,
Et incarnatus), Supraphon 1 12 0464 Venhoda.
17. MISSA O LUMEN ECCLESIE (O QUAM SUAVIS). 4 v.
ObrWrIII, no. 10, pp. 61-100; (ObrCW VIII).
Cantus firmus is antiphon "O quam suavis" (LU
917; but see HudsonOT 11 n. 13). Head-motive
from antiphon.
I. 1. Kyrie; 2. Christe; 3. Kyrie (133 mm.).
II. 1. Et in terra; 2. Gratias; 3. Qui tollis
(152 mm.).
III. 1. Patrem; 2. Et in unum; 3. Et incarna-
tus (3 v.); 4. Et resurrexit (239 mm.).
IV. 1. Sanctus; 2. Sanctus; 3. Pleni; 4.
Osanna; 5. Benedictus; 6. Osanna (166 mm.).
V. 1. Agnus Dei; 2. Agnus Dei; 3. Agnus Dei
(115 mm.).
Sources: Jena 22 (M. O quam suavis), Leipzig
51 (M. O quam suavis; T. and B. only), Rome
SMM 26 (anon.; M. O lumen ecclesie).
Literature: SalopM 11-15, SparksC 272-74 and
298.

18. MISSA PETRUS APOSTOLUS. 4 v. ObrW III, no.
    13, pp. 189-228; (ObrCW VIII). Cantus firmus
    is antiphon (LU 1547). Head-motive in S. A.
    of all movements.
    I. 1. Kyrie; 2. Christe (2 v.); 3. Kyrie (73
       mm.).
    II. 1. Et in terra; 2. Domine Deus (3 v.); 3.
       Qui tollis (211 mm.).
    III. 1. Patrem; 2. Et incarnatus (3 v.); 3. Et
       iterum (248 mm.).
    IV. 1. Sanctus; 2. Pleni (3 v.); 3. Osanna; 4.
       Benedictus (3 v.) (150 mm.).
    V. 1. Agnus Dei; 2. Agnus Dei (2 v.); 3. Agnus
       Dei (109 mm.).
    Sources: St. Gall 461 (Et incarnatus, without
    text), 1539[2]. Theorist: Zacconi 1592
    (Kyrie II, Patrem).
    Editions: GiesbertA 2: 106-7 (Et incarnatus);
    ObrW VII, no. 18, pp. 54-56 (Et incarnatus).
    Literature: MeierZ 295-96, SalopM 15-21 and
    134, SparksC 269-72, ToddR 64-65.
19. MISSA PFAUENSCHWANZ. 4 v. ObrW V, no. 19, pp.
    1-52 (Missa sine nomine); (ObrCW IX). Cantus
    firmus is popular melody (see setting by
    Barbingant).
    I. 1. Kyrie; 2. Christe (3 v.); 3. Kyrie (127
       mm.).
    II. 1. Et in terra; 2. Domine Deus (3 v.); 3.
       Qui sedes (260 mm.).
    III. 1. Patrem; 2. Et incarnatus (3 v.); Et
       resurrexit (278 mm.).
    IV. 1. Sanctus; 2. Pleni (3 v.); 3. Osanna; 4.
       Benedictus (3 v.) (228 mm.).
    V. 1. Agnus Dei; 2. Agnus Dei (3 v.); 3. Agnus
       Dei (132 mm.).
    Source: Modena a.M.1.2 (M. sine nomine).
    Literature: GombosiJ 116, SalopM 37-38,
    SparksC 254 and 294-98.
20. MISSA PLURIMORUM CARMINUM (I). 4 v. ObrW IV,
    no. 14, pp. 1-35 (Missa Adieu mes amours I;
    lacks Kyrie); no. 16, pp. 85-91 and 112-23
    (Missa Carminum; Kyrie & Sanctus only; Tracts
    on pp. 92-111 are not by Obrecht); (ObrCW X).
    Cantus firmi from chansons by Barbireau,
    Binchois, Busnois, Josquin, Ockeghem and
    others. (See identifications in GombosiJ 116-
    19.) Agnus is lacking in all sources (repeat
    of Kyrie?).

I. 1. Kyrie; 2. Christe; 3. Kyrie (126 mm.).
II. 1. Et in terra; 2. Qui tollis (279 mm.).
III. 1. Patrem; 2. Et incarnatus; 3. Et
    resurrexit; 4. Qui cum Patre (322 mm.).
IV. 1. Sanctus; 2. Pleni (3 v.); 3. Osanna; 4.
    Benedictus; 5. In nomine Domini (2 v.) (277
    mm.).
Sources: Dresden 1/D/505 (anon.), Linz 529
    (Credo and Sanctus, anon.; incomplete),
    Milan 2268 (Missa diversorum tenorum; lacks
    Kyrie; fac. of Patrem in NoblittF 126-27),
    Rome Sist. 35 (Kyrie, Sanctus).
Edition: BortoneJ 137-79 (lacks Kyrie).
Literature: GombosiJ 116-19, NoblittF, ReeseMR
    195-96, SalopM 86-88, SmijersM, SparksC 247.
21. MISSA PLURIMORUM CARMINUM (II). 4 v. ObrW IV,
    no. 17, pp. 129-78 (Missa Scoen lief), 179-88
    (Credo after Munich 3154); (ObrCW X). Cantus
    firmi in B. from S. of chansons by Barbireau,
    Compère, Martini and others. (See identifi-
    cations in StaehelinO 25-27.) StaehelinO
    proposes that the mass was written in 1487-88
    at Ferrara.
I. 1. Kyrie; 2. Christe (3 v.); 3. Kyrie (117
    mm.).
II. 1. Et in terra; 2. Qui tollis (130 mm.).
III. 1. Patrem; 2. Et ascendit; 3. Et unam
    sanctam (383 mm.).
IV. 1. Sanctus; 2. Pleni (3 v.); 3. Osanna; 4.
    Benedictus (3 v.) (222 mm.).
V. 1. Agnus Dei; 2. Agnus Dei (3 v.); 3. Agnus
    Dei (177 mm.).
Sources: Jena 31 (anon.; without title), Linz
    529 (Credo, Sanctus, Agnus; anon.), Modena
    a.M.1.2 (without title; fac. of Kyrie in
    HoornJ opp. p. 134), Munich 3154 (without
    title; Credo differs).
Literature: SalopM 88, StaehelinO 25-27,
    StrohmM 147.
22. MISSA ROSE PLAYSANTE. 4 v. (ObrCW IX).
    Cantus firmus from T. of chanson by Caron
    (Philippon, Dusart?); segmented. Unpublished
    except for Kyrie.
I. 1. Kyrie; 2. Christe (3 v.); 3. Kyrie (116
    mm.).
II. 1. Et in terra; 2. Qui tollis.
III. 1. Patrem; 2. Et incarnatus.
IV. 1. Sanctus; 2. Pleni (3 v.); 3. Osanna; 4.
    Benedictus (3 v.).

V. 1. Agnus Dei; 2. Agnus Dei (3 v.); 3. Agnus
Dei.
Sources: Modena a.M.1.2 (anon.), Munich 3154
(anon.; incomplete), Segovia.
Edition: SmijersV no. 13 (Kyrie).
Literature: ReeseMR 202-3, SparksC 266-68 and
300-3.
23. MISSA SALVE DIVA PARENS. 4 v. ObrO I, no. 5,
pp. 229-84; ObrW I, no. 5, pp. 193-244;
(ObrCW XI). Model, if any, unknown. Head-
motive (S. A. B.) in Kyrie, Gloria, Sanctus.
I. 1. Kyrie; 2. Christe; 3. Kyrie (92 mm.).
II. 1. Et in terra; 2. Domine Deus; 3. Cum
sancto Spiritu (234 mm.).
III. 1. Patrem; 2. Genitum non factum; 3. Et
incarnatus; 4. Qui cum Patre (2 v.); 5.
Confiteor (312 mm.).
IV. 1. Sanctus; 2. Pleni (3 v.); 3. Osanna; 4.
Benedictus; 5. In nomine (2 v.); 6. Osanna
(272 mm.).
V. 1. Agnus Dei; 2. Agnus Dei (3 v.); 3. Agnus
Dei (185 mm.).
Sources: Barcelona 5 (anon.), Leipzig 1494
(Kyrie, Gloria, Credo only; anon.), Linz 529
(Sanctus; anon.; incomplete), Rome Sist.
51 (anon.), Verona 761 (anon.), Vienna 15495
(fac. of Kyrie in BesselerS 114-15, MGG 9
Taf. 115), 18832 (Fuga = Qui cum Patre;
anon.), 1503 Misse Obreht, 1538⁹ (Pleni,
without text; anon.), 1545 (Qui cum Patre),
1590³⁰ (Fuga = Qui cum Patre). Theorists:
Heyden 1537, 1540 (Fuga = Qui cum Patre),
1547 Glareanus (textless = Qui cum Patre),
1553 Faber (textless = Qui cum Patre).
Editions: ObrW VII, no. 17, p. 53 (Qui cum
Patre); GlareanusD 323-24.
Literature: GombosiJ 122, JeppesenM 383,
StrohmM 148, StaehelinO 20-23, ToddR 62-64.
Recordings: Baroque 9004 Brown (Kyrie),
Collegium 102/3 Taruskin (Sanctus), Seraphim
6052 Otten (Monad = Qui cum Patre).
24. MISSA SCARAMELLA. 4 v. (ObrCW XI). Cantus
firmus from popular song (see settings by
Compère and Josquin). Probably composed in
1487-88 at Ferrara. Incompletely preserved
and unpublished.
Source: Kraków 40634 (A. and B. only).
Literature: HudsonT 299-300, ObrW V no. 23.

25. MISSA SICUT SPINA ROSAM. 4 v. ObrW II, no.
    11, pp. 101-40; (ObrCW XI). Cantus firmus is
    fragment of responsory "Ad nutum Domini" (AR
    130*). Head-motive in Kyrie and Sanctus, and
    the complete B. of Agnus, are from Kyrie of
    Missa Mi-mi by Ockeghem. A different head-
    motive in Gloria and Credo is based on the
    c.f. HudsonOT proposes that this mass was
    composed in memory of Ockeghem.
    I. 1. Kyrie; 2. Christe; 3. Kyrie (69 mm.).
    II. 1. Et in terra; 2. Qui tollis; 3. Qui
    sedes (154 mm.).
    III. 1. Patrem; 2. Et incarnatus; 3. Et
    resurrexit; 4. Et in Spiritum; 5. Confiteor
    (299 mm.).
    IV. 1. Sanctus; 2. Pleni; 3. Gloria tua; 4.
    Osanna; 5. Benedictus; 6. Qui venit (168
    mm.).
    V. 1. Agnus Dei; 2. Agnus Dei; 3. Agnus Dei
    (52 mm.).
    Sources: Jena 22, Rome Sist. 160 (anon.).
    Literature: BukofzerS 309, HudsonOT (most
    important), MeierZ 298, SalopM 28-33,
    SparksC 274-76.
26. MISSA SI DEDERO. 4 v. ObrW III, no. 9, pp. 1-
    54; (ObrCW XII). Cantus firmus from T. of
    motet by Agricola, segmented. Head-motive in
    Kyrie, Gloria, Credo, and Agnus III from
    motet.
    I. 1. Kyrie; 2. Christe (3 v.); 3. Kyrie (170
    mm.).
    II. 1. Et in terra; 2. Qui tollis (223 mm.).
    III. 1. Patrem; 2. Crucifixus (244 mm.).
    IV. 1. Sanctus; 2. Pleni (3 v.); 3. Osanna; 4.
    Benedictus (3 v.) (252 mm.).
    V. 1. Agnus Dei; 2. Agnus Dei (3 v.); 3. Agnus
    Dei (211 mm.).
    Sources: Florence 107bis (anon.; incomplete),
    Leipzig 1494 (incomplete), Munich 3154,
    Munich 374 (Sanctus, T. and B. only),
    Segovia (Christe), Uppsala 76e (S. only;
    Agnus III lacking), 1509[1], 1538[9] (Christe,
    without text; anon.). Tablatures: Chicago
    Newberry 107501 (Christe, anon.), 1507[6]
    (Christe, anon.).
    Literature: GombosiJ 120-22, MeierZ 290,
    NoblittT, ReeseMR 201-2, SalopM 126-28,
    SparksC 262-63 and 299-300, WagnerG 125-27.

27. MISSA SUB TUUM PRESIDIUM. 3-7 v. ObrO Missae
    VI; ObrW II, no. 6, pp. 1-40; (ObrCW XII).
    The principal cantus firmus is the antiphon
    "Sub tuum praesidium" (LU 1861). Additional
    cantus firmi employed in the Credo, Sanctus,
    and Agnus are cited in SparksC.
    I. (3 v.) 1. Kyrie; 2. Christe; 3. Kyrie (76
    mm.).
    II. (4 v.) 1. Et in terra; 2. Qui tollis (76
    mm.).
    III. (5 v.) 1. Patrem; 2. Et resurrexit (76
    mm.).
    IV. (6 v.) 1. Sanctus; 2. Benedictus (78 mm.).
    V. (7 v.) 1. Agnus Dei; 2. Agnus Dei; 3. Agnus
    Dei (78 mm.).
    Sources: Dresden 1/D/505 (fac. in ObrO), ca.
    1510 Concentus (fac. in ObrO). Theorist:
    Faber 1553 (Christe).
    Literature: EldersS 111 et passim, LenaertsM
    621, LockwoodN (most important), ReeseMR
    195, SalopM 3-6, SparksC 282-85, WagnerG
    118-20, WolffM 52-54.
    Recordings: Archive 198 406 Knothe, Bach Guild
    HM2 SD Gillesberger.

    (2)   Masses - Doubtful
1. MISSA VECI LA DANSE BARBARI. 4 v. (ObrCW
    XIII). Cantus firmus from popular song and
    anon. chanson. The Credo is also attributed
    to A. Rener. NoblittO proposes that the
    remainder of the mass is by Obrecht.
    Unpublished.
    Sources: Dresden 1/D/505 (Credo only, anon.),
    Jena 36 (Adam Rener, mass without title on
    this cantus firmus; its Credo = Credo of the
    present mass), Leipzig 51 (Jacobus Obrecht,
    mass without title, lacking Pleni and Agnus;
    T. and B. only).
    Literature: NoblittO, ObrW V no. 23,
    StaehelinO 11-14.

    (3)   Masses - Miscellaneous
    The three masses listed below are anonymous in
the sources but have been attributed with some
plausibility to Obrecht and are to be published in
ObrCW.

1. MISSA GRACUULY ET BIAULX. 4 v. (ObrCW XIII).
    Cantus firmus from T. of chanson by Barbireau.
    The mass is attributed to Obrecht in
    StaehelinM. Unpublished.
    Source: Modena a.M.1.2 (anon., without title).
    Literature: StaehelinM 85-86, StaehelinO 5-7.
2. MISSA JE NE SERAY PLUS. 3 v. (ObrCW XIV).
    Cantus firmus from S. of chanson by Philipet
    des Pres. Attributed to Obrecht in WardA.
    Unpublished except for Benedictus.
    Sources: Berlin 40021 (anon.), Hradec
    Králové II A 7 (anon.; Kyrie, Gloria,
    Credo only), Munich 260 (Benedictus;
    anon.), Vienna 18832 (Benedictus; anon.).
    Edition: BellinghamS 77-79 (Benedictus).
    Literature: JustM 1: 292-93, WardA.
3. MISSA N'ARAY-JE JAMAIS. 4 v. (ObrCW XIV).
    Cantus firmus, segmented, from T. of chanson
    by Morton. Attributed to Obrecht in
    StaehelinM. Unpublished.
    Sources: Berlin 40021 (anon.; without title),
    Dresden 1/D/505 (anon.; without title),
    Wrocɫaw I F 428 (anon.; without title).
    Literature: JustM 1: 297-338, StaehelinM 86-
    87, StaehelinO 3-5.

    (4) Motets - Authentic
    The following 26 works by Obrecht with Latin
title or texts are classified here as motets,
although a few may be instrumental works (nos. 21,
26). Generally regarded as authentic, they display
on the whole the same stylistic characteristics as
the masses. Strohm suggests that the "instrumental" motets may have been played by minstrels at
the Salve concerts in Bruges and elsewhere (StrohmM
86).
    Like the masses, most of the motets are based
on cantus firmi. These are discussed in NagleS,
and some also in SparksC. Little has been written
about the motets without identified cantus firmi.
A few motets can be dated around 1488 on the basis
of their texts (nos. 9, 13, 18). Two motets are
incomplete in the sources and remain unpublished
(nos. 12, 16). All motets will eventually be
published in ObrCW vols. 15-16.

1. ALMA REDEMPTORIS MATER. 2. Et stella maris; 3.
   Tu que genuisti; 4. Virgo prius; 5. Sumens
   illud. (213 mm.) 3 v. ObrW VI, no. 17a, pp.
   157-64; no. 17b, pp. 165-72 (Ego sum).
   Text and cantus firmus (in B.): antiphon
   B.M.V. (LU 277).
   Sources: London R.C. 1070, 1542[8] (Ego sum
   super Alma redemptoris).
   Literature: NagleS 56-61.
2. AVE MARIS STELLA. (53 mm.) 3 v. Text and
   cantus firmus (in T.): hymn (LU 1259).
   Source: Segovia.
   Editions: BakerU 2: 933-7, NagleS 42-44.
   Literature: NagleS 41-46.
3. AVE REGINA COELORUM. 2. Funde preces. (126
   mm.) 4 v. ObrO II, no. 6, pp. 75-81; ObrW
   VI, no. 6, pp. 64-8. Text and chant
   (paraphrased in S.): antiphon B.M.V. (LU
   1864). Cantus firmus in T. from T. of motet
   by Frye.
   Source: 1504[3].
   Edition: AmbrosG 5: 20-28 (incorrect text).
   Literature: NagleS 106-12.
4. BEATA ES, MARIA. 2. Ave Maria/Beata es. (137
   mm.) 4 v. ObrW VI, no. 7, pp. 69-74. Text
   and cantus firmus (in T.): devotional song,
   15th cent. (DrevesA 20: 256). The second part
   has as an additional cantus firmus (in A.) the
   sequence "Ave Maria . . . Virgo serena" (VP
   46).
   Source: 1505[2].
   Literature: NagleS 112-20.
   Recording: Archiv 2533 377 Turner.
5. BENEDICAMUS IN LAUDE JHESU. (44 mm.) 4 v.
   Text: Benedicamus trope. Cantus firmus (in
   S.): tone for solemn feasts, mode 2 (LU 124).
   Source: Segovia.
   Editions: BakerU 2: 778-83, NagleS 94-95.
   Literature: NagleS 92-96.
6. CUIUS SACRATA VISCERA (I). (44 mm.) 3 v.
   Text and cantus firmus (in T.): verse 2 of
   hymn, "Assunt festa jubilaea" (15th cent.;
   MMMA 1: 140).
   Source: Segovia.
   Editions: BakerU 2: 945-48; NagleS 35-37.
   Literature: NagleS 34-38.
7. CUIUS SACRATA VISCERA (II). (25 mm.) 4 v.
   Text and cantus firmus (in T.): verse 2 of

hymn, "Assunt festa jubilaea" (15th cent.;
MMMA 1: 140).
Source: Segovia.
Editions: BakerU 2: 784-48, NagleS 39-40.
Literature: NagleS 38-41.
8. FACTOR ORBIS /VENI, DOMINE. 2. Spiritus
Domini/Veniet fortior/Hodie scietis/Erunt
prava/Bethlehem es civitas. (227 mm.) 5 v.
ObrO II, no. 4, pp. 41-57; ObrW VI, no. 2, pp.
15-28. Multiple texts and cantus firmi from
chants of Advent (AM 218, AR 152*, LU 341 and
356-57, etc.)
Sources: Florence II.I.232 (fac. in HoornJ
148), Rome Sist. 42, 1508[1] (lacking A[2].).
Literature: BrownM 159, MeierZ 293, NagleS
130-40, ReeseMR 191, SparksC 304.
9. INTER PRAECLARISSIMAS VIRTUTES /ESTOTE FORTES
IN BELLO. 2. Eya propter/Estote fortes; 3.
Igitur hoc praesum. (326 mm.) 4 v. Cantus
firmus (in T.) is first phrase of antiphon (LU
118). Text (by Obrecht?) addressed to the
Pope (Innocent VIII?). Probably composed in
1488 at Ferrara.
Source: Segovia.
Editions: BakerU 2: 725-65; NagleS 159-72.
Literature: DunningS 14-17, NagleS 152-74,
SmijersT.
10. LAUDEMUS NUNC DOMINUM /NON EST HIC ALIUD. 2.
Cantemus Domino/Vidit Jacob scalam. (209 mm.)
5 v. ObrO II, no. 5, pp. 58-74; ObrW VI, no.
5, pp. 49-63. Cantus firmi (in T.) are
antiphons (LR 237, 241, 238).
Sources: Rome Sist. 42, 1508[1] (lacking A[2]).
Literature: LenaertsM 625-26, NagleS 140-52,
SparksC 304.
Recording: Seraphim 6104 Munrow.
11. LAUDES CHRISTO REDEMPTORI. 2. Haec est dies.
(192 mm.) 4 v. ObrW VI, no. 8, pp. 75-84.
Text: sequence attr. to Notker Balbulus
(DanielT 2: 178-79, KehreinL 88).
Source: 1505[2].
12. MATER PATRIS, NATI NATA /SANCTA DEI GENITRIX.
2. Ab eterno generatus/Sancta Dei genitrix; 3.
Virgo Mater/(Sancta Dei genitrix); 4. Maria
mater gratie/(Sancta Dei genitrix). 5 v.
(Ct[2] lacking). Text: sequence (KehreinL 232).
Cantus firmus in T. Unpublished.

Source: 1508[1].
Literature: StephanB 47.
13. MILLE QUINGENTIS /REQUIEM. 2. Cecilie ad
festum. (208 mm.) 4 v. ObrW VI, no. 20, pp.
179-88 (Requiem). Cantus firmus (in T.):
Introit, Mass for the Dead (LU 1807). Text
(by Obrecht?) laments death of the composer's
father, Willem, in 1488.
Sources: Florence Cons. 2439 (Requiem text
only), Segovia, 1504[1] (Requiem text only;
anon.).
Literature: BakerU 1: 13, NagleS 187-96,
SmijersM, SmijersT, SparksC 307, StephanB
47-48.
14. O BEATE BASILI /O BEATE PATER. 2. O beate
pater (3 v.); 3. O virum digne/Invisit
sanctus. (235 mm.) 4 v. ObrW VI, no. 9,
pp. 85-94. The same cantus firmus is also
used in Obrecht's Missa de Sancto Donatiano
(cf. hymn "Iste confessor," LU 1177).
Composed for Bruges? (StrohmM).
Sources: Florence 232, 1505[2].
Edition: HAM I, no. 76a (first part only).
Literature: NagleS 50-55, StephanB 48, StrohmM
145.
Recording: Pleiades 251 Brown (first part
only).
15. OMNIS SPIRITUS LAUDET. (78 mm.) 5 v.
Consists of 11 short sections alternating
S.S. and S.A.T.B.
Source: Segovia.
Edition: BakerU 2: 766-77.
16. O PRECIOSISSIME SANGUIS /GUBERNA TUOS FAMULOS.
2. Guberna tuos. 3. Te ergo quesumus. 5 v.
(Ct[2] lacking). Cantus firmi in T.
Unpublished. Composed for Bruges? (StrohmM).
Source: 1508[1].
Literature: StephanB 47, StrohmM 145.
17. PARCE DOMINE. 2. Parce Domine. (46 + 71 mm.)
3 (4) v. First part: ObrW VI, no. 10, pp. 95-
96; second part: ObrW VII, no. 27, pp. 79-80
(keyboard arr.). Text after Joel 2: 17,
Ecclesiasticus 2: 13. Cantus firmus in B.,
unidentified. (A similar c.f. is found in the
4 v. motet "Parce Domine" by Heinrich Isaac.)
According to Glareanus 1547 the original motet
is for three voices; an A. is added in
Petrucci's Motetti B (1503[1]) and in some MSS,

as indicated below. The second part is found,
in two versions, only in the Sicher organ
tablature (St. Gall MS 530). VellekoopP
demonstrates that this second part is integral
to the structure of the work.
Sources (first part only, unless otherwise
    noted): Amiens 162 (anon.), Bologna Q 17
    (anon.; lacks S.), Bologna Q 18 (anon.; with
    added A.), Brussels IV.90/Tournai 93 (anon.;
    lacks B.), Cambridge 1760, Copenhagen 1848
    (anon.), London 35087 (B. lacking; anon.),
    MunichU 322-25 (with added A.), St. Gall 463
    (lacks B.), Uppsala 76a (anon.), 1503[1] (with
    added A.), [c.1521][7] (T. only).
Tablatures: St. Gall 530 (anon.; also
    includes two versions of the second part,
    the second of which is attributed to
    Obrecht), Zurich 284a, 1531[5] (anon.).
Theorist: Glareanus 1547.
Editions (first part): BesselerC 9, GlareanusD
    327-28, ParrishM 55-57, RoksethT 25.
    (Second part): VellekoopP 46-47.
Literature: Buning-JurgensM, EldersS 137-38,
    NagleS 196-200, VellekoopP, VellekoopZ
    (the articles by Vellekoop are most
    important).
Recordings (first part only): Epic 3045 de
    Nobel, Haydn Soc. 9038 Møller, Telefunken
    8026 Ruhland (3 & 4 v. versions).
18. QUIS NUMERARE QUEAT. 2. Audivit ipse tamen; 3.
    Fundant preces. (252 mm.) 4 v. ObrW VI, no.
    13, pp. 120-30. Text celebrates the Treaty of
    Bagnolo, 1484; motet probably composed in
    1487-88 at Ferrara (DunningS).
    Source: 1505[2].
    Literature: DunningS 9-14.
19. REGINA CELI. (61 mm.) 2 v. Cantus firmus (in
    T.): antiphon B.M.V. (LU 275). Mensuration
    puzzle.
    Source: Segovia.
    Editions: BakerU 2: 998-1002, HewittS 70-71.
    Literature: HewittS, NagleS 174-81.
20. SALVE CRUX, ARBOR /O CRUX LIGNUM. 2. O crux
    lignum/Per signum crucis; 3. Mundi vera salus.
    (259 mm.) 5 v. ObrO II, no. 2, pp. 17-35;
    ObrW VI, no. 3, pp. 29-45. Cantus firmus (in
    T.) is v. 12 of sequence "Laudes crucis
    attolamus" (KehreinL 67-68; see NagleS 123);

second part has additional c.f. in 5ta:
antiphon (AM 1041). Text: sequence attr. to
Adam of St. Victor (DanielT 5: 90, KehreinL
76).
Source: 1520[4]. Theorist: Zacconi 1592 (T.).
Literature: AmbrosG 3: 185, NagleS 121-30,
SparksC 304, StephanB 47, StrohmM 145.
Recordings: Archiv 2533 377 Turner, Lyrichord
7273 Planchart.
21. SALVE REGINA (I). 2. Vita dulcedo; 3. Eia ergo;
4. Et Jesum; 5. O clemens; 6. O pia; 7. O
dulcis. (288 mm.) 3 v. ObrW VI, no. 16,
pp. 145-56. Instrumental work, composed at
Bruges? (StrohmM). Text and cantus firmus:
antiphon B.M.V. (LU 276).
Source: Regensburg B 216-19.
Edition: AmbrosG 5: 46-60.
Literature: NagleS 61-81, SparksC 307-10,
StrohmM 145, WolffM 134-45.
Recordings: Allegro 9019 Vielle Trio (parts 1,
2, 7, 5, 6), Telefunken 9498 Hildenbrand
(parts 1-3).
22. SALVE REGINA (II). 1. Vita dulcedo; 2. Ad te
suspiramus (3 v.); 3. Et Jesum; 4. O pia.
(149 mm.) 4 v. Text and cantus firmus (in
A.): antiphon B.M.V. (LU 276). Polyphonic
settings alternate with chant verses.
Source: Segovia.
Edition: SmijersV 3: 65-69.
Literature: NagleS 61-81.
23. SALVE REGINA (III). 6 v. ObrO II, no. 1, pp.
1-163; ObrW VI, no. 1, pp. 1-14. Text and
cantus firmus (in T. and S^2): antiphon B.M.V.
(LU 276). Polyphonic settings alternate with
chant verses.
I. 1. Vita dulcedo; 2. Ad te suspiramus (128
    mm.).
II. 1. Et Jesum; 2. O pia (106 mm.).
Sources: Munich 34, Regensburg C.98 (anon.).
Literature: NagleS 61-81, SparksC 304.
Recording: Archive 2533 377 Turner.
24. SALVE SANCTA FACIES /HOMO QUIDAM FECIT. 2.
Salve nostra gloria/Quia iam parata sunt.
(289 mm.). 4 v. ObrW VI, no. 12, pp. 108-
19. Text: sequence (DanielT 1: 341 and 2:
232, KehreinL 62). Cantus firmus (in S.):
responsory (AM 1189).

Source: Florence 232.
Literature: NagleS 82-88, StrohmM 145.
25. SI BONA SUSCEPIMUS. (64 mm.) 3 v. Text: Job
   2: 10, 1: 21.
   Sources: St. Gall 463 (S. only), 1541[2]
   (anon.).
   Edition: LoachA 2: 43-45.
26. SI SUMPSERO. (104 mm.) 3 v. ObrW VI, no.
   19, pp. 175-78; 194-96 (lute); 197-200
   (keyboard). Text: Ps. 138: 9, 22: 4.
   Instrumental?
   Sources: Augsburg 142a (anon., textless),
   Brussels 11239 (anon.), Florence 107bis
   (listed in index, lacking in MS; anon.),
   Greifswald 640-41 (anon.), Heilbronn X,2 (B.
   only), Paris 1597 (anon.; fac. in HewittB
   74-75), St. Gall 463 (S. only; anon.),
   1502[2], [c. 1535][14] (S. only; anon.), 1538[9]
   (anon.; textless). Tablatures: Berlin
   40026 (anon.), St. Gall 530 (Alexander),
   1536[13].
   Editions: HewittB 204-8, PickerC 467-71.
   Literature: PickerC 94-95.

(5) Motets - Doubtful
Of the works listed below, nos. 1, 2, and 4
are unica found in mid-16th century German sources
under Obrecht's name. The lateness of the sources
and their German provenance, together with the
stylistic discrepancies between these compositions
and Obrecht's authentic works, make the
attributions doubtful. Nos. 3 and 5 bear
conflicting attributions of approximately equal
weight.
1. DISCUBUIT JESUS. 2. (Et accepto); 3. (Edite et
   bibete) (2 v.). (109 mm.) 4 v. ObrW VI, no.
   21, pp. 189-93 (the missing A. is reconstruc-
   ted). Text and cantus firmus (in T.):
   responsory (German, 16th cent.; see NagleS 90-
   92). FinscherO-MGG and NagleS doubt the
   authenticity of this work.
   Source: Zwickau LXXXI,2 (lacks A.; textless).
   Literature: NagleS 88-92.
2. HAEC DEUM CAELI. (70 mm.) 5 v. ObrO II, no.
   3, pp. 36-40; ObrW VI, no. 4, pp. 46-48.
   Text: verse 2 of hymn "Quod chorus vatum" (VP
   103). Cantus firmus (in A., T., and S[2]) is
   the melody of hymn "Iste confessor" (LU 1196).

Source: 1542^{12}.
Editions: EDMR 21, no. 16; ReeserD 5-9.
Literature: NagleS 46-49, SparksC 304-6.
Recording: Seraphim 6104 Munrow.
3. JUDAEA ET JERUSALEM. 2. Cras egrediemini; 3.
Constantes estote. 4 v. Text and cantus
firmus (in B.): responsory (AM 1183-84).
Conflicting attributions to Isaac and Obrecht.
FinscherO-MGG and SparksO-NG list this as a
doubtful work of Obrecht. Unpublished.
Sources: Dresden 1/D/505 (Obrecht), Dresden 59
(A. T. only; anon.), Leipzig 51 (T. B. only;
anon.), Regensburg A.R. 838-43 (Isaac),
Zwickau XCIV,1 (anon.), 1538^7 (Isaac).
Literature: JustS 1: 137-38, 2: 51 (as work of
Isaac).
4. MAGNIFICAT. 1. Et exultavit; 2. Quia fecit; 3.
Fecit potentiam; 4. Esurientes; 5. Sicut
locutus est; 5. Sicut erat. (225 mm.) 4 v.
ObrW CI, no. 15, pp. 136-44. Text: Luc. 1:
46-55. Cantus firmus: Tone 5 (LU 210). Sets
the even-numbered verses, alternating with
chant. FinscherO-MGG doubts the authenticity
of this work.
Source: Dresden 1/D/505.
Literature: MeinholzU 47-50 and 146-55, NagleS
96-105.
Recording: Turnabout 34569 Cohen.
5. NEC MIHI NEC TIBI (HELAS). (101 mm.) 2 (3) v.
Text (or title?): 3 Reg. 3: 26. AtlasC
suggests that this is an instrumental duo by
Obrecht, to which Virgilius (perhaps the Ser
Vergilio active in Florence between 1507 and
1518; see D'AcconeS 281-82) added an A. The 3
v. version is attributed to Obrecht in
Segovia, and to Virgilius in the Florentine MS
Rome Giul. XIII.27. The title may be a
reference to their joint responsibility for
the work.
Sources: Florence 229 (anon.; textless),
Hradec Králové II A 7 (anon.; textless),
Perugia 431 ("Helas"; S. T. only; anon.),
Rome Giul. XIII.27 (Virgilius), Segovia
(Jacobus Hobrecht), Turin I.27 ("Duo. Nec
mihi nec tibi sed dividatire"; S. T. only;
anon.).
Editions: AtlasC 2: 34-38, BrownC 2: 638-42.

Literature: AtlasC 1: 131-33, AtlasCA 258-60,
BakerU 53-54, D'AcconeS 283-84.

(6) Motets - Spurious
Various sacred works ascribed to Obrecht in
16th century sources are attributed in more
reliable sources to other composers. The following
works included in ObrW are almost certainly not by
Obrecht.
1. O VOS OMNES. 3 v. ObrW VI, no. 18, pp. 173-
   74. Attributed to Obrecht in St. Gall 463 and
   to Compère in Bologna Q 17 and 1542[8], this
   work is undoubtedly by Compère. It bears
   the French rondeau text "Tant ay d'ennui" in
   some sources. FinscherO-MGG and SparksO-NG
   regard the attribution to Obrecht as false,
   and MaasT omits it from his worklist.
2. PASSIO DOMINI. 4 (6) v. ObrW VIII.
   Attributed to Obrecht in 1538[1] and some sixteen German manuscripts of the 16th century,
   and to La Rue in Dresden 1/D/505. However,
   the earliest source, Florence 232 (fac. in MGG
   10, Taf. 63) names Longaval as the composer,
   and Rome Sist. 42 and Toledo 23 name J. A la
   Venture (see SmijersM). FinscherO-MGG regards
   the attribution to Obrecht as false, while
   SparksO-NG and MaasT consider it doubtful.
   The work is probably by Longaval/A la Venture
   (whose names may refer to the same person).
3. PATER NOSTER. 4 v. ObrW VI, no. 14, pp. 131-
   35. Attributed to Obrecht in Leipzig 49/50,
   to Willaert in in the authoritative **Adriani
   Willaert . . . Music quatuor vocum, Liber
   secundus** (Venice, 1545) and many other
   sources. It is unquestionably by Willaert.
   FinscherO-MGG and SparksO-NG regard the
   attribution to Obrecht as false. MaasT omits
   this motet from his worklist.
4. SI DEDERO. 3(4) v. ObrW III, pp. 55-57
   (Agricola). Attributed to Obrecht by a 16th
   century hand in a copy of 1538[9] (probably
   through confusion with his Missa Si dedero),
   this work is attributed to Alexander Agricola
   in nine sources and to Verbonnet in one. Wolf
   (in ObrW III) regards Agricola as the
   composer. FinscherO-MGG and SparksO-NG regard
   the attribution to Obrecht as false. MaasT
   omits this motet from his worklist.

5. SI OBLITUS FUERO. 4 v. ObrW VI, no. 11, pp.
    97-107. Attributed to Obrecht in Dresden
    1/D/505, but to Ninot Lepetit in Florence 232
    and Jo. Lepetit in Rome Sist. 42. FinscherO-
    MGG and SparksO-NG regard the attribution to
    Obrecht as false; MaasT regards it as
    doubtful. The composer is probably Ninot/Jo.
    Lepetit.

(7) Secular Works - Authentic
Of Obrecht's 26 authentic works, 19 have
Flemish texts. Most of the Flemish pieces appear
to be based on popular songs. Five works have
French texts or incipits; of these, two are based
on one or more voices of a polyphonic model (nos.
3, 10), one on a popular song (no. 22), and two are
apparently freely composed (nos. 4, 19). One work
is based on an Italian popular song (no. 13).
    Most of the Flemish works are uniquely
preserved in the Segovia MS. They represent the
largest body of Flemish songs by a single composer
that come down to us from the 15th century.
Discovered too late for inclusion in ObrW, many are
published in SmijersV 3. All the secular works are
scheduled for publication in ObrCW 17.

1. ALS AL DE WEERELT. (84 mm.) 4 v. Based on
    popular song, primarily in T.
    Source: Segovia.
    Edition: SmijersV 3: 86-88.
2. DEN HAGHEL ENDE DIE CALDE SNEE. (59 mm.) 4 v.
    Source: Segovia
    Editions: LenaertsA 30-31, SmijersV 3: 78-79.
    Recording: Anth. Son. 5 Raugel.
3. FORS SEULEMENT. (72 mm.) 4 v. ObrW VII, no.
    6, pp. 14-16. Rondeau. Cantus firmus in A. =
    S. of chanson by Ockeghem.
    Sources: Florence Cons. 2439, Regensburg
        C.120, St. Gall 461, 1504[3].
    Editions: AmbrosG: 29-33, GiesbertA 1: 12-13,
        PickerF 8-11.
    Literature: GombosiJ 30-32, ReeseMR 187-88.
    Recording: Mus. Her. 1716 Harnoncourt, Mus.
        Her. 3859 Piguet.
4. HELAS MON BIEN. (49 mm.) 3 v. ObrW VII, no.
    7, pp. 17-18. Rondeau(?)
    Source: St. Gall 461.

Edition: GiesbertA 2: 62-63.
Recording: Harmonia Mundi 384 Clemencic.
5. IC DRAGHE DE MUTSE CLUTSE.   (84 mm.)   4 v.
Source: Segovia.
Editions: GreenbergA 214-21, SmijersV 3: 89-
91.
Recordings: Oiseau-Lyre 203/6 Rooley, Teldec
6.41053 Binkley.
6. HEBBE GHEEN GHELT.   (85 mm.)   4 v.
Source: Segovia.
Edition: SmijersV 3: 92-94.
Literature: ReeseMR 189.
7. IC HOERDE DE CLOCSKINS LUDEN.   (108 mm.)   4 v.
Source: Segovia.
Edition: SmijersV 3: 83-85.
8. IC RET MY UIT SPACIEREN.   (51 mm.)   4 v.   ObrW
VII, no. 22, pp. 69-70 (keyboard arr.).   Based
on popular song in T.
Source: St. Gall 530.
9. IC WEINSCHE ALLE SCOENE VROUWEN.   (67 mm.)   4
v.   Based on popular song, primarily in S. and
T.   Although attributed to Stoltzer in a
German print, this work is probably by
Obrecht, to whom it is attributed in the
authoritative Segovia MS.
Sources: Segovia (Hobrecht), Ulm 236 (anon.;
"Ich wünsch alln Frauen), 1544[20] (Thomas
Stoltzer, "Ich wünsch alle Frauen").
Editions: DTO 72: 72 (Stoltzer), PAPTM 1: 96-8
(Stoltzer), SmijersV 3: 95-96 (Hobrecht?).
Recording: Anth. Son. 5 Raugel.
10. J'AY PRIS AMOURS.   2 partes.   (232 mm.)   4 v.
ObrW VII, no. 8, pp. 19-28.   Instrumental?
Cantus firmi are S. T. of anon. rondeau.
Sources: 1502[2], [c. 1535][14] (S. only; anon.).
Editions: HewittB 94-105, TaruskinJ 37-44; B.
Thomas, ed., **The Art of the Netherlanders**,
10.   London: Pro Musica Editions, 1984.   8
pp.
Literature: ReeseMR 188.
11. LACEN ADIEU.   (58 mm.)   4 v.
Source: Segovia (fac. in **Musica** 15 [1961],
Taf. 12).
Edition: SmijersV 3: 76-77.
Literature: ReeseMR 189.
12. LAET U GENOUGHEN.   (81 mm.)   4 v.   Based on
popular song primarily in T.
Source: Segovia.

Edition: SmijersV 3: 70-72.
Literature: BrownM 160.
Recording: Mus. Her. 713 Weinhöpfel.
13. LA TORTORELLA. (49 mm.) 4 v. ObrW VII, no.
13, pp. 43-45. Based on popular song?
Probably composed in Ferrara ca. 1487-88.
Sources: Florence 164-67 (anon.), B.R.229,
Rome Giul. XIII.27, 1504[3].
Editions: AmbrosG 5: 36-39, BrownC 2: 389-91.
Literature: BrownC 1: 279-80, ReeseMR 187,
RubsamenF 64.
Recording: Epic 3263 de Nobel.
14. MA MENCHE VEL MA BUCHE. (48 mm.) 4 v. ObrW
VII, no. 23, p. 71 (keyboard arr.). Based on
popular song in S.(?)
Source: St. Gall 530 (tablature).
15. MARION LA DOULCE. 3 v. Unpublished.
Sources: Copenhagen 1848 (anon.), Hradec
Králové II A 20 (B. only, without
text).
Literature: StaehelinO 11.
16. MESKIN ES HU (ADIU, ADIU). (30 mm.) 4 (3) v.
ObrW VII, no. 1, pp. 1-2; no. 26, pp. 78-79
(keyboard arr.). Based on popular song,
divided between T. and A. in 4 v. version; in
T. in version for 3 v.
Sources (4 v. unless otherwise indicated):
Florence 178 (Adiu, adiu), B.R.229 (without
text; fac. in HoornJ opp. p. 168), Panc. 27
(3 v.; anon.), Segovia, St. Gall 463 (index
only), 1501 (anon.). Tablature: St. Gall
530 (anon.).
Editions: AmbrosG 5: 34-35 (without text),
BrownC 2: 383-84, HewittO 421.
Literature: BlackburnT 141-44, ReeseMR 189.
17. MOET MIJ LATEN U VRIENDELIC SCHIJN. (21 mm.)
3 v.
Source: Segovia.
Edition: BakerU 2: 942-44.
18. ROMPELTIER. (33 mm.) 4 v. ObrW VII, no. 2,
pp. 2-3. Based on popular song in T. The
absence of the composer's name in Petrucci's
later editions leads Hewitt to consider the
attribution in 1501 to Obrecht as doubtful.
Sources: Florence 121 (anon.), 1501 (anon. in
later editions).
Edition: HewittO 274.
Literature: BlackburnT 139-41.

Recordings: FSM 63904 Cross, Telefunken 8008
Muziekkring Obrecht.

19. SE BIEN FAIT. (62 mm.) 4 v. ObrW VII, no.
10, pp. 34-6.
Source: Rome Cas. 2856.
Edition: AmbrosG 5: 40-42.
Literature: ReeseMR 189.

20. SULLEN WIJ LANGHE IN DRUCKE. 4 v.
Unpublished.
Source: Segovia (B. incomplete).

21. T'ANDERNACKEN. (81 mm.) 3 v. ObrW VII, no.
3, pp. 3-7; no. 24, pp. 72-76 (lute arr.).
Based on popular song in T. Instrumental.
Sources: St. Gall 463 (S. only), Zwickau
LXXVIII,3 (anon.; without text), 1501.
Tablatures: 1533_1 (Der alt Tandernack;
anon.), 1536^{13}.
Editions: HewittO 366-68, TaruskinT 11-13.
Literature: HewittO 80-81, ReeseMR 189,
StrohmM 144.

22. TANT QUE NOSTRE ARGENT DURA. (43 mm.) 4 v.
ObrW VII, no. 11, pp. 36-38. Based on popular
song in T. and B.
Sources: Florence Cons. 2442, Munich 1516
(anon.), 1504^3.

23. TSAT EEN (CLEEN) MESKIN. 2 parts. (106 mm.)
4 v. ObrW VII, no. 4, pp. 7-11. Based on
popular song primarily in T.
Sources: St. Gall 461, 463 (index only),
Segovia, 1501.
Editions: GiesbertA 2: 102-3, HAM 1: 82-83,
HewittO 407-10.
Literature: HewittO 102, ReeseMR 189.
Recordings: Mus. Her. 1716 Harnoncourt, Mus.
Her. 4611 Sothcott, Anth. Son. 4 Cape, Bach
Guild 634 Cape, Pleiades 251 Brown, Seraphim
6104 Munrow.

24. WAER SIJ DI HAN. (78 mm.) 4 v. Based on
popular song primarily in T.(?)
Source: Segovia.
Edition: SmijersV 3: 73-75.

25. WAT WILLEN WIJ METTEN. 2 parts. (107 mm.) 4
v. ObrW VII, no. 9, pp. 29-33 (Maule met);
no. 12, pp. 38-42 (Vanilment).
Based on popular song primarily in T. B.(?)
Sources: Basel F.X.5-9 (anon.; without text;
A. lacking), Berlin 40021 (anon.; without
text), Hradec Králové II A 7 (Precanti-

bus; anon.), Rome Giul. XIII.27 (Maule
met), Segovia, 1502² (Vavilment).
Edition: HewittB 188-92.
Recording: Archive 3223 Harnoncourt.

26. WEET GHY WAT MIJNDER JONGHEN HERTEN.   (79 mm.)
    4 v. Based on popular song in T. (See
    settings by Ghiselin and anon.)
    Source: Segovia.
    Editions: SmijersV 3: 80-82, TaruskinI 47-49.
    Literature: KesselsB 96-97, ReeseMR 187.
    Recording: Telefunken 8008 Muziekkring
      Obrecht.

    (8) Secular Works - Doubtful
1. EIN FRÖLICH WESEN. (46 mm.) 4 v. ObrW VII,
   no. 20, pp. 61-63. S. T. B. from Lied by
   Barbireau; A. is a clumsly addition that is
   not likely to be by Obrecht.
   Sources: St. Gall 462, 463 (S. A. only).
   Editions: GeeringL 55-56, TaruskinE 22-23.
   Literature: GombosiO 126-27, KesselsB 92-94.
   Recording: Seraphim 6104 Munrow.
2. LA STANGETTA. (60 mm.) 3 v. ObrW VII, no.
   14, pp. 45-47. Instrumental. Parody of
   chanson? (Possible models include anon. "Ce
   n'est pas sans" in Bologna MS Q 16, and "D'un
   bon du cuer" publ. in BrownC 99-100, DrozT 42-
   43.) Also attr. to Isaac and Weerbecke. In a
   study devoted to this work, KämperL favors
   attribution to Weerbecke.
   Sources: Florence Panc. 27 (anon.), Heilbronn
     X,2 (B. only; anon.), Segovia (Ortus de
     celo, Ysaac), Zwickau LXXVIII,3 (Obrecht;
     without text), 1501 (Werbech; attribution
     lacking in later editions), [c. 1535]¹⁴ (S.
     only; anon.), 1538⁹ (anon.; without text).
     Tablatures: 1507⁶ (anon.), 1536¹³ (anon.).
   Edition: HewittO 325-26.
   Literature: KämperL, KämperS 71-72.
   Recording: Mus. Her. 4611 Sothcott.
3. T'MEISKIN WAS JONCK (DE TUSCHE IN BUSCHE). (48
   mm.) 4 (3) v. Based on popular song in T.
   Also attributed to Isaac and Japart, but the
   attribution to Obrecht in the Segovia MS has
   the greatest weight. Most sources give four
   voices, but London Add. 35087, lacking the A.,
   may represent the original to which a fourth
   voice was added.

Sources: Bologna Q 17 (De tous in busc;
anon.), Florence 107 (De tusch in busch;
anon.), 178 (De tusche in busche; Japart),
B.R.229 (anon.; without text), London Add.
35087 (A. lacking; anon.), St. Gall 463
(index only; anon.), Segovia (Jacobus
Hobrecht), 1501 (Isaac; attribution lacking
in later editions). Tablature: 1512^2
(Metzkin; Isack; arr. by Arnolt Schlick for
voice and lute).
Editions: BrownC 2: 339-41, DTO 28: 109, 159
(arr. voice and lute), 32: 203-4 (Isaac);
HewittO 277-78; IsaacO 7: 138-39; LenaertsN
(4-5) (Isaac); WolfL 20-21 (3 v.; Isaac).
Recording: Anth. Son. 5 Raugel (Isaac).

(9) Secular Works - Spurious
Two anon. settings of "Myn morken gaf," one
for 3 v. and the other for 4 v. with the same S.,
are listed as a single work by Obrecht in MaasT
106. The attribution may have originated in
SmijersVZ 170, where the 4 v. setting in Bologna MS
Q 18 is assigned to Obrecht without explanation.
All sources are anon. Modern editions include
WexlerMM 8-10 (both versions, anon.), WolfL 1 (3
v., anon.), HewittB 143-45 (4 v. anon.), LenaertsL
(5-6) (4 v., anon.).

(10) Works without Text
1. FUGA. (25 mm.) 4 v. ObrW VII, no. 19, pp.
    57-58. A 3-part canon over a cantus firmus
    derived from the canon.
    Source: Rome Cas. 2856 (notated as a single
    voice).
2. (TEXTLESS). (58 mm.) 3 v. ObrW VII, no. 15,
    pp. 48-49.
    Source: Munich 3154.
3. (TEXTLESS). (81 mm.) 3 v. ObrW VII, no. 16,
    pp. 50-52. Cantus firmus (unidentified) in S.
    Source: Florence B.R. 229.
    Edition: BrownC 490-92.
4. (TEXTLESS). 3 v. Unpublished. Cantus firmus
    (unidentified) in T.
    Source: Verona 757.
    Literature: StaehelinO 10.
5. (TEXTLESS). 3 v. Unpublished.
    Source: Verona 757.
    Literature: StaehelinO 10.

6. (TEXTLESS). B. only. Unpublished.
    Source: Hradec Králové II A 20.
    Literature: StaehelinO 11.

    (11) Fragmentary and Lost Works
1. MISSA(?) REGINA CELI. Composed 1503 for
    Maximilian I. "6 October, 1503, at Innsbruck.
    Master Martin gives to Jacob Opprecht 14 ells
    of good damask cloth for composing for us a
    Regina celi service (Ambt)." (StaehelinO 14-
    15.) Staehelin presumes that this is a mass
    rather than a single setting of the antiphon.
    No mass by Obrecht with this title is known.
    (For a 2 v. setting of the antiphon "Regina
    celi" by Obrecht, see the Work List above,
    Motet no. 19.)
2. TRATTI ET GRADUALI:
    ALLELUIA DELLA MADONNA DI SETTEMBRE
        (Nativitate B.M.V.).
    SEQUENZA DI S. GIOVANNI BATTISTA.
    SEQUENZA DELLA RESURRETTIONE (v. TE AGNUM SINE
        MACULA).
    [SEQUENZA DELLA VISITATIONE (v. TU NOS
        VISITA)] (by Isaac).
    The above titles of works attributed to
    Obrecht are cited in Zacconi 1592, with many
    short musical examples (fols. 42', 84, 109,
    155'). Some of these citations, but not the
    examples, are repeated in Cerone 1613.
    However Cerone gives a 4 v. example different
    from any of Zacconi's immediately following
    his discussion of works by Isaac, Senfl, and
    Obrecht (p. 957). Zacconi's attributions are
    cast into doubt by the identification of the
    "Sequenza della Visitatione" as a fragment of
    the sequence "Piae vocis" in the mass proper
    Visitationis Mariae by Heinrich Isaac
    (Choralis Constantinus II, no. 13; DTO 32:
    103). The other examples have not been
    identified.

Note: The Missa In nomine Jesu by "Jacomo" sent to
Duke Ercole d'Este at Ferrara in 1504 by the
Ferrarese ambassador in Florence (StaehelinO 15) is
probably not by Obrecht. The full name of the
copyist is given as "Jacopo Dini," and it is this
person that is evidently meant (StaehelinB).

III. SOURCES

The majority of Ockeghem's sacred works are found in the Chigi manuscript at the Vatican Library in Rome, a choirbook of Flemish origin dating from shortly after the composer's death in 1497 and perhaps intended as a memorial collection. His secular works are most strongly represented in the Dijon and Washington (Laborde) chansonniers, prepared while he was still living. Two volumes were devoted exclusively to Obrecht's masses in the sixteenth century: **Misse Obreht** published by Petrucci at Venice in 1503, during the composer's lifetime; and **Concentus harmonici quattuor missarum** . . . Jacobi Obrecht, published at Basel around 1510, some five years after his death. Obrecht is well represented in manuscript and printed anthologies from around 1480 to the early 1540's, after which there is a marked decline in representation. The most important single manuscript source of his music is a choirbook in the archive of the cathedral at Segovia, Spain, dating from the beginning of the sixteenth century. Many of his masses are found in the large and variegated MS Munich 3154, compiled at Innsbruck in the early sixteenth century, and in Modena MS a.M.1.2, written at Ferrara shortly after Obrecht's death in 1505 and probably intended as a memorial collection.

A. CHOIRBOOKS AND PART-BOOKS

1. Manuscripts

The library sigla given below are taken from RISM. For additional bibliographical data, see Census-Catalogue. All items are choirbooks unless otherwise noted.

AMIENS. BIBLIOTHÈQUE MUNICIPALE (F-AM).
  MS Mus. 162. Polyphony in parts I and III.
    France, ca. 1500.
    (Obrecht): Parce Domine
AUGSBURG. STAATS- UND STADTBIBLIOTHEK (D-AS).
    Catalogue: GottwaldA.
  MS 2° 142. Augsburg, ca. 1505-14.
    Literature: BenteN 230-42.
    (Obrecht: Si sumpsero)
BARCELONA. BIBLIOTECA CENTRAL DE CATALUÑA (E-Bc).
    Catalogue: PedrellC.
  MS 454. Spain, ca. 1500-35. Literature:
    AnglésM 1: 112-15.
    (Ockeghem): Missa Au travail suis
BARCELONA. BIBLIOTECA ORFEÓ CATALÀ (E-Boc).
  MS 5. Part I, devoted to masses: late
    fifteenth cent. Literature: AnglésM
    115, JosquinWM I: vii-viii, ObrO I:
    xxvii.
    (Obrecht): Missa Salve diva parens
BASEL. ÖFFENTLICHE BIBLIOTHEK DER UNIVERSITÄT
    (CH-Bu). Catalogue: RichterK.
  MS F.X. 5-9. 5 part-books. Basel, dated
    1535-46.
    (Obrecht): Wat willen wij
BERLIN. DEUTSCHE STAATSBIBLIOTHEK (former
    Preussische Staatsbibliothek) (D-Bds).
  MS Mus. 40098 (Glogauer Liederbuch). See
    under Kraków.
  MS Mus. 40634. See under Kraków.
BERLIN. STAATSBIBLIOTHEK DER STIFTUNG PREUSSISCHER
    KULTURBESITZ (D-B).
  MS Mus. 40021. Germany, dated 1495. (Mod.
    ed. to appear in EDMR.) Literature:
    EitnerC, JustM, ObrCW IV: xxvi.
    (Obrecht): Misse Fortuna desperata,
      Malheur me bat; (Wat willen wij)
    (Obrecht?): Misse Je ne seray plus,
      N'aray-je jamais
BOLOGNA. CIVICO MUSEO BIBLIOGRAFICO MUSICALE (I-
    Bc). Catalogue: GaspariC.
  MS Q16. Italy, after 1487. Literature:
    FullerA, PeaseB-MGG, PeaseR.
    (Ockeghem): La trentana (= L'autre
      d'antan)
    (Ockeghem?): Departes vous Malebouche,
      Dieu d'amours (= Malheur me bat)
    (Obrecht?): Ce n'est pas sans (= La
      stangetta)

MS Q17. Florence? ca. 1500. Literature:
       WexlerN.
       Ockeghem: D'ung aultre amer, J'en ay
           dueil
       (Obrecht): Parce Domine, (?) De tous in
           busc (= T'meiskin was jonck)
MS Q18. Bologna, early sixteenth cent.
       Literature: TorchiM 502-3, WeissM.
       (Ockeghem?): Malheur me bat
       (Obrecht): Parce Domine
BRUSSELS. BIBLIOTHÈQUE DU CONSERVATOIRE ROYAL DE
       MUSIQUE (B-Bc).
       MS 33.346. Flanders, late fifteenth cent.
           Literature: BorrenI 5: 178, OckCW I: xvi.
           (Ockeghem): Missa sine nomine (I), Kyrie
               (fragmentary).
BRUSSELS. BIBLIOTHÈQUE ROYALE ALBERT Ier (B-Br).
       General inventory: BorrenI.
       MS 228. Brussels or Mechlin, ca. 1516-23.
           Written for Margaret of Austria. Fac.
           ed.: Album. Modern ed.: PickerC.
           Literature: PickerCA.
           (Ockeghem): J'en ay dueil
       MS 5557. Flanders, 1459-80. Literature:
           KenneyO, OckCW I: xvi, II: xi, WegmanN.
           (Ockeghem): Missa sine nomine (= Quinti
               toni)
           Ockeghem(?): Missa Pour quelque paine
       MS 11239. Savoy, ca. 1500. Fac. ed.:
           Chansonnier. Modern ed.: PickerC.
           Literature: PickerCA, PickerN.
           (Ockeghem): (S'elle m'amera)/Petite
               camusette (S. T. only)
           (Obrecht): Si sumpsero
       MS IV 90. Bruges, 1511. (S. part-book only.
           Tournai 94 also belongs to this set.)
           Literature: HuysD 33-34, KesselsB.
           (Ockeghem): J'en ay dueil
           (Obrecht): Parce Domine
CAMBRIDGE. MAGDALENE COLLEGE, PEPYS LIBRARY (GB-
       Cmc).
       MS 1760. France, early sixteenth cent. (Fac.
           ed.: RMF 2.) Literature: FenlonC 123-26,
           MerrittC 91-99.
           Obrecht: Alma Redemptoris Mater, Parce
               Domine

CAMBRIDGE.   TRINITY COLLEGE LIBRARY (GB-Ctc).
    MS R.2.71.   France, ca. 1475.   Literature:
        FallowsJ.
        Ockeghem: Ma maistresse (S. T. only,
            incomplete)
COPENHAGEN.   KONGELIGE BIBLIOTEK (DK-Kk).
    MS Ny Kongelige Samling 1848-2⁰.   Lyons,
        ca. 1525.   Literature: PlamenacPS.
        (Ockeghem): Basies moy dont fort, D'ung
            aultre amer, Fors seulement contre,
            (Ma bouche rit, first part only)
        (Obrecht): Parce Domine, Marion la
            doulce
    MS Thott 291⁸.   France or Burgundy, ca. 1475.
        Modern ed.: JeppesenK.
        (Ockeghem): D'ung aultre amer, Prenez sur
            moi
DIJON.   BIBLIOTHÈQUE MUNICIPALE (F-Dm).
    MS 517.   France or Burgundy, after ca. 1475.
        Fac. ed.: PlamenacD.   Modern ed.: DrozT
        (partial).   Literature: PickerD.
        Ockeghem: D'ung aultre amer, Fors
            seulement l'attente, L'autre d'antan
            (anon.), Ma bouche rit (anon.),
            Mort tu as navré (anon.), (Prenez
            sur moi, missing), Presque transi,
            Quant de vous seul, S'elle m'amera/
            Petite camusette (anon.)
        Barbinguant (Ockeghem?): Au travail suis
        Busnoys (Ockeghem?): Quand ce viendra
DRESDEN.   SÄCHSISCHE LANDESBIBLIOTHEK (D-Dlb).
    Catalogue: SteudeM.
    MS Mus. 1/D/505 (Annaberg 1248).   Annaberg,
        ca. 1530.   (Modern ed. to appear in EDMR.)
        Literature: AlbrechtA-MGG, NoblittM; ObrW
        VI/3: vii, ObrO Missae VI, SteudeM 221-
        33.
        Obrecht: Missa Sub tuum presidium
        Obrecht(?): Credo (Missa Veci la danse
            barbari), Judea et Jerusalem,
            Magnificat, (Missa N'aray-je jamais)
        (Obrecht): Missa Plurimorum carminum (I)
    MS Grimma 59 (1-2).   A. T. part-books.
        Leipzig, dated 1548-50.   SteudeM 103-5.
        (Obrecht?): Judea et Jerusalem
EL ESCORIAL.   BIBLIOTECA DEL MONASTERIO (E-E).
    MS IV.a.24.   Naples, ca. 1465.   Modern ed.:
        HanenC.   Literature: SouthernE.

(Ockeghem: Ma maistresse, first part
     only); Hockengem(?): Quand ce
     viendra
FLORENCE. BIBLIOTECA NAZIONALE CENTRALE (I-Fn).
Catalogue: BecheriniC.
MS II.I.232 (Magl. XIX.58). Florence, ca.
     1515. Literature: BecheriniC 21-22,
     CummingsF, ObrO II/2: vii, ObrW VII: vii.
     Obrecht: Factor orbis, O beate Basili,
     Salve sancta facies
MS Banco rari 229. Florence, ca. 1491.
     Modern ed.: BrownF. Literature:
     BecheriniC 22-29.
     Martini (Ockeghem?): (Malheur me bat
     Obrecht: La tortorella, (Meskin es hu),
     (textless a 3)
     (Obrecht?): (Nec mihi nec tibi),
     T'meiskin was jonc
MS Magl. XIX.107bis. Florence, ca. 1512.
     Literature: BecheriniC 42-44, ObrW I no.
     3: vi, ObrCW IV: xxvi.
     (Obrecht): Missa Fortuna desperata
     (fragments), Missa Si dedero
     (fragments)
     (Obrecht?): De tusch in busch (=
     T'meiskin was jonc)
MS Magl. XIX.121. Florence, ca. 1500.
     Literature: BecheriniC 52-54, BlackburnT,
     JeppesenF 2: 52-53 and 144-45.
     (Obrecht): Rompeltier
MS Magl. XIX.164-67. Four part-books.
     Florence, ca. 1520. (Fac. ed.: RMF 5.)
     Literature: BecheriniC 69-71, ObrW VII:
     xi, PannellaC.
     (Obrecht): La tortorella
MS Magl. XIX.176. Florence, ca. 1480.
     Literature: BecheriniC 72-75.
     Ockeghem: La despourveue (anon.), Ma
     bouche rit
     (Ockeghem?): Quand ce viendra
MS Magl. XIX.178. Florence, ca. 1490.
     Literature: BecheriniC 75-77.
     (Ockeghem): D'ung aultre amer
MS Panc. 27. Northern Italy, early sixteenth
     cent. Literature: BecheriniC 118-22,
     JeppesenF 2: 37-42 and 122-25, ObrW
     VII: xi.
     Obrecht: Meskin es hu; (Obrecht?): La
     stangetta

FLORENCE. BIBLIOTECA RICCARDIANA E MORENIANA (I-
    Fr).
    MS 2356. Florence, ca. 1480. Literature:
        PlamenacS, PlamenacPS.
        (Ockeghem): D'ung aultre amer, Ma bouche
            rit
    MS 2794. France, ca. 1480-90. Modern ed.:
        JonesF. Literature: RifkinP.
        Okeghem: Alma Redemptoris Mater, Aultre
            Venus estes, D'ung aultre amer, Ung
            aultre l'a
        Hayne (Ockeghem?): Ce n'est pas jeu
FLORENCE. CONSERVATORIO DI MUSICA LUIGI CHERUBINI,
    BIBLIOTECA (I-Fc). Catalogue: BecheriniM.
    MS Basevi 2439. Brussels or Mechlin, ca.
        1510. Modern ed.: NewtonF. Literature:
        BecheriniM 257-60.
        Ockeghem: Basies moy dont fort, Fors
            seulement contre, J'en ay dueil,
            (S'elle m'amera)/Petite camusette
        Obrecht: Missa Fortuna desperata
            (fragments), Mille quingentis, O
            beate Basili, Fors seulement
    MS Basevi 2442. S. A. T. part-books; B.
        missing. Florence or France, early six-
        teenth cent. Literature: BecheriniM 266-
        68, BrownMS.
        Obrecht: Tant que nostre argent
GREIFSWALD. UNIVERSITÄTSBIBLIOTHEK (D-GRu).
    MS BW 640-41 (Eb 133). MS supplement to RISM
        1538[8]. S. B. part-books (A. T. missing).
        Germany, dated 1539-88. Literature:
        ObrW VII: xi.
        (Obrecht): Si sumpsero
HEILBRONN. STADTARCHIV, MUSIKSAMMLUNG (D-HB).
    MSS IV-V/2. Two part-books. Germany, after
        1575. Literature: SiegeleM 38-39.
        (Ockeghem?): Deo gratia (T. only)
    MS X,2. B. part-book (of original four). MS
        appendix to RISM 1541[2]. Copied from RISM
        [c. 1535][14]? Literature: ObrW VI/6: vii,
        SiegeleM 42-48, StaehelinZ.
        Obrecht: Si sumpsero; (?) La stangetta
HRADEC KRÁLOVÉ. KRAJSKE MUZEUM (CS-HK).
    Catalogue: CernýS. MS II A 7 (Speciálnik
    Codex). Prague, ca. 1500. Literature:
    CernýS 40-41.
        (Obrecht): Precantibus (= Wat willen wy)

(Obrecht?): Missa Je ne seray plus
(incomplete), (Nec mihi nec tibi)
MS II A 20. B. part-book only (of original
three). Czech, sixteenth cent.
Literature: CernýS 52.
Obrecht: (Marion la doulce), (textless)
JENA. UNIVERSITÄTSBIBLIOTHEK (D-Ju). Catalogue:
RoedigerG.
MS 22. Brussels or Mechlin, ca. 1500.
Literature: ObrW III no. 10, RoedigerG
N: 39-44.
Obrecht: Misse O quam suavis, Sicut spina
rosam
MS 31. Wittenberg, early sixteenth cent.
Literature: RoedigerG N: 73-79.
(Obrecht): (Missa Plurimorum carminum II)
MS 32. Wittenberg, early sixteenth cent.
Literature: ObrCW I: xi, III: xi,
RoedigerG N: 80-87.
(Obrecht): Missa Adieu mes amours, Missa
O beate pater Donatiane (= De S.
Donatiane)
MS 36. Wittenberg, early sixteenth cent.
Literature: RoedigerG N: 175-79.
Rener: (Missa sine nomine- Credo =
Obrecht?: M. Veci la danse barbari)
KRAKÓW. BIBLIOTEKA JAGIELLÓNSKA (PL-Kj).
Glogauer Liederbuch (formerly Berlin,
Preussische Staatsbibliothek, MS Mus.
40098). Three part-books. Glogau
(Silesia), ca. 1480. Fac. ed.: RMF 6.
Modern edition: EDMR 4, 8, 85, 86.
Literature: RingmannG.
(Ockeghem: Ma bouche rit)
MS Mus. 40634 (formerly Berlin, Preussische
Staatsbibliothek). A. B. part-books
only. Germany, first half of the
sixteenth century. Literature: ObrW V:
no. 23, ObrCW I: xi, OckCW I: xv.
Ockeghem: Missa Cuiusvis toni
Obrecht: Misse Adieu mes (amours),
Libenter gloriabor, Malheur me bat,
Scaramella
LEIPZIG. UNIVERSITÄTSBIBLIOTHEK (D-LEu).
MS 1494 (Apel Codex). Leipzig, before 1504.
Modern ed.: EDMR 32-34. Literature:
ObrO I: xxvii-ix, ObrW I no. 5,
RiemannM.

Obrecht: Misse Salve diva parens
(incomplete), Si dedero (fragments)
MS Thom. 51. (T. B. part-books; S. A.
missing). Leipzig, ca. 1550.
Literature: ObrCW V: xvii, ObrW III no.
10, VI/3: vi, OrfM, NoblittR.
Obrecht: Misse Je ne demande, O quam
suavis
(Obrecht?): Missa Veci la danse barbari,
Judaea et Jerusalem
Agricola (Obrecht?): Missa Malheur me bat
LINZ. BUNDESSTAATLICHE STUDIENBIBLIOTHEK (A-LIs).
MS 529. Austria, ca. 1500. Fragments.
(Obrecht: Misse Plurimorum carminum I, Salve
diva parens)
LONDON. BRITISH LIBRARY (GB-Lbl). Catalogue:
Hughes-HughesC.
MS Add. 35087. Flanders, early sixteenth
cent. Modern ed.: McMurtryB.
Literature: Hughes-HughesC I: 262,
II: 128-9, ObrW VII/2: vii.
(Obrecht): Parce Domine (Ct. only);
(?) T'meiskin was jonc
MS Royal 20.A.XVI. France, ca. 1490. Fac.
ed.: RMF 10.
Modern ed.: LitterickM.
(Ockeghem): J'en ay dueil; (?) Ce n'est
pas jeu
LONDON. ROYAL COLLEGE OF MUSIC (B-Lcm).
MS 1070. France, early sixteenth cent.
Literature: LowinskyM, LowinskyRC, ObrW
VI/6: viii.
Obrecht: Alma Redemptoris Mater
LOUVAIN. BIBLIOTHÈQUE DE L'UNIVERSITÉ.
MS 163. Ct. part-book only. Flanders, 1546.
Destroyed in 1914. Literature:
Prod'hommeI 485-87.
Ockeghem: (Requiem)- Rex gloriae
LUCCA. ARCHIVIO DI STATO, BIBLIOTECA MANOSCRITTI
(I-La).
MS 238. Bruges, ca. 1470-1500. Literature:
StrohmU, StrohmM 120-36, 192-200.
(Ockeghem?): Missa Pour quelque paine
(incomplete)
MANTUA. PALAZZO DUCALE, STUDIO DI ISABELLA D'ESTE.
Wood inlay. 1505. Literature: ReeseM 81-86.
Okenghem: Prenez sur moi

MILAN. DUOMO, CAPPELLA MUSICALE (I-Md).
    Catalogue: SartoriC.
    MS 2268 (Librone 2). Fac. ed.: RMF 12b.
        Milan, ca. 1490-1500. Copied by
        Franchino Gafuri and others. Literature:
        AMMM, JeppesenG, SartoriC 47-50.
        Obrecht: Missa diversorum tenorum (= M.
        Plurimorum carminum I)
MODENA. BIBLIOTECA ESTENSE (I-MOe). Catalogue:
    LodiC.
    MS alpha.M.1.2 (L457). Ferrara, ca. 1505.
        Literature: LockwoodM 208 and 226-27,
        LodiC 17, ObrW I no. 3, ObrO I/3: xvi,
        OckCW I: xvi.
        Ockeghem: Missa Ecce ancilla Domini
        Obrecht: Misse Caput, (Fortuna
            desperata), L'homme armé,
            (Pfauenschwanz), (Plurimorum
            carminum II), Rose playsante;
            (?) (M. Gracuuly et biaulx)
MONTECASSINO. ARCHIVIO DELLA BADIA (I-MC).
    MS 871N. Naples, ca. 1480. Modern ed.:
        PopeM.
        Oquegan: Mort tu as navré; Cornago-
        Oquegan: Qu'es mi vida
        (Ockeghem): (S'elle m'amera)/Petite
            camusette
        Dufay (Ockeghem?): Departes vous
            Malebouche
MUNICH. BAYERISCHE STAATSBIBLIOTHEK (D-Mbs).
    Catalogue: GöllnerB, MaierM.
    MS Germ. 810 (Schedel Liederbuch). Germany,
        1461-67. Fac. ed.: EDMR 84. Modern ed.:
        EDMR 74-75. Literature: BirminghamS.
        (Ockeghem: Ma bouche rit)
    MS Mus. 34. Flanders, ca. 1525. Literature:
        MaierM 58-59, ObrW VII: vii, ObrO II:
        iii.
        Obrecht: Salve Regina (III)
    MS Mus. 260. Flanders or Germany, mid-
        sixteenth cent. Modern ed.: BellinghamS.
        Literature: MaierM 110-13.
        (Obrecht?): (Missa Je ne seray plus-
            Benedictus)
    MS Mus. 1516. Four part-books. Germany,
        ca. 1540. Modern ed.: WhislerM.
        Literature: GöllnerB 92-101, MaierM
        114-17, ObrW VII: xii

Ockeghem: (S'elle m'amera)/Petite
      camusette
Obrecht: Tant que nostra argent dura
MS Mus. 3154. Innsbruck, late fifteenth or
      early sixteenth cent. (Mod. ed. to
      appear in EDMR.) Literature: MaierM 19-
      22, NoblittC, NoblittD, ObrW I: v, ObrO
      I/1: v, ObrCW II: xi; V: xvii-xviii.
Obrecht: Misse Beata viscera
      (incomplete), Je ne demande
      (incomplete), (Plurimorum carminum
      II), Rose playsante (incomplete), Si
      dedero; (textless a 3)
MUNICH. UNIVERSITÄTSBIBLIOTHEK (D-Mu).
      Catalogue: GottwaldM.
      MS 2° Art. 239. Appendix to F. Gafurius, De
      harmonia musicorum instrumentorum opus
      (Milan, 1518). Basel, 1514-17. Written
      by P. Tschudi and H. Glareanus.
      Literature: GottwaldM 100-1, ObrW V no.
      22, ObrCW IV: xviii.
      Obrecht: Missa Fors seulement
      MS 4° Liturg. 374 (1-2). Two part-books (T.
      B.) of Petrucci 1504[1] and 1509[1], with
      insertions by H. Glareanus. Basel, early
      sixteenth cent. Literature: ObrW III:
      viii.
      Obrecht: Missa Si dedero- Sanctus
      MS 8° 322-325. Four part-books. Basel, 1527.
      Copied for H. Glareanus. Literature:
      GottwaldM 70-75, ObrW VII/2: vii.
      Obrecht: Parce Domine
NEW HAVEN, CONNECTICUT. YALE UNIVERSITY, BEINEKE
      LIBRARY (US-NH).
      MS 91 (Mellon Chansonnier). Naples, ca. 1475.
      Fac. and modern ed.: PerkinsMC.
      Literature: BukofzerU.
      Ockeghem: L'autre d'antan, Ma bouche rit,
            (S'elle m'amera)/Petite camusette;
            (?) Quand ce viendra
PARIS. BIBLIOTHÈQUE NATIONALE, DEPARTEMENT DE LA
      MUSIQUE (F-Pn).
      MS fr. 1596. France, ca. 1495. Literature:
      WexlerM.
      (Ockeghem): Fors seulement contre
      MS fr. 1597. France, ca. 1500. Modern ed.:
      ShippC. Literature: CouchmanL.
      (Ockeghem): Fors seulement l'attente
      (Obrecht): Si sumpsero

MS fr. 2245. France, ca. 1495.
    Ockeghem: D'ung aultre amer, Fors
        seulement contre
    Haine (Ockeghem?): Ce n'est pas jeu
MS fr. 15123 (ms. Pixérécourt). Florence,
    ca. 1480. Modern ed.: PeaseE.
    Busnois (Ockeghem): D'ung aultre amer
    Ockeghem: La despourveue, L'autre d'antan
    (anon.); Ma bouche rit (anon.), Se
    vostre cuer eslongne; (?) Departes
    vous Malebouche
MS nouv. acq. fr. 4379, part 1. Originally
    part of Seville MS 5-I-43; see under this
    listing below.
MS Réserve Vmc 57 (Chansonnier Nivelle de la
    Chausée). France, ca. 1470. Fac. ed.:
    HigginsC. Literature: ThibaultC.
    Okeghem: D'ung aultre amer, Fors
        seulement l'attente (anon.,
        fragment), Ma bouche rit, S'elle
        m'amera/Petite camusette, Tant fuz
        gentement
    Okeghem(?): Au travail suis, Quand ce
        viendra (anon., erased)
MS Rothschild 2973 (Chansonnier Cordiforme).
    Savoy, ca. 1475. Modern ed.: KottickM.
    Literature: KottickC.
    (Ockeghem): L'autre d'antan, Ma bouche
        rit
PERUGIA. BIBLIOTECA COMUNALE AUGUSTA (I-PEc).
    MS 431 (G.20). Naples, ca. 1485. Literature:
    AtlasO.
    (Obrecht?): Helas (= Nec mihi nec tibi)
REGENSBURG. BISCHÖFLICHE ZENTRALBIBLIOTHEK,
    PROSKE MUSIKBIBLIOTHEK (D-Rp).
    MS A.R. 838-843. Regensburg, dated 1571-73.
    Isaac (Obrecht?): Judaea et Jerusalem
    MS B.211-215. Five part-books. Germany or
    Austria, 1538-43. Literature: MohrH.
    Okegus (Ockeghem?): Caeleste beneficium,
        Gaude Maria
    MS B.216-219. Three part-books. Salzburg?
    ca. 1550. Literature: MohrH, ObrW VI/6:
    viii.
    Obrecht: Salve Regina (I)
    MS C.98. Southern Germany or Austria, early
    sixteenth cent. Literature: ObrO II:
    iii.

(Obrecht): Salve Regina (III)
MS C.120 (Pernner Codex). Southern Germany or
    Austria, ca. 1520-25. Literature: ObrW
    VII: xii.
    Obrecht: Fors seulement
ROME. BIBLIOTECA CASANATENSE (I-Rc).
    MS 2856. Ferrara, ca. 1480. Modern ed.:
    WolffC. Literature: LlorensCC, LockwoodM
    224-25, 269-72, ObrW VII: xii.
    Ockeghem: D'ung aultre amer, L'autre
        d'antan, Ma bouche rit, Se vostre
        cuer eslongne; (?) Ce n'est pas jeu
    Malcort (Ockeghem?): Malheur me bat
    Obrecht: Se bien fait, Fuga (a 4)
ROME (VATICAN CITY). BIBLIOTECA APOSTOLICA
    VATICANA (I-Rvat). Catalogues: HaberlB,
    LlorensC, LlorensO, SherrP.
    Cappella Giulia MS XIII.27. Florence,
        ca. 1492. Literature: AtlasC, LlorensO
        43-48, ObrW VII: xii.
    Ockeghem: Dung (=Ung) aultre la
    (Ockeghem): D'ung aultre amer, Frayres y
        dexedes me (= Fors seulement
        l'attente), Ma bouche rit
    Martini (Ockeghem?): Malheur me bat
    (Hayne or Ockeghem): Se mieulx ne vient
        (= Ce n'est pas jeu)
    Obrecht: La tortorella, Maule met (= Wat
        willen wy)
    Virgilius (Obrecht?): Nec mihi nec tibi
    Cappella Liberiano di S. Maria Maggiore, MS 26
        (JJ. III.4). Rome, early sixteenth cent.
        Literature: HudsonN.
    (Obrecht): Missa O quam suavis
    Cappella Sistina MS 14. Naples? late
        fifteenth cent. Literature: LlorensC 18-
        20, OckCW I: xvi, RothZ 268.
    Ockeghem: Missa De plus en plus
    Cappella Sistina MS 26. Rome, ca. 1513-21.
        LlorensC 54-56, OckCW II:xi.
    Ockeghem: Credo sine nomine
    Cappella Sistina MS 35. Rome, ca. 1486-88.
        LlorensC 69-72, ObrCW III: xi, OckCW I:
        xvi-xvii, RothZ 267-68.
    Okeghen: Missa Cuiusvis toni; (Ockeghem):
        Missa L'homme armé, Intemerata Dei
        Mater

Obrecht: (Missa de S. Donatiano), (Missa
plurimorum carminum I)- Kyrie &
Sanctus
Cappella Sistina MS 41. Rome, ca. 1480-1507.
Literature: LlorensC 81-83, OckCW I:
xviii, II: xi, SherrP 225-33.
Ockeghem: Missa Au travail suis, Missa
Quarti toni (= M. Mi-mi)
Cappella Sistina MS 42. Rome, ca. 1503-12.
Literature: LlorensC 83-86, ObrW VI: vii,
ObrO II/2: vii, SherrP 234-48.
Okeghem: Salve Regina (I)
Obrecht: Factor orbis, Laudemus nunc
Dominum
Cappella Sistina MS 46. Rome, ca. 1507-21.
Fac. ed.: RMF 21. Literature: LlorensC
94-98, LowinskyMC 232, SherrP 283-86.
Jo. (Ockeghem): Alma Redemptoris Mater
Cappella Sistina MS 51. Naples? late
fifteenth cent. Literature: LlorensC
103-5, ObrO I no. 5, OckCW II: xi, RothZ
268.
Cornelius Heyns (Ockeghem?): Missa Pour
quoy (= Pour quelque paine)
(Obrecht): Missa Salve diva parens
Cappella Sistina MS 63. Rome, ca. 1480-1507.
Literature: LlorensC 119-20, OckCW I:
xviii, II: xi, SherrP 256.
Okeghem: (Missa Au travail suis), (Missa
Mi-mi)
Cappella Sistina MS 160. Brussels or Mechlin,
ca. 1518. Literature: LlorensC 187-89,
ObrCW I: xxii.
(Obrecht): Misse Ave Regina celorum,
Sicut spina rosam
MS Chigi C.VIII.234. Brussels or Mechlin,
1498-1503. (Fac. ed.: RMF 22.)
Literature: BesselerC-MGG, KellmannO,
OckCW I: xvii, II: xi, RussellM.
Ockeghem: Ave Maria, Intemerata Dei
Mater; Misse Au travail suis, Caput,
Cuiusvis toni, De plus en plus, Ecce
ancilla Domini, Fors seulement, Ma
maistresse, Mi-mi, Prolationum,
Quinti toni, Sine nomine (II),
Requiem
SEGOVIA. CATEDRAL, ARCHIVO CAPITULAR (E-SEG).
MS without number. Spain, ca. 1500. Fac.

ed.: Cancionero. Modern ed.: BakerU.
Literature: AnglésM 1: 106-12, ObrCW I:
xi, IV: xxvii, StrohmM 142-44, TaruskinE
4-5.
Scoen Heyne (Ockeghem?): Ce n'est pas
    jeu
Hobrecht: Misse Adieu mes amours
    (incomplete), Fortuna desperata,
    Libenter gloriabor, Rose playsante,
    Si dedero- Christe; Ave maris
    stella, Benedicamus in laude Jhesu,
    Cuius sacrata viscera (I, II), Inter
    praeclarissimas virtutes, Mille
    quingentis, Omnis spiritus laudet,
    Regina celi, Salve Regina (II);
    (?) Nec mihi nec tibi; Als al de
    weerelt, Den haghel ende die calde
    snee, Ic draghe de mutse clutse, Ic
    en hebbe gheen ghelt, Ic hoerde de
    clocskins luden, Ic weinsche alle
    scoene vrouwen, Lacen adieu, Laet u
    genoughen, Meskin es hu, Moet mij
    laten, Sullen wij langhe, Tsat een
    cleen meskin, Waer sij di han, Wat
    willen wij metten, Weet ghij wat
    mijnder; (?) T'meiskin was jonc
Ysaac (Obrecht?): Ortus de celo (= La
    stangetta)
SEVILLE. CATEDRAL METROPOLITANO, BIBLIOTECA
    CAPITULAR Y COLOMBINA (E-Sc).
    MS 5-I-43. Naples(?) ca. 1480. Paris 4379,
        part 1, originally belonged to this ms.
        Fac. ed.: PlamenacF. Modern ed.: MoerkS.
        Literature: PlamenacRF.
        (Ockeghem): D'ung aultre amer, Ma bouche
            rit, Ma maistresse
    MS 7-I-28. Spain, ca. 1490-1500. Modern
        eds.: GavaldáC, HaberkampW.
        Literature: AnglésM 1: 103-6.
        (Ockeghem): De la momera (= S'elle
            m'amera)/Petite camusette; (Cornago-
            Ockeghem): Qu'es mi vida
SIENA. BIBLIOTECA COMUNALE DEGLI INTRONATI (I-Sc).
    MS K.I.2. Siena, ca. 1481. Fac. ed.: RMF 17.
        Literature: D'AcconeL, ObrCW II: xi,
        ZiinoA.
        (Obrecht): (Missa Beata viscera,
            incomplete)

ST. GALL. STIFTSBIBLIOTHEK (CH-SG).
    MS 461 (Liber Fridolini Sicherii).
    Netherlands(?), before 1545. Mod. ed.:
    GiesbertA. Literature: ObrCW III: xxiii,
    ObrW VII: xii.
    Ockeghem: Fors seulement (contre), Fors
        seulement (l'attente); (?) Malheur
        me bat
    Obrecht: (Missa Petrus apostolus- Et
        incarnatus), Fors seulement, Helas
        mon bien, Tsat een meskin
    (Obrecht): (Missa De Sancto Martino)-
        Benedictus
    MS 462 (Heer Liederbuch). Paris and Glarus,
        ca. 1510-30. Modern ed.: GeeringL.
        Literature: ObrW VII: xii-xiii.
    Obrecht(?): Ein frölich Wesen
    MS 463 (Tschudi Liederbuch). S. A. part-books
        only. Switzerland, ca. 1540.
        Literature: LoachA, ObrW VII/2: viii.
    Obrecht: Parce Domine, Si bona
        suscepimus, Si sumpsero;
        (T')Andernacken; (index only:) Es
        sas ein meitschi (= Tsat een
        meskin), Meskin es hu, (?) T'meiskin
        (was jonck), (?) Ein frölich Wesen
STUTTGART. WÜRTTEMBERGISCHE LANDESBIBLIOTHEK (D-
    Sl).
    MS Mus. fol. I 47. Stuttgart, ca. 1507.
        Literature: GottwaldS 81-82, ObrCW III:
        xxiii-xxiv.
    (Obrecht): Missa (De Sancto Martino,
        incomplete)
TARAZONA. CATEDRAL, ARCHIVIO CAPITULAR (E-TZ).
    MS 5. Spain, early sixteenth cent.
        Literature: AnglésM 1: 15, RussellM 4,
        SevillanoC 157-58.
    (Ockeghem: Requiem)- Sicut cervus
TOURNAI. BIBLIOTHÈQUE DE LA VILLE (B-Tv).
    MS 94. Bruges, 1511. (T. part-book only;
        Brussels IV 90 also belongs to this set.)
        Literature: BorrenI 6: 119-21, KesselsB.
    (Ockeghem): J'en ay dueil
    (Obrecht): Parce Domine
TRENT. MUSEO DIOCESANO (I-TRmd).
    MS BL (93). Trent, ca. 1460. Fac. ed.: Codex
        Trid. 93. Literature: DTO 61: vi-x,
        FallowsST 174, SaundersD.
    (Ockeghem: Ma maistresse)

TRENT.   MUSEO NAZIONALE (I-TRmn).
    MS 88.   Trent, ca. 1460. Fac. ed.: Codex
        Trid. 88. Literature: DTO 14-15: 13-47,
        FallowsST 177, OckCW II: xi-xii.
        Ockeghem: Missa Caput
        Ockeghem (?): Missa Le serviteur
        (Ockeghem?): Gaude Mater (= Quand ce
            viendra)
    MS 90.   Trent, ca. 1460. Fac. ed.: Codex
        Trid. 90. Literature: DTO 14-15: 57-67,
        FallowsST 175-76, SaundersD.
        Ockeghem: O rosa bella
    MS 91.   Trent, ca. 1460-80. Fac. ed.: Codex
        Trid. 91. Literature: DTO 14-15: 67-75,
        FallowsST 179.
        (Ockeghem?): Gaude Mater (= Quand ce
            viendra)
TURIN.   BIBLIOTECA NAZIONALE UNIVERSITARIA (I-Tn).
    MS Ris. mus. I.27. Turin(?), ca. 1500. Fac.
        ed.: RMF 18.
        (Obrecht?): Nec mihi nec tibi
ULM.   VON SCHERMAR'SCHE FAMILIESTIFTUNG (D-Usch).
    MS 236a-d. Four part-books. Southern
        Germany, late sixteenth cent.
        Stoltzer (Obrecht?): I weinsche alle
UPPSALA.   UNIVERSITETSBIBLIOTEKET (S-Uu).
    MS 76a.   France, ca. 1500. Fac. ed.: RMF 19.
        Literature: BrownN.
        (Obrecht): Parce Domine
    MS 76e.   S. part-book only. Frauenberg, E.
        Prussia, after 1506. Literature:
        StaehelinO 33-34 (fn. 81), StevensonT
        100.
        (Obrecht): (Missa De Sancto Martino),
            Misse L'homme armé, Si dedero
VERONA.   BIBLIOTECA CAPITOLARE (I-VEcap).
    Catalogue: TurriniP.
    MS 757.   Northern Italy, ca. 1500. (Fac. ed.:
        RMF 24.) Literature: BrownC 196.
        Obrecht: (two textless pieces a 3)
    MS 759.   Northern Italy, ca. 1500.
        Literature: Kanazawa 176-79, OckCW I:
        xvii, PrestonS 351-56.
        Ockeghem, Missa sine nomine (I)
    MS 761.   Northern Italy, ca. 1500.
        Literature: ObrO I: xxviii, PrestonS
        367-68.
        (Obrecht): Missa Salve diva parens

VIENNA. ÖSTERREICHISCHE NATIONALBIBLIOTHEK (A-Wn). Catalogue: MantuaniT.
MS 11883. Flanders, early sixteenth cent. Literature: MantuaniT 7: 72-73, ObrCS IV: xi, ObrW V, nos. 20, 23, OckCW II: xii.
(Ockeghem): Missa sine nomine (= Prolationum)
Obrecht: (Missa De tous biens playne), Missa L'homme armé
MS 18832. Two part-books of original four. Flanders, ca. 1520. Literature: MantuaniT 240-42, NowakB, ObrCW IV: xviii.
(Obrecht): (Missa Fors seulement-Benedictus), (Missa Salve diva parens- Qui cum patre); (?) (Missa Je ne seray plus- Benedictus)
MS Suppl. Mus. 15495. Flanders, ca. 1510. Literature: ObrO I:xxix.
Obrecht: Missa Salve diva parens
WASHINGTON, D.C. LIBRARY OF CONGRESS (US-Wc).
MS M2.1.L25 Case (Laborde Chansonnier). France or Burgundy, ca. 1475-90. Literature: BushL, GutiérrezU.
(Ockeghem): D'ung aultre amer, Fors seulement l'attente, Il ne m'en chault, J'en ay dueil, La despourveue, Les desleaux, Ma bouche rit, Ma maistresse, Presque transi; (?) Ce n'est pas jeu
Busnois (Ockeghem?): Quand ce viendra
WOLFENBÜTTEL. HERZOG AUGUST BIBLIOTHEK, MUSIKABTEILUNG (D-W).
MS Extravag. 287. France or Burgundy, ca. 1475. Literature: BrownMGG-W, KonradM 38-39.
(Ockeghem): D'ung aultre amer, Fors seulement l'attente, Ma bouche rit, Ma maistresse, S'elle m'amera/Petite camusette
(Ockeghem?): Au travail suis, Quand ce viendra
WROCŁAW. BIBLIOTEKA UNIWERSYTECKA (PL-WRu).
MS I F 428.
(Obrecht: Missa Cela sans plus)
(Obrecht?: Missa N'aray-je jamais)
ZWICKAU. RATSSCHULBIBLIOTHEK (D-Z). Catalogue: VollhardtB.

MS LXXVIII,3. Three part-books. Zwickau(?),
    early sixteenth cent. Literature: ObrW
    VII: xiii, VollhardtB 28-30.
    (Obrecht: T'Andernacken); Obrecht(?): (La
    stangetta)
MS LXXXI, 2. Three part-books (A. missing).
    Germany, before 1550. Literature:
    VollhardtB 33-38.
    Obrecht(?): Discubuit Jesus.
MS XCIV,1. A. T. part-books of original
    four(?). Germany, dated 1590.
    Literature: VollhardtB 16.
    (Obrecht?): Judaea et Jerusalem

2. Prints

Sigla for the printed collection in the
following list are those in RISM B/I. All items
are choirbooks unless otherwise noted.

1501   **Harmonice musices Odhecaton A.** Venice:
              O. Petrucci. Later eds.: 1503^2,
              1504^2. Fac. ed.: New York, Broude
              Bros., 1973. Modern ed.: HewittO.
              Literature: BoormanF, SartoriB 34-42,
              52-56, 77-82.
              Ockeghem: Ma bouche rit; (?) Malheur
                  me bat
              Obrecht: Meskin es hu, Rompeltier,
                  T'Andernacken, Tsat een meskin
              Isaac (Obrecht?): T'meiskin was jonc
              Werbeck (Obrecht?): La stangetta
1502^2 **Canti B numero cinquanta.** Venice: O.
              Petrucci. Later eds.: 1503^2, 1513
              Quinquagena carminum (Mainz: P.
              Schöffer). Modern ed.: HewittB.
              Literature: SartoriB 42-44.
              Obrecht: Cela sans plus (= Osanna of
                  Missa), Si sumpsero, J'ay pris
                  amours, Vavilment (= Wat willen
                  wij)
1503   **Misse Obreht.** Venice: O. Petrucci.
              Four part-books. Literature: ObrW I,
              ObrCW V, RISM A/I/6 342, SartoriB 56-
              57.
              Obrecht: Misse Je ne demande,
                  Graecorum, Fortuna desperata,
                  Malheur me bat, Salve diva parens

1503[1]   **Motetti de passione** . . . B. Venice: O.
            Petrucci. Literature: SartoriB 58-60.
            Obrecht: Parce Domine (a 4)
1504[1]   **Motetti C.** Venice: O. Petrucci. Four
            part-books. Literature: SartoriB 82-
            85.
            (Ockeghem): Ut heremita solus
            Obrecht: Requiem (= Mille quingentis)
1504[3]   **Canti C No. cento cinquanta.** Venice: O.
            Petrucci, 1503 (= 1504 n.st.). Fac.
            ed.: New York, Broude Bros., 1978.
            Literature: SartoriB 69-74.
            Ockeghem: J'en ay dueil, Prenez sur
            moi, (S'elle m'amera)/Petite
            camusette
            Obrecht: Ave Regina coelorum, Fors
            seulement, La tortorella, Tant que
            nostre argent dura
1505[2]   **Motetti libro quarto.** Venice: O.
            Petrucci. Four part-books.
            Literature: SartoriB 99-102.
            Obrecht: Beata es Maria, Laudes
            Christo, O beate Basili, Quis
            numerare queat
1508[1]   **Motetti a cinque, libro primo.** Venice:
            O. Petrucci. Four part-books. (Ct[2]
            missing.) Literature: SartoriB 129-
            30.
            Obrecht: Factor orbis, Laudemus nunc
            Dominum, Mater Patris, O preciosis-
            sime sanguis
1509[1]   **Missarum diversorum auctorum, liber
            primus.** Venice: O. Petrucci, 1508 (=
            1509 n.st.). Four part-books.
            Literature: SartoriB 135-37.
            Obreth, Missa Si dedero
[ca. 1510] **Concentus harmonici quattuor missarum**
            . . . Jacobi Obrecht. Basel: G.
            Mewes, s.d. Four part-books.
            Literature: ObrCW III, IV; ObrO I,
            Misse 6; ObrW I no. 3, RISM A/I/6 342,
            StaehelinO 15-16.
            Obrecht: Missa Sub tuum presidium,
            Fortuna desperata, Maria zart, De S.
            Martino
1520[4]   **Liber selectarum cantionum quas vulgo
            Mutetas appellant.** Augsburg: Grimm &
            Wyrsung. Literature: ObrW VII: vii-
            viii.

Obrecht: Salve crux
[c.1521][7] **Motetti (novi) e canzone franzose.**
Venice, (1524). A. part-book only, of
original four (Bologna, Civico
Museo Bibliografico, Mus. R141[2]).
Literature: RubsamenM 88-89; ChapmanA
106.
Obrecht: Parce Domine
[c.1535][14] (Lieder). (Frankfurt/M.: C. Egenolff).
S. part-book only. Literature:
BridgmanC, StaehelinZ.
(Ockeghem?): Malheur me bat
1538[7]   **Modulationes aliquot quatuor vocum
selectissimae, quas vulgo motetas
vocant.** Nuremberg: J. Petreius. Four
part-books.
Isaac (Obrecht?): Judaea et Jerusalem
1538[9]   **Trium vocum carmina.** Nuremberg: H.
Formschneider. Three part-books.
Literature: BrownI 1538$_2$.
(Ockeghem): Fors seulement (contre),
Ma bouche rit; (?) Malheur me bat
(Obrecht): Missa Fortuna desperata-
Pleni; Missa Malheur me bat-
Christe, Pleni, Crucifixus, Agnus
II; Missa Salve diva parens- Pleni;
Missa Si dedero- Christe; Si
sumpsero; (?) La stangetta
1539[1]   **Liber quindecim missarum.** Nuremberg: J.
Petreius. Four part-books.
Literature: OckCW I: xviii.
Ockeghem: Missa Cuiusvis toni
1539[2]   **Missae tredecim quatuor vocum.**
Nuremberg: H. Grapheus. Four part-
books. Literature: ObrW III no. 12.
Obrecht: Misse Ave Regina coelorum,
Petrus apostolus
1541[2]   **Trium vocum cantiones centum.**
Nuremberg: J. Petreius. Three part-
books. Fac. ed.: RMF 26.
(Obrecht): Si bona suscepimus
1542[6]   **Tomus tertius psalmorum selectorum.**
Nuremberg: J. Petreius. Four part-
books. Literature: TeramotoP
(Ockeghem?): Deo gratia
1542[8]   **Tricinia.** Wittenberg: G. Rhaw. Three
part-books.
Obrecht: Ego sum super Alma
Redemptoris

1542^{12} **Sacrorum hymnorum liber primus.**
Wittenberg: G. Rhaw. Four part-books.
Literature: ObrW VI: viii.
Obrecht: Haec Deum coeli

1544^{20} **Hundert und fünfftzehen guter newer**
Liedlein. Nuremberg: J. Ott. Four
part-books. Modern ed.: PAPTM I-III.
Literature: Tenorlied 133-44.
Stoltzer (Obrecht?): Ic weinsche alle

1545^{7} **Secundus tomus biciniorum.** Wittenberg:
G. Rhaw. Two part-books.
Obrecht: Missa Salve diva parens- Qui
cum patre

1549^{16} **Diphona amoena et florida, selectore**
Erasmo Rotenbuchero, boiaro.
Nuremberg: J. Montanus & U. Neuber.
Two part-books.
Ockeghem(?): Vivit Dominus

1568^{7} **Cantiones triginta selectissimae . . .**
collectae et in lucem editae per
Clementem Stephani. Nuremberg: U.
Neuber. Four part-books.
(Ockeghem?): Deo gratia

1590^{30} **Selectae, artificiosae et elegantes**
fugae duarum, trium, quatuor, et
plurium vocum, partim . . . collectae,
partim compositae a Jacopo Paix.
Lavingen: L. Reinmichael. Later ed.:
1594^{3}. Literature: BrownI 1590_{6}.
Ockeghem: Fuga trium vocum (= Prenez
sur moi)
Obrecht: Fuga (= Missa Salve diva
parens- Qui cum patre)

B. TABLATURES

1. Manuscripts

BERLIN. STAATSBIBLIOTHEK PREUSSISCHER KULTURBESITZ
    (D-B).
    MS Mus. 40026 (Kleber organ book). Pforzheim,
        ca. 1521-24. Literature: LoewenfeldL.
        (Obrecht): Si sumpsero
CHICAGO. NEWBERRY LIBRARY (US-Cn).
    MS 107501 (Capirola lute book). Venice,
        ca. 1517. Fac. ed: Capirola. Modern
        ed.: GombosiC. Literature: RISM B/VII
        79-80.
        Obrecht: Missa Si dedero- Christe
ST. GALL. STIFTSBIBLIOTHEK (CH-SG).
    MS 530 (Sicher organ book). St. Gall, early
        sixteenth cent.
        Literature: MarxN, NefS, ObrCW IV:
        xxviii, ObrW VII: xiii.
        Obrecht: Missa Fortuna desperata-
            Benedictus; Parce Domine, Parce
            Domine (part 2), Si sumpsero; Ic ret
            my uit spacieren, Ma merche vel ma
            buche, Meskin es hu
ZURICH. ZENTRALBIBLIOTHEK (CH-Zz).
    MS S.248a. Keyboard tablature. Sixteenth
        cent.
        Obrecht: Parce Domine

2. Prints

1507^5 (Francesco Spinacino). **Intabolatura de**
            lauto Libro primo. Venice: O.
            Petrucci. Literature: BrownI 1507_1.
            (Ockeghem): Ma bouche rit
1507^6 (Francesco Spinacino). **Intabolatura de**
            lauto Libro secondo. Venice: O.
            Petrucci. Literature: BrownI 1507_2.
            (Ockeghem): D'ung aultre amer;
                (?) Malheur me bat
            (Obrecht): Missa Si dedero- Christe;
                (?) La stangetta
1512^2 Arnolt Schlick. **Tabulaturen etlicher**
            Lobgesang und Lidlein uff die Orgeln
            und Lauten. Mainz: P. Schöffer.
            Literature: BrownI 1512_1.
            Isack (Obrecht?): Metzkin (= T'meiskin
                was jonck)

1531^5 **Treze motetz musicaulx avec ung prelude,**
            le tout reduict en la tabulature des
            orgues, espinettes et manicordions.
            Paris: P. Attaingnant. Mod. ed.:
            RoksethT. Literature: BrownI 1531_7.
            (Obrecht): Parce Domine
1533^4 Hans Gerle. **Tabulatur auff die Laudten.**
            Nuremberg: H. Formschneider.
            Literature: BrownI 1533_1.
            (Obrecht): Der alt Tandernack (=
            T'Andernacken)
1536^{13} Hans Newsidler. **Das ander Theil des**
            Lautenbuchs. Nuremberg: J. Petreius.
            Literature: BrownI 1536_7.
            Obrecht: Si sumpsero, (T')Andernacken;
            (?) La stangetta
1545^{21} **Des chansons reduictz en tabulature de**
            lut. Louvain: P. Phalèse. Later
            ed.: RISM 1547^{20}. Literature: BrownI
            1545_3.
            (Obrecht): Een vrolic wesen

C. EXAMPLES IN THEORETICAL TREATISES

The following list is chronological.

TinctorisL
> Tinctoris, Johannes. **Liber de arte
> contrapuncti.** 1477. Sources: Bologna,
> Bibl. Universitaria, MS 2573; Brussels,
> Bibl. roy., MS I 4147. Modern eds.:
> CoussemakerS IV, TinctorisO II.
> Ockeghem: Missa La belle se siet (lost);
> Faugues (Ockeghem?): Missa Le serviteur

TinctorisP
> Tinctoris, Johannes. **Proportionale musices.**
> ca. 1473. Sources as above. Modern eds.:
> CoussemakerS IV, TinctorisO IIa.
> Ockeghem: L'autre d'antan

Gafurius 1496
> Gafurius, Franchino. **Practica musicae.**
> Milan: J. Petrus. Fac. eds.: Farnborough,
> Gregg Press, 1967; Bologna, Forni, 1972.
> English transl.: GafuriusP.
> Ockeghem: L'autre d'antan

Heyden 1537
> Heyden, Sebaldus. **Musicae, id est Artis
> canendi.** Nuremberg: J. Petreius.
> Obrecht: Missa Je ne demande (fragments of
> T.); Missa Salve diva parens- Fuga (= Qui
> cum patre)

Heyden 1540
> Heyden, Sebaldus. **De arte canendi.**
> Nuremberg: J. Petreius. (Second ed. of
> Heyden 1537.) Fac. ed.: New York, Broude
> Bros., 1969. Literature: OckCW II: xii,
> ReeseF 42-43.
> Ockeghem: Missa Prolationum, Prenez sur moi
> Obrecht: Missa Je ne demande (fragments),
> Missa Salve diva parens- Fuga (= Qui cum
> patre)

Glareanus 1547
> Glareanus, Heinrich. **Dodecachordon.** Basel:
> H. Petrus. RISM 1547[1]. Fac. ed.:
> Hildesheim, G. Olms, 1969. English transl.:
> GlareanD.
> Ockeghem: Missa Cuiusvis toni, Prenez sur
> moi
> Obrecht: Missa Fors seulement- Qui tollis,
> Sanctus; Missa Salve diva parens- Qui cum
> patre; Parce Domine

Faber 1553
    Faber, Gregor. **Musices practicae erotematum.**
    Basel: H. Petrus.   Literature: ObrCW V: xix
    Ockeghem: Prenez sur moi
    Obrecht: Missa Je ne demande- Gloria (T.),
        Missa Salve diva parens- Fuga (= Qui cum
        patre), Missa Sub tuum presidium- Christe
Zanger 1554
    Zanger, Joannes. **Practicae musicae praecepta.**
    Leipzig: G. Hantzsch.   Literature: OckCW II:
    xii.
    Ockeghem: Missa Prolationum
    Obrecht: Missa Ave Regina celorum- Osanna
Finck 1556
    Finck, Hermann. **Practica musica.** Wittenberg:
    Haeredum G. Rhaw. Fac. ed.: Bologna, Forni,
    1967.
    (Ockeghem): Ut heremita solus
Wilphlingseder 1563
    Wilphlingseder, Ambrosius. **Erotemata musices**
    practicae. Nuremberg: C. Heussler.
    Literature: ObrCW V: xix, OckCW I: xviii,
    II: xii.
    Ockeghem: Missa Cuiusvis toni- Kyrie; Missa
        Prolationum- Kyrie; Fuga (= Prenez sur
        moi)
    Obrecht: Missa Je ne demande (fragments)
Zacconi 1592
    Zacconi, Lodovico. **Prattica di musica.**
    Venice: G. Polo.   Later ed.: 1596.   Fac.
    ed.: Bologna, Forni, 1967.
    Ockeghem: See lost masses.
    Obrecht: Missa Ave Regina celorum
        (fragments), Missa Petrus apostolus- Kyrie
        II; Salve crux; see also fragmentary and
        lost works.
Cerone 1613
    Cerone, Pedro. **El melopeo y maestro.** Naples:
    J.B. Gargano & L. Nucci. Fac. ed.: Bologna,
    Forni, 1969.
    Obrecht: See fragmentary and lost works.

IV. BIBLIOGRAPHY

AfMw   **Archiv für Musikwissenschaft.**

AlbrechtA-MGG   Albrecht, Hans. "Annaberger Chorbücher."
                          MGG 1: 489-91.
                          Description of Dresden MSS I/D/505 and
                          1/D/506 (formerly Annaberg MSS 1126 and
                          1248).

Album   **Album de Marguerite d'Autriche.** Fac. ed.
                          of Brussels, Royal Library, MS 228, with a
                          Foreword by Martin Picker. Peer: Alamire,
                          1986.

AM   **Acta musicologica.**

AmbrosG   Ambros, August Wilhelm. **Geschichte der Musik.**
                          3rd ed., rev. Otto Kade. 5 vols. Leipzig:
                          Leuckert, 1887-1911. Reprint, Hildesheim:
                          G. Olms, 1968. ML160 A493.
                          An outstanding, pioneer scholarly history of
                          music, the first to offer a firmly-based
                          overview of fifteenth-century music (in vol.
                          3). Vol. 5 is an anthology of fifteenth and
                          sixteenth-century music, including a mass
                          movement of Ockeghem, a motet of Obrecht,
                          and secular works of both composers. An
                          index of names and subjects in vol. 3 covers
                          vol. 5 as well.

AMMM   **Archivium musices metropolitanum mediolanense.**
                          Ed. Luciano Migliavacca et al. Milan,
                          1958- . M2.A538.
                          Series of modern editions of music in Milan
                          Cathedral choirbooks.

AnglésM   Anglés, Higinio. **La música en la corte de los
                          reyes católicos.** Vol. 1, **Polifonia
                          religiosa.** Monumentos de la musica

115

española, vol. 1. Barcelona: Consejo
superior de investigaciones científicas,
1941. Reprint, 1960. M2.M4845 vol. 1.
An edition of sacred polyphony at the
Spanish royal courts, with a preface
describing MSS in Barcelona, Segovia,
Seville, and Tarazona, among others.

AnthM   **Anthology of Music: A Collection of Complete
               Musical Examples Illustrating the History of
               Music (= Das Musikwerk, eine Beispielsamm-
               lung zur Musikgeschichte)**. Cologne: Arno
               Volk Verlag, 1959-75. 47 vols. M2.M94512.

AntiphonaleM   **Antiphonale monasticum pro diurnis horis.**
               Benedictines of Solesmes, eds. Paris:
               Desclée, ca. 1934.
               Antiphonary containing chants for the
               monastic office in Gregorian notation, with
               an index of chants.

AntonowytschR Antonowytsch, Myroslaw. "Renaissance-
               Tendenzen in den Fortuna-desperata-Messen
               von Josquin und Obrecht." Mf 9 (1956): 1-
               26.
               Analysis and comparison of the two masses
               from the point of view of their unity,
               symmetry, and individual style.

ApfelK   Apfel, Ernst. "Der klangliche Satz und der
               freie Diskantsatz im 15. Jahrhundert." AfMw
               12 (1955): 297-313.
               Comparison of compositional styles in
               fifteenth-century music, including masses by
               Ockeghem.

AR   **Antiphonale sacrosanctae romanae ecclesiae.**
               Benedictines of Solesmes, eds. Tournai:
               Desclée, 1948.
               Modern edition of the Gregorian office
               chants.

AtlasC   Atlas, Allan. **The Cappella Giulia Chansonnier
               (Rome, Biblioteca Apostolica Vaticana,
               C.G.XIII.27)**. Musicological Studies, 27. 2
               vols. Brooklyn: Institute of Medieval
               Music, 1975-76. 293, 86 pp. ISBN 91-2024-
               23-2, -24-0.

Vol. 1 offers detailed commentary on this
important MS and its repertory, with indexes
of text incipits, composers, and sources,
and an extensive bibliography. Vol. 2
presents transcriptions of previously
unpublished works. This is a revised
version of a dissertation written at New
York University in 1971.

AtlasCA Atlas, Allan. "Conflicting Attributions in
Italian Sources of the Franco-Netherlandish
Chanson, c. 1465-c. 1505." **Music in
Medieval and Early Modern Europe.** Ed. I.
Fenlon. Cambridge: Cambridge Univ. Press,
1981, pp. 249-93. ML 172. ISBN 0-521-
23328-3.
Attempts to distinguish composers from
arrangers in cases of conflicting
attributions.

AtlasO Atlas, Allan W. "On the Neapolitan Provenance
of the Manuscript Perugia, Biblioteca
Comunale Augusta, 431 (G20)." MD 31 (1977):
45-105.
Includes inventory of MS and concordances.

BakerU Baker, Norma Klein. "An Unnumbered Manuscript
of Polyphony in the Archives of the
Cathedral of Segovia: Its Provenance and
History." Ph.D. diss., University of Mary-
land, 1978. 2 vols. 1082 pp. UM 79-15798.
Study of a MS especially rich in works of
Obrecht.

BankS Bank, J. A. "Some Comments on the Transcription of 'Pleni sunt coeli' in Jacob
Obrecht's Missa Maria Zart." TVNM 20
(1966): 170-77.
A criticism of van Crevel's edition in ObrO.

BecheriniC Becherini, Bianca. **Catalogo dei manoscritti
musicali della Biblioteca nazionale di
Firenze.** Kassel: Bärenreiter, 1959. 177
pp. ML136.F56B5.
Catalogue of musical MSS in the Florence
National Library. Indexes of titles and
text incipits, composers and theorists,
poets, and other names.

BecheriniM   Becherini, Bianca. "I manoscritti e le stampe
                  rare della Biblioteca del Conservatorio 'L.
                  Cherubini' di Firenze." **La Bibliofilia**, 66
                  (1964): 255-99.
                  Catalogue of musical MSS and rare prints in
                  the library of the Florence Conservatory.
                  Index of composers.

BellermannM   Bellermann, Heinrich. **Die Mensuralnoten und
                  Taktzeichen des 15. und 16. Jahrhunderts.**
                  Berlin: Walter de Gruyter, 1858. 4th ed.,
                  1963. Rev. by H. Husmann. ML174.B44.
                  Treatise on mensural notation, citing
                  examples from theorists of the fifteenth and
                  sixteenth centuries.

BellinghamS   Bellingham, Bruce, and Edward G. Evans, Jr.,
                  eds. **Sixteenth-Century Bicinia: A Complete
                  Edition of Munich, Bayerische Staatsbiblio-
                  thek Mus. Ms. 260.** Recent Researches in the
                  Music of the Renaissance, 16-17. Madison:
                  A.R. Editions, 1974. 192 pp. M2.R2384 v.
                  16-17.

BentD   Bent, Margaret. "Diatonic Ficta." **Early
                  Music History**, 4 (1984): 1-48.
                  Discusses a modulatory passage in the Kyrie
                  of Obrecht's Missa Libenter gloriabor (pp.
                  34-40).

BenteN   Bente, Martin. **Neue Wege der Quellenkritik
                  und die Biographie Ludwig Senfls.**
                  Wiesbaden: Breitkopf & Härtel, 1968.   391
                  pp. ML410.S463B5.
                  Study of sources for biography and works of
                  Senfl. Extensive bibliography, index of
                  sources, and general index.

BesselerA   Besseler, Heinrich, ed. **Altniederländische
                  Motetten von Johannes Ockeghem, Loyset
                  Compère und Josquin des Prez.** Kassel:
                  Bärenreiter, 1956. 23 pp. M2082.B48A4.
                  Small anthology of fifteenth-century motets.
                  Contains Ockeghem's "Alma Redemptoris."

BesselerC   Besseler, Heinrich, ed. **Capella: Meisterwerke
                  mittelaltlicher Musik.** Heft 1, **Drei- und
                  vierstimmige Singstücke des 15.Jahrhunderts.**

Kassel: Bärenreiter, 1950. 26 pp.
Anthology including Obrecht's "Parce
Domine."

BesselerC-MGG   Besseler, Heinrich.   "Chigi-Kodex."   MGG 2:
1194-97.   Description of Rome, Bibl. Vat.,
MS Chigi C.VIII. 232, the most important
source of Ockeghem's music.

BesselerM   Besseler, Heinrich.   Die Musik des Mittelalters und der Renaissance.   Handbuch der
Musikwissenschaft, ed. Ernst Bücken,
vol. 2.   Wildpark-Potsdam: Athenaeion, 1931.
Reprint, New York: Musurgia, ca. 1946.   337
pp.   ML160.B9B4.
Standard history of medieval and Renaissance
music by a distinguished authority.   See
especially pp. 230-40 (The Netherlandish
Era).   Bibliography and detailed index of
names and subjects.

BesselerS   Besseler, Heinrich, and Peter Gülke, eds.
Schriftbild der mehrstimmigen Musik.
Musikgeschichte in Bildern, vol. 3.
Leipzig: VEB Deutscher Verlag für Musik,
1973.   184 pp.   ML89.M9
Reproductions of pages from medieval and
Renaissance sources of polyphonic music,
some in color, with transcriptions and
commentary.   Good bibliographies and indexes
of sources, names and subjects.

BesselerV   Besseler, Heinrich.   "Von Dufay bis Josquin:
ein Literatur-Bericht."   ZfMw 11 (1928-29):
1-22.
A commentary on editions of fifteenth-
century music.

BlackburnT   Blackburn, Bonnie J.   "Two 'Carnival Songs'
Unmasked: A Commentary on MS Florence Magl.
XIX.121."   MD 35 (1981): 121-78.
A study of an early sixteenth-century
Italian MS containing Flemish songs by
Obrecht and other works.

BockholdtF   Bockholdt, Rudolf.   "Französische und
niederländische Musik des 14. und 15.
Jahrhunderts."   Musikalische Edition in

Wandel des historischen Bewusstseins, ed.
T. Georgiades, pp. 149-73. Kassel:
Bärenreiter, 1971. ML174.G46. ISBN 3-
7618-0059-2.
Study of the historical development of the
editing of early music. Includes facsimiles
and comparison of eighteenth-century
editions of Ockeghem's Fuga trium vocum
(Prenez sur moi) by Hawkins, Burney, and
Forkel.

BoormanF   Boorman, Stanley. "The 'First' Edition of the
               Odhecaton A." JAMS 30 (1977): 183-207.
               Bibliographical study of Petrucci's first
               publication (RISM 1501).

BoormanS   Boorman, Stanley, ed. Studies in the
               Performance of Late Medieval Music.
               Cambridge: Cambridge University Press, 1983.
               282 pp. ML 170. ISBN 0-521-248191.
               Specialized studies; see FallowsS,
               PlanchartP.

BorrenE   Borren, Charles van den. Etudes sur le XVe
               siècle musical. Antwerp: De Nederlandsche
               boekhandel, 1941. 287 pp. ML172.B64.
               Chapter 2 contains an important study of
               Ockeghem's masses as well as other works.

BorrenG   Borren, Charles van den. Geschiedenis van de
               muziek in de Nederlanden. 2 vols.
               Amsterdam: Wereld-bibliothek, 1949-51. 430,
               410 pp. ML295.B6.
               A history of music in the Netherlands. Vol.
               I, pp. 129-229, contains a survey of
               fifteenth century music, emphasizing
               Ockeghem and also discussing Obrecht.
               Index of names at end of vol. II.

BorrenI   Borren, Charles van den. "Inventaire des
               manuscrits de musique polyphonique qui se
               trouvent en Belgique." AM 5 (1933): 66-71,
               120-27, 177-83; 6 (1934): 23-29, 65-73, 116-
               21.
               A detailed inventory of MSS of polyphonic
               music in Belgian libraries, including those
               in Brussels and Tournai.

BorrenM   Borren, Charles van den. "Le Madrigalisme
               avant le madrigal." **Studien zur
               Musikgeschichte. Festschrift für Guido
               Adler**, pp. 78-83. Vienna: Universal-
               Edition, 1930.
               Discusses word-painting in fifteenth-century
               music, including masses of Ockeghem.

BrenetJ   Brenet, Michel. "Jean de Ockeghem, maitre
               de la chapelle des rois Charles VII et Louis
               XI." **Mémoires de la Société de l'Histoire
               de Paris et de l'Ile-de-France**, vol. 20.
               Paris, 1893.
               This essay, the primary study of Ockeghem's
               biography, was published in a revised
               version in BrenetM. According to PlamenacA
               28, this first version is more accurate than
               the second.

BrenetM   Brenet, Michel. **Musique et musiciens de la
               vieille France**. Paris: Félix Alcan, 1911.
               Reprint, Paris: Ed. d'Aujourdhui, 1978.
               249 pp. ML270.2.B7.
               Pages 21-82 contain the revised version of
               BrenetJ. Index of names and subjects.

BrennO   Brenn, Franz. "Ockeghems spiritueller
               Rhythmus." International Musicological
               Society, **Bericht über den Siebenten
               Internationalen Musikwissenschaftlichen
               Kongress, Koln 1958**, pp. 73-74. Kassel:
               Bärenreiter, 1959.
               Brief comment on the philosophical basis and
               implications of Ockeghem's rhythmic style.

BridgmanA   Bridgman, Nanie. "The Age of Ockeghem and
               Josquin." Chap. 8 in **Ars Nova and the
               Renaissance 1300-1540**, ed. Dom A. Hughes and
               G. Abraham, pp. 239-302. Vol. III of **The
               New Oxford History of Music**. London:
               Oxford University Press, 1960. 565 pp.
               ML160.N44. ISBN 0-19-316303-9.
               Includes surveys of Ockeghem's and Obrecht's
               works.

BridgmanC   Bridgman, Nanie. "Christian Egenolff,
               imprimeur de musique." **Annales
               musicologiques**, 3 (1955): 77-177.

Bibliographical study of a collection of
three song-books published by Egenolff (vol.
3 = RISM [1535][14]).

BrownC-NG   Brown, Howard M. "Chanson, 2. 1430 to about
                 1525." NG 4: 137-40; bibl. 144-45.
                 General survey.

BrownF   Brown, Howard M., ed. **A Florentine
                 Chansonnier from the Time of Lorenzo the
                 Magnificent.** 2 vols. Monuments of
                 Renaissance Music, 7. Chicago: University
                 of Chicago Press, 1983. 322, 645 pp.
                 M2.M489 v. 7. ISBN 0-226-07623-7.
                 Study and modern edition of Florence Bibl.
                 naz. MS Banco rari 229. List of sources,
                 indexes of composers and compositions.

BrownG   Brown, Howard M. "The Genesis of a Style: The
                 Parisian Chanson, 1500-1530." In HaarC, pp.
                 1-50.
                 Survey of the Parisian chanson, beginning
                 with Ockeghem's "Les desléaulx."

BrownI   Brown, Howard M. **Instrumental Music Printed
                 before 1600.** Cambridge, Mass.: Harvard
                 University Press, 1965. 559 pp.
                 ML128.I65B77. ISBN 0-674-45610-6.
                 Bibliography of printed instrumental music
                 in the Renaissance, including tablatures and
                 arrangements of vocal pieces. A standard
                 reference work. Extensive bibliography,
                 detailed indexes of libraries and their
                 holdings, types of notation, instrumental
                 media, names, and titles.

BrownIV   Brown, Howard M. "Instruments and Voices in
                 the Fifteenth-Century Chanson." In **Current
                 Thought in Musicology**, ed. John W. Grubbs,
                 pp. 89-137. Austin: University of Texas
                 Press, 1976. ML 3797.1.C87. ISBN 0-292-
                 71017-8.
                 Aspects of performance practice, with
                 illustrations.

BrownL   Brown, Howard M. "'Lord, have mercy upon us':
                 Early Sixteenth-Century Scribal Practice and
                 the Polyphonic Kyrie." **Text. Transactions**

of the Society for Textual Scholarship, 2:
93-110. New York: AMS Press, 1985.
P47.T48. ISBN 0-404-62552-5.
Concerns text underlay in Kyries of masses
by Ockeghem and others in MS Rome Chigi.

BrownM   Brown, Howard M. Music in the Renaissance.
            Prentice-Hall History of Music series.
            Englewood Cliffs: Prentice-Hall, 1976.   384
            pp. ML172.B86. ISBN 0-13-608497-4.
            Chapter 3 includes a survey of Ockeghem's
            work (pp. 66-83), and Chapter 6 of Obrecht's
            (pp. 156-60).
            Bibliographical notes and index of names.

BrownMS   Brown, Howard M. "The Music of the Strozzi
            Chansonnier (Florence, Biblioteca del
            Conservatorio di Musica, MS Basevi 2442)."
            AM 40 (1968): 115-29.

BrownN   Brown, Howard M. "A 'New' Chansonnier of the
            Early Sixteenth Century in the University
            Library of Uppsala: A Preliminary Report."
            MD 37 (1983): 171-233.
            Description and inventory of Uppsala MS
            76a.

BrownP-NG   Brown, Howard M. "Performing Practice. 4.
            15th- and 16th-Century Music." NG 14: 377-
            83 (bibliography pp. 390-92).

BrownR   Brown, Howard M. "A Rondeau with a One-Line
            Refrain Can Be Sung." Ars Lyrica, 3 (1986):
            23-35.
            Discusses performance of Ockeghem's
            "L'autre d'antan" as a rondeau, following
            GareyC.

BrownW-MGG Brown, Howard M. "Wolfenbüttler
            Handschriften." MGG 14: 810-11.
            Describes Wolfenbüttel MS Extravag. 287.

BukofzerC   Bukofzer, Manfred. "Caput: A Liturgico-
            musical Study." Studies in Medieval and
            Renaissance Music, pp. 217-310. New York:
            W.W. Norton, 1950. ML172.B9.
            A seminal study, comparing the Missae Caput
            of Ockeghem and Obrecht with the anonymous

English mass that served as their model.
Although Bukofzer erroneously believed that
the original Missa Caput was by Dufay, his
stylistic analyses and observations remain
fundamentally valid. The volume, in which
this is the principal essay, includes a good
general index.

BukofzerU   Bukofzer, Manfred. "An Unknown Chansonnier of
                the 15th Century." MQ 28 (1942): 14-49.
                Describes the Mellon Chansonnier at Yale
                University (New Haven).

Buning-   Buning-Jurgens, J. E. "More about Jacob
   JurgensM   Obrecht's 'Parce Domine'." TVNM 21 (1970):
                167-69.
                Concerns number symbolism in this motet.

BurkholderJ   Burkholder, J. Peter. "Johannes Martini and
                the Imitation Mass in the Late Fifteenth
                Century." JAMS 38 (1985): 470-523.
                Discusses the relationship of Obrecht's
                Missa Je ne demande to Martini's.

BushL   Bush, Helen E. "The Laborde Chansonnier."
                **Papers of the American Musicological
                Society, Annual Meeting 1940**, pp. 56-79.
                A.M.S., 1946.
                Describes Washington, Library of Congress MS
                M2.1.L25 Case.

Cancionero   **Cancionero de la Catedral de Segovia.**
                Facsimile. Ed. Ramon Perales de la Cal.
                Segovia: Caja de Ahorros y Monte de Piedad,
                1977. ca. 450 pp. M2.C226. ISBN 84-7231-
                353-0.
                Facsimile edition of an important fifteenth
                century MS containing many works of Obrecht.

CaraciF   Caraci, Maria. "Fortuna del tenor 'L'homme
                armé nel primo Rinascimento." NRMI
                9 (1975): 171-204.
                Study of early chansons and masses based on
                the popular song "L'homme armé."
                Ockeghem's Mass is compared to Dufay's. The
                "Caput" and "Fors seulement" Masses of
                Ockeghem and Obrecht are also discussed.

CasimiriC

Casimiri, Raffaelo. "Canzoni e motetti dei sec. XV-XVI." **Note d'archivio**, 14 (1937): 145-60.
Description and inventory of Rome MS Vat. lat. 11953.

CauchieV

Cauchie, Maurice. "Les Véritables nom et prénom d'Ockeghem." **Revue de musicologie**, 7 (1926): 9-10.
Discusses 1885 publication of a supposed autograph signature "Jo. Ockeghem."

Census-
Catalogue

Census-Catalogue of Manuscript Sources of Polyphonic Music, 1400-1550. Ed. Charles Hamm and Herbert Kellman. University of Illinois Musicological Archives, Renaissance Manuscript Studies, 1. 3 vols. to date. Stuttgart: American Institute of Musicology & Hänssler-Verlag, 1979- . 441, 493, 410 pp. ML135.C46. ISBN 3-7751-0645-6. (A 4th vol. is in press.)
Descriptive catalogue of Renaissance musical manuscripts, with full bibliographical references. Organized by location. Index of composers and general index. An indispensable research tool.

CernyS

Cerný, Jaromir. "Soupis hudebnick rukopisu muzea v Hradci Králové." **Miscellanea Musicologica**, 19 (1966): 9-67.
Inventory of musical MSS at Hradec Králové.

Chansonnier

Chansonnier of Marguerite of Austria. Peer: Alamire, 1984. ISBN 90-6853-002-X.
Fac. ed. of Brussels, Bibl. roy. MS 11239.

ClercxI

Clercx, Suzanne. "Introduction à l'histoire de la musique en Belgique (II)." RBM 5 (1951): 114-31.
Examines the question of Ockeghem's nationality in the light of historical evidence (pp. 120-31).

Codex Trid.

Codex Tridentinus 87 (-93). Rome: Bibliopola, 1969-70. 7 vols. ML96.T75.
Facsimile editions of MSS at Trent.

Codici   I codici musicali trentini a cento anni dalla
                  loro riscoperta. Ed. N. Pirrotta and D.
                  Curti. Trent: Provincia Autronoma di
                  Trento, 1986. ISBN 88-7702-011-3.
                  Report of a conference on the Trent codices
                  held in Trent in 1985. Includes FallowsST
                  and SaundersD.

CornagoC   Cornago, Johannes. Complete Works. Ed.
                  Rebecca L. Gerber. Recent Researches in the
                  Music of the Middle Ages and Early
                  Renaissance, 15. Madison: A-R Editions,
                  1984. xxx, 73 pp. M2.R2383 v. 15. ISBN 0-
                  89579-193-5.
                  Contains Cornago's "Qu'es mi vida
                  preguntays" and Ockeghem's arrangement of
                  it.

CouchmanL   Couchman, Jonathan Paul. "The Lorraine
                  Chansonnier." MD 34 (1980): 85-157.
                  Description of Paris, Bibl. nat. MS fr.
                  1597.

CoussemakerS   Coussemaker, Edmond de. Scriptorum de musica
     IV   medii aevi. Vol. 4. Paris: A. Durand,
                  1876. Reprints, Graz: Meyerhoff, 1898;
                  Hildesheim: Georg Olms, 1963. 498 pp.
                  ML170.C86.
                  Contains modern edition of treatises by
                  Johannes Tinctoris.

CrétinD   Crétin, Guillaume. Déploration de
                  Guillaume Crétin sur le trépas de Jean
                  Ockeghem. Ed. E. Thoinan. Paris: A.
                  Claudin, 1864. Reprint, London: H. Baron,
                  1965. 46 pp. ML410.O56S72.
                  Modern edition of a poem lamenting the death
                  of Ockeghem, originally published in 1527.

CrétinO   Crétin, Guillaume. Oeuvres poétiques. Ed.
                  K. Chesney. Paris: Firmin-Didot, 1932.
                  Contains modern edition of Déploration
                  (pp. 60-73).

CrevelS   Crevel, Marcus van. "Strukturgeheimnisse bei
                  Obrecht." Musica, 15 (1961): 252-25. (Also
                  in Dutch in TVNM 19 (1963): 86-88.)
                  Explains author's transcription method

employed in ObrO. See also the criticism of this method in DahlhausZ and FinscherS.

CrevelV   Crevel, Marcus van. "Verwante sequensmodula-
           ties bij Obrecht, Josquin en Coclico." TVNM
           16 (1941): 107-24.
           Discusses sequential passages in Obrecht's
           Missae Ave Regina, Salve diva parens, and
           Libenter gloriabor.

CrockerH   Crocker, Richard L. **A History of Musical
           Style**. New York: McGraw-Hill, 1966.
           Reprint, New York: Dover, 1986. 573 pp.
           ML430.5C76. ISBN 0-486-25029-6.
           Chapter 6 contains thoughtful stylistic
           analyses of many of Ockeghem's masses, with
           musical examples (pp. 156-69). The book
           includes a comprehensive general index, but
           no bibliography.

CummingsF Cummings, Anthony M. "A Florentine Sacred
           Repertory from the Medici Restoration." AM
           55 (1983): 267-332.
           Discusses Florence MS II.I.232. Includes
           description, inventory, history of the
           manuscript, bibliography.

CurryC   Curry, Jerry Lee. "A Computer-Aided
           Analytical Study of Kyries in Selected
           Masses by Johannes Ockeghem." Ph.D. diss.,
           University of Iowa, 1969. 224 pp. UM 70-
           4344.
           Not seen.

D'AcconeL D'Accone, Frank A. "A Late 15th-Century
           Sienese Sacred Repertory: MS K.I.2 of the
           Biblioteca Comunale, Siena." MD 37 (1983):
           121-70.
           Description, inventory, history, and dating
           of MS.

D'AcconeS D'Accone, Frank A. "Some Neglected Composers
           in the Florentine Chapels." **Viator**, 1
           (1970): 263-88.
           Discusses Obrecht/Virgilius "Nec mihi."

DahlhausM Dahlhaus, Carl. "Miszellen zu einigen
           niederländischen Messen." KmJb 63/64

(1979-80): 1-7.
Discusses Ockeghem's Missae Mi-mi and
Cuiusvis toni.

DahlhausO   Dahlhaus, Carl. "Ockeghems 'Fuga trium
vocum'." Mf 13 (1960): 307-10.
Discusses "Prenez sur moi."

DahlhausZ   Dahlhaus, Carl. "Zu Marcus van Crevels neuer
Obrecht-Ausgabe." Mf 20 (1967): 425-30.
Critical examination of van Crevel's
theories concerning tactus, notation, and
number symbolism in his edition of Obrecht's
Missa Maria zart (ObrO).

DanielT   Daniel, Hermann Adalbert. **Thesaurus
hymnologicus**. 5 vols. Halle & Leipzig,
1841-56. Reprint in 2 vols., Hildesheim:
Georg Olms, 1973. 364, 403, 295, 371, 411
pp. BV468.D36. ISBN 3-487-049139, 049147.
Standard anthology of medieval hymn and
sequence texts. General index in vol. 5.

DavisonE   **Essays on Music in Honor of Archibald Thompson
Davison**. Cambridge, Mass: Dept. of Music,
Harvard University, 1957. 374 pp.
ML55.D3H3.
Contains HewittS, MerrittC.

DeanO   Dean, Jeffrey J. "Ockeghem or Basiron? A
Disputed Salve Regina and a 'Very Notable'
Minor Composer." **Abstracts of Papers Read
at the Fifty-second Annual Meeting of the
American Musicological Society . . .** 1986,
pp. 46-47.
Demonstrates that the Salve Regina (II) is
by Basiron rather than Ockeghem.

DiehlP   Diehl, George K. "The Partbooks of a
Renaissance Merchant: Cambrai,
Bibliothèque municipale, MSS 125-128."
Ph.D. diss., University of Pennsylvania,
1974. 907 pp. UM 75-02,718.
Description, inventory, and study of a
sixteenth century Flemish manuscript.

DrevesA   Dreves, Guido M, C. Blume, and H. M.
Bannister, eds. **Analecta hymnica medii**

aevi. 55 vols. Leipzig, 1886-1922.
Reprint, New York: Johnson Reprint Corp.,
1961.
Register, ed. Max Lütolf. 3 vols. Bern:
Francke, 1978. BV 468.A622A5. ISBN 3-7720-
1430-5, -1431-3, -1432-1.
Standard edition of medieval hymn texts.
The **Register** is a comprehensive index.

DrozT   Droz, Eugénie, Geneviève Thibault, and
Yvonne Rokseth, eds. **Trois chansonniers
français du XVe siècle**, fasc. 1. Paris: E.
Droz, 1927. 125 pp. Reprint, New York: Da
Capo, 1978. M2.D78T8. ISBN 0-306-77561-1.
Partial edition of Dijon MS 517.

DTO   **Denkmäler der Tonkunst in Österreich**. Ed. G.
Adler. Vienna: Artaria (Universal), 1894-
Reprint Graz: Akademische Druck- u.
Verlagsanstalt, 1959-60. M2.D36.
14-15   Vols. 14-15 (Jg. VII). **Sechs Trienter
Codices**, 1. Ed. G. Adler & O. Koller.
Selections from Trent MSS. Includes
thematic catalogue of MSS 87-92.
38   Vol. 38 (Jg. XIX/1). **Sechs Trienter
Codices**, 3. **Auswahl**. Ed. G. Adler.
Includes Ockeghem's Missa Caput and the
Missa Le serviteur attributed to him.
72   Vol. 72 (Jg. XXXVII/2). **Das Deutsche
Gesellschaftslied in Österreich von 1480-
1550**. Ed. L. Nowak. Modern edition of
Renaissance Lieder.

DufayO VI   Dufay, Guilluame. **Opera omnia**. Ed. Heinrich
Besseler. CMM 1. Tom. VI, **Cantiones**.
Rome: American Institute of Musicology,
1964. 118 pp. M3.D84.
Critical edition of Dufay's works, including
doubtful ones. Volume 6 is devoted to the
secular works.

DunningS   Dunning, Albert. **Die Staatsmotette 1480-
1555**. Utrecht: A. Oosthoek, 1970. 361 pp.
ML240.D84.
A study of ceremonial motets in the
Renaissance. Includes a chronological list
of motets and their occasions; index of
composers, works, sources; bibliography.

EckertO   Eckert, Michael. "Ockeghem's Offertory:
             Mensural Anomaly or Structural Capstone?"
             **Abstracts of the Papers Read at the Forty-
             fourth Annual Meeting of the American
             Musicological Society** . . . **1978**, pp. 1-2.
             Discusses the structural and symbolic
             function of the final movement of Ockeghem's
             Requiem.

EckertS   Eckert, Michael. "The Structure of the
             Ockeghem Requiem." Ph.D. diss., University
             of Chicago, 1977. 78 pp.
             Analysis demonstrating the stylistic and
             structural unity of the work.

EldersJ   Elders, Willem. "Josquin's 'Absolve,
             quaesumus, Domine': A Tribute to Obrecht?"
             TVNM 37 (1987): 14-24.
             A speculative attempt to relate Josquin's
             funeral motet to the death of Obrecht.

EldersS   Elders, Willem. **Studien zur Symbolik in der
             Musik der alten Niederländer.** Bilthoven:
             A.B. Creyghton, 1968. 227 pp. ML265.E4.
             Detailed study of symbolism in fifteenth and
             sixteenth-century music by Netherlands
             composers, including Obrecht. Bibliography,
             index.

EDMR   **Das Erbe deutscher Musik.** Ser. 1,
             Reichsdenkmale. Leipzig: Breitkopf &
             Härtel, 1935-42. Kassel: Bärenreiter,
             1954- . M2.E68.
4   Vol. 4. **Das Glogauer Liederbuch.** 1. Teil,
             Deutsche Lieder und Spielstücke. Ed. H.
             Ringmann & J. Klapper. 1936; reprint 1954.
8   Vol. 8. **Das Glogauer Liederbuch.** 2. Teil,
             Ausgewählte lateinische Sätze. Ed. H.
             Ringmann & J. Klapper. 1937; reprint 1954.
21   Vol. 21. G. Rhaw, **Sacrorum hymnorum lib.
             primus.** 1. Teil. Ed. R. Gerber. 1942.
32   Vol. 32. **Der Mensuralkodex Nikolas Apel.**
             1. Teil. Ed. R. Gerber. 1956.
33   Vol. 33. Ibid., 2. Teil.
34   (Vol. 34. Ibid., 3. Teil.)
84   Vol. 84. **Das Liederbuch des Dr. Hartmann
             Schedel. Faksimile.** 1978.

85   Vol. 85. **Das Glogauer Liederbuch**. 3. Teil.
            Ed. C. Väterlein. 1981.
86   Vol. 86. **Das Glogauer Liederbuch**. 4. Teil.
            Ed. C. Väterlein. 1981.
            Volumes. 4, 8, 85, 86 comprise a modern
            edition of Kraków (Berlin) MS 40098;
            volume 4 also contains a thematic catalogue
            of the MS. Volume 21 is a modern edition
            of RISM 1542^{12}. Volumes 32-34 are a modern
            edition of Leipzig MS 1494. Volume 84 is a
            facsimile of Munich, Bay. St.-bibl. MS Germ.
            810; a modern edition of this source has
            been announced as vols. 74-75.

EinsteinI   Einstein, Alfred. **The Italian Madrigal**.
            Transl. Alexander H. Krappe, Roger H.
            Sessions, and Oliver Strunk. 3 vols.
            Princeton: Princeton University Press, 1949.
            Reprint 1971. 476 (888), 333 pp.
            ML2633.E32. ISBN 0-691-09112-9.
            Brilliant, detailed survey of Italian
            secular vocal music in the Renaissance.
            Ockeghem and Obrecht are mentioned only
            peripherally. Volume 2 contains indexes of
            names and places. Volume 3 is devoted to
            complete musical examples. The 1971 reprint
            includes revised song texts with English
            translations.

EitnerC   Eitner, Robert. "Codex Mus. Ms. Z21 der Kgl.
            Bibliothek zu Berlin." MfMg 21(1889): 93-
            102.
            Description and inventory of Berlin MS
            40021.

EM   **Early Music**.

FallowsE   Fallows, David. "English Song Repertories of
            the Mid-fifteenth Century." PRMA 103 (1976-
            77): 61-79. Survey of English songs
            ca. 1430-70, with reference to continental
            music including Ockeghem (pp. 67-68).

FallowsJ   Fallows, David. "Johannes Ockeghem: The
            Changing Image, the Songs and a New Source."
            EM 12 (1984): 218-30.
            A general discussion of Ockeghem's chansons
            and description of a newly-found MS source,

Cambridge R.2.71. One of the few general
surveys of Ockeghem's secular works.

FallowsP   Fallows, David. "The Performing Ensembles in
              Josquin's Sacred Music." TVNM 35 (1985):
              32-64.
              Much of the information in this article
              applies to Ockeghem and Obrecht as well as
              to Josquin. This is the most detailed study
              to date of performance practice in sacred
              music of the later fifteenth century.

FallowsS   Fallows, David. "Specific Information on the
              Ensembles for Composed Polyphony, 1400-
              1474." BoormanS, pp. 109-59.
              Concentrates on performance practices at the
              Burgundian court. Much of the information
              is applicable to Ockeghem's music.

FallowsST   Fallows, David. "Songs in the Trent Codices:
              An Optimistic Handlist." Codici, pp. 170-
              79.
              List of secular works in the Trent MSS.

FauguesCW   Faugues. **Collected Works**. Ed. George C.
              Schuetze, Jr. Brooklyn: Institute of
              Mediaeval Music, 1960. 178 pp. M3.F33.
              Includes the Missa Le serviteur, sometimes
              attributed to Ockeghem.

FauguesO   Faugues. **Opera omnia**. Introduction by George
              C. Schuetze, Jr. Publications of Mediaeval
              Musical Manuscripts, 7. Brooklyn: Institute
              of Mediaeval Music, 1959. M2.P95 no. 7.
              Facsimiles of the original MSS, including
              the Missa Le serviteur in Trent 88.

FeiningerF   Feininger, Laurence K. J. **Die Frühgeschichte
              des Kanons bis Josquin des Pres (um 1500)**.
              Emsdetten: H. & G. Lechte, 1937. 65 pp.
              Discusses the thirty-six voice canon "Deo
              gratia" attributed to Ockeghem.

FenlonC   Fenlon, Iain, ed. **Cambridge Music Manuscripts
              900-1700**. Cambridge University Press, 1982.
              174 pp. ML141.C3. ISBN 0-521-24452-8.
              Exhibition catalogue. Includes description
              of Cambridge, Pepys MS 1760 (pp. 123-26).

FétisB   Fétis, F. J. **Biographie universelle des
              musiciens**. 2nd ed., Paris, 1875. Reprint,
              Brussels: Culture et Civilisation, 1983.
              8 vols. ML105.F418.
              Articles on Ockeghem and Obrecht appear in
              volume 6. These are unreliable as a whole,
              but include some useful information. They
              should be read in relation to more recent
              scholarly studies.

FinscherO-MGG Finscher, Ludwig. "Obrecht, Jacob." MGG 9:
              1814-22.
              Good survey of life and works. Corrections
              in MGG 16: 1418.

FinscherS   Finscher, Ludwig. "Spekulationen über eine
              Obrecht-Messe." **Musica**, 19 (1965): 228.
              Critical review of van Crevel's edition of
              Obrecht's Missa Sub tuum presidium (ObrO).

ForkelA   Forkel, Johann Nicolaus. **Allgemeine
              Geschichte der Musik**. 2 vols. Leipzig:
              Schwikert, 1788-1801. Reprint, Graz:
              Akademische Druck- u. Verlagsanstalt, 1967.
              504, 776 pp. ML159.F3.
              Important early history. Discusses works of
              Ockeghem and Obrecht, especially with
              respect to their contrapuntal technique.

FoxB   Fox, Charles Warren. "Barbireau and
              Barbingant: A Review." JAMS 13 (1960): 79-
              101.
              Establishes the separate identities of these
              composers. Discusses their works, including
              the "Au travail suis" attributed to both
              Barbingant and Ockeghem.

FullerA   Fuller, Sarah. "Additional Notes on the 15th-
              Century Chansonnier Bologna Q16." MD
              23 (1969): 81-103.
              Supplements the information in PeaseR.

FrançonP   Françon, Marcel. **Poèmes de transition (XVe-
              XVIe siècles): Rondeaux du Ms. 402 de Lille**.
              Cambridge, Mass.: Harvard University Press,
              1938. 771 pp.
              Modern edition of a fifteenth-century
              manuscript of chanson poetry.

GaffuriusP   Gaffurius, Franchinus. **Practica musicae.**
                 Transl. Clement A. Miller. MSD 20.
                 American Institute of Musicology, 1968.   244
                 pp. ML171.G101.
                 Bibliography, index of names. See also the
                 next item.

GafuriusP   Gafurius, Franchinus. **The 'Practica musicae'
                 of Franchinus Gafurius.** Transl. and ed. by
                 Irwin Young. Madison: University of
                 Wisconsin Press, 1969. 273 pp.
                 ML171.G1216. ISBN 299-05180-3.
                 The preceding two items are English
                 translations of Gafurius 1496, an important
                 late fifteenth century treatise. Ockeghem
                 and Obrecht are briefly discussed, and
                 Ockeghem's "L'autre d'antan" is quoted. The
                 Young edition erroneously omits Obrecht's
                 name (pp. 154-55), which Miller includes (p.
                 144). The Young edition includes an index.

GareyC   Garey, Howard. "Can a Rondeau with a One-line
                 Refrain be Sung?" **Ars lyrica**, 2 (1983): 10-
                 21.
                 Discusses the unusual form of Ockeghem's
                 "L'autre d'antan." See also BrownR.

GaspariG   Gaspari, Gaetano. **Catalogo della biblioteca
                 del Liceo musicale di Bologna.** 5 vols.
                 Bologna, 1890-1943. Reprint, Bologna:
                 Forni, 1961. 417, 573, 389, 279, 560 pp.
                 ML136.B6L6.
                 Catalog of the library of Padre G.B.
                 Martini, given to the city of Bologna and
                 now in the Civico Museo Bibliografico
                 Musicale. It is especially rich in
                 fifteenth-century MSS.

GavaldáC   Gavaldá, M. Querol. **Cancionero musical de
                 la Columbina.** MME 33. Barcelona: Consejo
                 superior de investigationes cientificos,
                 Instituto español de musicología, 1971.
                 103 pp. M2.M4845 no. 33.
                 Modern edition of Seville MS 7-I-28.

GeeringL   Geering, Arnold, & Hans Trümpy, eds. **Das
                 Liederbuch des Johannes Heer von Glarus.**
                 Schweizerische Musikdenkmäler, 5. Basel:

Bärenreiter, 1967. 186 pp. M2.S397 v. 5.
Modern edition of St. Gall MS 462.

GiesbertA   Giesbert, Franz J., ed. **Ein altes Spielbuch
               aus der Zeit um 1500 (Liber Fridolini
               Sichery).** 2 vols. Mainz: Schott, 1936.
               108 pp.
               Modern edition of St. Gall MS 461.

GlareanD   Glarean, Heinrich. **Dodecachordon.** Transl.
               Clement A. Miller. MSD 6. American
               Institute of Musicology, 1965. 551, 223 pp.
               ML171.G543.
               English translation of Glareanus 1547, an
               important sixteenth-century treatise.
               Includes complete works and movements by
               Ockeghem and Obrecht, with discussions.

GöllnerB   Göllner, Marie Louise. **Bayerische Staats-
               bibliothek, Katalog der Musikhandschriften,
               2: Tabulaturen und Stimmbücher bis zur Mitte
               des 17. Jahrhunderts.** Kataloge bayerischer
               Musiksammlungen, 5/2. Munich: G. Henle,
               1979. 230 pp. ML136.M92B44 v. 5/2. ISBN
               3-87328-027-2.
               Catalogue of Renaissance manuscript
               tablatures and part-books in the Bavarian
               State Library, Munich.

GombosiC   Gombosi, Otto, ed. **Compositione di Meser
               Vincenzo Capirola. Lute-Book (circa 1517).**
               136 pp. Neuilly-sur-Seine: Sociètè de
               Musique d'Autrefois, 1955. Reprint, New
               York: Da Capo, 1983. M140.C3L8.
               Modern edition of Chicago, Newberry Library
               MS 107501, with extensive commentary.

GombosiJ   Gombosi, Otto. **Jacob Obrecht: eine
               stilkritische Studie.** Leipzig: Breitkopf &
               Härtel, 1925. 131 pp. plus 87 pp.
               Notenanhang. ML410.O27G76.
               A fundamental study of Obrecht's musical
               style in relation to his contemporaries.
               Appendix includes many complete works by
               fifteenth-century composers, including
               Ockeghem.

GottwaldA   Gottwald, Clytus. **Die Musikhandschriften der**
                   Staats- und Stadtbibliothek Augsburg.
                   Wiesbaden: Otto Harrassowitz, 1974. 328 pp.
                   ML136.A92. ISBN 3-447-01598-5.
                   Catalogue of music MSS in the Augsburg State
                   Library. Indexes of names, places,
                   subjects, incipits.

GottwaldM   Gottwald, Clytus. **Die Musikhandschriften der**
                   Universitätsbibliothek München. Wiesbaden:
                   Otto Harrassowitz, 1968. 127 pp.
                   Catalogue of music MSS in the University
                   Library, Munich. Indexes of names, places,
                   and subjects; textual incipits.

GottwaldS   Gottwald, Clytus. **Die Handschriften der**
                   Württembergischen Landesbibliothek
                   Stuttgart. Codices Musici, I. Wiesbaden:
                   Otto Harrassowitz, 1964. 184 pp. ML93.85C6
                   v. 1.
                   Catalogue of music MSS in the Württemberg
                   Landesbibliothek. Bibliography, index of
                   names, places, and subjects; textual and
                   musical incipits.

GR   **Graduale sacrosanctae romanae ecclesiae.**
                   Benedictines of Solesmes, eds. Solesmes,
                   1974. 918 pp.
                   Modern edition of Gregorian chants for the
                   mass, with indexes of chants and feasts.

GreenbergA   Greenberg, Noah, and Paul Maynard, eds. **An**
                   Anthology of Early Renaissance Music. New
                   York: W.W. Norton, 1975. 318 pp. M2.A517.
                   ISBN 0-393-02182-3.
                   Annotated anthology of music of the
                   fifteenth and early sixteenth centuries.
                   Well chosen and beautifully illustrated.
                   Contains works of Ockeghem and Obrecht.

GroutH   Grout, Donald Jay, with Claude V. Palisca. **A**
                   History of Western Music. 3rd ed., New
                   York: W.W. Norton, 1980. 849 pp.
                   ML160.G872. ISBN 0-393-95136-7.
                   Standard historical survey, with selective
                   bibliographies and extensive index.
                   Chapter 6 discusses Ockeghem's and Obrecht's
                   masses.

GutiérrezU   Gutiérrez-Denhoff, Martella.
"Untersuchungen zu Gestalt, Entstehung und
Repertoire des Chansonniers Laborde." AfMw
41 (1984): 113-46.
Study and inventory of the fifteenth-century
MS Washington, Library of Congress, M.2.1
L25 Case.

HaarC   Haar, James, ed. **Chanson and Madrigal, 1480-
1530.** Isham Library Papers, 2. Cambridge,
Mass.: Harvard University Press, 1964. 266
pp. ML180.I85. ISBN 0-317-09611-7.
Conference report; contains BrownG and
RubsamenF. Musical examples include
Ockeghem's "Les desléaulx." Index.

HaassS   Haass, Walter. **Studien zu den "L'homme
armé-Messen" des 15. und 16. Jahrhunderts.**
Kölner Beiträge zur Musikforschung, 136.
Regensburg: Gustav Bosse Verlag, 1984. 178
pp. ML3088.H112. ISBN 3-7649-2288-5.
Study of L'homme armé Masses, including
those of Ockeghem and Obrecht.

HaberkampW   Haberkamp, Gertraut. **Die weltliche Vokalmusik
in Spanien um 1500.** Münchener
Veröffentlichungen zur Musikgeschichte,
12. Tutzing: Hans Schneider, 1968. 341
pp. M2.H17W4.
Study of secular vocal music in Spain ca.
1500. Includes a complete modern edition of
Seville MS 7-I-28.

HaberlB   Haberl, Fr. X. **Bausteine für Musikgeschichte,
2. Bibliographischer und thematischer
Musikkatalog des päpstlichen Kapellarchives
im Vatikan zu Rom.** Leipzig: Breitkopf &
Härtel, 1888. Reprint, Hildesheim: Georg
Olms, 1971. 184 pp. ML 60.H12. ISBN 3-
487-04001.
Description and thematic index of the
Cappella Sistina MSS at the Vatican in Rome.
Indices of names, titles.

HAM   Davison, Archibald T., and Willi Apel, eds.
**Historical Anthology of Music, 1. Oriental,
Medieval and Renaissance Music.** Rev. ed.
Cambridge, Mass.: Harvard University Press,

1950. 258 pp. M2.D25H5 v. 1. ISBN 0-674-
39300-7.
Standard anthology. Contains works by
Ockeghem and Obrecht.

HanenC   Hanen, Martha K. **The Chansonnier El Escorial**
              IV.a.24. Musicological Studies, 36.
              Henryville, Pa.: Institute of Mediaeval
              Music, 1983. 3 vols. 170, 478 pp. M2.E75.
              ISBN 0-931902-17-3.
              Study and modern edition of a fifteenth-
              century chansonnier at El Escorial, Spain.

HarrisA   Harris, Russell G. "An Analysis of the Design
              of the 'Caput' Masses by Dufay and Ockeghem
              in their Metric and Rhythmic Aspects."
              Hamline Studies in Musicology, 1: 1-46.
              Minneapolis: Burgess Publ. Co., 1945.
              ML184K7.
              A student paper written under Ernst Krenek's
              direction, discussing the influence on the
              Masses of Gregorian chant rhythm as
              interpreted by the monks of Solesmes.

HawkinsG   Hawkins, Sir John. **A General History of the**
              Science and Practice of Music. 5 vols.
              London, 1776. New ed. in 3 vols., London:
              Novello, 1853. Reprint in 2 vols., New
              York: Dover, 1963. 963 pp. ML159.H39.
              Important early history of music. Includes
              quotations from treatises and extensive
              musical examples, including a canon by
              Ockeghem (p. 338; incorrectly realized).
              General index, indexes of musical examples,
              illustrations.

HayneO   Hayne van Ghizeghem. **Opera omnia.** Ed. Barton
              Hudson. CMM 74. American Institute of
              Musicology, 1977. lii, 45 pp. M3.H45.
              Collected works of the composer, including
              doubtful works.

HenzeS   Henze, Marianne. **Studien zu den Messen-**
              kompositionen Johannes Ockeghems. Berliner
              Studien zur Musikwissenschaft, 12. Berlin:
              Merseburger, 1968. 260 pp. ML410.O31H5.
              Study of Ockeghem's Masses, with emphasis on
              rhythmic analysis and number symbolism.

HewittB   Hewitt, Helen, ed. **Ottaviano Petrucci, Canti B numero cinquanta, Venice, 1502.** Monuments of Renaissance Music, 2. Chicago: University of Chicago Press, 1967. 242 pp. M2.M47 v. 2.
Modern edition with commentary. Indexes of composers and works.

HewittF   Hewitt, Helen. "'Fors seulement' and the Cantus Firmus Technique of the Fifteenth Century." PlamenacFS, pp. 91-126.
Survey of works based on Ockeghem's "Fors seulement."

HewittO   Hewitt, Helen, and Isabel Pope, eds. **Harmonice musices Odhecaton A.** Cambridge, Mass.: Mediaeval Academy of America, 1942. Reprint with corrections, 1946. 421 pp. M2.P39H3.
Modern edition of the first book of polyphonic music ever printed (by Ottaviano de' Petrucci, Venice, 1501). Mainly secular works by Franco-Flemish composers. Extensive commentary, with concordances. Indexes of composers and works.

HewittS   Hewitt, Helen. "A Study in Proportions." DavisonE, pp. 68-81.
A study of Obrecht's "Regina coeli," with transcription.

HeydenA   Heyden, Sebald. **De arte canendi.** Transl. C.A. Miller. MSD 26. American Institute of Musicology, 1972. 141 pp. ML171.H3813.
English translation of Heyden 1540, an important sixteenth-century treatise. Discusses works of Ockeghem and Obrecht, with examples.

HigginsC   Higgins, Paula. Introduction to facsimile edition of **Chansonnier Nivelle de la Chausée.** Geneva: Minkoff Reprint, 1984. xxvi, 180 pp. ISBN 2-8266-0752-9.
Description and facsimile of Paris, Bibl. nat. Rès. Vmc MS 57, one of the central sources of fifteenth-century chansons.

HigginsI   Higgins, Paula. "'In hydraulis' Revisited:
                New Light on the Career of Antoine Busnois."
                JAMS 39 (1986): 36-86.
                Documents the activities of Busnois at
                Tours, supporting the theory that Busnois
                was a pupil of Ockeghem.

HMS 3   The History of Music in Sound. Gerald
                Abraham, gen. ed. Vol. 3, Ars Nova and the
                Renaissance. Ed. Dom Anselm Hughes. New
                York: Oxford University Press, 1953. 82 pp.
                ISBN 0-19-323102-6.
                Booklet accompanying record album RCA 6016,
                supplementing the New Oxford History of
                Music (see BridgmanA).

HoornJ   Hoorn, L. G. van. Jacob Obrecht. The Hague:
                M. Nijhoff, 1968. 245 pp. ML410.027H7.
                Survey of Obrecht's life and works. Many
                statements are subjective or unreliable.
                However, it contains much useful information
                and cites important documents. This is the
                only monograph on Obrecht of its kind, but
                it must be used with caution.

HoughtonR   Houghton, Edward F. "Rhythm and Meter in
                Fifteenth Century Polyphony." Journal of
                Music Theory, 18 (1974): 190-212.
                Based on HoughtonRS, this deals in a general
                way with Ockeghem's rhythmic style.

HoughtonRS   Houghton, Edward F. "Rhythmic Structure in
                the Masses and Motets of Johannes Ockeghem."
                Ph.D. diss., University of California,
                Berkeley, 1971. 334 pp.
                Surveys Ockeghem's sacred music, examining
                its notational and mensural aspects in
                detail. Contains valuable observations on
                Ockeghem's style.

HudsonN   Hudson, Barton. "A Neglected Source of
                Renaissance Polyphony: Rome, Santa Maria
                Maggiore JJ.III.4." AM 48 (1976): 166-80.
                Description and inventory of an early
                sixteenth-century Roman MS.

HudsonO   Hudson, Barton. "On the Texting of Obrecht
                Masses." Abstracts of Papers Read at the

Fifty-second Annual Meeting of the American
Musicological Society . . . **1986**, pp. 18-19.
Finds that separate texts are to be sung to
the cantus firmi in at least three of
Obrecht's Masses, and probably five others.

HudsonOT   Hudson, Barton. "Obrecht's Tribute to
            Ockeghem." TVNM 37 (1987): 3-13.
            A study of Obrecht's Missa Sicut spina
            rosam, seen as a memorial to Ockeghem (d.
            1497) and placed in the context of Obrecht's
            stylistic development.

HudsonT   Hudson, Barton. "Two Ferrarese Masses by
            Jacob Obrecht." JM 4 (1985-6): 276-302.
            Discusses the dating, sources, and
            transmission of Obrecht's Misse Malheur me
            bat and Fortuna desperata; also the
            authorship of "Malheur me bat" (probably by
            Martini, but sometimes attributed to
            Ockeghem).

Hughes-   Hughes-Hughes, Augustus. **Catalogue of**
  HughesC   **Manuscript Music in the British Museum.** 3
            vols. London: British Museum, 1906-09.
            Reprints 1964; 1981. 615, 961, 543 pp.
            Z6816.B876. ISBN 0-7141-0425-6; -0426-4;
            -0427-2.
            Catalogue, arranged by genre, of music MSS
            in London, British Museum (now The British
            Library). Indexes of composers and titles.

HuschenM   Huschen, Heinrich, ed. **The Motet.** Transl.
            A.C. Howie. AnthM 47 (1975). 139 pp.
            M2.M94512 no. 47.
            Anthology of motets from the middle ages to
            the twentieth century. Includes examples by
            Ockeghem and Obrecht.

HuysD   Huys, Bernard. **De Gregoire le Grand à**
            Stockhausen. Brussels: Bibliotheque Albert
            Ier, 1966. 169 pp.
            Excellent exhibition catalogue of music in
            the Brussels Royal Library.

IMM   **Invitation to Medieval Music.** Ed. Thurston
            Dart and Brian Trowell. 4 vols. London:
            Stainer & Bell, 1967-78. 58, 58, 48, 48 pp.

ISBN 0-85249-316-9 (vol. 3), -317-7 (vol. 4). Small volumes containing examples of fifteenth-century music. Volumes 2-4 include works by Ockeghem and Obrecht.

IsaacO   Isaac, Henricus. **Opera omnia.** Ed. Edward R. Lerner. Corpus mensurabilis musicae, 65. 7 vols. to date. Stuttgart: American Institute of Musicology and Hänssler Verlag, 1974- . M3.I79. Includes "T'meiskin was jonck," attributed to Isaac and Obrecht, as model for Isaac's Mass in volume 7.

J   Josquin des Prez. **Proceedings of the International Josquin Festival-Conference . . . New York City, 21-25 June 1971.** Ed. Edward E. Lowinsky. London: Oxford University Press, 1976. 787 pp. plus 2 records. ML410.D36716. ISBN 0-19-315229-0. Contains many papers by leading authorities on music of Josquin and his contemporaries; includes KellmanJ, LenaertsM, and MendelT.

JAMS   **Journal of the American Musicological Society.**

Jardin   **Le Jardin de plaisance et fleur de rhetorique . . . (1501).** Facsimile edition, with introduction and notes by E. Droz and A. Piaget. 2 vols. Société des anciens textes français. Paris: Champion, 1910-25. ca. 500, 339 pp. PQ1307.J3. Reprint, with extensive commentary (volume 2), of an early sixteenth-century anthology of French poetry. Many of these poems served as texts for music. Contains bibliography and indexes of authors, titles, incipits, refrains, and names.

JeppesenF Jeppesen, Knud. **La Frottola.** 3 vols. Acta Jutlandica 41-43. Aarhus: Universitets-forlaget, 1968-70. 171, 349, 329 pp. AS281.A34 v. 41-43. Description of sources, with inventories and concordances, of music with Italian texts ca. 1500. Includes examples (in volume 3). Indexes of text incipits, composers.

Bibliography   143

JeppesenG   Jeppesen, Knud. "Die 3 Gafurius-Kodizes der
                Fabbrica del Duomo, Milano." AM 3 (1931):
                14-28.
                Descriptions and inventories of Milan MSS
                2266-69.

JeppesenK   Jeppesen, Knud, ed. The Copenhagen
                Chansonnier. New York: Broude Bros., 1965.
                Reprint, with additions, of Der
                Kopenhagener Chansonnier, originally
                published Copenhagen, 1927. M2.J58.
                ISBN 0-8450-0004-7.
                Modern edition of Copenhagen MS Thott 291[8],
                one of the central sources of fifteenth-
                century chansons.

JeppesenM   Jeppesen, Knud. Review of Music in the
                Renaissance by Gustave Reese. MQ 41 (1955):
                378-91. (See ReeseMR.)
                Major review, with additional information
                about Obrecht (pp. 382-83).

JM   Journal of Musicology.

JO   Johannes Ockeghem en zijn tijd. Tentoon-
                stelling . . . Dendermonde, 14 nov.-6 dec.
                1970. Dendermonde: A. De Cuyper, 1970.
                285 pp.
                Catalogue of the exhibition "Johannes
                Ockeghem and His Time," including essays and
                archival material. Contains new
                biographical data.

JonesF   Jones, George Morton. "The First Chansonnier
                of the Biblioteca Riccardiana, Codex 2794."
                Ph.D. diss., New York University, 1972. 2
                vols. 339, 316 pp. UM 72-31,090.
                Study and edition of an important fifteenth-
                century MS in Florence.

Josquin WM   Josquin des Pres. Werken. Ed. Albert
                Smijers. Missen. Amsterdam: Vereeniging
                voor nederlandsche muziekgeschiedenis, 1926-
                56. 2nd ed., Opera omnia, 1957 (only 2
                fascicles published). M3.D4, D44.
                Critical edition; includes models on which
                the Masses are based.

JustM   Just, Martin. **Der Mensuralkodex Mus. Ms.
               40021 der Staatsbibliothek Preussischer
               Kulturbesitz Berlin.** Tutzing: H. Schneider,
               1975. 2 vols. 347, 215 pp. ML93.J9. ISBN
               37952-01578.
               Critical study and inventory of important
               fifteenth-century MS. Bibliography, index
               of composers, list of sources.

JustS   Just, Martin. "Studien zu Heinrich Isaacs
               Motetten." Ph.D. diss., Eberhard-Karls-
               Universität, Tübingen, 1960. 2 vols.
               219, 132 pp.
               Study of Isaac's motets, including doubtful
               works. List of sources and works,
               bibliography.

KämperL   Kämper, Dietrich. "La Stangetta--eine
               Instrumentalkomposition Gaspars van
               Weerbecke?" **Ars musica, musica scientia:
               Festschrift Heinrich Huschen,** pp. 277-88.
               Ed. D. Altenburg. Beiträge zur rheinische
               Musikgeschichte, 126. Cologne, 1980.
               ML55.H87A7. ISBN 3-88583-002-7.
               Study of a work attributed to both Obrecht
               and Weerbecke, probably by the latter.

KämperS   Kämper, Dietrich. **Studien zur instrumentalen
               Ensemblemusik des 16. Jahrhunderts in
               Italien.** Analecta musicologica, 10.
               Cologne: Böhlau Verlag, 1970. 280 pp.
               plus 39 pp. music. ML465.K23. ISBN 3-412-
               01771-X.
               Study of music for instrumental ensembles in
               sixteenth-century Italy. Obrecht is
               mentioned in passing.

KanazawaT   Kanazawa, Masakata. "Two Vesper Repertories
               from Verona, c. 1500." **Rivista italiana di
               musicologia,** 10 (1975): 155-79.
               Study of Verona MSS, including nos. 758 and
               759.

KarpS   Karp, Theodore. "The Secular Works of
               Johannes Martini." **Aspects of Medieval and
               Renaissance Music: A Birthday Offering to
               Gustave Reese,** pp. 455-73. Ed. Jan LaRue.
               New York: W.W. Norton, 1966. Reprint, New

York: Pendragon, 1978. ML55.R4L4. ISBN 0-918728-07-X.
Stylistic study of Martini's secular music. Includes discussion of "Malheur me bat," attributed to both Ockeghem and Martini, without resolving the question of authorship.

KehreinL   Kehrein, Joseph. **Lateinische Sequenzen des Mittelalters.** Mainz: F. Kupferberg, 1873. Reprint, Hildesheim: Georg Olms, 1969. 620 pp. BV468.K4.
Anthology of medieval sequence texts. Index of incipits; glossary of medieval Latin words.

KellmanJ   Kellman, Herbert. "Josquin and the Courts of the Netherlands and France: The Evidence of the Sources." J 181-216.
Descriptions of MSS produced at the Netherlands court ca. 1495-1534 now in Brussels, Florence, Rome, Vienna, etc.

KellmanO   Kellman, Herbert. "The Origins of the Chigi-Codex." JAMS 11 (1958): 6-19.
A study of Rome, Vat. Chigi MS C.VIII.234, the most important source of Ockeghem's music. Some of its conclusions are revised in KellmanJ.

KenneyO   Kenney, Sylvia W. "The Origins and Chronology of the Brussels Manuscript 5557 in the Bibliothèque Royale de Belgique." RBM 6 (1952): 75-100.
A study of an important fifteenth-century choirbook containing sacred music by Ockeghem and his contemporaries.

KesselsB   Kessels, Leon. "The Brussels/Tournai-Partbooks: Structure, Illumination, and Flemish Repertory." TVNM 37 (1987): 82-110.
Study and inventory of an early sixteenth-century Franco-Flemish MS that includes works by Ockeghem and Obrecht.

KeyzerJ   Keyzer, Berten de. "Jacobus Obrecht en zijn vader Willem." **Mens en Melodie,** 8 (1953):

317-19.
A frequently-cited article containing
biographical data concerning Obrecht and his
father. Not seen.

KirschQ   Kirsch, Winifried. **Die Quellen der
               mehrstimmigen Magnificat- und Te Deum-
               Vertonungen bis zur Mitte des 16.
               Jahrhunderts.** Tutzing: H. Schneider, 1966.
               588 pp. ML128.M2K6.
               Critical catalogue of Magnificat and Te Deum
               settings to the middle of the sixteenth
               century, including a Magnificat doubtfully
               attributed to Obrecht.

KmJ   **Kirchenmusikalisches Jahrbuch.**

KonradM   Konrad, Ulrich; Adalbert Roth; and Martin
               Staehelin. **Musikalischer Lustgarten.**
               Wolfenbüttel: Herzog August Bibliothek,
               1985. 294 pp. plus 2 records. ISBN 3-
               88373-045-9.
               Catalogue of an exhibition of musical
               holdings of the Herzog August Bibliothek,
               Wolfenbüttel. Among these is MS Guelf.
               287 Extravag., a central source of fifteenth
               century chansons (pp. 38-39). Copiously
               illustrated.

KottickC   Kottick, Edward L. "The Chansonnier
               Cordiforme." JAMS 20 (1967): 10-27.
               A study of Paris, Bibl. nat. MS Rothschild
               2973, based on KottickM.

KottickM   Kottick, Edward L. "The Music of the
               Chansonnier Cordiforme: Paris, Bibl. Nat.
               Rothschild 2973." Ph.D. diss., University
               of North Carolina, 1962. 2 vols. 202, 133
               pp. UM 64-539.
               Description, discussion, and complete modern
               edition of an important fifteenth-century
               French MS.

KreitnerV   Kreitner, Kenneth. "Very Low Ranges in the
               Sacred Music of Ockeghem and Tinctoris." EM
               14 (1986): 467-79.
               Study of works notated for low voices.

Concludes that they are intended to be sung
as notated, without upward transposition.

KrenekD   Krenek, Ernst.   "A Discussion of the Treatment
               of Dissonances in Okeghem's Masses as
               Compared with the Contrapuntal Theory of
               Johannes Tinctoris." **Hamline Studies in
               Musicology**, 2 (1947): 1-26.
               A stylistic study by a distinguished
               modern composer.   Although narrowly
               focused on Ockeghem without taking into
               account the practices of other composers,
               this is a pioneer effort at defining
               Ockeghem's style and has not been
               superceded.

KrenekJ   Krenek, Ernst.   **Johannes Ockeghem**.   New York:
               Sheed & Ward, 1953.   86 pp.   ML410.O31K7.
               The only book on Ockeghem in English, this
               is evidently aimed at general readers and is
               superficial.   KrenekD is a more significant
               study.

KringsB   Krings, Alfred.   "Die Bearbeitung der
               gregorianischen Melodien in der
               Messkomposition von Ockeghem bis Josquin des
               Prez." KmJ 35 (1951): '36-53.
               A general survey of the ways in which
               fifteenth-century composers use Gregorian
               melodies in their masses.

KyriazisC   Kyriazis, Maria.   **Die Cantus firmus-Technik in
               den Messen Obrechts**.   Bern: Arnaud, 1952.
               76 pp.
               Dissertation, summarized in SparksC 466,
               n. 2.   Not seen.

LemaireC   Lemaire de Belges, Jean.   **La Concorde des deux
               langages**.   Ed. Jean Frappier.   Paris: Droz,
               1947.   112 pp.
               Critical edition of poem written in 1511.
               In it, the musical styles of various
               composers, including Ockeghem, are described
               (p. 18).   Introduction, notes, bibliography,
               glossary, and index of names.

LenaertsA   Lenaerts, René B., ed.   **The Art of the
               Netherlanders**.   AnthM 22 (1964).   117 pp.

Anthology of fifteenth- and sixteenth-
century music by Netherlands composers,
including Ockeghem and Obrecht.

LenaertsB   Lenaerts, Renè B. "Bemerkungen über
Johannes Ockeghem und seinen Kompositions-
stil." **Convivium musicorum. Festschrift
Wolfgang Boetticher zum sechzigsten
Geburtstag**, pp. 163-67. Ed. H. Hüschen and
D.-R. Moser. Berlin: Merseburger, 1974.
Comments on Ockeghem's style and its
origins. Suggests that Ockeghem came into
contact with English music at Bruges ca.
1450 or earlier and that its florid style
influenced him. Strohm questions this (see
StrohmM 177, n. 152).

LenaertsC   Lenaerts, Renè B. "Contribution à
l'histoire de la musique belge de la
renaissance." RBM 9 (1955): 103-20.
Includes an important biographical study of
Ockeghem (pp. 109-16). See also the
response by S. Clercx on pp. 120-21.

LenaertsM   Lenaerts, Renè B. "Musical Structure and
Performance Practice in Masses and Motets of
Josquin and Obrecht." J 619-26.
Discusses the implications of structure for
performance, especially the use of
instruments.

LenaertsN   Lenaerts, René B. **Het Nederlands polifonies
lied in de zestiende eeuw**. Mechelen: Het
Kompas, 1933. 173 pp. plus 129 pp. music.
ML2626.L56.
Study of Flemish polyphonic songs, with many
examples, including works of Obrecht.
Bibliography, list of sources, indexes of
names and text incipits.

LesureO   Lesure, François. "Ockeghem à Notre-Dame
de Paris (1463-1470)." PlamenacFS 147-54.
Summarizes recently-found documents relating
to Ockeghem's appointments and benefices in
Paris.

LevitanO   Levitan, Joseph S. "Ockeghem's Clefless
Compositions." MQ 23 (1937): 440-64.

Study of works that can be read in more than
one clef, primarily Missa Cuiusvis toni and
"Prenez sur moi."

LitterickM   Litterick Rifkin, Louise. "The Manuscript
                Royal 20.A.XVI of the British Library."
                Ph.D. diss., New York University, 1976.   319
                pp. UM 77-16,502.
                Study and edition of a late fifteenth-
                century French chansonnier, with discussion
                of related sources.

LitterickP   Litterick, Louise. "Performing Franco-
                Netherlandish Secular Music of the Late
                Fifteenth Century." EM 8 (1980): 474-85.
                Criteria for the use of instruments in
                performing untexted parts in fifteenth-
                century chansons, based on the sources.

LitterickR   Litterick, Louise. "The Revision of
                Ockeghem's 'Je n'ay dueil'." Le Moyen
                français, 5 (1980): 29-48.
                Compares different versions of the chanson,
                and concludes that Ockeghem made the
                revision himself.

LlorensC   Llorens, Josephus M. Capellae Sixtinae
                codices. Vatican City: Biblioteca
                apostolica vaticana, 1960. 555 pp.
                ML136.R72S57.
                Catalogue of Sistine Chapel MSS at the
                Vatican Library in Rome. Index of names,
                titles, and subjects. Facsimiles.

LlorensCC   Llorens, José M. "El Códice Casanatense
                2.856 identificado como el Cancionero de
                Isabella d'Este (Ferrara)." Anuario
                musical, 20 (1965): 161-78.
                Concerns provenance of chansonnier Rome,
                Bibl. Casanatense MS 2856.

LlorensO   Llorens, José M. Le Opere musicali della
                Cappella Giulia. 1. Manoscritti e edizioni
                fino al '700. Vatican City: Biblioteca
                apostolica vaticana, 1971. 412 pp.
                ML136.V252G6.
                Catalogue of music before 1800 from the
                Cappella Giulia at the Vatican Library in

Rome. Index of names, titles, and subjects.
Facsimiles.

LoachA   Loach, Donald G. "Aegidius Tschudi's Songbook
                (St. Gall MS 463): A Humanistic Document
                from the Circle of Heinrich Glarean." Ph.D.
                diss., University of California, Berkeley,
                1969. 2 vols. 470, 407 pp. UM 70-17,607.
                Study of a Swiss MS written by a student of
                Glareanus.

LockwoodA   Lockwood, Lewis. "Aspects of the 'L'homme
                armé' Tradition." PRMA 100 (1973-74): 97-
                122.
                Discusses L'homme armé Masses and related
                works, including Ockeghem's Mass and chanson
                "L'autre d'antan."

LockwoodM   Lockwood, Lewis. **Music in Renaissance Ferrara
                1400-1505.** Cambridge, Mass.: Harvard
                University Press, 1984. 355 pp.
                ML290.8.F45L6. ISBN 0-674-59131-3.
                Study of music and musicians at the Este
                court in Ferrara, one of the major musical
                centers of the Renaissance. Obrecht's
                association with Ferrara is reviewed (pp.
                207-10). Includes documents, bibliography,
                index, and many illustrations.

LockwoodMF   Lockwood, Lewis. "Music at Ferrara in the
                Period of Ercole I d'Este." **Studi musicali,**
                1 (1972): 101-30.
                Includes letters concerning Obrecht not
                reprinted in LockwoodM (pp. 112-13, 127-29).

LockwoodM-NG   Lockwood, Lewis. "Mass. 6. The Cyclic Mass in
                the Later 15th Century." NG 11: 784-86.
                Survey of Mass composition in the late
                fifteenth century, including the work of
                Ockeghem and Obrecht.

LockwoodN   Lockwood, Lewis. "A Note on Obrecht's Mass
                'Sub tuum praesidium'." RBM 14 (1960): 30-
                39.
                An important study, concentrating on the
                symmetrical design of the Mass and its
                implications for the study of Obrecht's
                other masses.

LodiC

Lodi, Pio. Catalogo delle opere musicali. Città di Modena. Biblioteca Estense. Bolletino dell'Associazione dei musicologi italiani, 8. Parma, 1923. Reprint, Bologna: Forni, 1967. 561 pp. ML136.M7B5. Catalogue of music in the Biblioteca Estense, formerly located in Ferrara but now in Modena.

LoewenfeldL

Loewenfeld, Hans. Leonhard Kleber und sein Orgeltabulaturbuch. Ph.D. diss., Friedrich-Wilhelms-Universität, Berlin, 1897. Reprint, with notes by Peter Williams, Hilversum: Frits Knuf, 1968. 82 pp. Study of Berlin MS 40026 (Kleber organ tablature).

LöpelmannL

Löpelmann, Martin, ed. Die Liederhandschrift des Cardinals de Rohan. Göttingen: Gesellschaft für romanische Literatur, 1923. 428 pp. Edition of fifteenth-century French poems in Berlin, Kupferstichkabinett, MS 78.B.17.

LowinskyC

Lowinsky, Edward E. "Canon Technique and Simultaneous Conception in Fifteenth-century Music." Essays on the Music of J.S. Bach and Other Diverse Subjects. A Tribute to Gerhard Herz, pp. 181-222. Ed. R.L. Weaver. Louisville: University of Louisville, 1981. 334 pp. ML55.H46. Discusses Ockeghem's Missa Prolationum among other examples.

LowinskyM

Lowinsky, Edward E. "Music in the Culture of the Renaissance." Journal of the History of Ideas, 15 (1954): 509-53. Reprinted in P.O. Kristeller and P.P. Wiener, eds., Renaissance Essays, pp. 337-81. Harper Torchbooks. New York: Harper & Row, 1968. A classic essay on the place of music in Renaissance thought.

LowinskyMB

Lowinsky, Edward E. "A Music Book for Anne Boleyn." Florilegium historiale: Essays Presented to Wallace K. Ferguson, pp. 160-235. Ed. J.G. Rowe and W.H. Stockdale. Toronto: University of Toronto Press, 1971.

Study of Cambridge MS 1070.   See also
LowinskyRC.

LowinskyMC   Lowinsky, Edward E.   **The Medici Codex of 1518.**
Historical Introduction and Commentary,
Transcription, and **Facsimile.**   Monuments of
Renaissance Music, 3-5.   3 vols.   Chicago:
University of Chicago Press, 1968.   245,
405, 309 pp.   M2.M489 v.3-5.   ISBN 0-226-
49480-2; -49481-0; -49482-9.
A study of Florence, Bibl. Med.-Laur., MS
Acq. e doni 666.   Although it contains no
works of Ockeghem or Obrecht, it does
include a unique version of Josquin's
Déploration on the death of Ockeghem.   The
Commentary volume is a wide-ranging
discussion of motet styles and composers
around 1500 and includes a list of sources,
notes on some little-known manuscripts, and
a comprehensive index.

LowinskyO   Lowinsky, Edward E.   "Ockeghem's Canon for
Thirty-six Voices: An Essay in Musical
Iconography."   PlamenacFS 155-80.
Discussion of the "Deo gratia(s)" ascribed
to Ockeghem.

LowinskyRC   Lowinsky, Edward E.   "MS 1070 of the Royal
College of Music in London."   PRMA 96 (1969-
70): 1-28.
Brief discussion of the MS treated at length
in LowinskyMB.

LowinskyS   Lowinsky, Edward E.   "'Secret Chromatic Art'
Re-examined."   **Perspectives in Musicology,**
pp. 91-123.   Ed. Barry S. Brook, Edward O.D.
Downes, and Sherman Van Solkema.   New York:
W.W. Norton, 1972.   ML55.B77.   ISBN 0-393-
02142-4.
A revue by Lowinsky of his theories of
chromaticism and modulation in sixteenth-
century music.   A long footnote discusses
the interpretation of a passage from
Obrecht's Missa Libenter gloriabor in
CrevelV (p. 119).   See also BentD.

LR   **Liber responsorialis pro festis I. classis.**
Ed. by the Benedictines of Solesmes.

Solesmes, 1895.
Selected Gregorian chants in modern square
notation, based on the earliest sources.

LU   The Liber Usualis, with Introduction and
            Rubrics in English. Ed. by the Benedictines
            of Solesmes. Tournai: Desclée, 1953 (also
            later eds., with slightly different contents
            and pagination). 1921 pp.
            Standard modern edition of Gregorian chants
            for Sundays and feast-days, in square
            notation. Indexes of chants and feasts.

MaasA   Maas, Hans. "A l'aventure." TVNM 23 (1973):
            92-102.
            Considers authorship of a Passion attributed
            to Obrecht, Longueval, and Alaventure.
            Found to be typical of neither Obrecht nor
            Longueval. Too little is known of
            Alaventure for certain attribution.

MaasT   Maas, Chris. "Towards a New Obrecht Edition.
            A Preliminary Worklist." TVNM 26 (1976):
            84-108.
            List of Obrecht's works and their sources,
            in preparation for ObrCW.

McMurtryB   McMurtry, William M. "The British Museum
            Manuscript Additional 35087: A Transcription
            of the French, Italian, and Latin
            Compositions with Concordance and
            Commentary." Ph.D. diss., North Texas State
            University, 1967. 229 pp. text plus 185 pp.
            music. UM 68-2781.
            Study and partial edition of a Flemish
            manuscript of the early sixteenth century.

MaierM   Maier, Jul. Jos. Die Musikalischen
            Handschriften der K. Hof- und
            Staatsbibliothek in Muenchen, 1. Die
            Handschriften bis zum Ende des XVII.
            Jahrhunderts. Munich: Palm'schen
            Hofbuchhandlung, 1879. 176 pp.
            Catalogue of musical manuscripts from the
            Bavarian court chapel at Munich, now in the
            Bayerische Staatsbibliothek.

ManiatesC   Maniates, Maria Rika. "Combinative Chansons
               in the Dijon Chansonnier." JAMS 23 (1970):
               228-81.
               Discussion of polytextual chansons in Dijon
               MS 517, including one by Ockeghem (pp. 238-
               43).

MantuaniT   Mantuani, Joseph. **Tabulae codicum
               manuscriptorum praeter graecos et orientales
               in Bibliotheca Palatina Vindobonensi
               asservatorum**, 9-10. **Codicum musicorum**.
               Vienna: Geroldi filius, 1897-99.
               Reprint, Graz, 1965. 2 vols. 420, 587 pp.
               ML136.V6H8 v.9-10.
               Catalogue of musical manuscripts in the
               Austrian National Library, Vienna.

MarixM   Marix, Jeanne, ed. **Les Musiciens de la cour
               de Bourgogne au XVe siècle, 1420-67**. Paris:
               Éditions de l'Oiseau-lyre, 1937. 240 pp.
               M2.3.F815.
               Edition of works by composers active at the
               Burgundian court at Dijon and contemporary
               with Ockeghem.

MartiniM   Martini, Johannes. **Magnificat e messe**. Ed.
               B. Disertori. AMMM 12. Milan: Fabbrica del
               duomo, 1964. 98 pp.
               Modern edition of works by Martini.
               Includes models for masses, among them
               Ockeghem's "Ma bouche rit."

MartiniS   Martini, Johannes. **Secular Pieces**. Ed.
               Edward G. Evans, Jr. Recent Researches in
               the Music of the Middle Ages and Early
               Renaissance, 1. Madison: A-R Editions,
               1975. 90 pp. M2.R283 v.1.
               Includes "Malheur me bat," also attributed
               to Ockeghem.

MarxN   Marx, Hans Joachim. "Neues zur Tabulatur-
               Handschrift St. Gallen Stiftsbibliothek,
               Cod. 530." AfMw 37 (1980): 264-91.
               Study of the Sicher organ book.

MD   **Musica disciplina**.

MeierC   Meier, Bernhard. "Caput. Bemerkungen zur
              Messe Dufays und Ockeghems." Mf 7 (1954):
              268-76.
              Concerns the modal/harmonic structures of
              two Missae Caput, the anon. English Mass
              formerly attributed to Dufay, and
              Ockeghem's Mass.

MeierH   Meier, Bernhard. "Die Harmonik im cantus
              firmus-haltigen Satz des 15. Jahrhunderts."
              AfMw 9 (1952): 27-44.
              Study of intervallic relationships in
              fifteenth-century music in relation to the
              contrapuntal theory of the period,
              especially in the work of Obrecht. One of
              the few important stylistic studies of this
              repertoire.

MeierS   Meier, Bernhard. "Studien zur Messkomposition
              Jacob Obrechts." Ph.D. diss., Freiburg/Br.,
              1952. 124 pp.
              Not seen. See MeierZ.

MeierZ   Meier, Bernhard. "Zyklische Gesamtstruktur
              und Tonalität in den Messen Jacob
              Obrechts." AfMw 10 (1953): 289-310.
              Study of the structural and stylistic
              features of Obrecht's masses. Based on
              MeierS.

MeinholzU   Meinholz, Josef. "Untersuchungen zur
              Magnificat-Komposition des 15.
              Jahrhunderts." Ph.D. diss., Cologne, 1956.
              220 pp. plus 37 pp. music.
              Includes analysis of Magnificat attributed
              to Obrecht.

MendelT   Mendel, Arthur. "Towards Objective Criteria
              for Establishing Chronology and
              Authenticity: What Help Can the Computer
              Give?" J 297-308.
              A brief but penetrating comment on the prob-
              lem of Ockeghem's style occurs on pp. 304-5.

MerrittC   Merritt, A. Tillman. "A Chanson Sequence by
              Fevin." DavisonE 91-99.
              Contains a description and inventory of
              Cambridge MS Pepys 1760.

Mf   Die Musikforschung.

MfMg   Monatshefte für Musikgeschichte.

MGG   Die Musik in Geschichte und Gegenwart.
              Allgemeine Enzyklopädie der Musik. Ed. F.
              Blume. Kassel: Bärenreiter, 1949-86. 17
              vols. ML100.M92. ISBN 3-7618-0641-8.
              One of the major music encyclopedias, with
              articles on composers, periods, musical
              forms, and many other subjects by experts.
              Volumes 15-16 contain supplementary
              articles, addenda, and corrigenda. Volume
              17 is a comprehensive index.

MillerE   Miller, Clement A. "Erasmus on Music." MQ
              52 (1966): 332-49.
              Discusses Erasmus's Naenia (lament) on the
              death of Ockeghem (pp. 341-43) and his
              reported study with Obrecht (p. 343).

MiyazakiN   Miyazaki, Haruyo. "New Light on Ockeghem's
              Missa 'Mi-mi'." EM 13 (1985): 367-75.
              Attempts to show that Ockeghem's Mass is a
              parody of his chanson "Presque transi."
              Unconvincing.

MMMA   Monumenta monodica medii aevi. 1. Hymnen (I).
              Ed. Bruno Stäblein. Kassel: Bären-
              reiter, 1956. 715 pp. M2.M48193.
              Critical edition of medieval hymn melodies.
              Indexes of text incipits, melodies, sources,
              names, and subjects.

MoerkS   Moerk, Alice Anne. "The Seville Chansonnier:
              An Edition of Sevilla 5-I-43 and Paris
              n.acq.fr. 4379 (Part I)." Ph.D. diss., West
              Virginia University, 1971. 2 vols. 179,
              412 pp. UM 72-5158.
              Study and edition of a fifteenth-century
              Italian MS containing works of Ockeghem.

MohrH   Mohr, Peter. Die Handschrift B 211-215 der
              Proske-Bibliothek zu Regensburg, mit kurzer
              Beschriebung der Handschriften B 216-219 und
              B 220-222. Schriften des Landesinstituts
              für Musikforschung, Kiel, 7. Kassel:
              Bärenreiter, 1955. 39 pp. plus 4 pp.

Notenanhang. ML93.M63.
Study and inventory of three sixteenth-
century MSS in Regensburg.

MorelotD   Morelot, Stéphen. "Notice sur un manuscrit
              de musique ancienne de la Bibliothèque de
              Dijon." **Mémoires de la Commission des
              antiquités du Département de la Côte-d'Or,**
              4 (1856): 133-60. Publ. separately as **De la
              musique au XVe siècle.**
              An early study of Dijon MS 517, an important
              source for Ockeghem's chansons.

MottaM   Motta, Emilio. "Musici alla corte degli
              Sforza." **Archivio storico lombardo,** ser.
              2, 4 (1887): 29-64, 278-340, 514-61.
              Reprint, Geneva: Minkoff, 1977.
              ML290.8.M4M7. ISBN 2-8266-0654-9.
              Archival study of musicians at the Sforza
              court in Milan. Cites a letter of 1472 from
              Galeazzo Maria Sforza to "Johannes Oken"
              (Ockeghem?) (pp. 305-6).

MPLSER 1/6   **Monumenta polyphoniae liturgicae sanctae
              ecclesiae Romanae,** ser. 1, tom. 1, fasc. 6.
              Johannes Ockeghem, **Missa super L'homme
              armé.** Ed. L. Feininger. Rome: Societas
              universalis Sanctae Ceciliae, 1948. 18 pp.
              M2.M4843.
              An edition of Ockeghem's mass in the
              original clefs and note values.

MQ   **The Musical Quarterly.**

MurrayJ   Murray, Bain. "Jacob Obrecht's Connection
              with the Church of Our Lady in Antwerp."
              RBM 11 (1957): 125-33.
              An important biographical study based on
              archival sources.

MurrayN   Murray, Bain. "New Light on Jacob Obrecht's
              Development: a Biographical Study." MQ 43
              (1957): 500-16.
              An important biographical study based on
              archival sources. This and the article
              preceding are among the most significant of
              those concerned with Obrecht's life.

NagleS   Nagle, Sister Mary Ellen. "The Structural
                Role of the Cantus Firmus in the Motets of
                Jacob Obrecht." Ph.D. diss., University of
                Michigan, 1972. 220 pp. UM 73-6889.
                A study of the 24 published motets by
                Obrecht based on a cantus firmus. Although
                weak in analysis, the study is valuable for
                identifying the source melodies and texts.

NefS   Nef, Walter Robert. **Der St. Galler Organist
                Fridolin Sicher und seine Orgeltabulatur.**
                Schweizerisches Jahrbuch für
                Musikwissenschaft, 7. Basel, 1938. 215 pp.
                ML5.S338 v.7.
                Study and inventory of St. Gall MS 530,
                including a thematic index (pp. 159-209).
                Bibliography, list of concordant sources,
                index of names.

NewtonF   Newton, Paul G. "Florence, Biblioteca del
                Conservatorio di Musica Luigi Cherubini,
                Manuscript Basevi 2439: Critical Edition and
                Commentary." Ph.D. diss., North Texas State
                University, 1968. 2 vols. 330, 275 pp. UM
                68-16,645.
                Study and edition of a Flemish manuscript of
                the early sixteenth century containing works
                of Ockeghem and Obrecht.

NG   **The New Grove Dictionary of Music and
                Musicians.** Ed. Stanley Sadie. London:
                Macmillan, 1980. 20 vols. ML100.N48. ISBN
                0-333-23111-2.
                The largest, most recent, and most important
                English-language musical encyclopedia.
                Comparable to MGG, it contains major
                articles on composers, forms, and sources by
                noted scholars, with ample bibliographies,
                musical examples, and illustrations.

NoblittC   Noblitt, Thomas. "Das Chorbuch des Nikolaus
                Leopold (München, Staatsbibliothek, Mus.
                Ms. 3154): Repertorium." AfMw 26 (1969):
                169-208.
                Study of an important fifteenth century
                German source containing major works of
                Obrecht.

NoblittCC   Noblitt, Thomas. "Chromatic Cross-Relations
             and Editorial Musica ficta in Masses of
             Obrecht." TVNM 32 (1982): 30-44.
             Editorial problems in Obrecht, by an editor
             of ObrCW.

NoblittD   Noblitt, Thomas. "Die Datierung der
             Handschrift Mus. ms. 3154 der Staatsbiblio-
             thek München." Mf 27 (1974): 36-56.
             Study of the dating of various layers of the
             MS, based on watermark evidence. See also
             NoblittC.

NoblittF   Noblitt, Thomas. "Filiation vis-à-vis Its
             Alternatives: Approaches to Textual
             Criticism." QMR 2, pp. 111-27.
             Concerns the relationships among the sources
             of Obrecht's Missa Plurimorum carminum I.

NoblittM   Noblitt, Thomas. "Manuscript Mus. 1/D/505 of
             the Sächsische Landesbibliothek Dresden."
             AfMw 30 (1973): 275-310.
             Study of a sixteenth-century German MS
             containing works of Obrecht.

NoblittO   Noblitt, Thomas. "Obrecht's 'Missa Sine
             nomine' and its Recently Discovered Model."
             MQ 68 (1982): 102-27.
             Identifies the model(s) as the popular song
             "Veci la danse Barbari" and an anon.
             polyphonic setting of the tune. Discusses
             the conflicting attribution of the Credo to
             Adam Rener and its implications for the Mass
             as a whole.

NoblittP   Noblitt, Thomas. "Problems of Transmission in
             Obrecht's 'Missa Je ne demande'." MQ 63
             (1977): 211-23.
             Study of the sources and variant versions of
             Obrecht's Mass.

NoblittR   Noblitt, Thomas. "A Reconstruction of Ms.
             Thomaskirche 51 of the Universitätsbiblio-
             thek Leipzig." TVNM 31 (1981): 16-72.
             Study of an incompletely preserved
             sixteenth-century German MS.

NoblittT   Noblitt, Thomas. "Textual Criticism of
                  Selected Works Published by Petrucci." QMR
                  1, pp. 201-44.
                  Study of Petrucci's readings of various
                  works, including some by Obrecht.

NowakB   Nowak, Leopold. "Eine Bicinienhandschrift der
                  Wiener Nationalbibliothek." ZfMw 14 (1931-
                  32): 99-102.
                  Description and brief study of Vienna MS
                  18832, containing duos from Obrecht masses.

NowotnyM   Nowotny, Rudolf. "Mensur, Cantus Firmus, Satz
                  in den Caput-Messen von Dufay, Ockeghem, und
                  Obrecht." Ph.D. diss., Munich, 1970. 3
                  vols. 124, 125, 13 pp.
                  Not seen.

NRMI   Nuova rivista musicale italiana.

ObrCW   Obrecht, Jacob. Collected Works (New Obrecht
                  Edition). Gen. ed. Chris Maas. Utrecht:
                  V.N.M., 1983- . M3.O27M3. ISBN 90-6375-
                  031-5. 17 vols. projected; 5 vols.
                  published to date.
                  1. Missa Adieu mes amours, Missa Ave Regina
                  coelorum. Ed. Barton Hudson. 1983. xxxv,
                  69 pp.
                  2. Missa Beata viscera, Missa Caput. Ed.
                  Thomas Noblitt. 1984. xxv, 85 pp.
                  3. Missa De Sancto Donatiano, Missa De
                  Sancto Martino. Ed. Barton Hudson. 1984.
                  xxxvi, 72 pp.
                  4. Missa De tous biens playne, Missa Fors
                  seulement, Missa Fortuna desperata. Ed.
                  Barton Hudson. 1986. liii, 91 pp.
                  5. Missa Grecorum, Missa Je ne demande. Ed.
                  Thomas Noblitt. 1985. xliii, 84 pp.

ObrO   Obrecht, Jacob. Opera omnia. Editio alterum.
                  Amsterdam: V.N.M., 1953-64. 4 vols. (no
                  more published). M3.O27V4.
                  1. Missae (1-5). Ed. A. Smijers. 1953-57.
                  284 pp.
                  2. Motetti (1-6). Ed. A. Smijers. 1956-58.
                  81 pp.
                  [3.] Missae, VI. Sub tuum presidium. Ed. M.
                  van Crevel. 1959. lxvii, 52 pp.

[4.] **Missae**, VII. Maria zart. Ed. M. van
Crevel. 1964. clxiv, 63 pp.

ObrW   Obrecht, Jacob. **Werken.** Ed. J. Wolf.
Amsterdam & Leipzig: V.N.M., 1908-21.
Reprint, Farnbrough: Gregg Press, 1968.   8
vols. in 7. M3.027W6.
1. **Missen (1-5).** Petrucci, **Misse Obreht,**
1503. 244 pp.
2. **Missen (6-8). Concentus harmonici.** 164
pp.
3. **Missen (9-13).** 228 pp.
4. **Missen (14-18).** 264 pp.
5. **Missen (19-23).** 184 pp.
6. **Motetten.** 200 pp.
7. **Wereldlijke Werken.** 100 pp. / 8. **Passio
Domini.** 48 pp.

OckCW   Ockeghem, Johannes. **Collected Works.** Ed.
Dragan Plamenac. American Musicological
Society, 1947- . 3 vols. projected; 2
published to date. M3.033.
1. **Masses I-VIII.** 2nd, corrected edition,
1959. 123 pp. (See OckSW for first
edition.)
2. **Masses and Mass Sections IX-XVI.** 1947.
2nd, corrected edition, 1966. 116 pp.
(3. Motets and Secular Works. Ed. D.
Plamenac and Richard Wexler, in press.)

OckSW   Ockeghem, Johannes. **Sämtliche Werke.** 1.
Messen I-VIII. Ed. Dragan Plamenac.
Publikationen älterer Musik, Jg. I^2.
Leipzig: Breitkopf & Härtel, 1927.
Reprint, Hildesheim: Georg Olms, 1968.   125
pp. M2.P961 v.1, pt.2. (See OckCW)

OrfM   Orf, Wolfgang. **Die Musikhandschriften
Thomaskirche Mss. 49/50 und 51 in der
Universitätsbibliothek Leipzig.**
Wilhelmshaven: VEB Deutscher Verlag für
Musik, 1977. 175 pp. ML136.L4U56. ISBN 3-
7959-0243-6.
Description and inventory of Leipzig MSS
49/50 and 51. Thematic index, indexes of
text incipits and names.

Ornitho-   Ornithoparcus/Dowland. **A Compendium of**
parcusC   **Musical Practice.** With a new Introduction,
                List of Variant Readings and Table of
                Citations of Theorists by Gustave Reese and
                Steven Ledbetter. New York: Dover
                Publications, 1973. 212 pp. MT6.07. ISBN
                0-486-20912-1.
                Facsimile editions of Andreas Ornithoparcus,
                Musici active micrologus (1517), and the
                English translation by John Dowland (1609).

PaliscaN   Palisca, Claude V., ed. **Norton Anthology of**
                Western Music, 1. New York: W.W. Norton,
                1980. 644 pp. M1.N825. ISBN 0-393-95143-
                X.
                Anthology of Medieval, Renaissance, and
                Baroque music for college students.
                Contains examples by Ockeghem and Obrecht.

PannellaC   Pannella, Liliana. "Le Composizioni profane
                di una raccolta fiorentina del cinquecento."
                Rivista italiana di musicologia, 3 (1968):
                3-47.
                Study and inventory of Florence MS 164-67.

PAPTM   **Publikationen alterer praktischer und**
                theoretischer Musik-Werke. Berlin:
                Gesellschaft für Musikforschung, 1873-
                1905. 29 vols.
                I-III. J. Ott. **Ein Hundert Fünfzehn**
                weltliche und einige geistliche Lieder. Ed.
                R. Eitner et al. 3 vols. Berlin: 1873-75.
                Reprint, New York: Broude Bros., 1966. 361
                pp. M2.G39.
                Modern edition of 1544[20].

ParrishM   Parrish, Carl, and John F. Ohl, eds.
                Masterpieces of Music before 1750. New
                York: W.W. Norton, 1951. 235 pp. M2.P25M3.
                ISBN 0-393-09739-0.
                Standard historical anthology. Includes
                works by Ockeghem and Obrecht.

PeaseB-MGG   Pease, Edward J. "Bologna, Civico Museo,
                Codex Q16." MGG 15 (Suppl.): 909-11.
                Describes a fifteenth-century chansonnier;
                see also PeaseR.

PeaseE | Pease, Edward J. "An Edition of the Pixérécourt Manuscript." Ph.D. diss., Indiana University, 1960. 2 vols. 127, 600 pp. UM 60-2831. Study and transcription of the fifteenth-century Italian MS Paris, Bibl. nat., fr. 15123.

PeaseR | Pease, Edward J. "A Report on Codex Q16 of the Civico Museo Bibliografico Musicale." MD 22 (1968): 231-34. Description and inventory of the MS. See also PeaseB-MGG.

PedrellC | Pedrell, Felipe. Catàlech de la Biblioteca musical de la Diputació de Barcelona. Barcelona: Palau de la Diputació, 1908-9. 2 vols. Catalogue of music and musical literature in the Central Library of the Province of Barcelona, with facsimiles, examples, and index.

PerkinsL | Perkins, Leeman L. "The L'Homme Armé Masses of Busnoys and Okeghem: A Comparison." JM 3 (1984): 363-96. An important study of Ockeghem's Mass and its models.

PerkinsM | Perkins, Leeman L. "Musical Patronage at the Royal Court of France under Charles VIII and Louis XI (1472-83)." JAMS 37 (1984): 507-66. Includes biographical information about Ockeghem based on archival sources, with transcriptions of original documents.

PerkinsMC | Perkins, Leeman L., and Howard Garey, eds. The Mellon Chansonnier. 1. The Edition. 2. Commentary. New Haven: Yale University Press, 1977. 2 vols. 204, 452 pp. M1495.M513M4. ISBN 0-300-01416-3. An exemplary study and modern edition of a fifteenth-century chansonnier at Yale that is an important source of Ockeghem's chansons. Includes a complete facsimile of the MS in volume 1. Detailed description of

concordant sources and variants, extensive
bibliography, and comprehensive index.

PerkinsM-NG   Perkins, Leeman L.   "Motet. II. Renaissance."
                NG 12: 628-37.
                Useful survey of the period.

PerkinsO-NG   Perkins, Leeman L.   "Ockeghem, Johannes."   NG
                13: 489-96.
                A fundamental survey of the life and works,
                with work-list and bibliography.

PickerC   Picker, Martin, ed.   **The Chanson Albums of
                Marguerite of Austria: MSS 228 and 11239 of
                the Bibliothèque Royale de Belgique,
                Brussels.**   Berkeley: University of
                California Press, 1965.   505 pp.   M2.P55.
                ISBN 0-520-01009-4.
                Study and edition of two early sixteenth-
                century chansonniers.   Index of composers.
                See also PickerCA.

PickerCA   Picker, Martin.   "The Chanson Albums of
                Marguerite of Austria."   **Annales
                musicologiques,** 6 (1958-63): 145-285.
                Study of Brussels MSS 228 and 11239.
                Contains information not contained in
                PickerC.

PickerD   Picker, Martin.   Review: "Dijon,
                Bibliothèque publique, Manuscrit 517.
                Facsimile edition."   JAMS 26 (1973): 336-40.
                Review of PlamenacD.   Contains inventory of
                MS.

PickerF   Picker, Martin, ed.   **Fors seulement: Thirty
                Compositions for Three to Five Voices or
                Instruments from the Fifteenth and Sixteenth
                Centuries.**   Recent Researches in the Music
                of the Middle Ages and Early Renaissance,
                14.   Madison: A-R Editions, 1981.   104 pp.
                M2.R2383.   ISBN 0-89579-135-6.
                Edition of Ockeghem's original rondeau and
                29 compositions based on it or on on one of
                its derivatives, including one each by
                Ockeghem and Obrecht.

PickerM   Picker, Martin. "The Motet Anthologies of
               Andrea Antico." **A Musical Offering: Essays
               in Honor of Martin Bernstein**, ed. E. H.
               Clinkscale and C. Brook, pp. 211-37. New
               York: Pendragon Press, 1977. ML55.B384.
               ISBN 0-918728-03-7.
               Bibliographical study of four books of
               motets published by Antico in 1520-21.

PickerMB   Picker, Martin, ed. with commentary. **The
               Motet Books of Andrea Antico.** Monuments of
               Renaissance Music, 8. Chicago: University
               of Chicago Press, 1987. M2.M489 v.8. ISBN
               0-225-66796-0.
               Modern edition of motets from four books
               published by Antico in 1520-21, with
               bibliographical notes and commentary.

PickerMR   Picker, Martin. "More 'Regret' Chansons for
               Marguerite d'Autriche." **Le moyen français**,
               5 (1980): 81-101.
               Includes discussion and transcription of an
               anon. "Tous les regretz," suggesting that it
               may be by Ockeghem.

PickerN   Picker, Martin. "A New Look at the 'Little'
               Chansonnier of Margaret of Austria." **Muziek
               aan het hof van Margaretha van Oostenrijk.
               Jaarboek van het Vlaamse Centrum voor Oude
               Muziek**, 3 (1987): 27-31. ISBN 90-6853-031-3.
               Revises views stated in PickerC and PickerCA
               regarding origins of Brussels MS 11239.

PickerS   Picker, Martin. "A 'Salve Regina' of
               Uncertain Authorship." QMR 2: 177-79.
               Concerns the "Salve Regina" (II) doubtfully
               attributed to Ockeghem but probably by
               Basiron.

PirroH   Pirro, André. **Histoire de la musique de la
               fin du XIVe siècle à la fin du XVIe.** Paris:
               Librarie Renouard, 1940. 371 pp.
               ML172.P56H5.
               Standard historical survey. Includes
               important biographical data and observations
               on the music of Ockeghem and Obrecht.
               Musical examples. Index of names.

PirroO   Pirro, Andrè. "Obrecht à Cambrai." TVNM
                  12 (1928): 78-80.
                  Contains valuable archival data for
                  Obrecht's biography.

PirrottaM   Pirrotta, Nino. "Music and Cultural
                  Tendencies in Fifteenth-Century Italy."
                  **Music and Culture in Italy from the Middle
                  Ages to the Baroque**, pp. 80-112. Cambridge,
                  Mass.: Harvard University Press, 1984. 485
                  pp. ML290.1.P57. ISBN 0-674-59108-9.
                  Reprint of an article originally published
                  in JAMS 19 (1966): 127-61.
                  Discusses contemporary criticism of
                  Renaissance composers, including Obrecht, by
                  Paolo Cortese (1510). Reprinted as chapter
                  7 in this edition of Pirrotta's collected
                  essays.

PiscaerJ   Piscaer, Anny. "Jacob Obrecht, geboortendatum
                  en andere bijzonderheeden." **Mens en
                  melodie**, 7 (1952): 329-33.
                  Speculates on the birthdate and family of
                  Obrecht.

PlamenacA   Plamenac, Dragan. "Autour d'Ockeghem." **Revue
                  musicale**, 9/4 (1928): 26-47.
                  Primarily concerns the thirty-six voice
                  canon attributed to Ockeghem. A major early
                  study by a leading Ockeghem scholar.

PlamenacD   Plamenac, Dragan. Introduction to fac. ed. of
                  Dijon, Bibliothèque publique, manuscrit 517.
                  Publications of Mediaeval Musical
                  Manuscripts, 12. Brooklyn: Institute of
                  Mediaeval Music, 1971. M2.P95 no. 12. ISBN
                  912024-12-7.
                  Excellent facsimile edition of a central
                  source of Ockeghem's chansons. See review
                  and index in PickerD.

PlamenacF   Plamenac, Dragan. Introduction to **Facsimile
                  Reproduction of the Manuscripts Sevilla 5-I-
                  43 and Paris n.a.fr. 4379 (Pt. 1).**
                  Publications of Mediaeval Musical
                  Manuscripts, 8. Brooklyn: Institute of
                  Mediaeval Music, 1962. M2.P95 no. 8. ISBN
                  0-912024-08-9.

Facsimile edition of the Seville
chansonnier. See PlamenacRF.

PlamenacFS   **Essays on Musicology in Honor of Dragan
              Plamenac on His 70th Birthday.** Ed. Gustave
              Reese and Robert J. Snow. Pittsburgh:
              University of Pittsburgh Press, 1969.
              Reprint, New York: Da Capo, 1977. 391 pp.
              ML3797.1.R44. ISBN 8229-1098-5; 0-306-
              77408-9.
              Essays honoring a leading Ockeghem scholar.
              Many deal with Ockeghem, including HewittF,
              LesureO, and LowinskyO. Concludes with a
              bibliography of "The Publications of
              Dragan Plamenac" by Thor Wood, pp. 385-91.

PlamenacJ   Plamenac, Dragan. "Johannes Ockeghem als
              Motetten- und Chansonkomponist." Ph.D.
              diss., University of Vienna, 1925.
              Unpublished and very rare, but the
              foundation of most modern Ockeghem
              scholarship and still the basic study of his
              motets and chansons.

PlamenacO-MGG Plamenac, Dragan. "Ockeghem, Johannes." MGG
              9: 1825-38. Additions and corrections in
              MGG 16: 1419-20.
              A basic survey of the life and works, with
              work-list and bibliography. Illustrated.

PlamenacO-R   Plamenac, Dragan. "Ockeghem." **Riemann Musik
              Lexikon**, 12th ed. Ed. W. Gurlitt. Mainz:
              B. Schotts Söhne, 1959-61. **Personenteil**,
              2: 335-36. ML100.R52.
              More succinct than the preceding, it also
              represents a somewhat revised view of the
              life and works, including the probable year
              of Ockeghem's birth.

PlamenacP   Plamenac, Dragan. "A Postscript to Volume II
              of the **Collected Works** of Johannes
              Ockeghem." JAMS 3 (1950): 33-40.
              Contains supplementary information relating
              to the first edition of OckCW II. This is
              incorporated into the second edition, but is
              presented here in somewhat greater detail.

PlamenacPS   Plamenac, Dragan. "A Postscript to 'The
                Second Chansonnier of the Biblioteca
                Riccardiana'." **Annales musicologiques**, 4
                (1956): 261-65.
                Supplements and corrects PlamenacS.

PlamenacR   Plamenac, Dragan. "On Reading Fifteenth-
                Century Chanson Texts." JAMS 30 (1977):
                320-24.
                Concerns texts to two chansons by Ockeghem,
                "Se vostre cuer eslongue" and "Ung aultre
                l'a."

PlamenacRF   Plamenac, Dragan. "A Reconstruction of the
                French Chansonnier in the Biblioteca
                Colombina, Seville." MQ 37 (1951): 501-42;
                38 (1952): 85-117, 245-77.
                Study of Seville MS 5-I-43/Paris n.a.fr.
                4379, pt. 1. See also PlamenacF.

PlamenacS   Plamenac, Dragan. "The 'Second' Chansonnier
                of the Biblioteca Riccardiana (Codex 2356)."
                Annales musicologiques, 2 (1954): 105-87.
                Study of a fifteenth century MS in Florence.
                See also PlamenacPS.

PlamenacZ   Plamenac, Dragan. "Zur 'L'homme-armé'-
                Frage." ZfMw 11 (1928/9): 376-83.
                Responding to an article by Otto Gombosi,
                this discusses the 'L'homme armé' tune and
                its use as a cantus firmus in Masses by
                Ockeghem and others, as well as its
                relationship to Ockeghem's chanson "L'autre
                d'antan."

PlanchartF   Planchart, Alejandro. "Fifteenth-century
                Masses: Notes on Performance and Chronolo-
                gy." **Studi musicali**, 10 (1981): 3-29.
                Discusses aspects of Ockeghem's Missa
                L'homme armé (pp. 9-13) and Obrecht's
                Missa Caput (pp. 13-17).

PlanchartG   Planchart, Alejandro. "Guillaume Dufay's
                Masses: Notes and Revisions." MQ 58 (1972):
                1-23.
                Discusses the relationship of the Caput
                Masses by Ockeghem and Obrecht to the Missa
                Caput attributed to Dufay. Here it is

suggested that the latter is actually an
English work, a view largely accepted today.

PlanchartM   Planchart, Alejandro., ed. **Missae Caput.**
Collegium Musicum, 5. New Haven: Dept. of
Music, Yale University, 1964. 182 pp.
M2.C6436 no. 5.
Good modern edition of the Caput Masses by
Dufay(?), Ockeghem, and Obrecht.

PlanchartP   Planchart, Alejandro. "Parts with Words and
without Words: The Evidence for Multiple
Texts in Fifteenth-century Masses."
BoormanS, pp. 227-51. Discusses Ockeghem's
Missa Ecce ancilla (pp. 250-51).

PlanchartR   Planchart, Alejandro. "The Relative Speed of
'Tempora' in the Period of Dufay." Royal
Musical Association, **Research Chronicle**, 17
(1981): 33-51.
Discusses mensural relationships in the
music of Ockeghem and Obrecht, as well as
Dufay, and the possible influence of
Ockeghem on Dufay.

PopeM   Pope, Isabel, and Masakata Kanazawa, eds. **The
Musical Manuscript Montecassino 871.** Oxford
University Press, 1978. 676 pp. M2.B14.
ISBN 0-19-816132-8.
Modern edition and study of a fifteenth-
century Neapolitan MS containing works by
Ockeghem and others.

PopeME   Pope, Isabel. "La Musique espagnole à la
cour de Naples dans la seconde moitié du
XVe siecle." **Musique et poésie au XVIe
siècle**, pp. 35-61. Paris: CNRS, 1954. 384
pp. ML3849.F73.
Discusses Ockeghem's arrangement of
Cornago's "Qu'es mi vida."

PrestonS   Preston, Alan H. "Sacred Polyphony in
Renaissance Verona." Ph.D. diss.,
University of Illinois, 1969. 376 pp. UM
70-954.
Study of choirbooks in Verona, principally
MSS 755-56, 758-61.

PRMA   **Proceedings of the Royal Musical Association.**

Prod'hommeI   Prod'homme, J.G. "Les Institutions musicales
                  (bibliothèques et archives) en Belgique et
                  en Hollande." **Sammelbände der Internation-
                  alen Musikgesellschaft,** 15 (1913-14): 458-
                  503.
                  Includes a description of Louvain MS 163,
                  destroyed in 1914 (pp. 486-87).

QMR   **Quellenstudien zur Musik der Renaissance,** ed.
1   Ludwig Finscher. 1. **Formen und Probleme der
                  Überlieferung mehrstimmiger Musik im
                  Zeitalter Josquins Desprez.** Wolfenbütteler
                  Forschungen, 6. Munich: Kraus, 1981. 281
                  pp. ML172.M9 1976. ISBN 3-601-00405-4.
2   2. **Datierung und Filiation von Musik-
                  handschriften der Josquin-Zeit.**
                  Wolfenbütteler Forschungen, 26.
                  Wiesbaden: Otto Harrassowitz, 1983. 269 pp.
                  ML172.D35. ISBN 3-447-02420-8.
                  Papers presented at symposia held in
                  Wolfenbüttel in 1976 (Forms and Problems
                  of Transmission of Polyphonic Music in the
                  Age of Josquin) and 1980 (Dating and
                  Filiation of Music Manuscripts of the
                  Josquin Period), including NoblittF,
                  NoblittT, PickerS, RothZ, StrohmQ. Many
                  examples and illustrations.

RahnO   Rahn, Jay. "Ockeghem's Three-Section Motet
                  'Salve Regina': Problems in Coordinating
                  Pitch and Time Constructs." **Music Theory
                  Spectrum,** 3 (1981): 117-31.
                  Analysis of the opening phrases of
                  Ockeghem's Salve Regina (I). Attempts to
                  explain the unique qualities of Ockeghem's
                  rhythmic style.

RBM   **Revue belge de musicologie.**

ReeseF   Reese, Gustave. **Fourscore Classics of Music
                  Literature.** New York: Liberal Arts Press,
                  1957. Reprint, New York: Da Capo, 1970. 91
                  pp. ML160.R33. ISBN 0-306-71620-8.
                  Describes eighty significant writings on
                  music from antiquity to the twentieth
                  century, among them treatises by Tinctoris

and Heyden, with selective bibliographies.
Indexes of authors and titles.

ReeseM   Reese, Gustave. "Musical Compositions in
                Renaissance Intarsia." **Medieval and**
                Renaissance Studies, 2: 74-97. Ed. John L.
                Lievsay. Durham, North Carolina: Duke
                University Press, 1968.
                Discusses Ockeghem's canon "Prenez sur moi"
                in an intarsia panel in the studio of
                Isabella d'Este at the Ducal Palace in
                Mantua. With illustrations and musical
                transcriptions.

ReeseMR   Reese, Gustave. **Music in the Renaissance.**
                New York: W.W. Norton, 1954. Revised ed.
                1959. 1022 pp. ML172.R42 1959. ISBN 0-
                393-09530-4.
                Classic survey of the period, containing
                more information than is usual in such
                works. Chapter 3 discusses Ockeghem (pp.
                118-36), and Chapter 5 discusses Obrecht
                (pp. 186-205). Extensive bibliography and
                general index. See review in JeppesenM.

ReeserD   Reeser, Eduard, ed. **Drie oud-nederlandse**
                motetten. Vereniging voor nederlandse
                muziekgeschiedenis, 44. Amsterdam: G.
                Alsbach, 1958. 32 pp.
                Includes modern edition of Obrecht's "Haec
                Deum coeli" (pp. 5-9).

RichterK   Richter, Julius. **Katalog der Musik-Sammlung**
                auf der Universitäts-Bibliothek in Basel.
                Beilage zu den MfMg 23-24 (1892). Leipzig:
                Breitkopf & Härtel. 105 pp.
                Catalog of music prints and MSS in the
                University Library at Basel. General
                index.

RiemannM   Riemann, Hugo. "Der Mensural-Codex des
                Magister Nikolaus Apel von Königshofen
                (Codex MS 1494 der Leipziger-Universitäts-
                bibliothek)." KJ 12 (1897): 1-23.
                Study of the Apel Codex (ca. 1500),
                containing works of Obrecht.

RifkinP   Rifkin, Joshua. "Pietrequin Bonnel and Ms.
               2794 of the Biblioteca Riccardiana." JAMS
               29 (1976): 284-96.
               Concerns an important fifteenth-century
               chansonnier in Florence containing works by
               Ockeghem.

RingmannG   Ringmann, Heribert. "Das Glogauer Liederbuch
               (um 1480)." ZfMw 15 (1932-33): 49-60.
               Describes Berlin MS 40098.

RISM   **Repertoire international des sources musicales**
               (International Inventory of Musical
               Sources).
A/I/6   A/I/6. **Einzeldrucke vor 1800**, 6.
               Montalbano-Pleyel. Ed. K. Schlage. Kassel:
               Bärenreiter, 1976. 670 pp. ML 113.I6
               v.AI6. ISBN 3-7618-0551-9.
               Bibliography of early printed music,
               arranged alphabetically by composer.
               Includes locations of copies. This volume
               contains Obrecht.
B/I   [B/I] **Recueil imprimés XVIe-XVIIe siècles,**
               1. **Liste chronologique.** Ed. F. Lesure.
               Munich-Duisburg: G. Henle, 1960. 639 pp.
               ML113.I6 v.BI.
               Bibliography of printed collections of music
               from the sixteenth and seventeenth centuries
               with basic descriptions and locations of
               copies. Indexes of publishers' and
               printers' names, titles and composers. A
               fundamental bibliographical reference tool.
B/IV/3   B/IV/3. **Handschriften mit mehrstimmiger
               Musik des 14., 15. und 16. Jahrhunderts, 1.
               Austria bis France.** Ed. K. von Fischer.
               Munich-Duisburg: G. Henle, 1972. 592 pp.
               ML113.I6 v.BIV3. ISBN 3-87328-007-8.
               Thematic catalog of MSS containing polyphony
               from the fourteenth to the sixteenth
               centuries. The first of two volumes
               alphabetically arranged by country. Index
               of text incipits and composers in volume 2.
B/VII   B/VII. Wolfgang Boetticher.
               **Handschriftlich überlieferte Lauten- und
               Gitarren-tabulaturen des 15. bis 18.
               Jahrhunderts.** Munich: G. Henle, 1978. 374
               pp. plus 12 pp. Suppl. ML113.I6 v.BVII.
               ISBN 3-87328-012-4.

Catalog of MS lute and guitar tablatures
from the fifteenth to the eighteenth
centuries arranged alphabetically by city.
Indexes by types of tablature and names (in
Supplement).

RMF   Renaissance Music in Facsimile. Gen. eds.
             Howard M. Brown, Frank A. D'Accone, and
             Jessie Ann Owens. New York: Garland, 1986-.
             29 vols. projected. M2.R248. ISBN 0-8240-
             1450 (-78).
2   (2. Cambridge, Magdalen College, Pepys
             1760.)
5   5. Florence, Biblioteca nazionale centrale,
             MSS Magl. XIX.164-167. Intro. by Howard M.
             Brown. 1987. 4 vols.
6   6. Glogauer Liederbuch. Kraków, Biblioteca
             Jagiellónska. Intro. by Jessie Ann Owens.
             1986. 3 vols.
10   10. London, British Library, Royal
             20.A.XVI. Intro. by Howard M. Brown. 1987.
12b   12b. Milan, Archivio della Veneranda
             fabbrica del duomo, Sezione musicale,
             Librone 2 (olim 2268). Intro. by Howard M.
             Brown. 1987.
17   17. Siena, Biblioteca comunale degli
             intronati, MS K.1.2. Intro. by Frank A.
             D'Accone. 1986.
18   18. Turin, Biblioteca nazionale
             universitaria, MS Ris. mus. I.27. Intro.
             by Frank A. D'Accone. 1986.
19   19. Uppsala, Universitetsbiblioteket,
             Vokalmusik i Handskrift 76a. Intro. by
             Howard M. Brown. 1987.
21   21. Vatican, Biblioteca apostolica vaticana,
             Cappella Sistina MS 46. Intro. by Jeffrey
             J. Dean. 1986.
22   (22. Vatican, Biblioteca apostolica
             vaticana, MS Chigiana C VIII 234.)
24   24. Verona, Biblioteca capitolare, MS
             DCCLVII. Intro. by Howard M. Brown. 1987.
26   26. Trium vocum cantiones centum . . . 1541.
             Intro. by Howard M. Brown. 1986. 3 vols.
             A new series of facsimile editions of
             manuscript and printed musical sources of
             the fifteenth and sixteenth centuries, with
             introductory essays.

RobertsonR   Robertson, Alec. **Requiem, Music of Mourning
                  and Consolation.** New York: Frederick A.
                  Praeger, 1968. 300 pp. ML3088.R62.
                  A survey of Requiem masses and similar
                  works. Includes a description of Ockeghem's
                  Requiem (pp. 29-36).

RoedigerG   Roediger, Karl Erich. **Die geistlichen
                  Musikhandschriften der Universitäts-
                  Bibliothek Jena.** Jena: Frommannsche
                  Buchhandlung, 1935. 2 vols.
N   **Notenverzeichnis.** 139 pp.
T   **Textband.** 107 pp.
                  Thematic catalog and study of a large
                  collection of sixteenth-century MSS from the
                  library of Frederick the Wise, Elector of
                  Saxony.

RoksethT   Rokseth, Yvonne, ed. **Treize motets et un
                  prelude pour orgue parus en 1531 chez Pierre
                  Attaingnant.** Paris: E. Droz, 1930. 61 pp.
                  Modern ed. of organ tablature 1531^5, with
                  transcriptions of the vocal models.
                  Includes Obrecht's "Parce Domine."

RossM   Ross, Ronald David. "The Motets of Jacob
                  Obrecht: A Stylistic Analysis." Ph.D.
                  diss., University of Cincinnati, 1973. 2
                  vols. 210, 264 pp.
                  Not seen.

RothA   Roth, Adalbert. "Anmerkungen zur Benefizial-
                  karriere des Johannes Ockeghem." (Projected
                  to appear in a Festschrift volume for Helmut
                  Hucke in 1988.)
                  A survey of papal benefices awarded to
                  Ockeghem at the request of King Louis XI of
                  France between 1463 and 1476, based on
                  documents in the Vatican archives. Includes
                  a previously unknown 1472 reference to
                  Ockeghem as a priest.

RothZ   Roth, Adalbert. "Zur Datierung der frühen
                  Chorbücher der päpstlichen Kapelle."
                  QMR 2, pp. 239-68.
                  Contains information on the date and
                  provenance of Rome, Vatican MSS Capp. Sist.
                  14, 35, and 51.

RubsamenF   Rubsamen, Walter H. "From Frottola to
                 Madrigal." HaarC, pp. 51-87.
                 Includes discussion of Obrecht's "La
                 tortorella."

RussellM   Russell, Eleanor. "The Missa In agendis
                 mortuorum of Juan Garcia de Basurto:
                 Johannes Ockeghem, Antoine Brumel, and an
                 Early Spanish Polyphonic Requiem Mass."
                 TVNM 29 (1979): 1-37.
                 Concerns a MS in Tarazona containing a
                 Requiem by Basurto that incorporates a
                 section of Ockeghem's Requiem Mass.

SaarL   Saar, Johannes du. **Het leven en de
                 composities van Jacobus Barbireau.** Utrecht:
                 W. de Hann, 1946. 210 pp. ML410.B24S2.
                 Compares Ockeghem's Missa Au travail suis to
                 its chanson model (pp. 137-43).

SalopE   Salop, Arnold. "The Early Development of
                 Harmonic Polyphony." Chapter 3 of **Studies
                 on the History of Musical Style**, pp. 81-102.
                 Detroit: Wayne State University Press, 1971.
                 ML430.5S24. ISBN 0-8143-1449-X.
                 Concerns the development of harmonic style
                 in fifteenth-century masses, principally
                 those of Ockeghem and Obrecht.

SalopJ   Salop, Arnold. "Jacob Obrecht and the Early
                 Development of Harmonic Polyphony." JAMS
                 17 (1964): 288-309.
                 A study of tonality in Obrecht's masses.
                 The analysis, using modern harmonic concepts
                 and terminology, is anachronistic but
                 musically perceptive.

SalopM   Salop, Arnold. "The Masses of Jacob Obrecht
                 (1450-1505): Structure and Style." Ph.D.
                 diss., Indiana University, 1959. 2 vols.
                 274, 324 pp., musical exx. UM 59-4034.
                 A study based on the twenty-two masses
                 published in ObrW and ObrO. Organized
                 according to the techniques employed, not by
                 individual works. There is no index.
                 Difficult to use, but thoughtful and
                 sensitive in its analyses. A summary is
                 given in SparksC 466-67, n. 2.

SantarelliQ   Santarelli, Cristina. "Quattro messe su tenor
               'Fors seulement'." NRMI 14 (1980): 333-49.
               Study of four masses based on Ockeghem's
               "Fors seulement," including those by
               Ockeghem himself and Obrecht.

SartoriB   Sartori, Claudio. **Bibliografia delle opere**
               musicali stampate da Ottaviano Petrucci.
               Florence: Leo S. Olschki, 1948. 217 pp.
               ML145.S22.
               Bibliography in chronological order of
               Petrucci's musical publications from 1501 to
               1520. Descriptions, tables of contents,
               locations of copies. Index of titles and
               bibliography. See also SartoriN.

SartoriC   Sartori, Claudio. **La Cappella musicale del**
               duomo di Milano: Catalogo delle musiche
               dell'archivio. Milan: Fabbrica del duomo,
               1957. 366 pp. ML136.M6D84.
               Catalog of MS and printed music in the
               archive of Milan Cathedral, including the
               Gafori codices, Librone 1-3 (pp. 43-53).

SartoriN   Sartori, Claudio. "Nuove conclusive aggiunte
               alla 'Bibliografia del Petrucci'."
               Collectanea historiae musicae, 1: 175-210.
               Florence: Leo S. Olschki, 1953.
               Additions and corrections to SartoriB.

SaundersD   Saunders, Suparmi E. "The Dating of Trent 93
               and Trent 90." Codici, pp. 60-83.
               Proposes dates for the copying of two Trent
               MSS, based on the watermarks. They include
               works of Ockeghem.

ScheringG   Schering, Arnold. **Geschichte der Musik in**
               Beispielen. Leipzig: Breitkopf & Härtel,
               1931. 481 pp. M2.S344.
               Standard anthology of early music. Includes
               Ockeghem's "Ut heremita solus." (The
               Obrecht motet in this volume is spurious.)

ScheringR   Schering, Arnold. "Ein Rätseltenor
               Okeghems." **Festschrift Hermann Kretzschmar**,
               pp. 132-35. Leipzig: C.F. Peters, 1918.
               ML55.K7F4.
               Study of Ockeghem's "Ut heremita solus."

Attempts to explain the puzzle-canon for
reading the tenor.

ScherliessM   Scherliess, Volker. **Musikalische Noten auf**
                   Kunstwerken der italienischen Renaissance.
                   Hamburg: K.D. Wagner, 1972. 164 pp.
                   ML85.S3. ISBN 3-921029-11-2.
                   Study and inventory of musical inscriptions
                   in Italian Renaissance art works. Discusses
                   Ockeghem's "Prenez sur moi" in the Ducal
                   Palace, Mantua (pp. 79-82; the transcription
                   is faulty.) Includes music, illustrations.

Schmidt-   Schmidt-Gorg, Joseph, ed. **History of the**
GörgH   **Mass.** English transl. by R. Kolben. AnthM
                   30 (1968). 118 pp.
                   Anthology of mass compositions, including a
                   movement from Ockeghem's Missa Prolationum.

SchuetzeI   Schuetze, George C., Jr. **An Introduction to**
                   Faugues. Musicological Studies, 2.
                   Brooklyn: Institute of Mediaeval Music,
                   1960. 94 pp. ML410.F25S38. ISBN 0-912024-
                   72-0.
                   Study of the music of Faugues, including the
                   Missa Le serviteur sometimes attributed to
                   Ockeghem.

SeayC   Seay, Virginia. "A Contribution to the
                   Problem of Mode in Medieval Music." **Hamline**
                   Studies in Musicology, 1 (1945): 47-68.
                   Includes a brief discussion of Ockeghem's
                   Missa Caput.

SevillanoC   Sevillano, J. "Catàlogo musical del
                   Archivio capitular de Tarazona." **Anuario**
                   musical, 16 (1961): 149-76.
                   Catalogue of musical MSS in Tarazona, Spain.
                   MS 5 contains the "Sicut cervus" of
                   Ockeghem's Requiem as part of a Requiem by
                   Basurto (pp. 157-58). See RussellM.

SherrP   Sherr, Richard J. "The Papal Chapel ca. 1492-
                   1513 and Its Polyphonic Sources." Ph.D.
                   diss., Princeton University, 1975. 307 pp.
                   UM 76-16,564.
                   Study of early MSS of the Sistine Chapel in
                   the Vatican Library, Rome.

ShippC   Shipp, Clifford M. "A Chansonnier of the
                  Dukes of Lorraine: The Paris Manuscript
                  fonds français 1597." Ph.D. diss., North
                  Texas State University, 1960. 580 pp. UM
                  60-6166.
                  Description and modern edition of a
                  fifteenth-century French MS.

SiegeleM   Siegele, Ulrich. **Die Musiksammlung der Stadt
                  Heilbronn.** Heilbronn: Stadtarchiv, 1967.
                  323 pp.
                  Catalog of the music in the Heilbronn City
                  Archive. Indexes of text incipits, titles,
                  names, and subjects. Illustrations.

SindonaE   Sindona, Enio. "É Hubert Naich e non Jacob
                  Hobrecht il compagno cantore del Verdelot
                  nel quadro della Galleria Pitti." AM 29
                  (1957): 1-9.
                  Corrects Einstein's mistaken identification
                  of a portrait in Florence as that of Obrecht
                  (see EinsteinI 1: 155-56).

SmijersM   Smijers, Albert. "De Missa Carminum van Jacob
                  Obrecht." TVNM 17 (1951): 192-94.
                  Concerns Missa Plurimorum Carminum (I) and
                  notes spurious movements included in ObrW.

SmijersMQ   Smijers, Albert. "Het Motet 'Mille
                  quingentis' van Jacob Obrecht." TVNM 16
                  (1942): 212-15.
                  Discusses the biographical information
                  contained in the text of the motet. See
                  also SmijersT.

SmijersT   Smijers, Albert. "Twee onbekende motetteksten
                  van Jacob Obrecht." TVNM 16 (1941): 129-34.
                  Concerns the reading and interpretation of
                  the texts of the motets "Inter praeclarissi-
                  mas" and "Mille quingentis" by Obrecht.

SmijersVZ   Smijers, Albert. "Vijftiende en zestiende
                  eeuwsche muziekhandschriften in Italië met
                  werken van nederlandsche componisten." TVNM
                  14 (1935): 165-81.
                  Identifies works by Netherlands composers in
                  fifteenth- and sixteenth-century MSS in
                  Italy.

SmijersW   Smijers, Albert. "Werken van Jacob Obrecht,
                 uitgeven door Prof. Dr. Joh. Wolf." TVNM
                 10 (1922): 182-84.
                 Critical review of ObrW with corrections.

SmithI   Smith, William Liddell. "An Inventory of pre-
                 1600 Manuscripts, Pertaining to Music, in
                 the Bundesstaatliche Studienbibliothek
                 (Linz, Austria)." **Fontes artis musicae**,
                 27 (1980): 162-71.
                 Includes brief description of MS 529 (p.
                 166).

SouthernE   Southern, Eileen. "El Escorial, Monastery
                 Library, Ms. IV.a.24." MD 23 (1969): 41-
                 79.
                 Study and inventory of a fifteenth-century
                 Italian MS containing works attributed to
                 Ockeghem.

SparksC   Sparks, Edgar H. **Cantus Firmus in Mass and
                 Motet, 1420-1520.** Berkeley: University of
                 California Press, 1963. Reprint, New York:
                 Da Capo, 1975. 504 pp. ML174.S7. ISBN 0-
                 306-70720-9.
                 A fundamental study of the techniques of
                 using borrowed melodies in fifteenth- and
                 sixteenth-century sacred music. Chapters 6-
                 7 deal with masses and motets of Ockeghem
                 and his contemporaries, and Chapter 9 is
                 concerned with Obrecht. Musical examples.
                 Comprehensive index.

SparksO-NG   Sparks, Edgar H. "Obrecht, Jacob." NG 13:
                 477-85.
                 Survey of Obrecht's life and works, with
                 work-list and bibliography. Musical
                 examples, illustrations.

StaehelinG   Staehelin, Martin. **Der Grüne Codex der
                 Viadrina.** Mainz: Akademie der
                 Wissenschaften, 1971. 68 pp. ML184.S7.
                 Study and inventory of Wrocław MS I F 428,
                 with thematic incipits. Index of text
                 incipits.

StaehelinV   Staehelin, Martin. "Möglichkeiten und
                 praktische Anwendung der Verfasserbestimmung

an anonym überlieferten Kompositionen der
Josquin-Zeit." TVNM 23 (1973): 79-91.
New information on works by fifteenth-
century composers, including Ockeghem and
Obrecht, based on study of the sources.

StaehelinO   Staehelin, Martin. "Obrechtiana." TVNM   25
                (1975): 1-37.
                New information on the life and works of
                Obrecht. See also Staehelin, "Berichtigung
                und Ergänzung zu 'Obrechtiana'." TVNM
                26 (1976): 41-42.

StaehelinZ   Staehelin, Martin. "Zum Egenolff-Diskantband
                der Bibliothéque nationale in Paris."
                AfMw 23 (1966): 93-109.
                Concerns the printed collection [c. 1535][14].

StamJ   Stam, Edward, ed. Josquin des Prez, **Qui
                habitat**, 24 vocum; Johannes Ockeghem, **Deo
                gratias**, 36 vocum. Exempla musica
                neerlandica, 6. Amsterdam: Vereniging voor
                nederlandse muziekgeschiedenis, 1971.   28
                pp. M2092.6.D47Q8.
                Modern edition of canonic compositions
                attributed to Josquin and Ockeghem.

StephanB   Stephan, Wolfgang. **Die burgundisch-
                niederländische Motette zur Zeit Ockeghems.**
                Heidelberger Studien zur Musikwissenschaft,
                6. Kassel: Bärenreiter, 1937. Reprint
                1973. 116 pp. ML178.S81B9.
                Important study of the late fifteenth-
                century motet. Musical examples, index of
                motets.

SteudeM   Steude, Wolfram. **Die Musiksammelhandschriften
                des 16. und 17. Jahrhunderts in der
                Sächsischen Landesbibliothek zu Dresden.**
                Quellenkataloge zur Musikgeschichte, 6.
                Wilhelmshaven: Heinrichshofen, 1974.   315
                pp. ML136.D78S37. ISBN 3-7959-0109-X.
                Catalog of musical MS collections of the
                sixteenth and seventeenth centuries in
                Dresden.

StevensonS   Stevenson, Robert. **Spanish Music in the Age
                of Columbus.** The Hague: Martinus Nijhoff,

1960. Reprint 1981. 335 pp. ML315.2.S74.
ISBN 0-88355-872-6.
Survey of Spanish music ca. 1480-1530.
Compares Ockeghem's setting of "Qu'es mi
vida" to Cornago's original (pp. 218-23).
Musical examples, bibliography,
comprehensive index.

StevensonT   Stevenson, Robert. "The Toledo Manuscript
             Polyphonic Choirbooks and Some Other Lost
             or Little Known Flemish Sources." **Fontis
             artis musicae,** 20 (1973): 87-107.
             Index to thirty-four choirbooks in Toledo as
             well as Uppsala MSS 76b-f and Copenhagen
             1848, arranged alphabetically by composer.

StraetenM   Straeten, Edmond vander. **La Musique aux Pays-
             Bas avant le XIXe siècle.** 8 vols.
             Brussels, 1867-88. Reprint, with new
             introduction by Edward E. Lowinsky, New
             York: Dover, 1969. 8 vols. in 4.
             ML106.N4S8. ISBN 486-21588-1.
             Contains scattered references to Ockeghem
             and Obrecht. Important archival material,
             loosely arranged and casually discussed.
             Indexes of names in each volume.

StrohmM   Strohm, Reinhard. **Music in Late Medieval
             Bruges.** Oxford: Clarendon Press, 1985.   273
             pp. ML265.2.S77. ISBN 0-19-316327-6.
             Survey of music and musical life in Bruges
             ca. 1380-1500. Obrecht's career in Bruges
             is treated in some detail (pp. 38-41), as is
             his music (pp. 144-48). Appendix B (pp.
             192-200) is an inventory of Lucca MS 238.
             Bibliography, index, illustrations.

StrohmQ   Strohm, Reinhard. "Quellenkritische
             Untersuchungen an der Missa 'Caput'." QMR
             2, pp. 153-76.
             Deals primarily with the Mass attributed to
             Dufay and comments on its relationship to
             Ockeghem's Mass.

StrohmU   Strohm, Reinhard. "Ein Unbekanntes Chorbuch
             des 15. Jahrhunderts." Mf 21 (1968): 40-42.
             Brief description of Lucca MS 238. See also
             StrohmM.

StrunkE   Strunk, Oliver. **Essays on Music in the
               Western World.** New York: W.W. Norton, 1974.
               200 pp. ML60.S862E8. ISBN 0-393-02178-5.
               Collected essays of a distinguished scholar.
               Includes Strunk0, StrunkR.

Strunk0   Strunk, Oliver. "Origins of the 'L'homme
               armé' Mass." **Bulletin of the American
               Musicological Society,** 2 (1937): 25-26.
               Also in StrunkE, pp. 68-69.
               Briefly discusses dependence of Obrecht's
               Mass on that of Busnois.

StrunkR   Strunk, Oliver. "Relative Sonority as a
               Factor in Style-Critical Analysis." **Studi
               musicali,** 2 (1973): 145-53. Also in
               StrunkE, pp. 70-78.
               Brief statistical study of the relative
               frequency of three- and four-part textures
               in selected fifteenth-century compositions,
               including one each by Ockeghem and Obrecht.

StrunkS   Strunk, Oliver. **Source Readings in Music
               History.** New York: W.W. Norton, 1950.
               Reprint 1965, in 5 vols. 919 pp.
               ML160.S89. ISBN 0-393-09742-0.
               Historical anthology of writings on music
               from the ancient Greeks to the nineteenth
               century in English translation. Includes
               prefaces to treatises by Tinctoris referring
               to fifteenth-century composers, including
               Ockeghem (pp. 193-99), and a selection from
               Glareanus referring to Obrecht (p. 221).
               Index of names and titles.

TaruskinA   Taruskin, Richard. "Antoine Busnois and the
               'L'homme armé' Tradition." JAMS 39
               (1986): 255-93.
               A wide-ranging study of fifteenth-century
               masses and settings of 'L'homme armé'
               with special reference to Busnois.
               Throughout there are observations about the
               L'homme armé Masses of Ockeghem and
               Obrecht.

TaruskinD   Taruskin, Richard, ed. **D'ung aultre amer.**
               Ogni Sorte Editions, RS 6. Miami: Arnold
               Grayson, 1983. 39 pp. plus 3 pp. Addendum.

A modern edition of Ockeghem's chanson and sixteen compositions based on it.

TaruskinE   Taruskin, Richard, ed. **Een Vrolic wesen.** Ogni Sorte Editions, RS 2. Miami: Arnold Grayson, 1979. 50 pp. A modern edition of fourteen settings of a popular Flemish song, with an extensive introduction and discussion of sources. Includes a setting by Obrecht (No. 2).

TaruskinI   Taruskin, Richard, ed. **In mynen zin.** Ogni Sorte Editions, RS 8. Miami: Arnold Grayson, 1984. 52 pp. A modern edition of seventeen settings of a popular Flemish song and related melodies. One of the latter is Obrecht's "Weet ghij" (No. 16).

TaruskinJ   Taruskin, Richard, ed. **J'ay pris amours.** Ogni Sorte Editions, RS 5. Miami: Arnold Grayson, 1982. 69 pp. A modern edition of twenty-eight settings based on an anonymous chanson, among them one by Obrecht (No. 17).

TaruskinT   Taruskin, Richard, ed. **T'Andernaken.** Ogni Sorte Editions, RS 7. Miami: Arnold Grayson, 1981. 44 pp. A modern edition of ten settings of a popular Flemish song, including one by Obrecht (No. 2).

Tenorlied   **Das Tenorlied: Mehrstimmige Lieder in deutschen Quellen 1450-1580.** Ed. Norbert Böker-Heil, Harald Heckmann, and Ise Kindermann. Catalogus Musicus, 9-11. Kassel: Bärenreiter, 1979-86. 3 vols.: 1. **Drucke.** 2. **Handschriften.** 3. **Register.** 397, 355, 567 pp. ML113.C35 v.9-11. ISBN 3-7618-0628-0, -0671-X, -0736-8. Thematic catalogue of prints and MSS of German songs of the Renaissance. Volume 3 contains indexes of publishers, composers, text incipits, and melodic incipits.

TeramotoP   Teramoto, Mariko. **Die Psalmmotettendrucke des Johannes Petrejus in Nürnberg (gedruckt**

1538-1542). Frankfurter Beiträge zur
Musikwissenschaft, 10. Tutzing: Hans
Schneider, 1983. 448 pp. ML2902.T47. ISBN
3-7952-0390-2.
Includes a study of 1542[6]. Bibliography,
index.

ThibaultC   Thibault, Geneviéve. "Le Chansonnier
                   Nivelle de la Chausée." **Annales**
                   musicologiques, 7 (1964-1977): 11-16.
                   A brief description of Paris MS Rés. Vmc
                   57, a central source of fifteenth-century
                   chansons, then owned by Mme. Thibault.
                   Includes many works by Ockeghem.

TinctorisA   Tinctoris, Johannes. **The Art of Counterpoint**
                   (Liber de arte contrapuncti). Transl. and
                   ed. by Albert Seay. Musicological Studies
                   and Documents, 5. American Institute of
                   Musicology, 1961. 141 pp. MT55.T5813.
                   A translation of the theoretical treatise
                   TinctorisL.

TinctorisO   Tinctoris, Johannes. **Opera theoretica.** Ed.
                   by Albert Seay. Corpus scriptorum de
                   musica, 22. American Institute of
                   Musicology, 1975-78. 2 vols. in 3. 198,
                   177, 60 pp. ML170.C6 no. 22.
                   Critical edition of Latin treatises by
                   Tinctoris, one of the most important
                   theorists of the fifteenth century.
                   Includes references to contemporary
                   composers, including Ockeghem and Obrecht,
                   and musical examples from Ockeghem's works.

ToddR   Todd, R. Larry. "Retrograde, Inversion,
                   Retrograde-Inversion, and Related Techniques
                   in the Masses of Jacobus Obrecht." MQ 64
                   (1978): 50-78.
                   A study of "serial" techniques employed in
                   six masses by Obrecht.

TorchiM   Torchi, Luigi. "I Monumenti dell'antica
                   musica francese a Bologna." RMI 13 (1906):
                   451-505, 575-615. Reprinted in Torchi,
                   Studi di storia della musica, Bologna:
                   Forni, 1969.
                   Describes MSS in Bologna, including Q 18
                   (143).

TreitlerS   Treitler, Leo. "Structural and Critical
Analysis." **Musicology in the 1980s**, ed. D.
Kern Holoman and Claude V. Palisca, pp. 67-
77. New York: Da Capo, 1982.
ML3797.1.M877. ISBN 0-306-76188-2.
A paper presented during panel discussions
held at the 1981 meeting of the American
Musicological Society. Discusses the
difficulty that Ockeghem's music poses to
the analyst and historian (pp. 76-77).

TrowbridgeS   Trowbridge, Lynn M. "Style Change in the
Fifteenth-Century Chanson: A Comprehensive
Study of Compositional Detail." JM 4 (1985-
86): 146-70.
Statistical analysis of melody and
counterpoint in fifteenth-century chansons,
including those of Ockeghem (p. 153). Facs.
of "Fors seulement" in Dijon MS 517 (p.
151).

TurriniP   Turrini, Giuseppe. "Il Patrimonio musicale
della Biblioteca capitolare di Verona dal
sec. XV al XIX." **Atti dell'Accademia di
agricoltura scienze e lettere di Verona**,
ser. 6, vol. 2, anno 1950-51 (Verona, 1952),
pp. 95-176.
Brief descriptions of Verona MSS 755-761,
with alphabetical index of contents.

TVNM   **Tijdschrift van de vereniging voor nederlandse
muziekgeschiedenis.**

VellekoopP   Vellekoop, Kees. "De Parce Domino-composities
van Jacob Obrecht." **Medelingenblad V.N.M.**,
23 (1967): 44-50.
Analysis and transcription of Obrecht's
"Parce Domine," second part.

VellekoopZ   Vellekoop, Kees. "Zusammenhänge zwischen
Text und Zahl in der Kompositionsart Jacob
Obrecht. Analyse der Motette 'Parce
Domine'." TVNM 20 (1966): 97-119.
Emphasizes number-symbolism in analysis of
Obrecht's "Parce Domine."

VollhardtB   Vollhardt, Reinhard. **Bibliographie der Musik-
Werke in der Ratsschulbibliothek zu Zwickau.**

Beilage zu den MfMg 25-28 (1893-96).
Leipzig: Breitkopf & Härtel, 1896. 299 pp.
Catalog of music in Zwickau. Includes
thematic incipits of anonymous works.
Indexes of subjects and names.

VP   **Variae preces.** Ed. by the Benedictines of
              Solesmes. 5th ed. Solesmes, 1901. 281
              plus 28 pp. M2154.V3.
              Modern edition of Gregorian chants for
              various occasions in the Roman liturgy.

WagnerG   Wagner, Peter. **Geschichte der Messe,** 1. Teil.
              Bis 1600. Kleine Handbücher der
              Musikgeschichte nach Gattungen, 11.
              Leipzig: Breitkopf & Härtel, 1913. 548
              pp. ML3088.W2.
              Standard survey of early masses. Out-of-
              date but scholarly and still useful.
              Chapter 3 deals with Ockeghem (pp. 101-110)
              and Obrecht (pp. 114-40). Musical examples,
              general index.

WallnerS   Wallner, Bertha. "Sebastian Virdung von
              Amberg: Beiträge zu seiner Lebens-
              geschichte." KJ 24 (1911): 85-106.
              Includes a letter of Virdung describing
              Ockeghem's thirty-six-voice canon (p. 97).

WardA   Ward, Tom R. "Another Mass by Obrecht?" TVNM
              27 (1977): 102-8.
              Attributes Missa Je ne seray to Obrecht.

WegmanA   Wegman, Rob C. "An Anonymous Twin of Johannes
              Ockeghem's 'Missa Quinti toni' in San Pietro
              B 80." TVNM 37 (1987): 25-48.
              Compares an anonymous Missa Ave Regina
              caelorum to Ockeghem's Missa Quinti toni,
              showing that the former is modeled on the
              latter and suggesting that it too may be by
              Ockeghem.

WegmanN   Wegman, Rob C. "New Data Concerning the
              Origins and Chronology of Brussels,
              Koninklijke Bibliothek, Manuscript 5557."
              TVNM 36 (1986): 5-25.
              Associates the MS, an important Ockeghem

source, with Bruges and the Burgundian court
ca. 1468-80.

WeinmannJ   Weinmann, Karl. **Johannes Tinctoris und sein
unbekannter Traktat 'De inventione et usu
musicae'**. Regensburg, 1917. Reprint,
Tutzing: Hans Schneider, 1961. 47 pp.
ML171.T4W45.
Study and edition of the surviving chapters
of Tinctoris's treatise on the history and
performance of music. Includes remarks on
Ockeghem's voice and character (p. 33).

WeissM   Weiss, Susan Forscher. "The Manuscript
Bologna, Civico Museo Bibliografico
Musicale, Codex Q 18 (olim 143): A
Bolognese Instrumental Collection of the
Early Cinquecento." Ph.D. diss., University
of Maryland, 1985. 2 vols. 537 pp. UM 86-
04237.
Study of an important Bolognese MS of the
early sixteenth century. Volume 2 contains
transcriptions of unica.

WexlerA   Wexler, Richard. "On the Authenticity of
Ockeghem's Motets." **Abstracts of the Papers
Read at the Fiftieth Annual Meeting of the
American Musicological Society** . . . 1984,
pp. 41-42. Philadelphia: A.M.S., 1984.
General discussion of the motets attributed
to Ockeghem, of which four are deemed
authentic.

WexlerM   Wexler, Richard. "Music and Poetry in
Renaissance Cognac." **Le moyen français**, 5
(1980): 102-14.
Contains description of Paris MS fr. 1596,
containing Ockeghem's "Fors seulement
contre."

WexlerN   Wexler, Richard. "Newly Identified Works by
Bartolomeo degli Organi in the MS Bologna Q
17." JAMS 23 (1970): 107-18.
Contains description and inventory of an
important early sixteenth-century Italian
MS.

WexlerO   Wexler, Richard. "Ockeghem's Canonic Chanson:
               A Reconstruction." **Abstracts of the Papers
               Read at the Forty-fourth Annual Meeting of
               the American Musicological Society** . . .
               1978, p. 1. Philadelphia: A.M.S., 1978.
               Brief discussion of "Prenez sur moi."

WexlerW   Wexler, Richard. "Which Franco-Netherlander
               Composed the First Polyphonic Requiem Mass?"
               **Papers from the First Interdisciplinary
               Conference on Netherlandic Studies** . . .
               1982, pp. 171-76. Ed. W.H. Fletcher.
               Lanham, Maryland: American Association for
               Netherlandic Studies, 1985. PF21.I57 1982.
               ISBN 0-8191-4707-9.
               Proposes that Ockeghem's Requiem was written
               on the death of King Charles VIII of France
               in 1461.

WhislerM   Whisler, Bruce Allen. "Munich, Mus. Ms. 1516:
               A Critical Edition." Ph.D. diss.,
               University of Rochester, 1974. 2 vols.
               360, 500 pp. UM 74-21,527.
               Study and edition of a sixteenth-century MS
               containing works of Ockeghem and Obrecht.

WitteM   Witte, Martin. "Ein Missdeuteter Rhythmus in
               Ockeghems 'Requiem'." Mf 23 (1970): 431-33.
               Proposes a correction to the edition in
               OckCW II.

WolfL   Wolf, Johannes, ed. **25 driestimmige oud-
               nederlandsche liederen uit het einde der
               vijftiende eeuw naar den codex London
               British Museum Add. MSS. 35087.** Vereeniging
               voor noord-nederlands muziekgeschiedenis,
               30. Amsterdam: G. Alsbach, 1910. 35 pp.
               Modern edition of late fifteenth-century
               Flemish songs, including "T'meiskin was
               jonck" attributed to Obrecht (here ascribed
               to Isaac).

WolfS   Wolf, Johannes, ed. **Sing- und Spielmusik aus
               älterer Zeit.** Leipzig, 1931. Reprint as
               Music of Earlier Times, New York: Broude
               Bros., 1946. 158 pp. M1.W85. ISBN 0-8450-
               2576-7.

Anthology of music, thirteenth to seventeenth centuries. Includes Ockeghem's "Ma bouche rit."

WolffC   Wolff, Arthur S. "The Chansonnier Biblioteca Casanatense 2856." Ph.D. diss., North Texas State University, 1970. 2 vols. 527, 459 pp. UM 71-08,696. Study and modern edition of fifteenth-century MS in Rome.

WolffM   Wolff, Hellmuth Christian. **Die Musik der alten Niederländer.** Leipzig: Breitkopf & Härtel, 1956. 272 pp. ML265.2.W6. Standard survey of music by Netherlands composers of the fifteenth and sixteenth centuries, organized by genre. Includes overview of Ockeghem and Obrecht. Many musical examples. Bibliography, general index.

WrightD   Wright, Craig. "Dufay at Cambrai: Discoveries and Revisions." JAMS 28 (1975): 175-229. Archival study. Presents evidence of direct contact between Dufay and Ockeghem (pp. 207-8).

WrightP   Wright, Craig. "Performance Practices at the Cathedral of Cambrai 1475-1550." MQ 44 (1978): 295-328. Archival study concerning performance practices at an important northern cathedral during the Renaissance. Relevant to the performance of sacred music by Ockeghem and Obrecht.

WrightV   Wright, Craig. "Voices and Instruments in the Art Music of Northern France during the 15th Century: A Conspectus." International Musicological Society, **Report of the 12th Congress, Berkeley 1977**, pp. 643-49. Ed. D. Heartz and B. Wade. Kassel: Bären-reiter, 1981. ML26.I6 1977. ISBN 3-7618-0649-3. Study of manuscript and iconographic evidence for performance practice during the period of Ockeghem and Obrecht.

ZfMw   **Zeitschrift für Musikwissenschaft.**

ZiinoA   Ziino, Agostino. "Appunti su una nuova fonte
                di musica polifonica intorno al 1500." NRMI
                10 (1976): 437-41.
                Brief description of Siena MS K.1.2.

ZimmermannS   Zimmermann, Reiner. "Stilkritische
                Anmerkungen zum Werk Ockeghems." AfMw 22
                (1965): 248-71.
                Stylistic analysis of Ockeghem's work, based
                primarily on his masses, with special
                attention to cadential structures. Suggests
                chronology of the masses and gives detailed
                analysis of the Christe of Missa Mi-mi.

V. DISCOGRAPHY

This discography is arranged alphabetically by record label and devoted mainly to long-playing records (LP), but a few recent cassette tapes and compact discs (CD) are included. Listings are of twelve-inch LPs unless otherwise stated. For currently available recordings in all formats consult the **Schwann** record and tape catalogue (Boston: Schwann Publications), published quarterly. For new CD issues, see the **Schwann Compact Disc Catalogue** (Boston: Schwann Publications), published monthly. For recordings of early music, the following reference works are especially useful:

James B. Coover and Richard Colvig. **Medieval and Renaissance Music on Long-playing Records.** Detroit Studies in Music Bibliography, 6. Detroit: Information Service, 1964. 122 pp.

_____: **Supplement (1962-71).** Detroit Studies in Music Bibliography, 26. Detroit: Information Coordinators, 1973. 258 pp. ISBN 911772-44-8.

Trevor Croucher, compiler. **Early Music Discography from Plainsong to the Sons of Bach.** Phoenix: Oryx Press, 1981. 2 vols. 273, 302 pp. ML156.2.C76. ISBN 0-89774-018-1.

Approximate dates of recording or issue are given, based on the information contained on the record jacket, in the Schwann catalogue, in the writer's memory, or on his best judgment. Dates of reissue are also given where known. Names and numbers of American companies precede those of European companies issuing the same recording. The most recent record number is given first followed by older numbers. Some recordings based on arbitrary musical arrangements or offering

seriously flawed performances have been omitted.
Many older recordings (and some more recent ones)
do not meet the highest standards either of
authenticity or musicianship, but the writer
believes that the recordings listed below
reasonably represent the music and can be heard
with profit.

Some recent recordings of high quality that
are especially recommended are: ARCHIVE 2533 377
(Obrecht: **Motets**; Pro Cantione Antiqua, Turner),
EMI/ANGEL 38188 (Ockeghem: **Requiem** and **Missa Mi-mi**;
The Hilliard Ensemble), MUSICAL HERITAGE 4026
(Ockeghem: **Missa Prolationum**; Cappella Nova,
Taruskin), MUSICAL HERITAGE 4179 (Ockeghem: **Motets**;
Cappella Nova, Taruskin), NONESUCH 71336 (Ockeghem:
**Missa Ma maistresse, Missa Au travail suis, Motets
and Chansons**; Pomerium musices, Blachly), OISEAU-
LYRE D186 D4 (**Le Chansonnier cordiforme**; Consort of
Musicke, Rooley), OISEAU-LYRE D254 D3 (Ockeghem:
Complete Secular Music; Medieval Ensemble of
London, Davies), SERAPHIM 6104 (**The Art of the
Netherlanders**; Early Music Consort, Munrow).

Finally, no claim is made that the list is
complete, although every effort has been made to
both see and hear at least one version of the
recording in question.

ACCORD (CD)149167 (1987). Ockeghem, **Missa Prolationum;
Chansons** (Ma bouche rit, Presque transi, Prenez sur moi,
Fors seulement l'attente, Maleur me bat, L'aultre
d'antan). Clemencic Consort.
ALLEGRO 9019 (72) (ca. 1949, reissued 1964). **Music of the
Gothic Period and the Early Renaissance**, vol. 1. The
Vielle Trio.
Obrecht: 3 Three-voiced Pieces (= Salve Regina I, parts
1, 2, 7, 5, 6, performed instrumentally).
AMADEO 5030. (See Musical Heritage 713)
AMADEO 6233. (See Musical Heritage 1716)
ANTHOLOGIE SONORE 4 (ca. 1939 on 78 rpm; reissued 1954). **The
15th Century**. Brussels Pro Musica Antiqua, S. Cape; M.
Meili, tenor; Paraphonistes de St-Jean des Matines, G.
de Van.
Ockeghem: Ma maistresse (Meili).
Obrecht: Missa Maria zart-Qui propter, Et incarnatus (de
Van); Tsat een meskin (Cape).
ANTHOLOGIE SONORE 5 (ca. 1939 on 78 rpm; reissued 1954).
Josquin des Pres and Other Composers of the Late 15th

and Early 16th Centuries. Netherlands Vocal Quartet, F.
Raugel.
Obrecht: Ic weinsche alle vrouwen eere; Den haghel ende
die calde snee.
ARCHIVE 3052 (1956). The Early Renaissance: Johannes
Ockeghem, 5 Chansons. Brussels Pro Musica Antiqua; S.
Cape.
Petite camusette; Ma bouche rit; Ma maistresse, Fors
seulement, L'autre d'antan.
ARCHIVE 73223/3223 (1963). Works from the Repertoire of the
Imperial Chapelle. Concentus Musicus, Vienna; N.
Harnoncourt.
Obrecht: Va vilment (= Wat willen wij, instrumentally
performed).
ARCHIVE 198 406 (1966). Ockeghem, Missa Mi-mi; Obrecht,
Missa Sub tuum praesidium. Cappella Lipsiensis; D.
Knothe.
ARCHIVE 2533 145 (1973). Ockeghem, Missa Pro defuntis
(Requiem). Pro Cantione Antiqua, Hamburger
Bläserkreis; B. Turner.
ARCHIVE 2533 377 (1978). Obrecht and de la Rue, Motets. Pro
Cantione Antiqua, London Cornett & Sackbut Ensemble; B.
Turner.
Obrecht: Salve Regina II, Beata es Maria, Salve crux.
ARION/PETERS 068 (1977). Ars Antiqua-Ars Nova. Ensemble
Vocal Français "Da Camera"; D. Meier.
Ockeghem: Missa Cuiusvis toni-Kyrie, Gloria, Sanctus,
Agnus; Déploration sur la mort de Binchois.

BACH GUILD 634 (ca. 1962). Music at the Burgundian Court
(1450-1500). Brussels Pro Musica Antiqua; S. Cape.
Ockeghem: D'un autre amer (performed instrumentally).
Obrecht: Tsat een meskin (performed instrumentally).
BACH GUILD HM2 SD (1972). Dufay, Mass, Se la face ay pale;
Obrecht, Mass, Sub tuum praesidium. Vienna Chamber
Choir, Musica Antiqua of Vienna; H. Gillesberger.
BAROQUE 9003 (ca. 1959). Magnificat. Renaissance Chorus of
New York; H. Brown.
Ockeghem: Credo Sine nomine.
Obrecht: Missa Je ne demande-Gloria, Credo.
BAROQUE 9004 (ca. 1959). Ockeghem, Missa Mi-mi; Obrecht,
Missa Salve diva parens-Kyrie. Renaissance Chorus of
New York; H. Brown.
BASF 21512. (See Harmonia Mundi 1 CO65-99600)

COLLEGIUM 102/3 (ca. 1975). Flemish and Burgundian Music in
Honor of the Blessed Virgin Mary. Columbia University

Collegium Musicum; R. Taruskin.
Obrecht: Missa Salve diva parens-Sanctus.
COUNTERPOINT/ESOTERIC 5601/601 (ca. 1963). **Music of the
Renaissance.** Vocal Arts Ensemble; R. Levitt.
Ockeghem: Fors seulement, Missa Fors seulement-Kyrie.

DECCA 79413/9413. (See MCA 2508)
DISCOPHILES FRANÇAIS 330.222-4 (ca. 1958). **Anthologie de la
chanson française de 1450 à 1550.** Ed. A. Seay.
Ensemble Vocal Roger Blanchard. 3 discs.
Ockeghem: Aultre Venus.

EMI/ANGEL 38188 (= His Master's Voice 27 0098 1; also
cassette) (1985). Ockeghem, **Requiem; Missa Mi-mi.** The
Hilliard Ensemble; P. Hillier. (Reflexe series.)
ENIGMA 53536. (See Mus. Her. 4611)
EPIC 3045 (= Philips 00678) (ca. 1955). Palestrina, **Missa
Papae Marcelli; Choral Music from the Lowlands.**
Netherlands Chamber Choir; F. de Nobel.
Ockeghem: Missa Sine nomine-Kyrie, Gloria.
Obrecht: Parce Domine.
EPIC 3265 (ca. 1956). **Dutch Folk Songs.** Netherlands Chamber
Choir; F. de Nobel.
Obrecht: La tortorella.

FSM PANTHEON 63904 (ca. 1975). **Songs and Dances of the
Renaissance.** Collegium Pro Musica; R. Cross.
Obrecht: Rompeltiere.

HARMONIA MUNDI (France) 384 (ca. 1970). **Rene Clemencic Plays
Flutes from the Middle Ages to the Baroque.** Clemencic
Ensemble.
Obrecht: Helas mon bien (performed instrumentally).
HARMONIA MUNDI (France) 990 (1976). **Musique à la cour de
Marguerite d'Autriche.** Clemencic Consort.
Ockeghem: Petite camusette.
HARMONIA MUNDI (France) 55998/998 (cassette 40998) (1977).
Obrecht, **Missa Fortuna desperata.** Clemencic Consort.
HARMONIA MUNDI (France) 55999/999 (= HNH 4013) (1975).
Ockeghem, **Requiem.** Clemencic Consort.
HARMONIA MUNDI (Germany) 1 CO65-99600 (= BASF 21512) (1973).
Ockeghem, **Missa Ecce ancilla Domini; Intemerata Dei
mater.** Pro Cantione Antiqua, Collegium Aureum, Hamburg
Wind Ensemble; B. Turner.
HAYDN SOCIETY 9038 (2071) (1953). **Masterpieces of Music
before 1750.** Record 1, **Gregorian Chant to the 16th
Century.** Copenhagen Boys' and Mens' Choir; N.
Møller.

Ockeghem: Missa Prolationum-Sanctus.
Obrecht: Parce Domine.
HNH 4013. (See Harmonia Mundi 55999/999)

JUBILATE 15211 (ca. 1975). Ockeghem, **Missa Cuiusvis toni.**
Frankfurter Madrigal-Ensemble; S. Heinrich.

LONDON INTERNATIONAL 91116 (10"; ca. 1955). **Musique du**
moyen-age à la Renaissance. Ensemble Monique Rollin.
Ockeghem: Les desléaux.
LYRICHORD 7108/108 (ca. 1965). Ockeghem, **Missa Mi-mi,**
Chanson and Missa Fors seulement. Berkeley Chamber
Singers, Wollitz Recorder Group; T. Zes.
LYRICHORD 7213 (ca. 1970). Ockeghem, **Missa Caput, Motets,**
Chansons. Capella Cordina; A. Planchart.
Motets: Ave Maria, Salve Regina II, Alma Redemptoris
Mater
Chansons: Ma maitresse, Ma bouche rit, Petitte
camusette.
LYRICHORD 7237 (1970). Ockeghem, **Missa Ecce ancilla.**
Capella Cordina; A. Planchart.
LYRICHORD 7273 (1973). Obrecht, **Missa Caput, Salve crux.**
Capella Cordina; A. Planchart.

MACE 9030 (1966). **Sacred Music of the Masters.** Aachen
Domchor; T.B. Rehmann.
Ockeghem: Missa Au travail suis-Kyrie.
MCA 2508 (= Decca 79413/9413) (1961; reissued ca. 1980). **XV**
Century Netherlands Masters: Isaac, Obrecht. New York
Pro Musica Motet Choir and Wind Ensemble; N. Greenberg.
Obrecht: Missa Fortuna desperata.
MUSIC GUILD 134 (7) (ca. 1961). Des Pres, **Missa Hercules;**
Okeghem, **Motets.** Ensemble Roger Blanchard. (The works
by Ockeghem are duplicated on Record Society 48.)
Ockeghem: Prennez sur moi, Intemerata Dei, Ut heremita.
MUSICAL HERITAGE 713 (= Amadeo 5030) (ca. 1964). **Secular**
Music of the Renaissance. Capella Monacensis; K.
Weinhöppel.
Obrecht: Laet u ghenoughen.
MUSICAL HERITAGE 1035 (ca. 1970). **Sacred Music in the**
Cathedral of Tours. "Jean de Ockeghem" Vocal Ensemble
and Choir; C. Panterne.
Ockeghem: Missa Cuiusvis tone-Kyrie, Sanctus, Agnus.
MUSICAL HERITAGE 1306 (= Valois 821) (1972). Ockeghem, **Les**
Motets à la Vierge. Prague Madrigal Singers; M.
Venhoda.
Salve Regina I and II, Intemerata Dei, Gaude Maria, Alma
Redemptoris, Ave Maria, Ut heremita.

MUSICAL HERITAGE 1716 (= Amadeo 6233) (ca. 1973). **Music at the Court of Maximilian I.** Concentus Musicus; N. Harnoncourt.
Obrecht: Fors seulement, Tsat een meskin (performed instrumentally).

MUSICAL HERITAGE 3859 (1978). **From Guillaume Dufay to Josquin des Pres.** Ricercare Ensemble, Zurich; M. Piguet.
Obrecht: Fors seulement (performed instrumentally).

MUSICAL HERITAGE 4026 (cassette 6026) (recorded 1978). **Johannes Ockeghem, Prince of Music.** Cappella Nova; R. Taruskin.
Missa Prolationum; Requiem-Hostias.

MUSICAL HERITAGE 4179 (1980). Ockeghem, **The Motets.** Cappella Nova; R. Taruskin.
Alma Redemptoris, Intemerata Dei, Salve Regina I and II, Ave Maria, Celeste beneficium, Gaude Maria.

MUSICAL HERITAGE 4472 (1981). Ockeghem, **Missa L'homme armé, Chansons** (Ma bouche rit, Mort tu as navre, Les desléaux, L'autre d'antan, S'elle m'amera). Cappella Cordina; A. Planchart.

MUSICAL HERITAGE 4611 (= Enigma 53536) (ca. 1975). **A Tapestry of Music for Christopher Columbus and His Crew.** St. George's Canzona; J. Sothcott.
Obrecht: Tsaat een meskin, La stangetta (performed instrumentally).

MUSICAL HERITAGE 830437 (ca. 1970). **History of European Music,** Part 2: **Music of the Middle Ages and the Renaissance.** Various singers and instrumentalists; D. Stevens.
Ockeghem: Missa L'homme armé-Kyrie, Agnus III, Ma maitresse, Ma bouche rit.

MUSIQUE FLAMANDE (ca. 1968). Records designed to accompany Roger Wangermée, **La Musique flamande dans la société des XVe et XVIe siècles** (Brussels, 1968). Derived in part from Archive 3052. 2 discs. Brussels Pro Musica Antiqua; S. Cape. Quatuor Vocale de Bruxelles, etc.
Ockeghem: Missa L'homme armé-Kyrie, L'autre d'antan, Ma maistresse.

NONESUCH 71336 (1977). Ockeghem, **Missa Ma maistresse, Missa Au travail suis, Motets and Chansons.** Pomerium Musices; A. Blachly.
Motets: Ave Maria, Alma Redemptoris.
Chansons: Ma maistresse, Au travail suis.

OISEAU-LYRE 50104 (1955). **Mass Attributed to Gilles Binchois; Secular Pieces.** Chapelle de Bourgogne; B.

van Eeckhout.
Ockeghem: Ma maitresse.
OISEAU-LYRE 203-6 (1975). **Musicke of Sundrie Kindes.** The
Consort of Musicke; A. Rooley. Florilegium series. 4
discs.
Obrecht: Ic draghe.
OISEAU-LYRE D186 D4 (1980). **Le Chansonnier cordiforme.** The
Consort of Musicke; A. Rooley. Florilegium series. 4
discs.
Ockeghem: L'autre d'antan, Ma bouche rit.
OISEAU-LYRE D237 D6 (1981). Dufay, **Complete Secular Music.**
The Medieval Ensemble of London, P. & T. Davies.
Florilegium series. 6 discs.
Ockeghem or Dufay: Departés vous.
OISEAU-LYRE D254 D3 (1982). Ockeghem, **Complete Secular
Music.** The Medieval Ensemble of London; P. & T.
Davies. Florilegium series. 3 discs.
OPUS MUSICUM 101/03 (1972). **Die Messe.** Vocal Ensemble "Pro
Musica Köln"; J. Hömberg. 3 discs.
Obrecht: Missa Beata viscera-Agnus.
OXFORD UNIVERSITY PRESS 128 (7"; recorded 1971). Recorded
examples accompanying Edward E. Lowinsky, ed., **Josquin
des Prez: Proceedings of the International Josquin
Festival-Conference . . . 1971** (London, 1976). Prague
Madrigal Singers; M. Venhoda. ISBN 0-19-315229-0.
Ockeghem or Martini: Malheur me bat.

PHILIPS 00678. (See Epic 3045)
PLEIADES 251 (ca. 1970). **Historical Anthology of Music in
Performance: Early and Late 15th-Century Music.**
University of Chicago Collegium Musicum; H.M. Brown.
Southern Illinois University Collegium Music; W.
Morgan.
Ockeghem: Missa L'homme armè-Kyrie, Agnus III; Ma
maitresse, Ma bouche rit.
Obrecht: O beate Basili; Missa Sine nomine (= S.
Donatiane)- Kyrie I, Agnus II; Tsaat een meskin.

RCA VICTOR 6016 (1953). **History of Music in Sound,** vol. 3.
Ars Nova and the Renaissance. 2 discs. Renaissance
Singers; M. Howard.
Ockeghem: Missa Fors seulement-Kyrie.
RECORD SOCIETY 48 (ca. 1961). Okeghem, **Missa Mi-mi, Prenez
sur moi, Intemerata Dei, Ut heremita.** Vocal and
Instrumental Ensemble; R. Blanchard. (Partially
duplicates Music Guild 134.)

SERAPHIM 6052 (1969). **The Seraphim Guide to Renaissance Music.** Syntagma Musicum of Amsterdam; K. Otten. 3 discs.
Ockeghem: Missa Quinti toni-Kyrie.
Obrecht: Monad (= Missa Salve diva Parens-Qui cum patre).
SERAPHIM 6104 (1976). **The Art of the Netherlands.** Early Music Consort of London; D. Munrow. 3 discs.
Ockeghem: Prenez sur moi, Ma bouche rit, Intemerata Dei.
Obrecht: Ein fröhlich wesen, Tsaat een meskin, Haec Deum caeli, Laudemus nunc.
SUPRAPHON 10412 (ca. 1965). **Dance Music of 4 Centuries, The Netherlands Masters.** Pro Arte Antiqua Ensemble.
Ockeghem: Ut heremita.
SUPRAPHON 1 12 0464 (1968). Obrecht, **Missa super "Maria zart".** Prague Madrigal Singers; M. Venhoda.

TELDEC 6.41053 (= Telefunken 9432) (ca. 1965; reissued ca. 1980). **Early Music in England, Flanders, Germany, and Spain.** Studio for Early Music; T. Binkley.
Obrecht: Ic draghe.
TELDEC 6.41155 (= Telefunken 9419) (1962; reissued 1981). In **Dulci Jubilo. Ancient Choral Music for Christmas.** Monteverdi-Choir, Hamburg; J. Jürgens.
Ockeghem: Alma Redemptoris.
TELEFUNKEN 8008 (7", 45 rpm; ca. 1959). **Musik der alten Niederländer.** Musikkring Obrecht.
Obrecht: Weet ghy, Rompeltier (performed instrumentally)
TELEFUNKEN 8026 (7", 45 rpm; ca. 1960). **Geistliche Musik des frühen 15. Jahrhunderts.** Capella Antiqua, Munich; K. Ruhland.
Obrecht: Parce Domine.
TELEFUNKEN 9419. (See Teldec 6.41155)
TELEFUNKEN 9432. (See Teldec 6.41053)
TELEFUNKEN 9498 (ca. 1966). **Historische Orgeln der Schweiz: Orgel der Burgkirche Valeria in Sion (Sitten), Wallis.** S. Hildenbrand. Das alte Werk series.
Obrecht: Salve Regina I, parts 1-3.
TURNABOUT 34569 (1974). **A Renaissance Christmas.** Boston Camerata; J. Cohen.
Obrecht: Magnificat.

UNIVERSITY OF ILLINOIS SCHOOL OF MUSIC 8 (ca. 1957). **Compositions by Johannes Ockeghem.** University of Illinois Collegium Musicum; G. Hunter.
Mass for the Dead (Requiem), Salve Regina I, Lament on the Death of Binchois.

VALOIS 764 (1965). Ockeghem, **Requiem**. Prague Madrigal
    Singers, Musica Antiqua of Vienna; M. Venhoda.
VALOIS 821. (See Musical Heritage 1306)
VALOIS 909 (ca. 1965). Ockeghem, **Missa Quarti toni Mi-mi**,
    Missa Ma maitresse. Ensemble Polyphonique de Paris; C.
    Ravier.
VALOIS 964 (ca. 1965). Ockeghem, **Missa Prolationum**. Prague
    Madrigal Singers, Musica Antiqua of Vienna; M. Venhoda.

WESTMINSTER 5347 (1953). Gallus, **10 geistliche Chöre**; Isaak,
    Choral Music. Vienna Akademie Kammerchor; F.
    Grossmann.
    Isaac or Obrecht: Mein Lieb war jung (= T'meiskin was
    jonck).

W.W. NORTON P8 15483 (1980). Recordings to accompany **A**
    History of Western Music and **Norton Anthology of Western**
    Music (New York, 1980). Album 1. 8 discs. ISBN 0-393-
    95161-8.
    Ockeghem: D'ung aultre amer (from Bach Guild 634).

INDEX OF NAMES

This index includes the names of historical personages mentioned in Chapters I, II, and III, excepting Ockeghem and Obrecht. It does not include the names of modern authors (i.e. after 1800), nor does it cover Chapters IV (Bibliography) and V (Discography).